Dale Brown

Former US Air Force captain Dale Brown was born in Buffalo, New York, and now lives in Nevada. He graduated from Penn State University with a degree in Western European History and received a US Air Force commission in 1978. While in the Air Force, he was a navigator-bombardier, flying over 2,500 hours in tactical and training aircraft and receiving several military decorations.

He was still serving in the Air Force when he wrote his highly acclaimed first novel, *Flight of the Old Dog*. Since then he has written a string of *New York Times* bestsellers, all of which are available from HarperCollins: *Silver Tower, Day of the Cheetah, Hammerheads, Sky Masters, Night of the Hawk, Chains of Command, Storming Heaven, Shadows of Steel, Fatal Terrain, The Tin Man, Battle Born, Warrior Class* and *Wings of Fire*.

He has also completed the first two of a new series of novels written with Jim DeFelice based around a high-tech weapons research centre in the Nevada desert: *Dale Brown's Dreamland* and *Dale Brown's Dreamland: Nerve Centre*.

'Brown serves up enough lethal hardware and over-the-top action to satisfy the most discerning technothriller fan.'   *USA Today*

'You have to hug the seat when reading Dale Brown. The one-time US Air Force captain navigates his way at such a fearsome pace it is impossible to take your eyes off the page.'   *Oxford Times*

'Like the thrillers of Tom Clancy, Stephen Coonts and Larry Bond, the novels of Dale Brown brim with action, sophisticated weaponry and political intrigue . . . first-rate.'   *San Francisco Chronicle*

'Brown is a master of this school of fiction, bringing life to his characters with a few deft strokes.'   *Publishers Weekly*

DALE BROWN

WINGS OF FIRE

HarperCollinsPublishers

HarperCollins*Publishers*
77–85 Fulham Palace Road,
Hammersmith, London W6 8JB

www.**fire**and**water**.com

Published by HarperCollins*Publishers* 2002
Special overseas edition 2002
1 3 5 7 9 8 6 4 2

First published in the USA by
G.P. Putnam's Sons 2002

A catalogue record for this book
is available from the British Library

ISBN 0 00 710987 3
ISBN 0 00 710988 1(trade pbk)

Typeset in Meridien by Palimpsest Book Production Limited,
Polmont, Stirlingshire

Printed and bound in Great Britain by
Clays Ltd, St Ives plc

ACKNOWLEDGMENTS

Thanks to all the folks I met and spoke with at the Air Force Research Laboratory Directed Energy Directorate and Airborne Laser Special Projects Office, Kirtland Air Force Base, Albuquerque, New Mexico. Special thanks to my old friend Colonel Ellen Pawlikowski, ABL SPO commander, for inviting me to visit her incredible staff and facilities; Lieutenant Colonel Joel Olsen, Lieutenant Colonel Mark Neice, Major Steve Smiley, Captain Carey Johnson, Captain Barrett McCann, Captain Dave Edwards, Captain Lynn Anderson, and Tim Foley, ABL SPO; and Rich Garcia, Lieutenant Colonel Tom Alley, Captain Eric Moomey, Conrad Dziewalski, Dr Bob Fugate, Mike Connor, and Dr Kip Kendrick of the Directed Energy Directorate.

Special thanks to Ken Englade, AFRL/ABL SPO public affairs, for all his hard work in setting up a great tour of all the facilities at Kirtland.

Thanks to David and Cheryl Duffield, Susan Bailey, Dean and Meredith Meiling, Sandy Scarcella and Ed Bolecky for their extraordinary generosity.

Thanks to Robert Gottlieb, Neil Nyren and Suzanne Tarantino for their help and support.

As always, to Diane for her love and support.

*To the memory of the victims of the terrorist
attacks on September 11, 2001,
and to the men and women who have answered
the call to arms in the war on terror.*

AUTHOR'S NOTES

This is a work of fiction. Any resemblance to real-world persons, places, events, or organizations is coincidental.

Your comments are welcome! Please visit www. megafortress.com on the World Wide Web to leave your comments and to learn about upcoming works, projects, appearances or events. I read every comment.

REAL-WORLD NEWS EXCERPTS

WAITING ON CAIRO
STRATFOR Intelligence Update, www.stratfor.com, October 13, 2000 –
Within the Arab world, the Egyptians occupy a unique position, the
very reason that they have been propelled to the center of the situation. Although it wields one of the largest Arab militaries, Cairo is also
the largest Arab state to continue ties with Israel; even Morocco has
called its diplomatic representative home for consultation . . .
 . . . Arab nations – even those that have signed peace agreements
with Israel – are under intense pressure to join together and take a
unified stand against Israel . . .

US AID FUELING THE DEVELOPMENT OF MODERN EGYPT
Washington Post, December 26, 2000 – Egypt, a preoccupation of US
foreign policy for the last quarter-century, has been the second-largest
recipient of American foreign aid during that period. The $52 billion
program, so far, has rebuilt mosques, constructed new schools, promoted
family planning and transferred high-tech weapons like F-16 warplanes
and M1-A1 tanks at a $2-billion-a-year clip . . .

CONSEQUENCES OF A NEW US DEFENSE STRATEGY
STRATFOR Global Intelligence Update, http://www.stratfor.com, March 1,
2001 – In Washington, an internal Pentagon review of American defense
strategy is likely to call for a dramatic reduction in US troops deployed
overseas . . . Such a historic shift would reduce the vulnerability of US
forces to attack and lower the profile of a seemingly imperial military
presence. Over the long term, however, such a strategy may force allies
and adversaries alike to build new regional alliances or adopt independent, antagonistic defense strategies . . .

LIBYA: GAINING LEVERAGE IN CENTRAL AFRICA
STRATFOR, June 5, 2001 – Chad and Libya reportedly deployed several
hundred troops, attack helicopters and other military equipment to the
Central African Republic on May 30, the BBC reported.
 . . . The unsuccessful uprising has opened the door for Libyan leader
Muammar Qadhafi to send Libyan troops into central Africa and closer
to Chad's southern oil fields . . .

AIR FORCE TURNS 747 INTO HOLSTER FOR GIANT LASER
Washington Post, July 22, 2001 – USAF plans to shoot down a Scud-type missile with a giant laser fired from a modified 747 within two years. That test would be to prove the feasibility of destroying an attacking missile in the 'boost' phase shortly after launch.

3 STUDIES FOCUS ON CUTTING OVERSEAS DEPLOYMENTS
Washington Times, July 25, 2001 – Secretary Rumsfeld ordered three Pentagon reviews of foreign troop engagements in order to determine how best to reduce the type of overseas deployments that mushroomed during the Clinton era.

Prologue

Over central Libya

'This has got to be the most insane idea in the history of aviation,' retired Navy commander John 'Bud' Franken muttered. 'Let it go and let's get this over with.'

Retired Air Force brigadier general Patrick McLanahan smiled, then fastened his oxygen visor in place with a snap. 'That's the spirit, AC,' he said happily. 'It only seems insane because no one's ever done it before.'

'Yeah, right. Just unzip your pants over there and let's go home.'

'Here it comes,' Patrick said. He hit a small stud on his computer trackball and spoke: 'Deploy array.' The computer acknowledged the command, and the attack was under way.

Far behind them, in a fairing between their aircraft's twin V-tails, a small oblong cylinder detached itself from its mounting and began to trail behind the aircraft on a thin carbon-fiber-reinforced fiber-optic cable. The tiny object, soon trailing several hundred feet behind the AL-52, was an ALE-50-towed electronic countermeasures decoy. Just three feet long and six inches in diameter, it was invisible to the Libyan air defense radars that surrounded them at that moment.

The aircraft was a modified B-52 Stratofortress bomber – not a US Air Force warplane, but an experimental aircraft modified by Patrick's company, Sky Masters Inc, called an AL-52 Dragon. The warplane he was sitting in was so advanced that even Patrick, who had been involved in its development both in and out of the Air Force for years, was truly amazed. What he was really sitting in, he realized with a mixture of awe and glee, was . . . the future. 'Star Wars' was no longer a Reagan-era pipe dream or the name of a hugely successful science-fiction motion picture series – it was right here, right now. The AL-52 Dragon combined the absolute state-of-the-art in laser technology, high-speed computers, miniaturization, stealth systems, and systems integration to produce the world's first true twenty-first century weapon system, using technology that had never been deployed on an aircraft before.

The airframe itself was based on the EB-52 Megafortress modification of the B-52H Stratofortress bomber, with stealthy composite fibersteel skin and frame, four powerful turbofan engines replacing the original eight turbofans, a V-tail stabilator replacing the big cruciform tail, and an advanced self-protection suite, including radar and infrared jammers, towed arrays, decoys, and Stinger aerial land mines. The original six-person crew had been replaced by enough state-of-the-art computers and artificial intelligence systems that now only two crew members, an aircraft commander and a mission commander, were required to be on board – and, in an extreme emergency, either could bring the plane home alone.

The Megafortress was designed as a stealthy flying battleship, able to penetrate heavily defended targets deep behind enemy lines and employ every air-launched weapon in the American arsenal – and a few that had been dreamed up just for it – with great precision. The Dragon variant of the Megafortress battleship retained the conventional attack capabilities – it could carry up to twelve thousand pounds of ordnance on wing hardpoints, including cruise missiles, air-to-air missiles, and even antisatellite and antimissile weapons. Patrick knew all about the devastating warfighting capabilities of the EB-52 Megafortress – he had spent more than fifteen years of his life working on it. Sky Masters Inc still flew several versions of the EB-52 for flight test and research purposes, still hoping that the Air Force would someday take the roughly one hundred B-52H Stratofortress bombers in flyable storage out of mothballs and have the company convert them to either EB-52 Megafortresses or AL-52 Dragons.

'Here we go, Bud,' Patrick said. To the computer, he said, 'Activate array.' In an instant, the towed array, which normally was all but invisible to radar, blossomed to the electromagnetic equivalent of a Boeing 747.

That move had its desired and expected effect: All of the Libyan air defense radars, which had just been searching the skies seconds before, almost immediately locked on to the towed decoy. Now instead of peaceful search and air traffic control radars, Patrick's

4

threat scope was suddenly alive with dozens of antiaircraft threats – surface-to-air missile sites, antiaircraft artillery, and fighter-intercept radars. *'Warning, SA-10 acquisition mode, ten o'clock, twenty miles,'* the computer responded. *'Warning, SA-9 acquisition mode, two o'clock, ten miles . . .'* The warnings kept coming, until: *'Warning, missile launch, SA-10, ten o'clock, nineteen miles . . . warning, missile launch, SA-10, ten o'clock, nineteen miles . . .'* – the SA-10 missiles always launched in pairs. *'Countermeasures not activated.'*

'Commit Dragon,' Patrick spoke. He had to consciously bring his breathing and voice under control. In all the times he had been on an attack run, this was the first time he did not react when a threat came up. If this didn't work, they'd be dead in fifteen seconds.

'Caution, Dragon activated . . . caution, Dragon engaging,' the computer responded. Patrick watched in fascination as the newest and most sophisticated computer system ever placed aboard any aircraft automatically began prosecuting the attack and activating the most devastating airborne weapon ever produced.

The AL-52 Dragon's LADARs, or laser radar arrays, which electronically scanned hundred of thousands of cubic miles of space in every direction thirty times per second, tracked the Soviet-made SA-10 missile with millimeter precision. At the same time the LADAR also instantly measured the dimensions of the rocket, determining where its motor section was. Tracking computers then began measuring the rocket's speed, altitude, and direction – even predicting its probable impact point and relaying the data to friendly forces downrange.

At the same moment, the Dragon itself came to life.

Turbopumps in the belly of the AL-52 Dragon immediately began pressurizing hydrogen peroxide and potassium hydroxide inside a reaction chamber. Chlorine gas and helium from storage tanks in the cargo section of the modified B-52 bomber were then sprayed under pressure into the chamber, forming an energized substance called singlet delta-oxygen. In another reaction chamber, iodine and helium were injected into the substance, which released the high-energy photons from the gas, creating laser light.

At the same time, the AL-52's laser radar locked onto the rocket rising through the atmosphere and immediately began to send

5

target airspeed, altitude, direction, acceleration, and flight path data to targeting computers. The computers immediately fed the data to the gimbaled turret in the nose of the AL-52, and the turret unstowed itself from inside the bomber's nose and turned and swiveled until the laser's telescope and four-foot-diameter mirror were aimed at the rocket. The pilots could feel a slight rumbling under their toes as the huge fifteen-foot-high turret slewed toward the target, but otherwise it did not affect the flight characteristics of the heavy bomber.

When all this information was received, processed, analyzed, and instructions sent – eight seconds after target detection – Patrick received a simple 'LASER READY' computerized voice in his headphones. 'Cockpit's ready for launch.'

'Roger. COIL in attack mode . . . now.'

The attack was purely automatic – there was no big red 'FIRE' button anywhere on the plane. The laser radar system instantaneously measured the exact size of the SS-12 rocket and aimed the laser at the rocket motor section, the point of maximum pressure on the missile. The laser radar also provided an atmospheric correction to the laser telescope's deformable mirror to adjust for temperature gradients from the Dragon to the target. Finally, the big COIL, or chlorine-oxygen-iodine laser, fired. A four-foot-diameter beam of high-energy laser light shot from the nose of the AL-52 and was focused by the deformable mirror down to a spot the size of a basketball on the motor section of the first rocket. The beam was completely invisible to the cockpit crew – they could see the mirror turret moving slightly, tracking the target, but nothing else.

Patrick switched the large full-color supercockpit display on the right-side instrument panel to the telescope view. He was now looking right down the barrel of the laser, watching an optical presentation of what the laser attack computer was looking at. The SA-10 missile was clearly visible, tracked and illuminated by the laser radar arrays and focused to razor-sharp clarity by the deformable mirror. The crosshairs in the center of the display were dead on the rear one-third of the missile – the center of the SA-10's rocket motor. Patrick increased the magnification and was even able to read markings on the side of the missile.

6

As the missile flew higher and higher in the sky, its thermo-dynamic pressures were building as well – pressure from the force of the engines, pressure from the atmosphere, pressure from gravity, pressure from building speed, and pressure created by the guidance system acting through the rocket's fins and gyros. Finally, the heat from the laser burned through the missile's skin enough that the skin surrounding the motor section couldn't contain the immense internal pressures or structurally hold the outside air pressures, and the missile ripped apart like a rotten banana and exploded.

'Missile destroyed!' Patrick shouted. 'We got it!'

The attack computer immediately shifted to the second SA-10 missile, launched seconds after the first, and the result was just as successful and just as spectacular. 'Missile two destroyed! Towed array in standby . . . laser's ready to shoot again, all threats down. Hot damn!'

Sky Masters Inc needed a realistic real-world test of its airborne laser technology, so Patrick McLanahan, overseeing the program, thought of the easiest and fastest way to test it out – fly over a country that liked to shoot missiles without warning and see if it worked. Libya filled the bill nicely. Libya had the best military hardware its oil money could buy, and they were notorious for firing on stray aircraft without warning. Plus, most of Libya south of Tripoli was open desert, so there was little risk of anyone being hurt by falling debris or misses – or, if the test didn't work, falling pieces of the AL-52 Dragon.

'Have we had enough, boss?' Franken asked. 'I sure have.'

'I don't want to hang around here any more than I have to, Bud,' Patrick said. 'But I'd sure like to wring the laser out a little more.' At that moment, both crew members received a warning message on their threat receiver, one of the multifunction displays in the center of the Dragon's instrument panel. 'Just got swept by fighter radar,' Patrick said. 'I think it might be time to head home.'

'Good deal,' Franken said. He started a slow left turn to the north, mindful of the towed array still extended behind them – they could easily turn quickly enough to wrap themselves up in their own array's cable. 'Just keep those puppies off us.'

'LADAR coming on,' Patrick said. He activated the laser radar for only a few seconds, but the laser radar's power and tight

7

resolution drew an amazingly detailed picture of all air targets within a hundred miles. 'We've got a flight of two MiG-29 interceptors, coming from Tripoli,' Patrick said. 'When you roll out, they'll be at your nine-thirty position, sixty-one miles, high. Heading zero-one-zero will put them at your nine o'clock.' The pulse-Doppler radar on the MiG-29, another Libyan purchase from the Russians, could not detect a target with a closure rate equal to the aircraft airspeed.

This was not looking good, Patrick noted immediately. *'Warning,'* the female-voiced threat computer reported, *'MiG-29 nine o'clock five-zero miles, flight level three-three-zero, acquisition mode. Warning, trackbreakers are in standby.'*

'Either this guy is very lucky, or very good,' Patrick said. 'The leader is coming right in on us. Something's not right.' He hit the voice command stud: 'System status.'

'All monitored systems are functioning normally,' the computer said after a slight pause. Then: *'Warning, MiG-29 at nine o'clock, forty miles, tracking.'*

'Oh, shit,' Patrick said. 'Trackbreakers coming on.' But it was then that he found the problem: 'The ECM system faulted – it shut itself down completely.' Patrick powered it back up.

'Warning, towed array not in coordinated flight,' the computer reported.

'That's what happened,' Patrick said. 'When we made the turn, it must've knocked the array out of whack and faulted the system. It's been back there spinning away like a great big pinwheel. I'm cutting it loose.' But that didn't work. 'The array won't jettison. It's totally faulted. I'm going to try an ECM system reset. LADAR coming on. It'll be the only threat warning we have now.'

'Warning, MiG-29 at seven o'clock, thirty miles . . .' But moments later, they heard, *'Warning, missile launch detected on radar, nine o'clock, twenty-six miles. Time to intercept, fifty seconds.'*

'Break left!' Patrick shouted. Franken shoved the throttles to full military power and yanked the control stick full left, rolling the AL-52 up on its left wing in a tight ninety-degree bank turn – they had to risk flying into their own cable to try to defeat the incoming radar-guided missile. At full bank, he started to apply back pressure to tighten the turn even more, presenting the smallest possible radar cross-section on the MiG-29's radar. He let

up on the back pressure when the computer issued a stall warning and started to pull the control stick forward. Meanwhile, Patrick was frantically trying every countermeasures switch he could. 'ECM is completely dead – chaff, flares, jammers, everything.'

Out the cockpit window, the sight was horrifying. They could clearly see a trail of fire arcing across the sky – the Libyan radar-guided missile, heading right for them. There was no time to turn, no time to try anything, no time to even speak . . .

The missile dove right at them – then passed just behind them, making a direct hit on the spinning array, missing them by less than three hundred feet. To the two men in the cockpit of the AL-52, it looked as if the missile had been aiming right at the middle of their foreheads.

'Lost . . . lost contact with the towed array,' Patrick said, gasping for breath – he thought he had bought the farm that time. 'The missile hit it dead-on.'

'Well, that's one way to cut the array loose,' Franken said.

Patrick switched his supercockpit display to the tactical view. 'These suckers aren't going to get a chance to get another shot off at us,' he said.

'Are you going to try to hit the missiles as they come off the rails?'

'I'm not going to let them get off the rails,' Patrick said. To the attack computer, he said, 'Commit Dragon.'

'No TBM targets,' the computer responded.

Patrick touched the MiG-29 icon on the supercockpit display and spoke, 'Attack target.'

'Stinger airmines out of range,' the computer responded. The AL-52 Dragon kept the built-in defensive weapons of the EB-52 Megafortress, including the Stinger airmines – small guided missiles fired from a cannon in the tail that created clouds of shrapnel in the path of enemy fighters tail-chasing the bomber. But the airmines could only attack targets within two miles of the bomber in the rear quadrant.

'Designate airborne target as TBM target,' Patrick commanded. 'Commit Dragon.'

'Stand by,' the computer responded. It was something never attempted – shooting down an aircraft with the airborne laser. Patrick didn't even know if the programming existed for the attack

9

computer to take a non-TBM, or tactical ballistic missile, target and process a laser attack against it. But he received his answer moments later: The supercockpit display was suddenly filled with the image of the southernmost MiG-29. The laser radar had locked onto the rear one-third of the aircraft, the same spot that it would normally lock onto a missile. *'Caution, target velocity data not within limits.'*

Patrick remembered that the laser attack computer was programmed to lock onto only fast-moving targets, like ballistic missiles – the MiG was flying much more slowly than a rocket. 'Override velocity data.'

There was another long, nervous pause; then: *'Caution, target velocity parameters overridden. Laser ready.'*

Patrick zoomed the image in until he was looking directly into the cockpit of the Libyan MiG; then he used his trackball and moved the crosshairs to the left side of the fighter, right on the nose of the largest missile he came across – he remembered that MiG-29s usually fired missiles off the right side first. He could see it clearly: a huge R-27 radar-guided on the number-three hardpoint. 'Lock onto target and attack laser,' he commanded.

'Warning, laser attack, stop attack,' the computer said. The Megafortress's antiaircraft attack logic had taken over for the Dragon's anti-ballistic missile attack logic and successfully started treating the chlorine-oxygen-iodine laser as another air-launched weapon. Seconds later, the computer reported, *'Laser firing.'*

The results were spectacular. Less than three seconds after the 'laser firing' warning, the R-27 missile on the MiG-29's hardpoint exploded in a blinding flash of light. The entire left wing of the lead MiG sheared off in the explosion. Patrick expanded the optronic view on the supercockpit display just in time to watch the Libyan pilot eject from his stricken fighter. The laser radar display showed the second MiG peel off sharply to the north.

'We got it!' Patrick crowed. He quickly locked up the second MiG-29. The supercockpit display now showed the diode laser locked onto the center top fuselage section of the second MiG. 'Attack target laser,' he commanded.

'Attack target laser, stop attack,' the computer warned. The second shot took several seconds longer, but soon Patrick could see a stream of smoke trailing from the MiG's fuselage – and then

suddenly the fuselage seemed to disintegrate from the inside, with ribbons of flames trailing from several cracks and tears in the upper-fuselage fuel tanks right above the number-one engine. The MiG-29 was into its second flat spin, its left engine burning hotly, before the pilot ejected.

'Wow, that was very cool,' Franken exclaimed. 'A laser powerful enough to shoot down a MiG-29 fighter. Very cool.'

'Let's try the last part of the test,' Patrick said. He quickly entered commands into the attack computer. It had stored information on the launch point of the SA-10 missile they had shot down, computed from tracking information by the laser radar arrays. Patrick slaved the laser telescope to the launch point coordinates, starting with a wide image. There, on the multifunction supercockpit display, he saw the entire SA-10 'Grumble' surface-to-air missile battery – the mobile engagement radar, the command post and low-altitude radar vehicle, a reload vehicle, and the four-round transporter-erector-launcher vehicle. Two rounds had obviously been fired from that vehicle. Patrick focused the telescope until the crosshairs were centered on one of the still-loaded launch tubes. The image was not as clear as the others were – the image was out of focus and wavered. Obviously it was harder for the adaptive optics to focus the image while shooting down through the atmosphere than it was to shoot across or up.

'C'mon, baby, let's see what you can do,' Patrick said. He hit his voice command button: 'Attack target,' he ordered.

'*Attack command received, stop attack,*' the computer responded.

'Commit Dragon.'

'*Laser commit . . . laser engaging.*'

But the results were not quite as pleasing this time. The crosshairs were dead on the target, and the diode laser was firing at full power, but the target remained. Patrick left it on for a full ten seconds before terminating. 'Didn't blow the launch tube. Not enough power to shoot down through the atmosphere at this range.'

'Please don't suggest we get any closer.'

'Don't worry – I think we're close enough. But we've got to figure out a way to pump more power into the system.'

'You're disappointed because your big laser couldn't slice, dice, and julienne every target? Too bad, sir,' Franken joked. 'Can we

11

terminate the test and go home now before they empty those last two missiles on us?'

'You got it, AC. Test terminated,' Patrick said after a sigh of relief. He quickly punched up the initial point of the air refueling anchor into the navigation computer, then replotted the flight path to take them well clear of Libyan airspace. 'Center up and let's go home.'

Al-Azhar Mosque, Cairo, Egypt
that same time

Al-Azhar Mosque and University was the oldest university in the world, a solemn and beautiful place in the Islamic section of Cairo. Muslim students from all over the world came here to study the Quran and listen to the world's most noted authorities on Islam. All Egyptian clerics had to study here, some as long as fifteen years, in the traditional Socratic method – a tutor and his pupils, asking and answering questions until both were satisfied that it was time to progress to the next lesson.

The three-acre compound was a mixture of early Islamic, Mamluk, and Turkish architecture, representing the dynamic history of the place. Al-Azhar was also the focal point of international celebrations of the birth of the Prophet Muhammad in late June. Islamic scholars and leaders from all over the world assembled here to an all-night *mulid*, or prayer festival, to tell stories, make speeches, teach, and pray.

The guests were assembled in the Madrasa and Tomb of Amir Atbugha, a grand hall inside the Gates of the Barbers that housed the university's collection of ancient manuscripts. Guests were served *shai* and *ahwa* – no alcohol at all, not even for foreigners – and a luscious assortment of *mezze* appetizers while they talked of politics, religion, and Muslim life, viewed the rare manuscripts, and waited for the festivities to begin.

The chief of the general staff of the United Kingdom of Libya, General Tahir Fazani, had waited a discreet distance apart from the heads of state. This was a time of worship and reflection, not state business, so he would not be permitted to address his president first. Fazani simply choked down his impatience, stayed in

12

the shadows, appeared as if he was praying or simply observing a moment of silence, and waited for his president to come to him. Fazani came from a long line of career military officers, but he had spent most of the last twenty years in Russia, Syria, and China studying military technology and modern warfighting – and staying out of the grasp of the previous Libyan dictator, Colonel Muammar Qadhafi. He was an expert political survivor – he knew when to make his voice heard and when to blend into the shadows, like now.

The new president of the United Kingdom of Libya, Jadallah Salem Zuwayy, sauntered over to Fazani, barely acknowledging his presence, only casting enough of a glance in his direction to order him to follow. Zuwayy was a tall, light-skinned man in his late thirties, with dark eyes, a thin mustache, and a dark beard that grew to a satanic point to the base of his long, thin throat. He was a former army officer who reportedly engineered the military coup that overthrew Qadhafi. Like Qadhafi before him, Zuwayy liked to wear different outfits depending on the occasion and his audience: Today he wore traditional Bedouin garb, rich-looking silks and muslins, bordering on opulent. Most times, Zuwayy was in desert-style battle dress uniform, often wearing tanker's boots and carrying a variety of weapons, from antique, ornate curved cavalry swords to live grenades.

'What is it, Fazani?' Zuwayy asked sternly.

'*He* wants an update on the deployment,' the chief of staff replied. He then held out a secure cellular telephone.

Zuwayy felt like telling Fazani to throw the phone into the garbage – but he dared not. The man on the other end of that secure connection had very long fingers – more like very long claws. 'Everything is ready?' the tall, thin, ethereal cleric asked in a low, monotone, disembodied voice.

'Yes, Highness,' Fazani reported. 'Just yesterday. All units are in full readiness.' He handed the cellular phone to Zuwayy and bowed.

Zuwayy smiled, then touched a preselected code on the phone's keypad. 'You'd better have some good news for me, Zuwayy,' a voice said angrily. 'You've been dodging me long enough.'

'All is in readiness,' Zuwayy said. 'My troops are in place, and the units are ready.'

'It took you long enough, Zuwayy,' the voice on the other end of the phone warned. 'They should have been in place days ago.'

'Come here and try dragging those things across the desert yourself, my friend,' Zuwayy said. 'You will see how easy it is.'

'I gave you plenty of time and money to set those units up, Zuwayy,' the voice said. His foreign accent was thick, but his meaning was all too clear. 'You had better not screw this up, or the first casualty in this war will be you.' And the call was abruptly terminated.

Zuwayy did not disguise a look of utter contempt on his face as he handed the phone back to Fazani. 'I look forward to meeting him in person,' Zuwayy muttered. 'I should like to see how black his heart really is.' He erased the scowl on his face, replacing it with a serene smile, as he noticed an entourage heading toward him. 'Now I must suffer this lackey.'

'Peace be upon you, Mr President,' the host of this celebration said warmly. President Kamal Ismail Salaam was the fourth elected Egyptian president since the Nasserite revolution in 1952. Tall, slender, and energetic, appearing more Italian than African, Salaam was the minister of finance under former president Muhammad Hosni Mubarak and leader of the National Democratic Party upon Mubarak's retirement from politics. Like Mubarak, Salaam was a military veteran, serving as the commander in chief of the Egyptian Air Defense Force Command.

'*Es salaem alekum!* Peace upon you, brother!' Zuwayy said loudly so the whole room could hear, spreading his hands far apart as if to embrace his host even from across the room. He stepped quickly across the richly carpeted floor toward his host. Walking the requisite three paces behind him was the Libyan Secretary of Arab Unity – the closest Libya came to a foreign minister – Juma Mahmud Hijazi.

Two of President Zuwayy's bodyguards quickly stepped up to President Salaam and stared at his hands and those of the others around him, looking for drawn weapons. It was a little irritating, but Salaam let the feeling go. The hall here at the Al-Azhar Mosque in Cairo, Egypt, was filled with dignitaries, diplomats, and celebrities from all over the world, here to celebrate the Prophet Muhammad's birthday. There was a lot of security in the place already – two Egyptian soldiers inside and outside every

14

doorway, along with a dozen Presidential Guard snipers watching from catwalks overhead – but Zuwayy was the only one to bring his own bodyguards into the great hall.

Salaam clasped Zuwayy's shoulders and embraced him in a traditional Arab greeting. '*Ahlan wa sahlan. Tasharrafna!* Hello and welcome. We are pleased and grateful by your presence, Mr President.' This was the first time meeting the new leader of neighboring Libya, and it was about what he expected, given Zuwayy's reputation. Zuwayy's lips turned tense and hard, and his hands disappeared perturbedly inside the billowing cuffs of his ornate silk robes.

Zuwayy's Minister of Arab Unity looked positively horrified. 'Pardon me, Mr President,' Secretary Hijazi said in a low but stern voice, 'but my lord prefers to be addressed as "His Royal Highness" or as "King Idris the Second." I am sure my office made the proper notifications to your office in a timely manner. And touching his highness without his permission is *absolutely* forbidden.'

'Of course,' Salaam replied. 'Yes, I was so notified.' He bowed to Zuwayy. 'My apologies, Highness.'

It was a joke, of course – everyone knew it. Jadallah Zuwayy claimed to be a descendant of the *sheikhs* of the al-Sanusi dynasty, the tribe of powerful desert nomads that united the three kingdoms of Tripolitania, Cyrenaica, and Fezzan under Islam during the Turkish occupation and formed the kingdom of Libya. It was Muammar Qadhafi, after oil was discovered in Libya, who led a military coup that overthrew King Idris al-Sanusi in 1969 and formed a military dictatorship; the al-Sanusi sheikhs were driven underground by Qadhafi's death squads and formed the Sanusi Brotherhood, a monarchist insurgency group. Now Zuwayy claimed to avenge his family's honor by taking the country back from Qadhafi in the name of the Sanusi Brotherhood.

His claims were utterly baseless. Born and raised in Tripoli, the son of an oil executive and housewife, Zuwayy was an ex-army officer who had been serving in relative obscurity as an infantry-training officer, specializing in demolition, breeching, and minelaying. It was widely suspected, though never confirmed, that Zuwayy joined the Libyan Islamic Fighting Group, an extension of the Mujahadeen – ultranationalist rebel groups spread out across the Middle East and Asia dedicated to the overthrow of

15

existing governments and replacing them with fundamentalist Muslim religious governments. Much of his financial backing came from Mujahadeen organizations in Iran and Sudan collectively known as the Muslim Brotherhood, with whom Zuwayy had formed a close alliance.

He had no royal blood in him, and his family never was part of the al-Sanusi clan, a great nomadic tribe that fought Turks, Italians, and Germans to win freedom for their people. The remnants of the al-Sanusi dynasty were scattered across Africa and the Middle East, fearing the Libyan assassination squads that pursued them under orders from Colonel Qadhafi. Although Zuwayy claimed to restore the monarchy to the al-Sanusi dynasty, his reputation as a ruthless, fanatical sociopath only drove them deeper into hiding. No one in Africa or the Middle East dared challenge his reign. The Western press scoffed at his claims and repeatedly offered much evidence that he was not a Sanusi, but the evidence was largely ignored, especially within Libya itself.

President Salaam stifled a smirk at the aide's remarks about Zuwayy's grandiose title and motioned beside him. 'Highness, may I present my wife, Susan Bailey Salaam. Madame, it is my pleasure to introduce His Highness, King Idris the Second, President of the United Islamic Kingdom of Libya.'

Susan Salaam stepped forward, curtsied deeply, averted her eyes, and extended her right hand upward. 'Welcome to Egypt, my lord. We are honored by your presence.'

It was obvious that her husband thought this too much of a show, even for Zuwayy. He was surprised when Zuwayy offered her a very pleased smile, the first he had ever seen or depicted of him. Could this man, could *any* man, be so vain . . . ? 'Please rise, woman,' Zuwayy said. 'We are privileged to be here on this glorious occasion.'

Susan rose – and Zuwayy looked into the most beautiful, most breathtaking, most alluring face he had ever seen. Her head was veiled, as it should be, but the sheen and luster of her deep black hair underneath could not be concealed. She wore no makeup that Zuwayy could detect, but her lips were deep red, her eyes dark and mesmerizing, her cheekbones high, her mouth perfectly formed. Her skin was perfect, light brown with slightly darker cheeks from exposure to sun, almost African. She took one look at the Libyan pretender, and even his rock-hard heart began to melt.

She was not African – Zuwayy knew she was an American, born to southern European emigrants – but this creature was the most beautiful he had ever seen on the planet. She could not be human – she had to be a goddess, or a gift from the loins of Allah himself. He also knew she was much more than just a thing of great beauty. She was once an American air force military officer, rising in the ranks from a lowly security police officer to deputy chief in charge of intelligence for the US Central Command. During the War for the Liberation of Kuwait, what the rest of the world called the Persian Gulf War of 1991, she acted as an intelligence liaison to the Egyptian military, which is how she and Kamal met. Zuwayy had been told that she was a woman of many talents: She could pilot a jet airliner, drive a main battle tank, fire a rifle, and argue both common and Shari'a law in any courtroom in the world in four languages.

Susan Salaam quickly averted her eyes again, not daring – properly – to gaze into the eyes of another man, as was proper Islamic custom. Zuwayy had to force his own eyes from her, realizing – then not caring – that he had let them linger on her too long. She must be a gift from God, Zuwayy told himself again . . .

. . . a gift for a man blessed enough to have such high favor of Allah. And Salaam was not, *could not*, be that man. 'It is a pleasure to meet you, my child,' Zuwayy said finally, fighting to control his breathing. He did not use the more formal address for a married woman, *ya sayyida*, but instead the more intimate expression *dahab*.

'Thank you, Your Highness,' Susan said, again letting those beautiful eyes flash up toward his. 'May the blessings of the Prophet, praise his holy name, be upon you and all of us today.'

'*Insha'allah*.' He had to tear himself away from looking at her, so instead concentrated on her husband, looking Kamal Ismail Salaam up and down disapprovingly. Salaam was wearing a simple white and blue traditional headdress, but was otherwise dressed in a conservative gray double-breasted Western-style business suit, with a single gold chain around his neck. 'You do not appear to be prepared for prayer, brother.'

'I have been asked to give a few remarks to our guests before

17

the prayers of celebration begin, Highness,' Salaam replied. 'My duties require that I be elsewhere during the prayers of celebration.' He motioned to his left. 'The chancellor of Al-Azhar University and chief justice of the Arab Republic of Egypt's Supreme Judicial Council, Ulama Khalid al-Khan, will lead the prayer celebration in my place.'

Khalid al-Khan bowed deeply to Zuwayy, then took the Libyan's extended hand and touched it tenderly to both cheeks. Al-Khan was in his late forties, a fundamentalist Sunni Muslim cleric who led the fight in 1980 as a firebrand – some said fanatic – to make the Shari'a, the Islamic legal code, the basis of Egyptian law; before that, the law had been a mishmash of English common law and even Napoleonic code, with a healthy dose of Turkish law thrown in to confuse everyone. The highest-ranking cleric in Egypt, al-Khan was an advocate of an even greater role of fundamentalist Islamic rule in Egypt and was very vocal in his opposition to both the Mubarak and Salaam governments. Al-Khan was dressed similarly to Zuwayy, with traditional Arab robes and turban.

'Majesty, it is an honor to meet you,' al-Khan breathed. 'May the blessings of the Prophet be upon you forever and always.'

'And to you, my son,' Zuwayy replied. He looked aghast at Salaam as if to say, 'That is how you pay proper respect to your superior.' 'The Prophet of course allows the faithful to pray anywhere,' Zuwayy said to Salaam, 'but He always looks with extreme favor on those who join together with their brothers in prayer.'

'My apologies, Highness,' Salaam said.

'I see you prefer to wear the clothing of a *mushrikun* as well,' Zuwayy added. 'You have also shaved your beard, of which Allah almighty also disapproves. At least you still observe the *adab al-imama*,' he added, motioning to Salaam's turban, 'although it does not appear to be the proper length, as prescribed by His Holiness the Prophet. You shall be instructed as to –'

'Mr President . . . er, Highness,' Salaam interjected, purposely getting his title wrong just to irk the Libyan, 'Allah, praise his name, knows the hearts and minds of all men. I am his servant, and I serve him in my own way.'

'The Prophet has told us how we must serve God,' Zuwayy responded sternly. 'If it is in our power, we must obey. Please do

18

not mock the Prophet or the faithful by telling us that not joining in prayer is a proper way to praise Allah. You must –'

'I'll take that under advisement, Highness,' Salaam interrupted again. He bowed to Zuwayy, as did his wife; neither the Libyan nor al-Khan acknowledged his gesture. 'If you'll excuse me, I must prepare for my welcoming address. Until this evening.' He turned and stepped away before Zuwayy could say anything else.

The two greeted other guests and visitors, but were soon escorted by staff members to the front of the great hall and were quickly instructed on the day's events. 'It is not a good idea to anger Zuwayy, Kamal,' Susan said to her husband in a low voice. 'He commands much respect in North Africa and elsewhere. The fundamentalists love him, and most of his enemies fear him.'

'He is a popinjay and a pretender,' Salaam said disgustedly. 'We all thought Colonel Qadhafi was a ruthless dictator, but Zuwayy is a hundred times worse. I had hoped a real al-Sanusi had taken over the Libyan government – then perhaps we'd see peace in our lifetime. Unfortunately, Egypt and most of Europe has to prepare to defend itself against whatever power-mad move he and his Mujahadeen crackpots will come up with.' He glanced over his shoulder and noticed al-Khan still speaking with Zuwayy. 'Or maybe we should be defending ourselves against the enemy right in our own house.'

'Khalid al-Khan may not be one of your staunchest supporters, Kamal,' Susan said, 'but he represents the loyal opposition.'

Salaam smiled, then squeezed his wife's hand tenderly. 'My wife, you are one of the most intelligent and thoughtful women I have ever known, on a par with the greatest minds in our great country, but you know so little of power politics,' Salaam said. 'Ten years in the US Air Force as an intelligence officer is indeed impressive but insignificant experience compared to one year sitting across a People's Assembly chamber arguing with men like Zuwayy and al-Khan. They and other members of the "loyal opposition" would just as soon throw a punch or an insult as they would squish a fig.'

'You think I am really that innocent, Jamal?' Susan asked playfully.

Salaam basked in the unearthly glow of her sly smile. 'I would never accuse you of being "innocent," my love,' he said. 'But even scholars and *ulamas* like Khan have no compunction about going outside the law to get what they want. There is too much at stake for them, both in this world and in the next. They are fanatical – they believe they are on a mission, their actions fully justified and sanctioned by God. The nation, the land, even their homes, mean nothing to them compared to what they perceive as the will of Allah. That vision obscures everything.' His eyes narrowed, and his grip on his wife's hand tightened. 'Always be watchful for the enemy. Trust no one. Question everything.'

'All I have to do to learn about the real world is watch you, Kamal,' Susan said. 'The one thing I trust is your love for your country and your people.'

'And my love for you, Sekhmet,' Salaam said, using the ancient Egyptian nickname he had given her, which meant 'huntress.' 'My love comes before the people, the country, even before God. Never forget that.'

'And my love for you is greater than all of our enemies and evil anywhere in the world,' Susan said. 'When you think all are against you, I will always be by your side.'

'Unfortunately, your place now needs to be behind me,' Salaam said, giving his wife a smile when he noticed her exasperated expression. 'You may be loved by everyone in Egypt, but you are still expected to walk behind your husband, not beside him, at least on this holy day.'

'Of course, my husband,' she replied. Susan gave her husband another soft kiss on the side of his lips, then stepped back the required two paces behind and to her husband's left, her hands folded before her, her eyes averted. She knew her place well: Dwelling in a nation torn between the past, the present, and the future, it was best to not give traditionalists like Zuwayy, al-Khan, and their followers any reason to question the loyalty or morals of their country's leaders. A few moments later, the Republican Guard security forces opened the doors of the great hall, indicating that the procession was about to begin.

Past the Gates of Sultan Qayt Bay, a large courtyard with several ornate minarets and *qibla* prayer walls separated the Madrasa from the main sanctuary, where the speeches and prayer services for President Salaam's guests would take place. The path through the courtyard from the tomb to the sanctuary was lined with soldiers, with clergy and other invited guests pressing against the soldiers to watch the procession.

It was Susan, not Kamal, who noticed two unusual things as they proceeded across the courtyard: First, the soldiers lining the procession route were not Presidential Guards, assigned to the protection of the president, but paramilitary soldiers from a unit she did not recognize; and second, they were facing the procession, their backs to the crowd instead of facing them. She turned to look for the Presidential Guard captain who had been stationed at the door to the Madrasa, but he was nowhere to be seen.

As she looked, her eyes caught those of Jadallah Zuwayy, walking several steps behind her. He nodded reassuringly to her, then glanced at Khalid al-Khan and nodded. Susan turned and looked at al-Khan, noticing the silent signal between the two. What was going on here? Why were they –?

Bedlam suddenly erupted. A soldier shouted something from the Madrasa – someone had been killed? Is that what he shouted? It was hard to tell – his voice was strained with pain or fear. There was purposeful movement in the crowd of onlookers, not a random milling about but a determined surge forward. The soldiers guarding the procession line, their backs to the crowd, noticed nothing – even when two men in traditional *thawb, sirwal, rida,* and turbans burst past them.

'Kamal!' Susan shouted. 'Look out!' But suddenly she was grabbed from behind. It was al-Khan. He held her tightly by the arms, pressed her toward him, leered hungrily at her, then shoved her forcefully back toward Zuwayy. The Libyan pretender-king grasped her, then said something in a low, soft voice. 'What are you doing, Majesty? What is going on?'

'I said, do not worry, my child,' Zuwayy said. 'Allah the almighty shall protect all true believers and servants of God.'

Susan spun around until she was facing Kamal, still in Zuwayy's grasp but being pulled backward, away from her husband. Up ahead of her, one of the strangers who had crashed unchecked through the security line grabbed President Salaam from behind, while another grasped him from in front. Once the man in front had a firm grip on Salaam, the man behind turned, raised his hands, and shouted, 'Death to all *kuffar*! Death to all enemies of God! The Muslim Brotherhood is Allah's sword of justice this day!'

The man in front of Kamal opened his cloak – and revealed several sticks of explosives and a detonator strapped to his abdomen.

'*La!*' Susan screamed in Arabic. '*Imshi!* Get away! Kamal!' She twisted easily away from Zuwayy. One of the paramilitary soldiers beside Zuwayy tried to grab her. She clawed her way free and took a running step toward her shocked husband . . . just as a brilliant flash of light, an impossibly loud explosion of sound, and an incredible blast of heat erupted right in front of her. She had a momentary image of Kamal Ismail Salaam's body and that of his attacker being blown apart like firecrackers, before a giant invisible force threw her backward and darkness closed over her. . .

Chapter One

Blytheville, Arkansas

The dark-clad figure turned, slowly, smoothly, menacingly. The blank, staring eyes were expressionless, robotic. The figure lifted a weapon from the floor, an immense M168 six-barreled Vulcan cannon, and pointed it right at Patrick McLanahan. From less than thirty meters away, he could not miss. The cannon, normally mounted on a large vehicle like an armored personnel carrier, could fire hot-dog-sized shells at up to three thousand rounds a minute – there would be nothing left of his body, even after only a one-second burst, to clean up with a sponge.

Patrick heard a clink of metal – the Gatling gun ammunition feed mechanism as the figure adjusted his grip. He couldn't see a trigger – the Vulcan cannon was normally electrically operated – so he could not even guess when the gun would start firing. It wouldn't matter anyway – at this range, he'd probably be dead before he heard the sound.

'Feels good,' the figure said, his voice electronically distorted. In rapid succession, he elevated the cannon straight up into the air, side to side, and around in all directions. The movements were smooth, mechanical, effortless, as if the one-thousand-pound cannon were little more than a wooden stick. He set the big gun down on the floor, then unfastened some latches, removed his helmet, and handed it to a technician standing nearby to help him. 'I feel like a damned clown miming on the street, but it works pretty well.'

Patrick looked at Hal Briggs but said nothing. Hal was wearing the new and improved Tin Man battle armor, and he looked as if he was thoroughly enjoying it.

The first version of the electronic armor was designed to protect the wearer from bullets or bombs – fast-moving blunt trauma or shock – but did nothing to enhance strength. The new suit added a fibersteel exoskeleton structure with microhydraulically operated joints at the shoulders, elbows, hips, knees, and ankles, with stress supports on the hands, fingers, and feet. The suit's onboard computers read and analyzed all of the body's normal muscle movements and amplified them through the exoskeleton, giving the wearer unbelievable physical strength, speed, and enhanced agility.

'Now, let's see if it fits in its convenient carrying case.' Hal entered a code into a small panel on his left gauntlet, which powered down the exoskeleton and released the bindings. The exoskeleton remained standing like some sort of metal sculpture or futuristic scarecrow. He entered another code into a small control panel inside the frame on the spine, and the exoskeleton started to fold itself. In less than thirty seconds, it had collapsed down to the size and weight of a small suitcase. Hal placed the folded exoskeleton into a padded duffel bag and slung it over his shoulder – because of its composite construction, it was light and easy to carry, although the fibersteel components were many times stronger than steel. 'Very cool. Every kid should have one.'

Hal stepped over to Patrick, the duffel bag slung on his back, and clasped his longtime friend on the shoulder. 'You okay, Muck?' he asked.

Patrick shrugged. 'It just feels like one of those days when you know something's not going to go right.'

'Well, Wendy did a good job getting this thing tuned up,' Hal said, motioning to the bag on his shoulder. 'It's very cool. I want to start putting it through its paces right away, before Masters decides to invest production money on something else.'

'That may be sooner than you think,' they heard a voice say. The voice belonged to Kevin Martindale. He was watching the demonstration from a corner of the test chamber. The young, handsome, energetic former president stepped over and greeted Patrick and Hal. Kevin Martindale, also a former vice president, had stayed only one term in the White House. He was a strong military advocate, but was voted out of office mostly because of actions he failed to take when the United States was threatened. What the public did not know was that Martindale preferred to use secret, unconventional forces to destroy an enemy's ability to make war before the situation grew worse.

Now Martindale was head of a secret organization called the Night Stalkers, composed of former military men and women, who performed similar unconventional-warfare missions around the world. But these operations were neither ordered nor sanctioned by any government – Martindale and his senior staff decided which missions to perform and how to perform them. In addition, squeezing or outright stealing money, weapons, and equipment from their defeated opponents usually funded these operations.

'Very impressive,' Martindale said, a fascinated gleam in his eye. These days, Kevin Martindale wore his hair much longer than he did in his days in the White House or Congress, and he had grown a goatee. He looked and acted quite a bit differently than his more conservative, buttoned-down government persona: Patrick hadn't yet decided if he liked the new Kevin Martindale. 'One of Jon Masters's new toys?'

'An old toy with some new tricks,' Hal responded, handing the duffel bag over to Martindale.

He was surprised at how lightweight it was. 'That's it? Everything but the armor and backpack?'

'That doubles the weight – still very transportable.'

'Excellent. We should talk to Jon and see if he can make a few units available to the Night Stalkers.'

'I'm sure that can be arranged,' Patrick assured him.

'With the usual three-hundred-percent markup,' Hal chimed in with a broad smile as he finished removing the Tin Man battle armor and stowing it in the duffel bag.

'Fine with me – I'm not paying for it,' Martindale responded dryly.

The comment bugged Patrick – it summarized all of Patrick's misgivings about being part of the Night Stalkers. Yes, they were doing important work – capturing international drug dealers and criminals like Pavel Kazakov, the Russian oilman and Russian Mafia chieftain, who had the incredible audacity to bribe generals in the Russian army to invade and occupy Balkan states so he could build a pipeline across those countries and make it more profitable for him to ship oil to the West. They had captured Kazakov and dozens of other terrorists, drug dealers, assassins, and international fugitives in less than a year.

But no one in this group was independently wealthy. They had to do an old infantry soldier's trick taken a few steps further:

raid the land as they marched across it. Patrick himself had threatened Pavel Kazakov, one of the world's most wealthy but most dangerous individuals, with taking his life in exchange for the tidy sum of half a billion dollars – he still made sure he was tossed into a Turkish prison, but he also threatened to kill him instead if he didn't pay up. They had stolen guns, computer equipment and data, vehicles, aircraft, ships, and hacked into hundreds of bank accounts of known international criminals to raise money for their operations. The logic was simple: Not only did they arrest the bad guys, but they also substantially reduced their ability to carry on their criminal or terrorist enterprises.

Patrick tried to tell himself that it was all for the common good – but those words kept on ringing hollow.

'Good to see you came through your "test flight" over Libya all right,' Martindale said to Patrick as they made their way out of the test lab. 'But may I respectfully suggest you just get Dr Masters to schedule some range time with the Air Force or Army on their ranges in North America to shoot down some missiles.'

'Unfortunately, we can't blame that one on him, sir,' Patrick admitted. 'The test flight idea was mine. Jon wanted to make a big splash to impress the Pentagon, and I picked the closest country I thought would take a shot at us without starting World War Three. It turned out to be one of the most successful test flights we've ever made in a Megafortress, and certainly the most successful one for the Dragon airborne laser.'

'Not too shabby for you either.'

'Sir?'

'I suppose you haven't heard – I heard it from very back-channel sources,' Martindale said. 'You know, of course, that President Thorn has never chosen a national security adviser.'

'Yes, sir. He claims that the purpose of the President's cabinet is to not only administer the government but to advise the President,' Patrick said. 'He claims it's the way our government was set up. He thinks bureaucrats like national security advisers distort and politicize the decision-making process.'

'What do you think of that?'

'I think any leader, especially the leader of the free world in the twenty-first century, needs all the advisers he can get,' Patrick replied. His eyes narrowed, and he looked at Martindale carefully. 'Why?'

'Because your name was being bandied about as being on the President's list for national security adviser.' Patrick stopped and looked at Martindale in complete surprise. 'He's putting together his reelection campaign, and the word is that folks would be more comfortable with him in a second term if he had a more identifiable, complete set of advisers – national security adviser being the number-one pick. That, it appears, is *you*.'

'*Me?* That's insane!' Patrick retorted.

'Why insane?' Martindale asked. 'After you put together and then commanded that Air National Guard EB-1C Vampire unit over United Korea, you're one of the most popular and well-known military guys out there. Some folks equate you with Jimmy Doolittle putting together the Tokyo air raids in World War Two, or with Colin Powell. The guys who have access can look at your record and just be amazed and awestruck at the stuff you've done. Plus, you have one more advantage.'

'What's that?'

'You're not Brad Elliott,' Martindale said with a smile. 'They look at what you and your team did over Russia and Romania in the Kazakov incident, over Korea, over China, over Lithuania, and all the other secret missions you've been involved in over the years, and they realize that you were fighting for your people – that shows pride, determination, and tenacity. Brad Elliott didn't fight for his people – Brad Elliott gladly sacrificed his people to do whatever he wanted. They know where you're coming from. Thorn likes that. I know you disagree with Thorn on military policy . . .'

'"Disagree"? It goes way beyond "disagree," Mr President! Thorn was the one who had me involuntarily retired from the Air Force! Thorn ordered my wife and daughter arrested by the FBI, and his Justice Department has got agents watching and listening in on Sky Masters Inc night and day. Thorn and I have absolutely nothing in common except loathing for each other.'

'In case you haven't noticed, Thorn likes surrounding himself with advisers that disagree with him,' Martindale said. 'In fact, I can't think of one person in his entire administration that thinks like him or is even remotely simpatico with his throwback

Jeffersonian ideology. Even his close friend Robert Goff and he constantly butt heads.'

'I'd work with Goff, Kercheval, or even Busick any day,' Patrick said. 'But there is no way in hell I'd ever serve under Thorn.'

'Why?'

'We don't just disagree – I feel his views of the military and America's role in the world suck,' Patrick said. 'America has the moral wisdom to use its military forces to protect peace and freedom around the world. This "stick-your-head-in-the-sand" attitude is causing widespread uncertainty in the world, and scumbags like Pavel Kazakov are crawling out of the woodwork and taking advantage of it.'

'Then why wouldn't you go to the White House and tell Thorn what you think?'

'Because you can't talk to guys like Thorn. He's a fanatic, an extremist ideologue. I'd be arguing real-world situations and alternatives to crises that require fast responses, and he'd be quoting Thomas Jefferson and Benjamin Franklin. No, thanks.'

'You would decline to accept the nomination?'

'Loudly and publicly,' Patrick said finally.

Martindale nodded. 'Good. You're the heart of this team, Patrick – I hope you know that,' he said sincerely. 'We'd exist without you, but we wouldn't be the same – not nearly as dedicated, not nearly as hard-charging. I'd move heaven and earth to keep you here.'

'Thank you, sir,' Patrick said. 'That means a lot.'

Patrick and Hal followed Martindale into a secure conference room in the main headquarters building of the Sky Masters Inc campus, a large industrial and research center in what was the old Blytheville Air Force Base in Arkansas, now called the Arkansas International Jetport. They warmly greeted Patrick's brother Paul, one of the first members of the Night Stalkers and the most experienced Tin Man battle armor user, along with Chris Wohl, a retired Marine Corps master sergeant and Hal Briggs's longtime partner. Martindale took his place at the apex of the conference table while Patrick secured the room, then motioned for Chris Wohl to begin.

'We are closely monitoring developments on the border between Libya and Egypt,' Wohl began. 'Libya has recently sent several thousand troops to the Sudan, on Egypt's southern border, supposedly to support the president of the Sudan against rebel insurgents that are using Chad as a safe haven. However, the insurgency was crushed last year, and Libyan forces remain deployed in three Sudanese bases – all within a day's armored vehicle march of five major Egyptian oil fields. Egypt has reinforced its armed forces in the region and maintains a rough parity with Libyan forces.'

'So Libya wants to take Egypt's oil fields?'

'That's nothing new,' Martindale said, 'although they've preferred in the past to try to form a partnership with Egypt in developing its oil reserves. However, Egypt wants to form a consortium with some Western oil companies to tap its oil fields.'

'Lots more money that way, I'd guess,' Briggs offered.

'Exactly right – and ExxonMobil and Shell don't bring troops with them to the contract-signing ceremonies,' Martindale said. 'The consortium wants to build a four-hundred-and-sixty-mile-long pipeline from southern Egypt to the Mediterranean Sea capable of shipping two million barrels of crude per day, along with building refineries. It's a three-billion-dollar project that Libya desperately wants to get involved with.'

'Doesn't Libya already export oil?' Paul McLanahan asked.

'Yes, but with US sanctions still in place, they don't ship much to the West,' Martindale replied. 'The new president of Libya, who calls himself King Idris the Second, is even worse than Muammar Qadhafi. Idris, whose real name is Zuwayy, has reorganized the Muslim Brotherhood, the group of Muslim fanatics that seeks to make every Arabic-speaking nation in the world a theocracy – governed and steered by strict fundamentalist doctrine. Libya, Sudan, and Yemen are solidly in his hip pocket; Palestine, Lebanon, Syria, Iraq, Saudi Arabia, and Jordan are leaning toward him; Kuwait, Bahrain, Qatar, the United Arab Emirates, Oman, and Egypt so far oppose him.'

'And the Muslim Brotherhood has been linked with the assassination of President Salaam of Egypt and his wife,' Hal Briggs added. 'Sounds like recruitment by intimidation to me. Join – or else.'

'It looks like Zuwayy's going further than just assassination,' Martindale said. 'Sergeant Wohl?'

31

'Intelligence experts suspect that Libya has imported surface-to-surface missiles from someone – China, Pakistan, Russia, we don't know for sure yet – and has set up several bases from which to stage attacks into Egypt to destroy their military forces,' Wohl went on. 'The rumor is, the missiles have chemical, biological, and nuclear warheads, as well as conventional high-explosives. We have been tasked to find those missiles, identify them, and destroy them if possible.'

'"Intelligence experts"?' Patrick asked suspiciously. 'Who might they be, sir? I know we're not getting any cooperation from US agencies.'

Kevin Martindale looked at Patrick with a mixture of irritation and surprise in his features. 'A group hired by the Central African Petroleum Partners,' Martindale replied uneasily.

'You mean the oil consortium with a stake in the Egyptian oil fields?'

'Do you have a problem working for them, General?' Martindale asked.

'Sir, I want to head off trouble as much as anyone,' Patrick said. 'And I certainly don't like Zuwayy any more than I liked Qadhafi and the terrorist organizations they sponsor. But I don't like the idea of being a hired gun for an oil cartel, either.'

'Would you like them better if I told you we would be getting our first paychecks out of this?' Martindale asked. 'That's the difference between this mission and all the others – we are given a target, but we're also well compensated for our services.'

Patrick fell silent, but the eagerness was evident in Hal Briggs's and Paul McLanahan's eyes. The reason was clear: They had the most to lose and the most to gain out of this. Martindale, Patrick, and Chris Wohl all had government pensions waiting for them; in addition, Patrick was a vice president of Sky Masters Inc, for which he was very well paid. But Hal Briggs resigned his Air Force commission well before retirement age, and Paul McLanahan had only a small disability check from the Sacramento Police Department, where he was a sworn officer for only a few weeks before being retired with a one-hundred-percent disability. Neither of them had earned any money in many months, and had been relying on gifts from Martindale and Patrick.

'How much are we talkin' about here, Mr President?' Hal asked.

'I accepted a twenty-million-dollar contract for our services, plus a bonus for complete destruction of all known missile installations,' Martindale replied. 'I will pay every man in this room twenty-five thousand dollars a day, beginning as soon as you accept this mission.'

'Per . . . *day* . . . ?'

'Our support team members will earn ten thousand dollars . . . and yes, that's per day, tax free,' Martindale went on. 'The Night Stalkers will pay Sky Masters Inc full retail price for the equipment and supplies we use. Sound okay with you, gentlemen?' Hal slapped his hands together excitedly, and Paul looked jubilant – even Chris Wohl nodded in approval, even though he wore his same expressionless warrior's mask. Martindale studied their faces, then settled on Patrick's. 'All right with you, General?' he asked.

Patrick looked at Paul and Hal's happy faces. Paul gave his brother an excited slap on the back – it had been a long time since he had seen him smile like that. 'Yes, sir,' Patrick finally responded. 'It's okay with me.'

'Outstanding,' Martindale said. He punched up instructions into a computer, and the results were projected onto a large flat-panel monitor on the conference-room wall. 'The intelligence we've received indicates several new Libyan missile bases scattered around the country. I'll leave it up to you and your support team to figure out the best way to proceed, but after speaking with Master Sergeant Wohl here, he suggests a soft probe of the most likely bases, followed by an unmanned aircraft strike to soften up the base's defenses, followed by a hard-target penetration. It's up to you – but I hasten to remind you of a substantial performance bonus for each one of you if the danger to the consortium's pipeline is eliminated. Enough said. Good luck, and good hunting.'

As was his custom, Martindale never stuck around for the details – the planning, training, organization, logistics, or movement of the Night Stalkers was never something he was concerned about. He gave marching orders, then left it to the teams to carry out the plan. Within minutes, they heard his helicopter depart, on its way to his next meeting. Patrick had little idea what he did, where he went, or whom he spoke to as the former president of the United States.

'Now we're talking *serious* bucks!' Briggs exclaimed happily. 'Man, I was hoping we'd get into jobs like this – I was thinking I'd have to go back to Georgia and help my granddad in his kennels and get a real job.'

'I'm not happy about accepting this job,' Patrick admitted. 'Some big oil cartel is asking us to put our asses on the firing line to help them keep their profits safe. We don't know anything about the cartel; and since the assassination of President Salaam, we don't know which way the Egyptian government is going to go. And I don't trust any intelligence info we get from private sources. They answer to investors and bosses, not to the grunts.'

Hal fell silent, looking at the ground. Chris Wohl nodded. 'All good points, sir,' he said. 'Our first priority would be to get our own intel – a few overflights from some NIRTSats should do it.' NIRTSats, or Need It Right This Second Satellites, were small, low-Earth orbit photo and radar reconnaissance satellites designed for a specific mission. They were extremely valuable in passing detailed intelligence information to tactical units; but because they were in very low orbits, their duration was usually only a few days or a couple of weeks, and they carried only small positioning thrusters and very little fuel, so their orbits could not be changed or even fine-tuned to any great extent. He looked at Patrick evenly, then added, 'If you agree to do it with us.'

'You don't need my approval, Chris.'

'Pardon me, sir, but I do . . . *we* do,' Wohl said.

''Fraid so, Muck,' Hal said. 'The Night Stalkers may be a private nonmilitary unconventional action team, but the bottom line is: We're a *team*.'

'We don't do anything unless we all agree to do it,' Paul chimed in. 'One person has veto power. One "no," even one "I'm not sure," and we scrub the mission.'

'That's the SOP, sir,' Wohl agreed. 'We all do it, or no one does it.'

Patrick hesitated. Something deep within him still maintained that this was wrong. He was trained to fight, trained to use his brains and his training and experience to fight and win battles – but this was not one of the battles he had in mind. He wasn't defending his home or his country or his family. This mission was to destroy one country's supposed threat to disrupt commerce in order to help a multinational corporation earn more money. This was a job for a private security company – or a mercenary force.

The obvious question: Was Patrick turning into a mercenary? Was he going to start fighting not for home or country or family, but for money?

Maybe he was, at least for the moment. If his own military didn't want him, maybe it was time to fight for what he felt was right – and accept a little money to do it.

'I'm in,' Patrick heard himself say. 'I'll get a NIRTSat constellation up right away, and get a few FlightHawks ready for air support.' The FlightHawks were Sky Masters's unmanned combat aircraft, capable of ground, air, or ship launch, and equipped to carry a wide variety of sensors, cameras, radio gear – or munitions. They were stealthy, accurate, and very effective.

'We're *gone*!' Paul McLanahan shouted excitedly, his electronically synthesized voice amplifying his happiness. 'Let's go kick some Libyan rocket-launching ass!'

Samāh, Libya
several days later

'Nike, say status,' Patrick McLanahan whispered into the secure satellite link. A warning indicator on his electronic visor had just advised him that one of his men had already engaged the enemy. Just a few minutes into what was supposed to be a quick, silent recon, they were made.

'Bad guy came out of nowhere, and this damned suit blasted him before I could stop it,' retired US Marine Corps master sergeant Chris Wohl explained. 'I'm secure, and I'm moving in.'

'This is supposed to be a soft probe, Nike, not an assault. We can come back.'

'If they're alerted, they might move all their assets, and then we'd have to locate them all over again,' Wohl protested. 'I think only one guy saw me, and I don't think he's a sentry, so we still might have time. Besides, you made this suit, not me. If you wanted a soft probe, you should've showed me how to shut off the auto-bugzapper feature. I'm secure, and I'm moving in.'

Once a flamethrowing kick-ass Marine, always a kick-ass

Marine, Patrick thought as he checked the God's-eye view display on his helmet-mounted electronic visor. Patrick McLanahan was kneeling in a shallow gully just a few yards inside the perimeter fence surrounding a newly discovered Libyan military base near Samāh, about two hundred miles south of Benghazi. The mission was to sneak in from three different points, doing a soft probe on this remote desert base. Initial intelligence reports said Samāh was a terrorist training camp, but a few unconfirmed reports received from the private intelligence sources said Samāh was a rocket base set up recently to secretly attack targets in Egypt, Chad, Europe, or in the Mediterranean Sea, possibly with medium-range Russian- or Chinese-made rockets with chemical or biological warheads.

The plan was for all three infiltrators to go in simultaneously, take infrared or night-vision digital images with their equipment, uplink it all to reconnaissance satellites back to their headquarters, and get out without anyone knowing they were there. If the Libyans discovered they had been infiltrated, they might pack everything up and turn the base into an unassuming training base.

But Chris Wohl was by far the most experienced and well-trained commando among them – and he ran on his own timetable, which was several steps ahead of everyone else, constantly thinking and planning and reacting, leading the way. Patrick should have known that Chris Wohl would want to make first contact.

The God's-eye overhead images that Patrick was studying were being transmitted via satellite from stealth unmanned combat aircraft called FlightHawks. Two FlightHawks had been launched from a Sky Masters Inc DC-10 launch aircraft over the Mediterranean Sea while on a normal, routine flight from Bahrain to Madrid. The FlightHawks were autonomous UCAVs, or unmanned combat air vehicles; although a ground controller could fly them, they were designed to fly a preprogrammed flight plan and automatically react to threats or new target instructions. One FlightHawk carried a LADAR, or laser radar, that took images as crystal-clear as a high-resolution digital photograph, then beamed those images down to Wendy on the *Catherine* as well as the men on the ground in Libya.

The FlightHawk's ground monitors and controllers were Patrick's wife and electronics wizard, Wendy Tork McLanahan, as well as Patrick's longtime partner and friend, engineering expert David Luger, based aboard a converted salvage ship a hundred miles off the Libyan coast in the Mediterranean Sea. The team's infiltration and exfiltration aircraft, a CV-22 Pave Hammer tilt-rotor aircraft, could take off, land, refuel, and be serviced on the cargo ship in hiding. The ship, a Lithuanian-flagged and fully registered and functioning rescue and salvage vessel named SS *Catherine the Great*, had a contingent of fifty highly trained commandos and enough firepower on board to start a small war.

The commandos on this mission also had another high-tech weapon in their arsenal: their improved 'Tin Man' electronic battle armor. Also developed by Sky Masters Inc, the armor used a special electroreactive technology that caused ordinary-looking and -feeling fabric instantly to harden to several times the strength of steel when sharply struck. The suit also contained self-contained breathing apparatus, temperature control, communications, long-range visual and aural detection and tracking sensors, mobility enhancers – compressed-air jump jets in the boots – and self-protection weapons. The self-defense weapon was an electrical discharge device that disabled the enemy with a bolt of high-voltage energy; it operated automatically, tied to the suit's sensors, and was able to fire instantly in any direction out to thirty feet from electrodes on both shoulders if an enemy was detected.

The newest feature of their battle armor: a microhydraulically controlled fibersteel exoskeleton that gave the wearer the strength and power of a multimillion-dollar robot. The exoskeleton ran along the back, shoulders, arms, legs, and neck, and amplified the wearer's muscular strength a hundred times; yet the exoskeleton and its control systems weighed only a few pounds and used very little power.

The armor could save its wearers from most small- and medium-sized infantry attacks and even some light armored attacks, but every attack drained precious power from the suit quickly, and they were several hundred miles from help. The Tin Man technology was designed to save its wearer from attack long enough to escape a defensive, patrol, or security engagement, not

37

to press an assault against a superior fighting force. The longer Wohl stayed in the area after the alarm was sounded, the more danger he was in.

Through his electronic visor, Patrick could see that Wohl had stopped just outside an area that had previously been identified in satellite photos as a garbage dump, known by its map coordinate Bravo Two. The area was unguarded and unsecured, and military and civilian personnel passed by it constantly without being stopped or challenged by anyone – there was no reason to suspect it was anything else but a garbage dump. Patrick had dismissed it in their search. 'Nike, what are you doing at Bravo Two?'

'I want to check this place out,' Wohl replied. 'I'm secure.'

'Nike, let's stick with the recon plan, shall we?'

'I'll be back on schedule in no time.'

'Stalkers, looks like there's some activity on this side of the base – your guy might have missed a bed check or something,' ex-Air Force security officer and commando Hal Briggs reported. The commandos on this mission were spread out around the sprawling, isolated desert base in strategic support locations, and moving from one spot to another without attracting any attention took time. 'They're doing a search around the perimeter. Might as well let Nike poke around a bit more – he's safe there for now.'

'If the alarm's been sounded, we need to bug out of here,' Patrick said. 'Your best exit point now is Alpha One, Nike. Get moving.' To Briggs, he added, 'Taurus, can you cover him?'

'Dammit, Castor, we traveled too far to turn around the moment someone has a bad dream,' Wohl radioed. 'I'm secure, and I think I found something interesting, so I'm staying put for sixty lousy seconds longer. The FlightHawks will have to RTB in less than fifteen minutes anyway – they might not complete a full reconnoiter, and there won't be time to recover, refuel, and relaunch them before daybreak. I'm *staying*. If you don't like it, come in here and try to drag me back. Nike *out*.'

McLanahan cursed again – it seemed as if he was doing that a lot lately – and wished for one of his long-range bombers loaded with smart bombs to be flying overhead right about now. Twice retired from the United States Air Force – the last time involuntarily – Patrick had been a one-star general, the deputy commander of one of the world's most secret weapons development and testing facilities, the High Technology Aerospace Weapons Center (HAWC), Elliott Air Force Base, Groom Lake, Nevada. The weapons from that facility had many times been used in real-world conflicts, from Russia to China to America and everywhere in between, and Patrick had been a part of the action originating there for over a decade. Patrick had seen and experienced the best – and worst – of both human suffering and technological amazement.

But they would probably not see action within a decade, if ever, because few politicians and bureaucrats – including, in Patrick's estimation, the current administration of US President Thomas Nathaniel Thorn – had the guts to use them. Just one of HAWC's Megafortress bombers could destroy several dozen armored vehicles and keep an entire battalion of troops at bay, without being detected on radar and without exposing itself to undue risk; if they were given the order, one Megafortress could destroy the entire base without so much as rustling an innocent civilian's tent flap, if there were any here. They had already proven the value of a small commando team paired up with one stealth bomber in the skies over Russia, right near Moscow itself.

But since then, Thorn had all but shut down HAWC and had sent most of America's fleet of bombers to the Boneyard, along with about a third of the active-duty military and other deep cuts in tactical weapons and units. McLanahan and the other commandos here at Samāh were not here under government sanction. It was dirty, difficult, and dangerous work.

No wonder Patrick found little to smile about these days.

'Don't give me that "Nike out" crap,' McLanahan radioed back. 'This is supposed to be a soft probe, not a search-and-destroy – that's why we have the FlightHawks overhead. I want you out *now.*'

'Then I guess I'll just ignore this SS-12 battery I just found.'
'*What?*'
'Pretty damned clever, hiding it in a garbage dump,' Wohl said. He moved closer to the area. There was a short ramp on the west end of the pit, ostensibly to make it easier for the dump truck drivers to enter the pit. But on closer inspection, he saw that the

garbage was piled not on the ground inside the pit but atop a retractable net. 'Normal overhead imagery shows a garbage dump. It's unguarded like a garbage dump – and the organic waste gives off enough heat to block infrared and radar imagery.' Wohl examined underneath the net with his infrared sensors. 'And there it is, boys – the aft end of a MAZ-543 transporter-erector-launcher and an SS-12 Scaleboard rocket, still in its marching sheath. I'll bet there are at least three more TELs in this pit, and if I check the other garbage pits, I'll find more. Not to mention the TELs hidden in some of the service buildings.'

'The damned Libyans have SS-12s,' Briggs breathed. 'Holy shit.' The SS-12 tactical ballistic missile, NATO code name 'Scaleboard,' was the upgraded version of the ubiquitous mobile 'Scud' surface-to-surface missile, in service with almost a dozen nations around the world. The SS-12 was larger, had three times the range of a Scud, was more accurate – and it carried a one-point-three-megaton nuclear warhead. As far as anyone knew, this was the first known instance of an SS-12 missile based outside of Russia. 'Can you see the warhead, Nike? Is it a nuke?'

'Stand by, Taurus. I'll check.'

'Nike, clear out of there,' McLanahan repeated. 'We'll have the FlightHawks take them out.' The first FlightHawk UCAV carried only the laser radar array, but the second FlightHawk was armed with four antitank BLU-108 SFW sensor-fuzed weapon bomblets and four antipersonnel Gator cluster bomb munitions. They were devastating weapons: A single SFW could destroy as many as three dozen main battle tanks, and a single Gator could kill, injure, or deny enemy access across an area twice the size of a football field. 'Base, you copy? Stand by to arm up the 'Hawks.'

'We have a good location on Nike,' Wendy McLanahan radioed from the Catherine out in the Med. The Tin Man battle armor contained a transponder to allow Wendy on board the command ship to track and monitor all the commandos. 'Ready to come in hot.'

'Negative, Base, negative,' Wohl interjected. 'The junk they got these things buried under will keep the SFW from detecting them, or they might lock onto some other hot object; and the junk might block the bomblets' blast effects. We're going to have to expose them enough so the SFWs and Gators can do their job, or destroy them one by one by hand. I'm moving in.'

No use in trying to hold him back, Patrick thought, he's on the warpath. It's not every day that you're sent in just to take a few pictures and end up coming across a bunch of nuclear-tipped missiles. Wohl must be salivating in his battle armor. 'Roger, Nike. Stalkers, let's move in together. One coordinated attack. Stand by.'

But Chris Wohl wasn't going to 'stand by' – he was already on the move.

He hurriedly checked for a sentry. There were sentry shacks on all four sides of the garbage pit, but through his infrared sensors he could see that all were deserted. He descended down the incline toward the rear of the rocket . . .

. . . and the second he reached the floor of the pit and touched the net covering the rocket, four huge ballpark lights illuminated the entire garbage pit, and a siren sounded. There were no sentries because the entire garbage pit was alarmed. Time had run out.

From his observation point, Patrick saw the lights come on. 'Oh, shit,' Patrick murmured. 'Taurus, move in, check the garbage pit at Alpha Two,' he radioed. 'I'll check Golf Six. Pollux, create a diversion around Tango Five. Base, order the FlightHawks in to attack.'

'Roger that, Castor,' Patrick's younger brother, Paul, responded. One of the original members of the Night Stalkers and the acknowledged expert in the use of the Tin Man battle armor, he was the fourth man on this spy team, taking the east side of the Libyan base.

'Copy, Castor,' Wendy replied. 'They're coming in hot, two minutes out, SFWs and Gators. Light up the targets as much as you can.'

Meanwhile, Wohl dashed to the body of the SS-12 rocket, grabbed a cable running down the side, and pulled. The SS-12 missile was encased in a plastic transport sheath that protected it during transit but popped off easily during launch; it was simple to peel it off now. It was a real SS-12 rocket – no decoys here. He dashed forward, unzipping the sheath as he ran, then climbed up onto the cab until he reached the warhead. It looked real enough too, although he had never seen a live nuclear warhead before. 'Castor, I just cracked open the warhead. Take a look and tell me what it is.'

Patrick commanded his electronic helmet visor to lock in on Chris Wohl's visor image, transmitted from his suit's electronics suite via satellite. He recognized it instantly: 'It's the real thing, folks – a Russian NMT-17 Mod One warhead, one-megaton-plus yield.'

Wohl turned at a sudden sound behind him and saw soldiers rushing to the edge of the garbage pit, gesturing inside. The best proof he had a live warhead here wasn't McLanahan's assessment – it was the fact that none of the Libyans surrounding him dared raise a rifle muzzle in his direction or even come any closer to him. They were afraid of creating a nuclear yield if they hit the missile with a bullet. Wohl knew it took a lot more than one bullet to set one of these things off – but then again, maybe they knew something he didn't. 'How do I disable it, Castor?'

'You can't, unless you brought a whole truckload of Snap-On Tools,' Patrick replied. 'Your best option is to create a heat source and let the FlightHawks finish the job.'

'I can do that,' Wohl said. He jumped down from the front of the TEL and searched until he found the diesel fuel refilling port, between the third and fourth set of wheels on the right side. The fuel tank itself was underneath the chassis and protected very well by slabs of steel, but he didn't need it. He opened the filler port, stepped back a few paces, and activated his self-protection weapon, sending a bolt of electrical energy from electrodes on his shoulders directly into the fuel port. A few moments later, Patrick saw a flash, and a second later heard an explosion, then another just a few moments later. So much for their little sneak-and-peek operation.

'All right, Nike, you dropped your drawers – we might as well have some fun too,' Hal Briggs chimed in. 'I'm in.'

'Go for the fuel filler port on the right side between the rear wheels,' Wohl said as he moved to the third SS-12. 'The TELs aren't grounded, and there aren't any flame suppressors in the filler tube.'

'Hey, Castor,' Briggs asked, 'what's the chance of one of those babies popping off with a yield in a fire?'

'Very slim,' Patrick replied. 'If they have no safeties in them or if the ones the Russians installed haven't been maintained by the Libyans, the worst that will happen is that the high-explosive

42

jacket surrounding the core will cook off and scatter radioactive debris around.'

'What if the trigger gets activated by a concussion or even by our shock beams?'

'I don't know,' Patrick said. 'Try not to hit the warhead with your beams. But there would have to be no pressure or acceleration safeties and pretty unstable triggers that then happen to work perfectly to produce a yield. Don't worry about it. Expose your missiles with a heat source as best you can so the FlightHawk can drop on them, and let's get out of here.'

Several seconds later, Patrick saw another explosion, this time farther north. 'Hot damn, that works good!' Briggs crowed. 'I'm liking this!'

Patrick started running for the perimeter fence, then hit his boots' jump-jets. A shot of compressed air propelled him twenty feet into the sky and almost a hundred feet forward. When he landed, he jogged forward while scanning the area with his helmet-mounted sensors. Libyan soldiers were pointing in his direction. He had to run several yards until the accumulators built up enough pressure, then propelled himself with ease over the perimeter fence. His sensors and self-protection weapons worked automatically – any soldiers within thirty feet were knocked unconscious by a bolt of energy strong enough to start a jet aircraft.

Two more jumps and six blocks later, Patrick was at the southernmost garbage pit. It was exactly as Chris Wohl described it: a strong net, steel or even Kevlar, with enough real trash piled atop it to hide a huge wide truck carrying a large rocket. One step inside the pit revealed a second transporter about fifty yards away. He immediately found the fuel filler port and set the first SS-12 afire just as Wohl and Briggs did, and the TEL's right rear wheels blew apart, sending the SS-12 rocket rolling right off its launch rail. In a few seconds it was going to be covered in burning diesel fuel – he hoped the nuclear warhead would just melt away and not cook off. He had no idea how sophisticated the Russians' nuclear warhead safety mechanisms were, or how well the Libyans had maintained them, so he had to assume that the explosive material surrounding the nuclear core would explode and scatter radioactive debris everywhere. He wanted to be off the base before any of them did just that.

Patrick quickly attacked the other two SS-12 launcher vehicles. Now there were explosions everywhere, mostly in the north where Hal Briggs was creating havoc. He turned just as his battle armor's defensive weapon downed another Libyan soldier that had run out from an underground shelter, an AK-47 raised and ready to fire. 'Base, status of the FlightHawk?'

'Inbound sixty seconds, coming in hot,' Wendy McLanahan responded. 'FlightHawk One has good imagery of all three garbage pits and good downlink to FlightHawk Two. You guys can bug out anytime. I took the liberty of calling for the Hammer too.' The 'Hammer' was the CV-22 Pave Hammer tilt-rotor aircraft. Accompanied by another tilt-rotor aircraft acting as an aerial refueling tanker, the Pave Hammer had flown them in across Egypt from the SS *Catherine the Great* in the Mediterranean Sea and had been waiting for them about a hundred miles to the south in the Sahara Desert.

'Good thinking, Base. Stalkers, rendezvous at Sierra One.' The team had buried caches of battery packs, spare parts, water, and medical supplies in various places in the desert for their withdrawal; if they were not used within three days, explosive charges would destroy the evidence.

'Taurus copies.'

'Nike copies.'

'Pollux copies.' Patrick had just turned to start jumping out of the base when he heard Paul cut in, 'Wait, Stalkers. I found something.'

'What do you got, Pollux?'

Paul McLanahan was too stunned to take cover – he was standing out in the open in front of three shabby-looking tin service buildings. Just before he was going to jet away, the big overhead doors to each building opened – and two MAZ-543 transporter-erector-launchers carrying an SS-12 Scaleboard nuclear rocket started to roll out. 'Stalkers, I'm staring at six huge rockets coming out of those service buildings. I think they're the same SS-12s you guys have been setting on fire. Should I –?'

And then he stopped – because all six of the huge vehicles stopped, and the SS-12 missiles started to rise up off the truck bed, and large steel legs began to extend to the ground to steady the vehicle. Warning lights began to blink, and soldiers and ground

44

crew members that had been running around before now started to take cover.

'Hey, guys, I think the Libyans are going to launch these puppies,' Paul said.

'Oh, crap,' Patrick murmured. 'Base, ETA on the FlightHawks?'

'Less than ninety seconds, Castor.'

Patrick had no idea how long it took to launch an SS-12, but he assumed that once it was elevated into launch position, it would take just a few moments. 'Stalkers, converge on Pollux. Let's take those SS-12s out before they can launch!'

'I can take them!' Paul shouted. 'You can't make it here in time! Continue the evacuation!'

'Stalkers, converge on Pollux *now*!' Patrick repeated. At the same time, he jet-jumped to the east in Paul's direction. 'Base, have the Hammer meet us at Tango Ten exfil point.'

'Roger,' Wendy replied. 'FlightHawks are sixty seconds out. Hammer's ETA to Tango Ten is two-zero minutes.'

Paul's electrical defensive weapon went off as several Libyan soldiers approached. He felt heavy-caliber bullets pounding into him from many directions, all on full automatic and some with very heavy rates of fire – a Minigun or antiaircraft gun aimed at him. Seconds later, he got a low-power warning. The Tin Man battle armor was not designed to sustain a heavy attack, and heavy-caliber automatic-weapons fire drained power quickly. Paul had only seconds to get away.

A loud siren sounded. Paul turned toward the SS-12 rocket just to the right of him just as restraining clamps that held the rocket to the launch rail released and the rocket started to eject some gases from its nozzles. It looked like it was going to launch at any moment.

Instead of jet-jumping away, Paul commanded a full-thrust jet – right into the rocket, just a few feet below the warhead section. Unrestrained by its road-march hold-down bar, the rocket easily toppled off the launch rail. Just as it hit the ground, the single-stage liquid rocket propellant ignited. The rocket streaked across the ground, slammed into the SS-12 unit beside it, and exploded. In rapid-fire succession, all six SS-12 Scaleboard rockets exploded in a wall of flame several hundred feet high and nearly a half-mile long. Every building within a mile was torn apart in the concussion.

Patrick did not just see and feel the six nearly simultaneous explosions – he was knocked off his feet from the concussion and earthquake-like tremors, even though he was more than a mile away. The eastern sky lit up like a millennium fireworks display. He didn't bother getting up from the ground, but low-crawled behind a doorway that led to yet another passageway underground. 'Stalkers, status check,' he ordered. He knew where the big explosion was, knew who had been assigned to attack that area, and he dreaded what he was going to learn . . . 'Castor is secure.'

'Nike secure.'

'Taurus secure. I got my bell rung, but I'm secure.'

'Pollux?' No reply. 'Pollux? *Paul?*' Patrick checked his electronic display for any sign of Paul's transponder. Nothing. 'Castor is en route to Pollux's last location,' he said. He hit his jump-jets and quickly propelled himself toward the massive explosions to the east. Patrick didn't have to check his heads-up display to know that Briggs and Wohl were on their way to join him.

But there was no way to reach Paul's last location. An area the size of at least four square city blocks was totally engulfed in flames – the very streets seemed to be rivers of fire, and the sky was thick with roiling waves of heat and smoke. Patrick was able to move forward another half-block with great difficulty before system failure warnings and low-power warnings started to ring. There were several Libyan soldiers in the area, but they seemed stunned both by the devastation and by the strangely armored figure before them.

'Patrick.' It was Hal Briggs, suddenly appearing beside him as if from nowhere.

'I'm going in.'

'You can't. No one can survive that, not even in a BERP suit.'

'I'm not leaving my brother behind,' Patrick said. 'I left David Luger behind in Siberia, and he survived only to be tortured for five years by the KGB. I won't let that happen to my own brother.'

'You can't do it. It's suicide.' He paused, studying his electronic visor and downlinking the status of Patrick's battle armor system. 'You only have ten minutes of power remaining, and that'll get sucked away fast inside that inferno. My power is down to three minutes. Let's go back to the exfil point and recharge the suits.

By then, maybe the fire will have been knocked back, and we can all go in and find Paul.'

'No. I'm going in.'

'How are you going to find him in *that*?'

'I don't know, but I'll find him.' Patrick didn't know what was guiding him – it wasn't any sensor scan or transponder beacon. He had always believed there was some sort of bond, like a telepathic link, between him and Paul, but it was something he always dismissed as simply two guys being raised together in a house full of women. Whatever it was, Patrick was relying on it now. As Hal Briggs and the amazed and terrified Libyan soldiers looked on, Patrick jet-jumped into the hellish flames.

System warnings flashed in his electronic visor, and his skin felt as if it was going to vaporize right off his body, but he kept going. Moving inside the fire was actually easier than he had thought. His battle armor's sensors detected any large debris around him, so he was able to sidestep the pieces of vehicles and buildings without walking into a burning trap. The multiple blasts had leveled most everything, so all he had to do was avoid the larger pools of burning rocket fuel and continue on. Three or four jumps, and he was in the center of the inferno.

His power was nearly gone. The last estimate he had was five minutes remaining, but the estimate just a minute before that said ten minutes, so in reality he had only a few minutes to get out before the battle armor completely shut down. Patrick knew if that happened, he would be instantly baked alive inside the armor like a potato in a microwave oven – crispy on the outside, well-done on the inside.

One more jump, and he found him – or, rather, what was left of him. Patrick could only stare at his brother, not in horror but in sorrow. He had to have been right atop the SS-12 when it detonated, because the blast had torn right through the Tin Man battle armor. It had been all but peeled off his body, stuck on here and there like clumps of dirt. The intense fires had taken care of the rest. Patrick lifted the body of his younger brother as gently and as completely as he could, then jetted away to the east via the shortest way out of the flames.

The Libyans were getting meaner and bolder now. As Patrick jump-jetted again just a few dozen yards from the perimeter fence, he felt heavy-caliber bullets hitting him from his sides and back. He had commanded the self-defense electrical beams not to fire to save energy, but his power was all but exhausted. One more jet propelled him over the fence, and the last of his energy reserves drained away.

The fence kept him and the Libyans separated for now, but that didn't last long. Already troops were streaming out, angry voices piercing the night sky, drowning out even the roar of the huge fires behind them. Their blood lust was evident – they were out for revenge and retribution, not capturing prisoners. Patrick had nothing left with which to fight. He could not avoid capture now . . .

Suddenly, there was a string of explosions between him and the advancing Libyans, stirring up the desert floor like an instant sandstorm. Without the protection of his fully charged armor, Patrick was knocked off his feet as he was pelted with super-sonic-blasted sand and rock. Stunned, he lay on the desert floor, knots of pain dotting all around his body. Writhing in pain, he saw the dark profile of his dead brother lying beside him. Both McLanahans, killed in one day, on the same mission. Shit.

He heard a loud roar and felt, rather than saw, more sand being kicked up. The Libyans were closing in, this time with helicop-ters or armored vehicles, hunting down Wohl and Briggs. The mission was a success, but they might all be wiped out, Patrick thought wearily. Once captured, their bodies put on display along with the remnants of their armor, the Night Stalkers would be dead, the United States would be embarrassed again, and . . .

'Patrick?' He willed his eyes to open and was surprised when they worked. He was looking directly at the alien-looking helmet worn by Hal Briggs. 'You okay, man?'

'Am I shot?'

'You sure as shit got fragged pretty good by the Gators, but I don't see any holes,' Briggs said. Patrick moved his arms and legs and found they all functioned, so he struggled to his feet. 'Wendy sent in FlightHawk Two right in the nick of time, and she laid down a carpet of cluster bombs and mines right in front of about a hundred Libyan regulars. The armor protected you from the fragments. We're safe right now, but we gotta move.' Briggs quickly got to work, snapping a fresh battery pack onto Patrick's backpack. He looked down, examining the body lying in the sand. 'You got Paul out. Good work. I'm so sorry, my friend. I'm gonna miss working with him. He's a hero.'

Patrick reached for the secure latches to his helmet, but Briggs stopped him. 'Better not, man,' he said seriously. 'FlightHawk One has detected radioactive and chemical agents in the area.' He motioned toward the Libyan soldiers lying dead in the aftermath of FlightHawk Two's raid. 'If the mines hadn't got them, the radioactivity or nerve agents would have. That replacement battery pack should give you enough juice to hop out of here and be far enough away for the Pave Hammer to safely pick us up. We'd better go.'

Patrick nodded, thankful to be alive. The noise Patrick heard was not a Libyan helicopter or tank, but the CV-22 Pave Hammer, making a high-speed pass over the area to check for pursuit. He reached down to pick up his brother again, but Chris Wohl carefully, gently pushed him away, and picked up Paul's body. Together the three commandos and their dead partner jetted eastbound into the desert.

They unearthed one of their prepositioned resupply caches a few minutes later. Fifteen minutes later they were far enough away so that radioactive and chemical weapon residue levels disappeared. Only then could the CV-22 land and extract them, first eastward into Egypt and then northwest out over the Mediterranean Sea.

It was a long, sad, quiet flight back to the *Catherine*.

Akranes, Iceland
that same time

'What in hell are you whining about now, Zuwayy?' the Russian shouted on the secure satellite channel. 'This had better be important.'

'My missile base at Samāh was attacked and nearly destroyed by commandos! *American commandos!*' President Jadallah Salem Zuwayy of Libya shouted in passable Russian. He was wearing a polyester blue and red warm-up suit, with no shoes – the clothes that had been thrown to him as his security officers burst into

49

his bedroom and snatched him literally out of bed into a waiting helicopter. At first, he thought it was an assassination squad – rampant fear was finally being replaced with white-hot anger as he realized he was safe. 'They have set eighteen of the missiles on fire! There are nerve agents and radioactive materials spreading all across my desert!'

'*Zakroy yibala!* Shut your fucking mouth and stop blabbering on this line!' the voice shouted back. 'This may be a secure channel, but if the Americans are indeed running an operation on you, they may have figured out how to crack the encryption codes. After all, they built the system we are using.'

'Did you hear what I said, *tovarisch*?' Zuwayy retorted. 'I am under attack! Thousands of square kilometers of my desert have been contaminated! Hundreds of my soldiers are dead! And the Americans certainly know all about those missiles and where I got them!'

'They know nothing of the sort,' Pavel Gregorevich Kazakov responded. Kazakov was sitting at a desk in a small, private apartment in Akranes, Iceland, a few kilometers north of the capital Reykjavík, sipping a cup of tea that an assistant had just fixed for him. His aide, a beautiful young Russian former army officer named Ivana Vasilyeva, deputy chief of staff to the former chief of staff of the army of the Russian Federation – who was just as talented on the pistol range and in a judo *dojo* as she was in bed – set a tray of sweet rolls and honey on the desk, gave Pavel an enticing smile, then departed. 'If they knew anything at all, they would have destroyed the entire base. Just a few commandos – they could have come from anywhere – Israel, Algeria, even your so-called allies Sudan and Syria. Now, shut up and calm yourself.'

Kazakov took a sip of tea as Zuwayy started blathering something in half Russian, half Arabic. A phone call an hour before dawn? Kazakov thought bitterly as he sampled one of the pastries. Outrageous. Being in the witness protection program was hell indeed.

One of the world's richest and certainly one of the world's most dangerous men, thirty-nine-year-old Pavel Kazakov, the son of one of the Russian Federation's most highly decorated and most respected army generals, was under house arrest in Iceland, charged with hundreds of counts of murder, conspiracy, fraud, extortion, grand larceny, drug trafficking, and a laundry list of other crimes against several nations from Kazakhstan to the United States. He had been captured by some as yet unidentified commandos, probably Americans, and sent to a Turkish prison. But since so many other countries had lodged charges against him, the World Court ordered that he stand trial in the International Crimes Against Humanity Tribunal in The Hague. With some good lawyers – backed up by generous bribes – Kazakov got some valuable concessions. Turkey usually does not allow extradition of its capital prisoners, but Kazakov agreed to waive his extradition rights in exchange for no death penalty, and he was transferred to a maximum-security facility in the Netherlands.

Then Kazakov started to talk. Within days, Interpol had made dozens of major arrests around the world of suspected narco-traffickers, money launderers, con artists, and gem and art thieves. The authorities had confiscated millions of dollars of stolen weapons, valuables, property, stocks and bonds – even nuclear weapons – in a very short period of time. Pavel Kazakov, still considered the world's most dangerous criminal mastermind, was quickly turning into the biggest and most important informant ever in the history of law enforcement. Some of the world's most feared terrorists, notorious drug smugglers, and slipperiest criminals – men that had been on the run for years, some for decades – had been captured. As much as Pavel Kazakov had cost the world in loss of life and destruction of property, the value of the property alone that his information caused to be recovered or captured topped it by a factor of one hundred.

But, of course, Pavel saw it differently. To him, it was a way to save his own skin, get out of prison – and eliminate the competition. Besides, what did the World Court care about ethnic fighting in Albania or Macedonia, or military men in Turkey, or polluted waters in Kazakhstan? They gladly traded information on drug dealers in Europe and North America for reducing, and then eventually eliminating, Kazakov's prison sentence.

Details of his plea bargain with the World Court were kept top secret. As far as anyone knew, Kazakov was in complete isolation in a prison in Rijssen, the Netherlands, awaiting trial. No one ever suspected that any court would even consider releasing him, and the World Court did not have a witness protection program. But in short order, one was created for him – and Pavel Kazakov was free.

Yes, he was nearly broke – but 'nearly broke' for him still meant more wealth than some Third World countries. It still offered him an opportunity to do what he did best – build his wealth back up again any way he could, whether it meant dealing drugs, weapons, humans, or oil. Plus, he could do it all from an untraceable apartment and telephone, with a new fully documented identity – all bought and paid for by the World Court in exchange for having the World Court eliminate his enemies for him.

'It is you who is responsible for this!' Zuwayy shouted, finally switching back to full Russian. 'My troops could have executed this entire operation without your damned missiles! Now the Americans are breathing down my neck! You must pay for the loss of my base and compensate me for the loss of my soldiers! You must –!'

'Shut your scum-sucking mouth, Zuwayy,' Kazakov interrupted hotly. 'I spent ten million dollars of my own money to put those missiles in place – but not in Samāh! I ordered that the missiles be placed in Al-Jawf, not Samāh!'

'I put missiles in Al-Jawf – and there they sit, useless, while my men roast in the damned Sahara Desert!' Zuwayy retorted. 'You make me pay fifty million dollars for missiles pointed at nothing but wasteland! I say no! Egypt is our true enemy! We need to threaten much more than just the Salimah oil fields.'

'You moved some of those missiles to Samāh, against my orders,' Kazakov said.

'The missiles at Al-Jawf are useless, worthless!' Zuwayy repeated. 'From Samāh, those missiles can reach Cairo, Alexandria, Israel, even Italy. Moving some of the missiles *that I purchased* does not affect your plan against the Salimah oil fields.'

'I'm not interested in attacking Israel, and I'm sure as hell not interested in attacking Italy with shitty first-generation rockets with chemical warheads!' Kazakov shouted. 'Are you out of your mind? If we attack Israel, it will bring the Americans into the region with a vengeance. My oil terminals on the Adriatic Sea are directly downwind of any bases we would attack in Italy –

besides, some of my best customers are in Italy! I did not pay you to put those missiles in Libya so you can threaten your neighbors or satisfy your thirst for global conquest.

'I'm glad those missiles in Samāh were destroyed, Zuwayy – perhaps now you'll stop going off on your own and listen to what I tell you to do. I will pay you to replace those missiles and warheads – but only if you dismantle any other bases that you put missiles other than Al-Jawf, and only if you stop being a jackass and do as I tell you to do from now on.'

'You may not talk to me this way,' Zuwayy said haughtily. 'I am the king of Libya. I am the leader of the Muslim Brotherhood, the lord of the Muslims. I am –'

'You are nothing but a back-stabbing opportunistic traitor who would sell his wife, mistresses, children, and even your own mother on the streets of Benghazi for money,' Kazakov interjected. 'You can use that cockamamie I-am-royalty story to impress your people and baffle the rest of the world, but to me you're nothing but a two-bit thug.

'Now shut up and listen. Your primary objective is the Salimah oil fields in Egypt, not to obliterate Cairo or Tel Aviv. Your job is to keep on moving your troops to Sudan, keep their readiness high, and keep on putting pressure on the Egyptian forces opposing yours without starting a shooting conflict yourself. If they are stupid enough to attack, you can simply walk in and wipe them up. Until then, I will continue to push the Central African Petroleum Partners to accept Libya and Metyorgaz as a partner, help develop some of your oil resources, and break the embargo on oil exports from Libya to Europe.'

'I do not understand,' Zuwayy said, hopelessly confused. 'Why don't we just go in, invade Egypt, and take the oil fields ourselves? No one will oppose us.'

'You idiot, *everyone* will oppose us,' Kazakov said. 'No one will intervene, but we will be drowning in oil because no one will buy what we are pumping, not even on the black market. Besides, if you invade, Central African Petroleum Partners will pull out, and neither you nor I have the money right now to build a thousand-kilometer-long pipeline across the Sahara Desert. We want the pipeline in place and operating before we take over.'

'In the meantime, you sit safe and sound in hiding while

American commandos destroy my military base,' Zuwayy cried. 'What am I supposed to do – hold my breath until the poison gas dissipates?'

Kazakov thought for a moment while he watched the former Russian army major Vasilyeva move as she straightened up his desk. She was like a tiger stepping soundlessly through the jungle hunting its prey, every movement graceful and with complete economy. She sensed him looking at her, turned her head to him, smiled, then turned her body so he could see her breasts, squeezing them together with her arms the way he liked to do.

He suddenly realized he had spent too much time with this Libyan popinjay.

'I don't give a shit what you do,' Kazakov said. 'Someone just invaded your country – it seems like the perfect time to do just about anything you wish to do. Use your armed forces, track those commandos down – you know they're not going to walk out of the damned desert, so track their aircraft down – and then destroy whatever base they came from with everything you've got. You'll be totally justified in whatever action you take – and you might even earn a bit of respect from your enemies. Now, stop bothering me – and you place those missiles where I tell you to place them, or the next biochem warhead you hear about will be falling on *your* head.' He slammed the phone down so hard, his teacup rattled in its saucer.

Zuwayy was dangerous, even unstable, Kazakov thought. He was a warmonger, ready to lash out at anyone, for any reason or no reason at all. He hoped Zuwayy would keep it together long enough, until the delicate negotiations with the Central African Petroleum Partners were concluded. Libyan forces were just a subtle threat to Egypt, and vice versa – neither country had any semblance of a real fighting force. But if anyone tried to attack Libya, the rockets were in place and ready to completely wipe out any opposition and guarantee that no outside forces were going to interfere.

In any case, Kazakov was going to get enough of a foothold in the African oil market to force out the other companies and eventually take over. He didn't have the power he had just a few short months ago – but it was just a matter of time. Once firmly in place in Africa, with the money pouring in, he could move

54

back into the vast untapped oil resources in the Caspian Sea region again.

He was so engrossed in his own heated thoughts that he did not notice Ivana Vasilyeva standing beside his desk, staring at him. Her full red lips were parted as if she were panting heavily, and her eyes were wide and glassy. He smiled at her.

'You speak to other men, even this king of Libya, as if he were a street sweeper who had just soiled your shoes,' Vasilyeva breathed. Her left hand drifted up to her breast, and her fingers teased a nipple underneath her sweater. 'You are an extraordinary man. I am pleased that you have chosen me to be by your side.'

He stood, walked over to her, reached behind her head with his left hand, and yanked her chin upward by pulling her hair. Her left hand did not move from her breast, so he fondled her right breast until her nipple sprang to life. 'I keep you here with me because of your contacts in the Russian government and army,' Kazakov said. He looked into her eyes as they grew wider, as if in fear, but her breathing was becoming heavier, more excited. 'I also keep you here because you can kill faster and more efficiently and in more ways than I.'

He pushed her aside roughly, then took his seat once again. 'Stop this foolishness and straighten up, Major,' Kazakov ordered her. She stood before him, watching him with half-closed eyes, her expression contrite yet inviting at the same time. 'I do not believe for one moment that you get orgasmic just by watching me yell at a strutting simpleton like Zuwayy. He is not one-tenth the soldier or leader you are – if he was, I would send you to Tripoli and have you assassinate him immediately. He is a bug to be squashed as soon as he fulfills his part, which is to force either a settlement or a war between the central African oil cartels and us. Your job is to watch my back and collect information, not to play with yourself in my office. If I need a whore, I'll call one.'

'I am here to do whatever you wish, Pavel –'

'I am Comrade Kazakov to you, Major,' he corrected her. 'And there should be no doubt in your mind that you are here to do whatever I wish, or else your fate would be the same as your last boss, General Zhurbenko – thirty years at hard labor in Siberia. But you are a highly trained soldier and a keen tactician, not a *zblidavattsa.* If I ever get another indication that you fancy your-self as anything else but my chief of security and my aide-de-camp, you will find yourself digging coal in Siberia beside Zhurbenko – or at the bottom of an Icelandic fjord.'

'Yes, Comrade Kazakov,' Vasilyeva said. But her eyes blazed as she went on, 'But now I wish to tell you something.'

'You do so at your own peril, Major.'

'Very well,' she said. She took a bold step forward; Kazakov's eyes warned her away, but he knew it would take more than a stare to make this woman back off. 'You say you chose me, Comrade. But now I tell you this: *I* chose *you* as well.'

'*Zasrat mazgi?* Oh, really?'

'Yes, Comrade,' Vasilyeva said confidently, with only a hint of a smile on her beautiful but army-hardened face. 'I chose General Zhurbenko the same way: He was a man that could get me the things I wanted – power, prestige, money, land, and status. If I had to let the old bastard feel me up or be his *min'etka* every now and then, it was all part of my plan to get what I wanted.

'I feel the same way about you, Comrade – you are a man that can get me what I want. You have the power – you *still* have the power, even here, in exile in Iceland. I can dedicate myself to a man such as you.'

'Frankly, Major, I was not too impressed with how well you protected your other mentor.'

'I noticed your power the moment I first met you in the general's car. I knew you were the one for me, the man with even more power than Zhurbenko, the one who could get me the things I want,' Vasilyev said. 'Besides, he gave me to you – it was clear he no longer needed me. It was easy to switch loy-alties. If the general showed the same loyalty to me when your plan started to become exposed, I would have used my powers to protect him as well – but he decided to be a good soldier and take his punishment, protecting his wife instead of me. That will cost him his life.'

She stepped closer to him again, and this time he saw some-thing more sinister in her expression – not just confidence, but a warning as well. 'I have given myself to you, Comrade. I am yours. Betray me, and I will bring you down like I brought down

Zhurbenko. Remain loyal to me, and you can do with me as you want – *anything* you want – and I will do anything for you.'

Pavel Kazakov had to suppress a thrill of dread that came over him again. The old feeling had come back – the feeling of impending danger. Every time he had listened, the feeling had saved him. Every time he ignored it, failed to break off his plans, run, and protect himself, he went down in disaster and defeat.

But before he could respond, she reached out to him, took his hands, and placed them on her breasts. Her eyes were demanding, commanding, riveting – and irresistible. She had always been irresistible. This wasn't loyalty, and certainly not love – this was plain old-fashioned ambition, desire, and a willingness to do anything, and allow anything to be done to her, to get what she wanted.

Of course, he failed to listen to the danger signal. He was helpless to heed it now.

'Well,' he said with a smile as she reached behind her neck to unzip her sweater, 'if you put it that way, Major . . .'

Zuwayy slammed the phone down hard. *'Saghf tarak khord!'* he cursed. 'That bastard! How dare he order me around like a child!' But Kazakov was right about one thing: This was a good opportunity to lash out at someone and prove he wasn't going to be pushed around. And he would be fully, completely justified in doing so.

He dialed a special secure pager number, then sat and waited. Several minutes later, a call was put through to him: 'Speak.'

'This is Ulama al-Khan, Majesty,' Khalid al-Khan, the chief justice of the Egyptian Supreme Court and the leader of the main opposition party, responded. 'God be with you.'

'And to you, Ulama,' Zuwayy said. This guy had to be the biggest idiot in all of Egypt and probably all of northern Africa, Zuwayy scoffed to himself. Khan saw himself as an Islamic holy man, a true believer who fancied himself a spiritual master and leader. He was so zealous in his beliefs – and so enamored of himself – that he couldn't see danger when it was right in front of his face. His ambition would quite possibly drive him into the Presidential Palace – but he had no concept of how to lead a government, except to send out his henchmen in the Egyptian Republican Guards and assassinate a political enemy. He truly believed that God would absolve him of all his sins, no matter how heinous his crimes.

But most times stupidity and ambition made for a pliant coconspirator, and that's what Zuwayy had in Khan. The Egyptian cleric thought it was in the best interest of all concerned for Egypt to join the Muslim Brotherhood – a loose confederation of Libya, Sudan, and Yemen, with major support in Syria, Jordan, Iraq, and Lebanon, and with some wealthy supporters in such pro-Western states such as Saudi Arabia, Oman, the United Arab Emirates, and even Kuwait. Jadallah Zuwayy, as ruler of the most powerful military in the alliance, was the leader of the Muslim Brotherhood. Their sworn mission: to replace all of the secular governments in the Middle East with religious-based governments firmly grounded in traditional Muslim beliefs. Egypt joining the Muslim Brotherhood would be the crown jewel in strengthening the organization and convincing other undecided nations to join – Egypt had the most powerful military force in the entire region, almost on a par with Israel quantitatively.

Zuwayy found a ready and willing ideological slave in Khalid al-Khan. Obviously the cleric never read anything but propaganda sheets – for he truly believed that Zuwayy was descended from the Prophet Muhammad and was the savior and sword of Islam. Zuwayy nurtured that fiction every chance he could, and Khan was obviously enjoying and benefiting from the attention. It did not take long to lodge al-Khan firmly under Zuwayy's thumb.

'I have a request of you, Ulama,' Zuwayy said.

'Ask anything of me, Majesty,' Khan replied devoutly.

'A sneak attack by unidentified commandos was perpetrated against Libya tonight.'

'I have heard of this, Majesty. Are you safe?'

'Perfectly safe, Ulama.'

'I swear this to you, Majesty, that the terrorists that did this deed will be hunted down like the dogs they are and punished!'

'You would tell me if these terrorists came from Egypt, Khalid?'

'Of course, Majesty!' Khan cried. 'I would notify you the instant I found out, even if I risked violating state secrets. You are descended from the loving Prophet – none may seek to harm you! All true believers know this to be true!'

58

'Thank you for your words of comfort, Khalid,' Zuwayy said. 'But I need your help to find the terrorists.'

'Anything, Majesty.'

'I believe that the terrorists crossed into Egypt to make their escape. I need your military forces to provide me with radar and patrol data so that I may track them down.'

'It shall be delivered to you by daybreak, Majesty.'

'And whatever my military forces may do, Ulama, I do not want your military forces to intervene,' Zuwayy said. 'I will not attack Egyptian soil without first notifying you – but I do not want any Egyptian forces to respond to attacks elsewhere.'

'I will give the orders myself, Majesty,' Khan said. 'It is easily done. The commanders of our largest military bases are friends to me and our cause.'

'Very good, Khalid. My war ministers will be in touch with your office within the hour. On behalf of all the faithful, I thank you.'

'It is my honor, Majesty,' Khan said. 'I am pleased to tell you, Highness, that I shall place my name in nomination before the People's Assembly for president of Egypt, *insh'allah.*'

'Excellent, Ulama,' Zuwayy said. His defense ministers and generals were entering the room – he had to shut this zealot off, quick. 'You have my full support and blessings. Anything my government or I can do to support you, it is yours.'

'Of course, joining the Muslim Brotherhood is my main goal, Majesty,' Khan said. 'I wish to strengthen ties with all of our Muslim brothers and force all of the foreigners out.'

'The foreigners are draining the strength out of all the faithful. We need to formalize our union, Ulama. When you are named president, we shall work together to eliminate the Westerners from our land. The oil they pump from our land is ours, not theirs. Libya took control of our oil fields, Khalid – Egypt should do the same. I will accept any information you can give me, and God will tell me His wishes.'

'As you wish, Majesty,' Khan said. 'It shall be sent to you without delay.'

Good little tool, Zuwayy thought, good little tool.

Aboard the SS *Catherine the Great*, in the Mediterranean Sea that evening

'I apologize for having to do this,' Patrick McLanahan said as he entered the briefing room. The other members of his team were already there, waiting. 'I know none of us feel much like debriefing right now. But we have a report to file. Let's get to it.' He looked over to his wife, Wendy. 'What have you got for us?'

Wendy looked on her husband sadly, her eyes wet with tears. Concentrating on recovering the commando team, with the body of her dead brother-in-law aboard, was one of the most difficult things she ever had to do. But Patrick was all business – never shed a tear, never sulked, never really looked at his brother once they were brought aboard. He helped carry the litter off the CV-22 Pave Hammer tilt-rotor aircraft until two other men took the body away, and then he got right back to work. She could feel the pain inside him, even though his face and features didn't show it.

Patrick issued a voice command, and his fibersteel exoskeleton automatically detached itself from his body. He stepped out of it and pressed a code into a hidden keypad, and the exoskeleton folded itself up into a package about the size of a small suitcase. He plugged the pack into a wall outlet to recharge it, set the exoskeleton aside, sat down at the head of the conference table, then plugged his battle armor into another available outlet. Patrick, Wendy noticed, still had Paul's blood on his hands, his wrists, his arms, and his face – he hadn't even slowed down long enough to wash it off.

'We launched a FlightHawk recon aircraft while you were on your way back, Patrick,' Wendy began in a low monotone voice. 'We did detect radioactive elements in the atmosphere over Samāh consistent with a number of nuclear warheads, so some of the rockets you destroyed were nuclear. The bad news is, we also detected VX nerve agents, also consistent with a number of warheads, maybe as many as a half-dozen.'

60

'Holy shit,' Hal Briggs breathed. 'With an SS-12 they could hit Rome, Athens, Istanbul, Tel Aviv . . .'

'Or Cairo, Alexandria, or the Suez Canal,' Patrick added. 'And Libya has a number of ex-Russian long-range bombers, tactical fighters, coastal antiship, and ship-borne weapon systems capable of delivering those warheads too. They could hold all of southern Europe at risk.' Patrick looked at his intelligence briefing notes. 'Our private intelligence sources told us there might be as many as six other bases, including two more secret bases like Samāh, hiding ballistic missiles armed with nuclear or chemical warheads. I'd like to set up a complete reconnaissance schedule with as many FlightHawks as we can, scanning every square foot to try to locate the other missiles.'

'Agreed,' Chris Wohl said. 'We can have a strike team standing by either offshore or in Egypt to move as soon as targets are located.'

'We should also push to upgrade the sensors on the recon FlightHawks,' Wendy added. 'We can put an ultra-wideband radar on a FlightHawk to let us scan for underground bunkers and communications lines under the sand.' The ultra-wideband radar, or UWBR, was one of the most significant advances in surveillance and reconnaissance: a radar capable of seeing through some medium-density objects. The system normally fit only on a full-size aircraft, but Jon Masters had redesigned it to fit on board a small, unmanned aircraft. 'The FlightHawks will have only a few hours' loiter time because of the size of the UWBR system, but we'll be able to scan the country quicker and more efficiently.'

'Then let's get it all moving this way immediately,' Patrick said. 'I don't want to give the Libyans a chance –'

Just then, an electronic warning tone sounded – the collision warning. Everyone in the briefing room immediately shot to their feet and headed out to their emergency stations. At the same moment the phone from the bridge sounded; Patrick picked it up before the second ring. 'Go ahead, Brian.'

'We got a situation, General,' Brian Lovelock, the captain of the *Catherine*, responded. 'We're receiving distress signals from two vessels within thirty miles of our position, saying they're under attack from unidentified aircraft. No warning given. The attackers appear to be moving from east to west – in our direction.'

'Got it,' Patrick replied. He pressed another button, this one hooked directly to the Combat Information Center and his long-time friend and partner, David Luger. 'Dave, what do you have?'

'We're just now picking up four high-speed aircraft bearing one-zero-five, altitude less than one thousand feet, heading west at four hundred eighty knots,' Luger responded. The *Catherine* had an entire combat radar system hidden aboard the salvage ship, disguised as standard navigation radars – it was as combat-capable as many world navies' warships. 'Sorry we didn't pick them up earlier, Muck, but they are right down on the friggin' deck. Their ETE is four minutes.'

'Sound general quarters, everyone to air defense positions,' Patrick ordered. 'Better start a complete data dump to the satellite and then destroy the classified. Someone's on the warpath out here, and I think we're next.' On his subcutaneous microtransceiver, he said, 'Patrick to Wendy . . . Wendy, I want you aboard the Pave Hammer, along with the civilians.'

'I'm staying,' Wendy said. 'I can have a FlightHawk armed with air-to-air missiles airborne in three minutes.'

'Wendy, no argument. You're evacuating with the other civilians.' He paused, then said, 'Bradley is waiting for you.'

There was a slight pause, but Patrick knew invoking the name of their son would do it. 'All right.'

'We'll hold them off as best we can,' Patrick said. He hit the hidden switch on his exoskeleton, stepped into it after it stood itself up, attached it to his body, locked his helmet in place, then ran up on deck. He immediately dashed over to the bow of the *Catherine*, which was facing east, in the direction from which the attackers were coming. 'Combat, this is Castor,' Patrick radioed. 'Range to bandits?'

'Twenty-two miles and closing. ETE less than three minutes.'

As he searched the morning sky with his helmet-mounted sensors, three crewmen trotted over to him, wheeling a large crate on a cart. Patrick unlocked the crate and with one hand extracted the weapon inside. It was an immense M-168 six-barreled Vulcan cannon. Normally mounted on a big Humvee or M-113 armored personnel carrier, the eight-hundred-pound Vulcan cannon was designed for use against ground targets and fast-flying helicopters at ranges out to a mile and a half. It had a maximum rate of fire of one hundred rounds per *second* – anything it hit would be chopped to hamburger in the blink of an eye.

'Combat, Castor,' Patrick radioed as he hefted the big cannon. The hydraulically powered exoskeleton made it ridiculously easy to level the big gun and move it smoothly and precisely in any direction. 'Where are they?'

'Bearing one-zero-two, range eighteen miles, low.'

Patrick activated all of his battle armor's sensors and began scanning at maximum range. 'Roger. Nike, Taurus, Pollux, you guys up?'

'Nike up in ten seconds,' Wohl replied.

'Taurus will be up in twenty.'

No reply from Pollux – and Patrick realized that there never would be one either, ever again. 'Roger, Stalkers,' he said sadly. 'Report when you're ready to engage.' At that moment, several of their commandos, wearing lightweight non-electronic battle armor, began to set their Stinger MANPADS (Man-Portable Air Defense System) up beside Patrick. The Stinger MANPADS was a portable shoulder-fired heat-seeking antiaircraft missile. Other commandos brought caskets of reloads. 'My MANPADS is up on the bow. Hammer, what's your status?'

At that moment, Patrick heard the low, steadily quickening roar of the CV-22 Pave Hammer's engines starting up behind him. It had been raised up on deck from its hold faster than Patrick could ever imagine. 'Hammer is starting engines. We'll be airborne in two minutes.'

'Make it one minute, Hammer,' Patrick ordered. 'Combat?'

'Bearing zero-niner-seven, range fifteen miles . . . stand by, aircraft turning slightly, range decreasing rapidly . . . We're being highlighted by X-band airborne radar. They got a lock on us.'

'Get the Hammer off the deck *now*,' Patrick shouted.

'Sixty seconds. All civilians are aboard.'

Patrick felt a rush of relief – and then a thrill of fear as his sensors picked up the aircraft. He saw two at first, then three. 'Contact, range nine miles and closing fast.' The roar of the Hammer's engines increased – it was close to liftoff speed. 'Eight miles . . . seven miles . . . bandits climbing slightly . . . six miles . . .'

'Sparkle! Sparkle!' Luger shouted. Everyone knew what that meant – they were being highlighted by a targeting laser.

Just then, Patrick saw another target appear – much smaller and much faster. 'Stalkers, *missiles inbound*! Missiles inbound! I've got two in sight!' Patrick raised the big Vulcan cannon and snapped off the safety with a quick thought-command. The two missiles were coming in fast, wavering slightly up and down in altitude but coming in straight and true. 'Dave, countermeasures starboard *now*!'

Behind him, two rockets streaked from hidden launchers. Each rocket was an electronic decoy, designed to broadcast radio and infrared signatures several thousand times larger and brighter than the ship. They drifted up slowly, making inviting targets. Would they be inviting enough . . . ?

They were. Both missiles veered to the right, chasing the decoys. Patrick tracked them with ease. The first missile hit the first decoy – but the second decoy must've crashed or malfunctioned, because the second missile only jinked slightly right and then veered left, back on the *Catherine*. Patrick issued an electronic command, and the big Vulcan cannon opened fire. A shaft of fire fifteen feet long belched from the muzzle, and a hundred empty cartridges showered onto the deck in front of the Stinger crew. Off in the distance, the second enemy missile exploded in a cloud of fire.

'Forward MANPADS up!' Patrick shouted. As he placed the Vulcan cannon on the deck as gently as if he were setting a golf bag down on the fringe of the green, the team of commandos stepped forward and placed the Stinger launcher on his shoulder. Patrick immediately locked onto the incoming fighter, waited until it got within range, then fired.

The lead fighter must've seen the launch immediately, because it immediately banked hard right and started ejecting decoy flares. But the second fighter was not as quick. He made a gentler turn, obviously hesitant to get too close to his leader at night and low to the ocean, and did not pop any decoy flares until it was far too late. The Stinger missile flew a smooth, unerring arc right up the fighter's hot tailpipe and exploded. The Stinger crew could not see anything so far away at night, but through his millimeter-wave imaging radar and infrared sensors, Patrick could see the second fighter dip precariously close to the ocean, regain altitude, dip again, climb, then plunge almost straight down into the dark Mediterranean. He saw no ejection seat blast free, or any parachute.

'Splash one,' Patrick announced. After all the death, destruction, and pain he had seen that day, the crash of this unidentified attacker meant absolutely nothing to him. 'First bandit is bearing zero-eight-zero, twelve miles, turning east.'

At that moment, he heard the CV-22 Pave Hammer tilt-rotor aircraft lift off the deck. Thank God, he breathed, Wendy was going to be safe, as long as they were able to keep those fighters off its tail until they were safely wave-hopping away.

'Taurus has three bandits, bearing two-five-zero, range nine miles,' Hal Briggs shouted on the command network. 'Comin' in low and smoking.'

'Nike has contact on the bandits at two-five zero,' Chris Wohl chimed in. 'Switching to Stinger. Taurus, you hang on to the Vulcan.'

'How about we both take a Stinger?' Briggs suggested. 'I can grab the Vulcan and knock down any stragglers after I launch.'

'Rog.'

'Stalkers, I have a surface contact, bearing two-two-three, range twenty-nine miles,' Dave Luger announced. 'He's hitting us with an India-band Plank Shave surface search radar and an India-band Hawk Screech fire-control radar. I make this a Koni-class frigate, probably Libyan. He's coming in fast, almost thirty knots. He could be within missile range at any time.'

'Should've known it was the Libyans,' Wohl muttered on the command net.

'Think they might be pissed at us for blowing up their nukes?' Briggs chimed in.

'Pissed enough to attack every ship close enough to have based the chopper,' Patrick said. 'Let's deal with the fighters first, then the frigate.' He didn't have to say the obvious – they were going to have a fight on their hands, one they had very little chance of surviving.

Stinger missiles soon began rippling from the starboard deck and fantail as the Libyan fighters closed in. Only the combination of the Vulcan cannons and decoys was able to keep the *Catherine* from being hit. Even so, one missile came close enough to rattle the deck with bits of shrapnel, caught at the last possible moment by a last-instant blast from Hal Briggs's cannon. But their efforts finally paid off. 'Stalkers, air search radar is clear,' Luger announced. 'Good shooting. No radar contacts. The rest RTBed.'

'I got a problem over here, boys,' Briggs said. 'I'm real low on ammo. Maybe two or three more bursts and I'm out.'

'Same here,' Wohl said.

Patrick checked his magazine and found he had just a handful of rounds remaining – not enough for even a half-second burst. 'How about your Stingers?'

'One on the fantail.'

'Two starboard.'

'One on the bow,' Patrick said. 'And there's no way we can outrun that frigate.'

'I just got a call – the Egyptian Navy is dispatching two Perry-class frigates,' Luger reported. 'ETE sixty minutes. They've launched patrol aircraft and helicopters, too.'

That was good news, Patrick thought, but they wouldn't be on time before the Libyan warship struck.

He hesitated, but only for a moment. For the second time, he was going to lose another base ship to enemy attack. The Iranians had sunk another commando carrier, the SS *Valley Mistress,* in the Persian Gulf, killing several dozen men. That incident had brought Patrick out of his first retirement to start a campaign of revenge against the Iranian Revolutionary Guards that had captured the survivors. He was determined not to allow that loss of life again. 'Abandon ship,' Patrick ordered. 'All crewmen to lifeboats. Right now.'

'Patrick –' Dave Luger began.

'This means you, Dave,' Patrick interrupted. 'We'll stay up here with whatever weapons we have left and hold off that frigate as long as possible. Then we'll –'

Suddenly, Hal Briggs shouted, 'Hey, Dave, is that a FlightHawk on the launcher over on the starboard side raising up to launch position?'

'A FlightHawk?' Patrick asked. 'Dave, how did you get a FlightHawk ready so fast?'

'I didn't do it, Muck,' Luger replied. 'I just noticed it elevating too. It's already spun up its guidance system. I didn't do it from here. I don't know . . .' He paused, then shouted, *'Missile inbound!* A missile just lifted off from that frigate . . . *a second missile just launched*! Two missiles inbound! Sea-skimmers, accelerating to point nine Mach, range twenty-five miles!'

'Get your asses on those lifeboats *now*!' Patrick shouted to the two MANPADS crew members with him, pushing them toward the lifeboat stations on the port side. He grabbed his last Stinger missile and dashed down the starboard side of the salvage ship. He saw the FlightHawk on the amidships launch rail, but he couldn't see what weapons, if any, it was carrying, or any other markings that would tell him which UCAV it was. Just as he reached the fantail alongside Briggs and Wohl, the FlightHawk unmanned combat air vehicle blasted off from its launcher on deck. 'Good job, Dave,' Patrick said. 'Now get to the lifeboats.'

'I'm telling you, Muck, I didn't –'

'Contact! Here they come!' Briggs shouted. 'Man, they're damned low. I don't know if the Stingers will be able to lock on them.' But he raised his Stinger, aimed, and fired. Seconds later, the first antiship missile, a Russian-made SS-N-2C Styx missile, exploded in a brilliant ball of fire. Patrick's Stinger missile missed the second antiship missile, but Chris Wohl was ready with his Vulcan cannon and destroyed it seconds before it hit. This time, the starboard side of the *Catherine* was showered with unspent rocket fuel and fiery bits of the obliterated warhead. It was a very close call.

'Lifeboats away,' they heard Dave Luger report. 'One lifeboat starboard, another on the port side, ready and waiting for you guys.'

'How many of those big missiles does that frigate carry?' Briggs asked.

'Koni-class frigates carry four SS-N-2s,' Luger responded.

'Then I'll stay to see if they fire any more missiles,' Patrick said.

'I'm staying too,' Hal Briggs said.

'I'm not leaving,' Chris Wohl said with pure titanium in his voice. 'We've got two Stingers and some ammo left – that should be enough for the last two SS-N-2s.'

Patrick nodded. He was happy to have such good fighters and close friends on that fantail with him. He had no way to fight off two big antiship missiles by himself, but he had been ready to order both of them to the lifeboats anyway.

'Here they come, guys,' Hal shouted. It seemed as if he barely had time to raise his Stinger missile before he fired. The antiaircraft missile missed, plunging into the sea without ever locking onto the target. Wohl's cannon fire hit the missile, but it still continued on, skipping across the ocean like a stick of dynamite thrown across a pond before slamming into the *Catherine* near the bow. Patrick's last Stinger missile shot missed as well, and the second SS-N-2 Styx missile hit just aft of the first missile's impact point. The ship shuddered, which soon progressed with terrifying speed to an earthquake-like trembling. The deck heeled upward, slammed down hard, then heeled up again. The bow was already going under.

It took every bit of strength for the three commandos to struggle to the port-side lifeboats. Luger had already lowered a boat to the water and had its engines started, and it took only seconds for the three to climb down, unfasten their lines, and motor away from the *Catherine*.

Through his electronic visor, Patrick could see the big Libyan frigate on the horizon. It was already turning toward them – the rapidly sinking salvage ship could no longer screen them. The lifeboat could only putter along, barely making five or six knots – the frigate would catch up to them in no time. Moments later he saw a muzzle flash, and seconds later a huge geyser of water erupted just a few dozen yards away – the Libyan frigate was already firing on them!

Wohl was twisting and pulling the lifeboat's tiller, trying to spoil their targeting. 'Come and get us, sucker,' he muttered. 'Just hope there's nothing left of me when you catch up to me.' Another geyser of water and an earsplitting *BOOM!* erupted, closer this time – they were getting the range. Another couple shots and . . .

Suddenly a fountain of fire appeared on the horizon. 'Something hit the Libyan frigate!' Patrick shouted. 'The FlightHawk! It must've kamikazied on the frigate! Not a moment too soon!' On the command net, he radioed, 'Wendy, this is Castor. Are you in contact with the Egyptian patrol ships? They should be able to screen you against any other Libyan fighters. Are you heading toward Egypt?' No response. 'Wendy, you copy?'

'This is the Hammer,' the pilot of the CV-22 Pave Hammer tilt-rotor aircraft replied. 'Are you trying to call us?'

'I was wondering if Wendy got in contact with the Egyptian navy.'

'Wendy's not on board, Castor,' came the response.

Patrick's mouth turned instantly dry, and his knees wobbled, even though his legs were supported by the high-tech exoskeleton. '*Say again*, Hammer?'

'Sir, Wendy is not on board,' the pilot acknowledged. 'She told some of our passengers to lift off without her, that she was going in a lifeboat after she got a FlightHawk ready to attack.'

'*Wendy?*' Patrick shouted. 'Can you hear me? Where are you? Answer me!' He was breathing so hard into his helmet that he was in danger of hyperventilating. 'I want a search of every lifeboat and every square inch of the Hammer! Turn this boat around! We're going back!'

But by the time they turned around, the SS *Catherine the Great* had slipped beneath the dark burning waters of the Mediterranean Sea. They searched for several minutes until they heard patrol helicopters from the Libyan frigate heading in their direction and they were forced to withdraw. The Libyans pursued them until Egyptian navy patrol planes forced the Libyan helicopters to return to their stricken ship, but by the time Patrick, Briggs, and Wohl were picked up by an Egyptian frigate, the area where the *Catherine* had gone down was surrounded by Libyan coastal patrol ships. There was no way they could return, and they easily out-numbered the Egyptian patrols. Patrick interrogated Wendy's sub-cutaneous microtransceiver, checking for life signs or even a position, but there was no reply.

Patrick could not bear to turn away from the spot where the *Catherine* had gone down. He didn't care if the whole world heard the strange high-tech-looking commando sobbing inside his battle armor.

Chapter Two

Blytheville, Arkansas
early the next morning

'I can't take a meeting today. Can't you see this place is a mad-house?' Jon Masters shouted when his assistant, Suzanne, inter-rupted him for the third time in the past hour.

'Jon, the Duffields have been waiting since yesterday . . .'

'I asked to reschedule the meeting.'

'They've already rescheduled twice,' Suzanne reminded him. 'They've flown out all the way from Nevada each time. They're trying to accommodate you all they can.'

'Have them try harder.' He jabbed a finger at the door, dis-missing her, then recited more commands into his voice-command computer terminal.

Suzanne sighed and gave up, but as she departed Jon's wife, Helen, who was the chairman of the board of their high-tech defense contractor aerospace company, Sky Masters Inc, walked in. Helen was several years older than her husband, but these days their age difference seemed to grow less and less noticeable. Helen was now wearing her dark hair a bit shorter, accentuating her long neck, slender face, and dark mysterious eyes; through the magic of laser surgery, she was also able to forgo the thick matronly-looking glasses she had worn since childhood. 'Jon, we have that meeting with the Duffields right now. Let's go.'

'I just got done telling Suzanne –'

'I know what you're telling Suzanne, but I'm telling you – we can't put this off any longer,' Helen insisted. 'Just a couple hours, that's all. A quick tour, review the prospectus, meet and greet, perhaps talk about the reorganization . . .'

'Helen,' Jon began, rubbing his temples quickly with his fingers, 'give me a break, okay?' He put his head down and concentrated on his self-massage, and Helen waited patiently for him to finish. Jon Masters was only in his mid-thirties, but his short, frizzy,

73

rather unkempt hair looked like it was already turning gray at the temples, and many speculated he rubbed his temples more and more these days to rub the gray off. He had stopped wearing ball caps and drinking from big thirty-two-ounce squeeze bottles like a preschooler; and Helen, his wife of only a few years, noticed that her younger husband was starting to feel his age as well as look it.

It was about time, she thought. Jon Masters's entire life had been one adventure after another: his first of several hundred patents at age ten; his first million-dollar tax return by age eleven; his first PhD, from the Massachusetts Institute of Technology, at age thirteen; control of the company, the one she had slaved for years to build, before age thirty. He had completely bypassed childhood and gone from infant to adult. Jon had never really known failure or pressure in his young life – he was always the one in control. Even in his clumsy, boyish, but charming courtship of her, he managed to learn how to charm and please a woman quickly enough to avoid losing her completely. He did not make her feel like just another conquest – he had learned well enough to avoid that trap.

'In case you've forgotten, Helen,' Jon muttered, 'Paul is dead; Wendy is missing; and Patrick, Hal, and Chris are being detained in Egypt.' Sky Masters Inc was the secret major weapons and technology supplier to former president Kevin Martindale's commando force, the Night Stalkers. It was not a closely guarded secret: Wendy, Patrick, Hal Briggs, and Chris Wohl were all employees of Sky Masters Inc, and Paul McLanahan, although employed as an attorney in California, had worked closely with Sky Masters for years on development of the Tin Man battle armor and other weapons. 'I'm a little preoccupied right now.'

'But the Duffields don't know any of that,' Helen said, closing Jon's office door behind her. 'We can't tell them several of our people are involved in secret commando attacks in Libya. We have to carry on as if everything is okay. If we don't, it'll look like we're just blowing them off – and we *definitely* don't want to do that.'

'Helen, I thought all this shareholder and ownership and corporate-resolution stuff was your responsibility,' Jon whined. 'All I want to do is be an inventor, work in the labs, design stuff . . .'

'You are also chief operating officer and the majority share-holder, so you have a say in everything that goes on,' Helen reminded him. 'Of course, you can always transfer all your shares to me, and then I can relieve you of your position as COO and largest shareholder and you can be just a regular salaried employee – just like you did to me six years ago.'

'C'mon, now – you're still not mad about that, are you?' Jon asked with a faint smile.

'A guy eight years my junior who had never even owned a *car* before marches into the company I mortgaged my parents' house to start and takes over in just a couple years – what do I have to be mad about?' Helen responded. But she smiled at him and said, 'Actually, I was impressed by what you did, even though I squawked and hollered every step of the way until I was purple, and I'm proud and pleased with what you've done with my company since then. You're a good guy, Jon. That impish spoiled-brat personality is almost gone, and you've turned into a regular guy.' She paused, her smile warm and genuine. 'The guy I love.'

Jon looked up and smiled back. 'And I love you, Helen.' He sighed, then added, 'And you can have the stock and the title. I don't want it. It's not worth that much these days anyway.'

'Bull, Dr Masters,' Helen said. 'If you didn't want it, you would have given it away long ago, or put it into a trust for the child you keep promising to make with me – if you'd ever go home and spend a night in bed with me. And don't worry about the stock value. Sure, it's gone down in recent months with the down-turn in the NASDAQ, but with the sweetheart stock option deals you finagled, you're still a rich guy.' She stepped over behind him and gently massaged his shoulders. 'Besides, giving up the stock and your position in the company wouldn't relieve you of worrying about our friends, or mourning Paul McLanahan.'

'No. I guess it wouldn't.' Jon sighed. 'I can't believe Paul's gone. We were almost the same age. He was teaching me how to sail. We were buddies. I felt closer to him than I did to Patrick.'

She massaged his shoulders a bit more until he moaned with pleasure, then patted his shoulder, hard, in the direction of his office door. 'Let's go, Doctor. Let's meet the Duffields.'

'Remind me who they are again?'

'You know who they are,' Helen said, rolling her eyes with

mock exasperation. 'Conan David Duffield is the retired founder of SumaTek, the largest very-high-speed integrated-circuit design company in the world and the pioneer of nanotechnology. We have used SumaTek chips in our designs for ten years. He's in his late forties, degrees from Rutgers and Cornell, he's into French and Napa Valley wine, humane treatment of animals, and private schools, including providing scholarships to good students who otherwise couldn't afford a private-school education. His new acquisition company is called Sierra Vistas Partners. He's the money guy – he buys, rehabilitates, grows, and sells distressed high-tech companies.'

'Hey, this company is not "distressed."'

'I'm not saying it is, Jon,' Helen said quickly. But they both knew better – the combination of a downturning stock market, a glut of fairly modern Russian and Chinese weapons on the global arms market, and vastly lower defense spending had depressed stock values and affected thousands of defense-related companies all over the world, including Sky Masters, Inc.

'His wife is Dr Kelsey D. Duffield, PhD,' Helen went on. 'I don't have that much info on her – she keeps more to herself. I hear she's much younger than he is. She's the front person: she investigates and evaluates companies, then reports to him.'

'What's her degree in?'

'Which one? She has six or seven of them, including two PhDs – electrical engineering, math, physics, computer-language design, chemistry, and a couple others. Speaks seven languages, plays concert-quality piano, writes music, and is an expert-level downhill skier and chess player. They have one child – I don't know her name.'

'Sheesh, is this the definition of a dysfunctional family, or what?' Jon quipped. Helen scowled at him. 'I'm only kidding. Sounds like a perfectly wonderful, albeit super-overachieving family unit. Wonder what the little girl's going to grow up like?' Helen looked at him with a knowing smile – she was looking at him. 'Don't answer that.'

'Can we go now?'

'All right, all right, let's meet the whiz family. But after this, no more meetings until our guys are safe.'

'Deal.'

'And we are *not* selling them the company,' Jon added. Helen said nothing. The answer to that question, at least for the time being, was not up to them. 'Let's go.'

They walked out of Jon's office, and Suzanne escorted them to the conference room. The folks waiting for them stood politely when they entered. Kelsey Duffield was a pretty woman in her mid-thirties, her reddish-blond hair tied back behind her neck. She wore a simple silk business suit and carried a thin briefcase, and she had a good, strong handshake and a confident, pleasing smile.

'Very pleased to meet you, Dr Duffield,' Jon said as he stepped quickly into the room, extending a hand and shaking hers enthusiastically. 'I've heard a great deal about you.'

The woman's eyebrows furrowed. 'I'm not a doctor, Dr Masters. Just a lowly CPA.' Jon glanced at Helen, a bit confused and surprised by her misinformation – Helen usually didn't get the details wrong. Duffield turned and nodded to the man standing beside her. 'This is my associate and chief financial officer, Neil Hudson. Neil, this is Dr Jon Masters, COO, and Dr Helen Kaddiri Masters, chairman of the board.'

As they shook hands, they heard a clatter. 'Oh, dear, please be careful. Ladies and gentlemen, my daughter. She seems to have a case of the dropsies today.' Duffield rushed over to a sideboard, where a cute little brunette girl of nine or ten had just spilled a cup of orange juice on her dress. The little girl studied Jon for a long moment while her mother cleaned her up. Jon smiled at her, and she smiled back. He found it cute that she had spilled juice on a copy of a technical journal that she had in her lap. Her mother put the engineering journal aside and put a well-worn copy of a children's book of airplanes on her daughter's lap.

Jon noticed that the girl was still staring at him, the smile gone, as Duffield returned to the group. Jon winked at her, but she did not respond. Well, Jon never did click well with little kids – probably why he was hesitating having some of his own.

'Would your daughter be more comfortable in the day-care center, with some other children her age?' Helen asked. 'It's just across the courtyard.'

'Or I'd be happy to take her to the park,' Suzanne offered.

Both the elder and younger Duffields looked a bit confused. 'No, she's fine here,' the elder Duffield said coolly. The numbers guy, Hudson, looked a little aghast for a moment; then, after Duffield glanced at him, he appeared as if he was suppressing a chuckle. 'Shall we get started?'

'Of course,' Helen replied. They all took seats around one end of the conference table. 'On behalf of everyone here at Sky Masters Inc, welcome to Blytheville and the Arkansas International Jetport. We have a tour of the facilities planned, then lunch, then a briefing on our current projects and plans for future growth. Suzanne?' Suzanne handed her two folders. 'Here is our current audited financials and company statements, including the latest Department of Defense and Congressional Budget Office audits and financial condition statements. I'm sure you'll find that Sky Masters Inc is well positioned to ride out the short-term economic slowdown and market situation and get ready to take advantage of new opportunities.'

'So, if you'll excuse me,' Jon said, rising quickly to his feet. 'I've got to head back to the labs. But I'll see you for lunch at twelve-thirty, and then I will make myself available for questions afterward. I hope you have a nice –'

'We've already taken the tour, Dr Masters,' Duffield said. 'We arrived yesterday, remember? You set that up for us then.'

'And we've already downloaded a copy of your financials from your website and from the Defense Department's audit department,' Hudson said. 'Your staff should be commended, Doctors. Your own marketing information parallels the government data exactly, neither overstating nor understating your situation.'

'Situation?' Jon asked defensively. He remained standing. 'There's no "situation."'

Duffield looked down at the table, paused for a moment as if steeling herself for the confrontation she knew had to occur, then spread her hands and looked sternly at Jon. 'With all due respect, Dr Masters, your company is, shall we say, running a little peaked.'

'"Peaked"? What does that mean?'

'In our analysts' view, your company is spending lots of money, acquiring equipment and real estate, flying aircraft, and making space launches – all without any obvious possibility of translating the activity into a government contract,' Duffield said. 'You're a publicly traded company with apparently no responsibility or accountability to your shareholders.'

'I guess you just don't know us as well as you think.'

'Your outlays for new equipment don't even come close to your contracts,' Hudson said. 'You have projects on two-, three-, five-, even ten-year timelines with no contract, no requests for proposals, not even draft technology memos.'

'We're a research firm as well as a design-and-development center,' Helen said. Jon took his seat, gearing himself up to defend his company alongside his wife, trying to present a unified front. 'Jon and I have spent most of our careers in advanced research, most of it begun completely in-house with no government inputs. Jon has written over a thousand papers on dozens of emerging technologies, things the government has never dreamed of before.'

'*We* make the RFPs and technology memos happen, folks,' Jon said pointedly, 'not the other way around. They read our research abstracts and come up with ideas based on our research. That's why they come to us when they want something.'

'But they haven't been coming,' Hudson said. 'Contracts have all but dried up.'

'We line up four or five new technology-maturation grants and feasibility study funds every month,' Helen said. 'They may not be long-term big-ticket contracts, but they pay the bills and allow us to do what we do best – design and develop cutting-edge technology. The contracts will come. Everything takes time.'

'Then we're in the dark, Doctors, because the numbers don't balance,' Hudson pressed. 'You're running a slight deficit, showing large sums borrowed from investors, shareholders, and company officers. But we look around your facility and we see at least three times the capital outlays just at this facility. And we know you have at least one other design center and three operations facilities. Where does the money come from, Doctors?'

'It's all in the audit. Read it again.'

'How much does your company involve itself in classified government projects?' Duffield asked.

'That's classified,' Jon replied. 'I could tell you, but then I'd have to kill you.' He chuckled at his own joke, but none of them laughed back. The little girl looked up from her reading – the technical journal was back on her lap, opened up to a picture of

79

a particle accelerator in Texas, probably the only pretty full-color photo in the entire magazine – but also did not smile.

'We have a top-secret security clearance,' Duffield said. 'We've also received permission from DoD and the Justice Department to talk –'

'Not that I know of,' Jon shot back. 'As soon as I have my security folks brief me on your security status, and we verify it with the FBI and DoD, we can talk.'

'Your chief of security seems to be on hiatus,' Duffield observed. 'So are most of your senior development and operations staff. We wanted to meet the McLanahans especially.'

'They're out of the country. On business.'

'What business?' Duffield asked. 'Company business? Or is it classified?'

'I don't want to discuss it.'

'We also wanted to see some of your research aircraft, particularly the FlightHawk unmanned attack aircraft, the Megafortress flying battleship, and the airborne laser penetrator aircraft,' Duffield went on. 'None of those aircraft are on the field, or at any of your other facilities as well. Where are they?'

'They must be flying,' Jon replied. 'They do that a lot, you know.'

'They certainly do – a lot more than we'd expect of a system still in design phase,' Hudson said. 'A quick glance at your petroleum bills alone and one would think you ran a tactical air wing.'

'One would be wrong.'

'You certainly have the computer capabilities to do extensive computerized flight testing on all of your aircraft, weapons, and spacecraft,' Duffield said. Jon and Helen noticed that the little girl had gotten out of her seat and walked over beside her mother, her little hands clutching the upside-down technical journal, intently watching Jon. 'In fact, your systems rival companies twice as large as yours – again, far more capability than your income stream suggests you need. You certainly use the computers you have, but for what we're not quite certain – apparently not for advanced design and development, since you seem to fly the aircraft to test them.'

'Something wrong with that?' Jon asked testily. 'Or is that a typical bean-counter question?'

'Most companies would lease additional computer systems – you purchased them, and you spend twice as much as most other companies in upscaling them yearly,' Hudson said. 'Why is that, Doctors?'

'It has to do with our security classification,' Helen offered. 'Leased systems usually means getting a security evaluation for the leasing company's personnel as well, which we end up paying for and becoming responsible for maintaining.'

'Besides, we like to have the best,' Jon responded testily. 'Is this interrogation going somewhere? Let's get to the bottom line, shall we?'

Duffield sat back in her seat, folding her hands on her lap. 'Maybe we got off on the wrong foot here, Doctors.'

'Maybe *you* have.'

'Sierra Vistas Partners are not corporate raiders,' she said.

'My butt tells me otherwise.'

'Jon, please,' Helen quietly admonished her husband. She turned to Duffield. 'What is it you wish, Mrs Duffield?'

'My company is looking to invest in a small but solid high-tech research-and-development firm like yours, to help launch the absolute newest innovations in aerospace, electronics, communications, materials science, and advanced weapon design,' Duffield said. 'We're not interested in improving current technologies – we want to develop the next-generation technologies. We know Sky Masters Inc is on the cutting edge. We want to tap into that. We're prepared to offer a sizable capital investment as well as contributions in personnel and abstracts to be a part of it.'

'Abstracts? You mean, buy into my company with a bunch of *ideas*?' Jon retorted. 'Why would I need that? I've got plenty of ideas of my own, thank you very much.'

'Lately, you seem to be stuck on improving existing designs rather than breaking out new ones,' Duffield said. 'We can help. We have some of the finest new engineers waiting to start.'

'In this current economic and budgetary climate,' Hudson said, 'we find it easier and better to merge with an existing firm that might be . . . how should we say it . . . ?'

'You already said "peaked,"' Jon said accusingly.

'"Peaked,"' the little girl parroted. 'That's what Mommy said.' Jon gave her a sideways smile.

81

'It's a win-win situation for all of us,' Duffield went on. 'We contribute to Sky Masters's continued success and sustained future growth, positioning you as the company of the future while all the other contractors are struggling to hold their heads above water.'

'We're not struggling,' Helen said. 'Read our prospectus – we feel we're more than adequately capitalized to hold us for –'

'Two months? Maybe another quarter? Two quarters at the most?' Hudson interjected. 'That's all we foresee.'

'Is that right?' Jon retorted. 'Well, the company is not for sale, and we don't need investors or outside hacks.'

'You're a publicly traded corporation, about to be delisted from the NASDAQ exchange because of low trading volume and frequency-of-trading restrictions, including halted trades and non-openings,' Duffield said. 'We've researched your personal holdings as well. You have tried to buy back your company stock and failed every time. Your personal net worth is good, but you've leveraged many of your assets to help try to acquire your company stock. The stock has been on a slide for months, and it's hurting your own personal holdings. You're piloting a sinking ship, Doctors.'

'Thanks for the financial advice, but we don't need it.'

'As you know, we've already been in contact with a good number of your larger shareholders,' Hudson said. Jon knew, all right – that was the reason for this meeting in the first place. 'No one came right out and said it, but there is a lot of uneasiness about the company and your stewardship of it. The shareholders have not met or voted, but have informally indicated to us that they might be willing to consider a merger, stock swap, or buyout. As Mrs Duffield said, we're not corporate raiders, but we do know a company ripe for acquisition – hostile or otherwise. Sky Masters Inc is it.'

'Your shareholders told us that there's always a need for fresh blood, new faces, and innovative leadership,' Duffield added. 'Sierra Vistas Partners has a long track record of successfully reorganizing and reenergizing companies of all sizes, while providing maximum value and benefits for shareholders and employees alike. We want to be part of the future, Doctors. We have an opportunity to use our talent and innovation to design our country's next-generation technologies at a minimal cost.'

'Talent? What talent?' Jon asked irritably. 'You keep on saying you have all this great and wonderful talent. Where did you find it? We have a staff of recruiters that travel ten months out of the year interviewing quality engineers and students all over the world. If they're out there, we've already identified them, and if we can, we get them to come here or to our other design center in Las Vegas. I know all of them by heart – I've met and spoken with all the top names in our related fields.'

'Mommy?' It was the little girl, holding up the magazine to her mother.

'Just a moment, sweetheart . . .'

'Maybe it would be better if your daughter waited outside,' Jon suggested coolly. He reached for the intercom on the phone on the conference table.

Duffield smiled at Jon; then, still watching him, she bent down to her daughter. 'Yes, dear?'

'Look.' She indicated one of the articles in the journal.

'Oh, I see that. Isn't that a nice picture.' Duffield took the journal out of her daughter's hands. '*Journal of the International Association of Applied Energy Engineers.* The "Zap Mag," I believe you call it?' she asked Jon.

'I guess.' To the intercom, he said, 'Suzanne, could you come and get little . . . little . . .' Jon realized he did not know the little girl's name. '. . . Mrs Duffield's daughter for us for a few moments?'

'And I see it's an article about . . . what does it say?' Duffield said to her daughter, still looking at Jon. Jon and Helen both looked at the woman in total puzzlement. What was she doing, including her daughter in this conversation about an article in a technical journal? 'It says, "Conditions for improved propagation of laser energy fields in the lower atmosphere." How interesting. Have you read this article, Dr Masters?'

'No, I haven't. Suzanne . . . ?'

'It's a fascinating article,' Duffield said, almost in mock excitement. 'I believe you were the one who developed the science that allowed the rollout of the first viable plasma-yield weapon system, isn't that right, Dr Masters? But it can generally only be used in the upper atmosphere because of the distortion of the plasma wave by rare gases under higher pressures in the lower atmosphere. This tells about how laser energy fields are more effective in tactical battlefield scenarios.'

Jon looked at Duffield in surprise, then accepted the magazine when she offered it to him. Jon read the name of the writer, his brows knotting in confusion. '"By Dr Kelsey Duffield"? But I thought you said you were an accountant?'

'I am,' the woman said. 'But my name is *Cheryl* Duffield.' She motioned to the little girl standing beside her with a smile. 'Dr Masters, *this* is Dr Kelsey Duffield.'

Jon made a little puffing sound with his mouth, as if he was about to laugh but instantly knew the joke was on him. 'You . . . *you're* Kelsey Duffield?' Helen asked incredulously.

'Yes, Dr Helen,' the little girl replied with a tiny giggle.

'Don't be too embarrassed – people make incorrect assumptions all the time,' Hudson said. 'Cheryl likes stringing along the charade as long as she can.' He smiled mischievously and added, 'I think this was a record.'

'This was no "incorrect assumption." You did this deliberately,' Jon argued.

'This article has *your* picture on it, Mrs Duffield,' Helen pointed out perturbedly.

'Would you read an article that had the picture of a nine-year-old girl over it?' Cheryl asked. 'Most scientists and engineers wouldn't. Even with as much as one percent of today's masters and doctoral candidates five or more years below the average age – and Kelsey was *twenty-three* years below the average for her first doctorate – few accept young savants as anything else but freaks. Besides, we thought it was funny.'

'I don't appreciate the humor in it, or your subterfuge for this meeting, intended or not,' Helen said pointedly. 'These meetings rely on a great deal of mutual trust and professionalism, neither of which you've displayed. Jon?' She looked over at her husband, expecting him to say something or even storm out of the room. But he suddenly looked totally confused, at first reading bits of the journal article, then looking quizzically at Kelsey Duffield. 'Jon?' Jon opened his mouth, closed it, pointed at the magazine, made a sound as he tried to say something again, then started staring off into space. Helen was confused and a little frustrated – her 'good cop/bad cop' act was not happening here. '*Jon* . . . ?'

'It looks like you have a question, Dr Jon,' Kelsey observed, with that impish smile – too similar to Jon's, Helen noted with immense dismay. 'About the article?'

'I . . .' He looked like a fish out of water. Now, Helen thought wryly, she knew what some of the members of his doctorate boards must've looked like as he spoke to them about technologies that wouldn't become realities for a generation to come – Jon Masters, the supergenius, was finally having to deal with his own little supergenius. 'A *laser* energy field? A plasma energy field excited by a laser? That's impossible. They don't exist at the same space-time. They *can't* exist together.'

'You're still working around the notion of noninterchangeable space-time continuums, Dr Jon?' little Kelsey asked, truly surprised at the notion. She shrugged, then nodded knowingly. 'Well, I guess if you still subscribe to the idea that matter and energy exist in only one space-time as defined by things like frequency, mass, and acceleration, then it's true – they can't exist together. But I think there are an infinite number of continuums that exist in each measurable space-time.'

'That's . . . that's ridiculous,' Jon said, but even as he said it, he couldn't convince himself it was so ridiculous. 'Measurement, predictability, quantification – all those are space-time equivalents. Mathematically anything can be proven or disproven, but you can't build – or sell – something that only exists as an equation on the blackboard. Even Einstein couldn't do that.' At that, Kelsey Duffield's smile grew even broader. 'Okay. How?'

'How much is it worth to you to find out?' Hudson asked.

'*Excuse me?*' Jon said, purposely raising his voice. 'You're going to start haggling like we're buying souvenirs in a marketplace in the Bahamas or something?'

'I didn't mean to sound impertinent,' Hudson said. 'But although I don't understand a fraction of what Kelsey does or says most of the time, she has over and over proven to me that what she says is *real* and can work. I've invested most of my personal fortune in her and her work, as I'm sure you guessed that her parents have.

'But the Duffields know anyone can build a lab – the difficult part is getting the products of the lab to be accepted and turned into something useful and important. As much as Kelsey's theories and experiments are revolutionary, they will never gain

85

acceptance in the real world because of who she is. Sky Masters has a good reputation – the best in the world. That's why we've come to you.'

Jon Masters looked at his wife, to Hudson, then finally to the Duffields. Kelsey stood quietly, her tiny little hands folded neatly before her. He then looked back at his wife, his eyes silently asking the question he dared not verbalize. Helen nodded, trying to reassure him with a faint smile. Jon turned back to Kelsey. 'You're going to tell us everything? Lay it all out for us? Explain everything?'

'Yes,' Hudson said. 'For a third.'

'What did you say?'

'We're going to share, Jon,' Kelsey said. The more she spoke, the faster she seemed to age – in just a few seconds it suddenly seemed as if her voice, her mannerisms, even the look in her eyes had all grown up. 'You and Helen and I –'

'That's Dr Masters to you, little girl,' Jon admonished her.

'I feel much closer to you than all these boring titles, Jon and Helen,' Kelsey said, her eyes smiling – maybe laughing, Jon thought. 'I like you. I like you both very much. You're like my big brother, and Helen is like my big sister.'

'You and Dr Masters now own seventy-three percent of the outstanding stock,' Cheryl Duffield said. 'You will sell thirty-three percent of it to Sierra Vistas Partners and then divest seven percent back to the company. You will then cancel all other stock option deals you have with the corporation so you can have no more than one-third of the outstanding stock. We will reapportion the board accordingly – one-third controlled by you, one-third by Sierra Vistas Partners, and one-third by the other shareholders.'

'What kind of crazy scheme is this?' Jon retorted. 'This is *my* company. I didn't just acquire the stock – I didn't even buy most of it. I *earned* it. I took my compensation in stock when the stock was worth less than a dollar a share. I'm not going to just give it up, especially to strangers.'

'The stock options that you've negotiated in place of salaries and other compensation have ensured you total control of the company for many years, Dr Masters,' Hudson said. 'Good or bad, you control the company because you control the stock –'

'I'm also the chief designer and engineer,' Jon interjected. 'I built this company by taking chances and by developing technologies that work and remain on the cutting edge. I've given my life to this company, and I've taken nothing but the paper value out. My shareholders *are* my shareholders because they like that arrangement.'

'That's not what I hear,' Cheryl Duffield said. 'Your shareholders are not happy about this, but there was nothing they could do about it – they either stuck with you or got nothing. But now they're riding the company with you into the ground.'

'That's your opinion,' Jon said heatedly.

'It's a fact,' Cheryl said. 'Well, the tables are turned. Refuse this tender offer, and you risk losing all your shareholders, bankrupting your company, and opening yourself up to a lawsuit. Sierra Vistas Partners will be there to pick up the pieces. If you accept our offer, you recoup some of your losses, you gain my daughter's knowledge and wealth of ideas, and your company survives. No corporate raiders I know will give you a better deal.'

'The stockholders won't go for it,' Jon said. 'The board will never vote to approve it. None of this will stand up in court. You'd be wasting your time.'

'I think we can make an offer attractive enough for most of your shareholders,' Cheryl said. 'As far as the courts – well, the last thing you need in this market climate is a lawsuit. It'll sink your company fast.'

'What's stopping me from just taking the cash you give me and buying more stock?'

'Your promise not to do so, not to upset the one-third balance,' Hudson replied. 'This arrangement is based on trust. . .'

'You have a funny way of showing it, *Mrs* Duffield.'

'We feel a one-third split is best for the company – neither of us gains a majority unless our ideas and proposals sufficiently sway the other shareholders to side with one or the other,' Hudson went on. 'Once news hits the street that you've given up your stock options, the value of the stock will soar.'

'So what's preventing you from selling your shares and cleaning up?'

'We restrict the stock we own for one year,' Cheryl Duffield replied. 'If either of us wants out, we have to promise to offer it to the other shareholders first, at a prenegotiated price. But that's not what we're doing this for. We certainly don't need the money, and we're not stock speculators. We're building a future for ourselves and Kelsey by building a partnership with you and Helen and the other talented folks you have here.'

'We'll work together, Jon,' Kelsey said. 'It's more fun that way.'

'Fun? You think any of this is fun? Do you have any idea what we do around here, little girl?'

'I'm Kelsey,' she said, smiling at him. 'We'll make things, Jon and Helen. We'll make things other people have never dreamed of. Fantastic, unbelievable, wonderful things. We'll make people happy and make people's lives better.'

'Are you for real?' Helen Masters asked. 'Do you have any idea what you're getting yourself into?'

Kelsey Duffield walked over between Jon and Helen and took their hands into hers. 'We're friends now, right?' she asked. 'We're going to be together and build things so incredible, no one will believe it. Right?'

Neil Hudson opened his briefcase and extracted several documents – including a check. 'Value of your stock at its thirty-nine-week average price per share – exceedingly generous given the current stock price. You agree to sell the seven percent back to the company at the same price, you give up your stock options, and you agree to make Sierra Vistas Partners your partner. Dr Duffield comes on board as co-chief operating officer and co-chief engineer, sharing responsibilities and privileges equally with Jon Masters. Dr Helen Masters stays on as president for one year, at which time there will be elections for officers.'

Jon took the check, looked at all the zeroes typed on it, then looked at the Duffields. 'I . . . I have to think about it.'

'Please, Jon?' Kelsey asked. 'It'll be fun. I promise.' Jon hesitated, looking at Helen, then staring at nothing. Kelsey smiled and said in a low voice, almost a whisper, 'I'll tell you about the laser field, Jon. When I tell you, you'll be *so* mad.'

'Mad? Why?'

'Because you already know how it works.'

'What did you say?' Jon asked. 'Know how what works? How can I know how it works if I've never even heard of it before!'

'You already know how it works, I'll bet,' Kelsey said. 'You just don't believe it. You keep on saying "no" because you don't believe it could be so simple. I'll tell you, Jon, and then we'll build it, and then we'll build other things you've already thought about but don't believe either. It'll be fun.'

Jon sat back in his chair, visibly deflated. That was the last word he had expected to hear this morning: the word 'fun.' He wanted so badly to tell this little superbrained girl that he had already lost a friend, may have lost another close friend, and several more friends were in serious danger. He wanted to tell her that what happened to the company didn't matter – it was what his company was trying to do for the people of the United States and the world that was important. But she was here, with her mother and CPA and her father's SumaTek money, ready to create alternate universes inside lasers and other such fantasy gadgets. He wanted to tell her to just go away and let the adults get back to work.

But then Jon's brain registered the feel of the check between his fingers, and he thought of all those zeroes on it. He couldn't do a thing if he went bankrupt or if this cute little savant walked off with his company. Paul would still be gone, Wendy would still be missing, and the others would still be in trouble – except then they wouldn't have any of Sky Masters's technology to help them.

'I need to tell you something,' Jon said slowly. 'I need to verify your security clearance, so I can't tell you everything, but I can tell you this: Your security clearance is not going to prepare you for what you'll learn. We do a lot of very interesting things here, but it's not what I would call "fun." In fact, I'd say most of it is downright horrifying.'

'My daughter doesn't design talking dolls and little robot voice-controlled dogs and dream about a life filled with roses and sunshine,' Cheryl said. She reached over and stroked Kelsey's hair and shoulders, smiling warmly at her. 'She designs laser weapons and dreams about stopping enemy airplanes with force fields. No one ever told her what to do, what to focus on. She just did it.

'My husband and I brought her up like any other young girl – at least, we tried to. We dressed her in pink dresses and little black shoes and put ribbons in her hair. We read Dr Seuss and *Goodnight Moon* and Harry Potter books to her.

'But by the time she was one year old, at the same time

other kids were just starting to walk, she was reading the *Wall Street Journal* and *Aviation Week & Space Technology*. The first book she read wasn't Nancy Drew or Powerpuff Girls at six years old – it was Drexler's *Nanosystems: Molecular Machinery, Manufacturing, and Computation* at *thirteen months*. The year after that, she was one of the contributors to Drexler's updated edition.'

Cheryl paused, her eyes adopting a far-off look as if she was replaying all the many moments, pleasant and otherwise, in her memory. 'We knew we couldn't treat her like an ordinary child,' she went on. 'By age six she was discussing weapons, theories, devices and formulas that were making advisers to presidents sweat and four-star generals lick their lips. She's been asked to teach nanotechnology at Cornell's Duffield Hall, the engineering research facility my husband built – a nine-year-old professor of nanoengineering, teaching at her father's school. Do you think she'd be scared to learn how many persons a plasma-yield warhead can kill, or that one of your NIRTSats can direct a two-thousand-pound bomb to hit its target within six inches? She's already figured out how to build supercomputers the size of an amoeba and turn the Moon into a photonic energy source that will supply the entire Earth with energy for a millennium. She talks to herself about the energy requirements for teleportation while she plays with Barbie dolls. At first I was worried about her being taken seriously – now I'm worried about her talents going to waste or, worse, falling into the wrong hands.'

Cheryl looked up at Jon, then at Helen, and asked in a quiet voice, 'Do you have children?' They shook their heads. 'All you want for them is the best,' she went on. 'You would give your own life to save theirs, sacrifice your own happiness to ensure their happiness. But what do you do if what your child is doing, the thing that makes her the happiest, might upset – or even destroy – your world? Do you let her have that experience?'

Her voice lowered almost to a whisper. 'Sometimes when she'd fall off her bike or trip on the stairs or come down with a fever, I'd pray that the accident or illness would turn her back into a normal child,' she said sadly. 'But, of course, it never did – in fact, I think it made her even more intelligent, as if the bacteria or viruses were millions of new brains talking to her, telling her more and more of the secrets of the universe.

'But you are a child genius too, Dr Masters,' she said to Jon. 'You understand what Kelsey's going through. You had parents that encouraged you to think beyond your age, beyond the levels where others thought you should be. We chose you because you've gone through what Kelsey is just starting to experience. I think it was hard for you, breaking down all the institutional and bigotry barriers, but you did it. You can be much more than a partner to Kelsey – you can be a mentor, a guide. No one else in the United States can do that for her. Only you.'

Cheryl Duffield looked up at the Masterses, and the steel returned to her eyes and voice. 'She knows all about what you do, what you build, and whom you build them for,' she said. 'She wants to help you build the next two generations of weapon systems, far better than you or I or anyone yet born can imagine. Her father and I said we'd help her do that, because in a way, that's what parents do for their kids. It's not ballet or baseball, but parents are supposed to help their kids follow their dreams. Right?'

Jon looked at Kelsey. To his immense shock, while her mother was talking, Kelsey had been writing out a long mathematical formula on a sheet of notepaper. When she noticed Jon was looking at her, she held up the piece of paper for him. For about the third or fourth time in that meeting, Jon's mouth dropped open.

'It's not finished,' Kelsey said, smiling.

'I . . . don't . . . believe . . . it . . .' Jon breathed, his eyes flitting across the symbols and numbers. He pointed to one section, and his eyes narrowed, then widened, then nearly bugged out. 'I . . . you . . . this . . .'

Kelsey handed it over to Jon, and he accepted it as if she had just handed him a thirty-pound bar of solid gold. 'We'll finish it together, okay, Dr Masters?' she said, her eyes twinkling.

'Jon. Call me Jon,' he said, smiling, his voice cracking with the sheer enormity of what he had just witnessed. Jon looked at the piece of paper, then at Kelsey, then at her mother. 'Do you realize what this is?'

'Of course. It's the future,' Cheryl said matter-of-factly, almost in a whisper. She looked down at the conference table, then added, 'God help us.'

On the Mediterranean Sea, ten miles northwest of Mersa Matrûh, Egypt that same time

The crew of the Egyptian warship *El Arish*, an American-built Oliver Hazard Perry-class guided missile frigate, treated the rescued members of the SS *Catherine the Great* as any other ship-wreck survivors, offering them water, blankets, strong hot tea, and *ful* – pita sandwiches stuffed with fava and black beans fried together with meat, eggs, and onions. They were kept in the hel-icopter hangar on the aft end of the ship, out of sight of most of the rest of the crew. Several of the Night Stalkers received medical treatment for burns and shrapnel wounds by the Egyptian ship's corpsman.

David Luger acted as the spokesman for the team when approached by the captain of the frigate, Commander Raouf Farouk, while Patrick, Hal, and Chris stayed away from the Egyptians in the center of the helicopter hangar, surrounded by commandos. 'We are grateful to you for helping us, Captain,' David said as the captain approached. 'You have saved our lives.'

'*Afwan*. You are welcome,' Farouk said. He looked at the men carefully. 'And your name?'

'I'm Merlin.'

'Your full name, rank, and nationality?'

'Just Merlin,' Luger replied. 'No rank or title. We are all Americans.'

'Keeping that information secret is an insult for those of us who have just saved your lives,' Farouk admonished him. 'Now, I order you to tell me your real name and rank, or I will throw you in my brig.'

'I'm sorry, sir, I will not,' David replied. 'I will tell you that we are crew members of the SS *Catherine the Great*, a salvage vessel based in Klaipeda, Lithuania. I'm sorry, but our ownership papers and letters of transit were lost in the attack.'

'I understand,' Farouk said. There was no doubt in Farouk's

mind that these were soldiers – they looked, acted, and even moved like fighting men. And they were not sailors, either. 'The bastardly Libyans think they own the Mediterranean. I am told you do not carry passports, either.'

'Sorry, sir. They went down with our ship as well.' That was true, but the passports that went down with the ship were all fakes. 'We are all American merchantmen. As I told your first officer, if you allow me to call the American embassy in Cairo, they can help verify our identities.'

'This is a military matter now, and we have specific procedures to follow to verify your identities,' Farouk said, obviously angry at Luger's lack of cooperation. 'You will be placed in custody at our home base of Mersa Matrûh and questioned. You will be treated fairly, I assure you, but since you were obviously involved in some military conflict with the Libyans, we can take no chances.' He motioned to the three men surrounded by the commandos. All three put their heads down while Egyptian intelligence officers snapped pictures of them and the other commandos. 'And then there is the question of those three gentlemen. Unless they are spacemen from Mars and an oxygen atmosphere is poisonous to them, they must remove their equipment immediately.'

'The devices they are wearing are life-support equipment,' Luger lied. He turned toward the three, and they all took off their helmets with a gentle hissing sound. Photo strobes flashed despite their efforts to hide their faces. 'They are under some distress if they take their helmets off. May they please put them back on, Captain?'

'My ship's doctor will examine the men with their outfits off,' the captain said. 'If they are in distress, they will be airlifted to the appropriate medical facility in Egypt for treatment – all the way to Cairo if necessary. They will be well treated, I assure you. But since that outfit is unknown to me, it will be removed, examined, and placed in secure storage at Mersa Matrûh until we can ascertain that it is safe and no threat to us.'

Luger nodded. 'Yes, sir. I'll tell them that right now. It will take a few moments to remove their outfits.' Luger bowed slightly to the captain, then went over to McLanahan, Briggs, and Wohl. 'Bad news, guys,' he said. 'The captain wants you to ditch the

93

armor. He's going to have his doc examine you; then he's going to place us all into custody at Mersa Matrûh.'

'We can't wait until we dock before we do something, sir,' Chris Wohl said in a low voice. Although they were all civilians now, retirees, Chris Wohl would never even consider calling McLanahan, Luger, or Briggs anything else but 'sir,' although he might put a definite sneer in his voice if he disagreed with their orders – as he did now. 'Mersa Matrûh is a combined-forces base – they have close to fifty thousand troops stationed there from all three services.'

'We're not supposed to be fighting the Egyptians,' David Luger said. 'Once we contact the American embassy, we'll be let go. But if we get into a shit storm with the Egyptians, they're just as likely to kill us.'

'Our embassy has no idea why we're here,' Patrick said. 'No real passports, no visas – and the President already tried once to have us all arrested. We can't go running to the embassy for help.'

'I'm forced to agree with the master sergeant, Muck,' Hal Briggs said. 'They'll treat us like captured terrorists. Our cover will be blown wide open.'

Patrick thought for a moment longer; then: 'Sarge, how many sailors on this ship?'

'About two hundred total. The US Navy doesn't usually carry Marines on little frigates, but the Egyptians do. Usually two marine platoons max, thirty or forty men – those will be the best-trained counterforces. We've seen one platoon in here already, but only a dozen of them armed.'

Luger tensed up as he saw movement nearby – the captain was getting tired of waiting and was getting his men together to start taking them into custody. The commandos surrounding the three leaders were trying to look casual and relaxed, but they could sense their tension. 'Looks like the captain's coming over here. Time's up.'

'How do you want to play it, sir?' Wohl asked Patrick.

Patrick got to his feet, turned away from the oncoming Egyptian captain, and hefted his helmet. 'Let's take this boat,' he said, and he quickly slipped his helmet into place.

'Hoo-rah,' Wohl said tonelessly as he and Briggs got to their feet. 'Good decision, sir.'

'*An iznukum!*' Farouk shouted when he saw Patrick put on the helmet. '*Min fadlukum!*' But when he saw Briggs and Wohl also put their helmets on, he knew things were turning ugly. '*Wa'if!*'' He motioned to his marine guards. '*Ihataris! Wa'if!*'

The three armored commandos moved out in a triangle formation, opposing the three main bodies of guards. At the same instant, the commandos also fanned out, moving with surprising speed since it seemed as if they were so relaxed and tired mere moments ago. The electronic energy bolts fired, striking the armed guards, and almost before the stunned guards hit the steel helicopter hangar deck, the Night Stalker commandos had their weapons in their hands. In less than fifteen seconds, every armed Egyptian sailor in the hangar was unconscious, and the commandos were closing, dogging, and guarding the steel hangar doors and hatches, weapons in hand.

'*What are you doing? What are you doing here?*' Farouk shouted as he saw his men drop to the nonskid deck, their bodies quivering from the electric shocks they received. He pointed an angry finger at Luger. 'You told me you meant us no danger!' He saw Patrick approach and turned his anger towards him. 'Are you the one responsible? I will see to it that you are put to death for this act of aggression! We saved you and your men from the Libyans, and now you dare do *this*!'

'Captain, I am Castor,' Patrick said. He paused as he listened to instructions Wohl issued to his men. The Night Stalker commandos quickly began to remove the Egyptian sailors' uniforms and put them on. 'My men and I won't hurt you, and we have no desire to take your ship, unless you do not cooperate with us.'

'Won't hurt us? Won't take my ship? You are terrorists! Saboteurs! Spies!' Farouk screamed. 'Putting on the uniform of another country's army is not permitted!'

'This is not war, Captain, and we are not soldiers,' Patrick said. 'Sir, I'm going to ask one more time for your cooperation.'

'I refuse. You may kill me if you wish.'

'I don't want to kill you, Captain,' Patrick said. 'I want you to contact your headquarters on Mersa Matrûh. Tell them I have taken you hostage and warn them not to approach this ship.'

'I told you, I will not cooperate,' Farouk said. 'I order you to put down those weapons and surrender.'

'That's not likely to happen, Captain,' Patrick said. 'But I'm sure you'll reconsider my offer to contact your headquarters once we reach the bridge.'

'The bridge?' Farouk gulped. 'You . . . you think you will *take my bridge?* You will all be dead in ten minutes.'

'Maybe so,' Patrick said. 'But in five minutes, we'll have control of your bridge.' He switched the view on his electronic visor to an electronic briefing Chris Wohl was giving to the Night Stalkers. Patrick saw that Wohl had called up an electronic blueprint of the US-made Perry-class frigate and was briefing his men on their assault. In less than five minutes, they were ready. Wohl took the port-side rail, Briggs the starboard rail, followed by fifteen Night Stalkers each; Patrick went atop the hangar and made his way forward along the upper gun deck with twenty commandos.

Because of the tense situation in the Med following the Libyan raids, the deck was full of lookouts, all armed with American-made machine guns. They were all doing exactly what they were supposed to be doing – searching the sea, continually scanning for threats using night-vision goggles and infrared sniperscopes – so it was easy to simply step within a few feet of them unnoticed, quietly knock them unconscious with a quick zap, disable or capture their weapons, and move on. McLanahan's, Briggs's, and Wohl's electronic visors showed each crewman on deck in stark relief several yards away, and their amplified hearing equipment allowed them to take cover before a crew member came through a hatch or unexpectedly appeared around a corner.

On the bridge, the officer of the deck, or OOD, was making a log entry when suddenly the frigate's propeller simply stopped. 'Sir, sudden loss of propulsion!' the helmsman reported.

The OOD immediately picked up the 1MC phone direct to Engineering. 'Engineering, bridge, what's happening down there?' No reply. 'Engineering, bridge, respond!' Still no reply. The OOD turned to the chief petty officer. 'Sound general quarters, all hands to battle stations, no drill.' He picked up another phone, the one direct to the captain's quarters. 'Captain to the bridge. Emergency.' The OOD had picked up another phone. 'Combat, bridge . . . Combat, can you hear me?' There was no reply. 'What in hell is going on here?' He turned to the chief petty officer and shouted, 'And why haven't you sounded general quarters, dammit?'

'I activated the alarm, but it did not sound, sir!' The chief petty officer turned to one of the watchstanders and shouted, 'Start a running message relay right now, general quarters, battle stations, this is not a drill. Go!'

'*Ma'lesh*,' they heard behind them. 'It doesn't matter.'

The OOD and chief petty officer turned and saw Commander Farouk step onto the bridge. 'Sir, we've lost propulsion,' the OOD reported, 'and I cannot raise Engineering or Combat and I cannot sound general quarters. I . . .' But then he noticed the surprised expressions of the helmsman and the other watchstanders as the captain stepped onto the bridge. 'Sir . . . ?'

Farouk was roughly pushed toward his captain's chair in the center of the bridge, and then the place seemed to explode in chaos. Men in Egyptian naval uniforms pointed automatic weapons at the bridge crew, shouting in English. At the same moment, the access door from the center of the bridge burst open, and more English-speaking men rushed in; behind the OOD and chief, the port-side weather door also whipped open, and more strange men entered. Once the bridge crew was gathered up, they were placed down on the deck, hands behind their necks. Four of the commandos stayed on the bridge, while others took up security positions outside and in the inside passageway.

Patrick entered commands into the frigate's computerized helm station, and the ship turned away from the Egyptian coast, increasing power to maximum. He then picked up the captain's telephone and held it out to Farouk. 'I need you to tell your crew that we will be delayed in returning to Mersa Matrûh and to not interfere with my men.'

'I refuse.'

Patrick seemingly did not react – but moments later, Farouk's body began to do a strange jerking quiver in his seat, and his eyes began to roll up into his head. The spasm lasted for several moments, then Farouk's body went limp. The Egyptian captain appeared as if he had just been beaten up, his breath coming in deep gasps, although no one had touched him. 'It will be harder on you if you do not comply,' Patrick said in an electronically synthesized voice.

Farouk held out his hand, and Patrick placed the telephone in it. The Egyptian took several deep breaths, then spoke in Arabic.

97

After he had finished, Patrick turned to one of the Night Stalkers and asked, 'What did he say?'

'He said the bridge and probably Engineering and Combat have been taken by American commandos. He ordered his crew to resist us to the maximum extent possible.'

'The only ones that will be hurt will be your men, Captain,' Patrick said. He spoke into his helmet communications system, then handed the phone back to Farouk a few moments later. 'We have made contact with your headquarters, Captain. Tell them anyone approaching this ship will be attacked and killed. This is your only warning.' Farouk relayed the message, recommending that all forces be dispatched immediately to disable his ship and prevent it from falling into terrorist hands.

'Well, now the Egyptians know we're here,' Briggs radioed to Patrick via their battle armor comm system. 'Half the crew is ready to rush us from every corner of the ship, and soon half the Egyptian military will be barreling down on us. What's the plan?'

'We need to get in contact with Martindale, have him get every asset we have available searching for Wendy,' Patrick said. 'I want to turn this ship inside out looking for weapons, I want everyone to get fully recharged and rearmed, and then I want a plan of action to go in and rescue her.'

'Patrick,' Briggs said softly, 'we still don't know if she's alive.'

'She's alive. I know it.'

'But we don't –'

'I said, she's *alive*, dammit!' Patrick cried angrily. 'I'm going to find her even if I have to move every grain of sand in the desert to do it.'

Over the Mediterranean Sea
that same time

'You cannot go back, Sekhmet,' said retired Egyptian army general Ahmad Baris, President Kamal Ishmail Salaam's national security adviser and longtime trusted friend of the family. Fifty-three-year-old General Baris lost most of his right leg in the 1973 Arab-Israeli War, burned off in a tank explosion, but he stayed in government to serve his country as best he could, rising through the

98

ranks from onion-peeler and tailor to intelligence coordinator to tactician to presidential military advisor. 'It is too dangerous. Al-Khan's henchmen and the Muslim Brotherhood assassins are everywhere.'

'Not even to bury my husband?' Susan Bailey Salaam said in a low voice. Her head and arms were swathed in bandages, and an Egyptian army doctor had inserted an intravenous tube into a vein in her leg because the second-degree burns on her arms would not allow it.

'Especially not for a funeral,' Baris said sadly. 'Trust me. You would not be safe. There will be a simple ceremony for your husband, no more. It is too dangerous otherwise.'

Susan Salaam and General Baris were on board an Egyptian army helicopter, zooming low over the Mediterranean Sea westward, about five miles off the coast. Ahmad Baris had engineered an alternate escape plan for Susan to get out of the city after the attack so secret that not even the Presidential Guards knew about it. After the men and women killed or injured in the attack were taken away by ambulance from the mosque, Baris had Susan taken in several different ambulances to a waiting army helicopter and whisked out of the city.

'I feel like a coward. I feel as if I have abandoned my husband,' Susan said stonily.

The retired general sighed softly, then repositioned his right leg to ease the pain a bit, which easily got Susan's attention. 'Your husband is dead, Sekhmet,' he said softly, like a father speaking to his young daughter. 'Being killed at his grave site by more Muslim Brotherhood assassins would not help him or Egypt.' He paused, then added softly, 'You know I would follow your husband into hell, and I pledge the same to you. Tell me what you wish, and I will do everything in my poor powers to help you do it.'

'What do you suggest, General?'

'We are heading toward Mersa Matrûh, our largest military base outside Cairo, about three hundred kilometers west,' Baris replied. 'I can have a foreign ministry transport waiting for us there. The plane can take us anywhere in western Europe – Portugal, England, Belgium, Ireland. From there, we can request protection from the American embassy – you are a dual national as well as a credentialed Egyptian ambassador, so that will not be a problem.'

'I will not leave Egypt,' Susan said sternly. 'It is my home now, not America.' She glared at him with her one unbandaged eye. 'I'm surprised you would even suggest it, General.'

'I am sorry, Madame. I was only thinking of your safety. I apologize if I have offended you or dishonored the memory of the president by suggesting you flee the country.'

'You are still one of the most respected men in all of Egypt, perhaps in the entire Arab world,' Susan said, reaching up and taking Baris's hand. 'Your loyalty is unquestioned, as is your heart.' She looked at Baris, paused as if considering her words, then said, 'You could be president, or prime minister, if you so chose. But you stay in the shadows. Your people need you, General. When will you stand up and lead them?'

'I have led men only once, at the head of a formation of tanks in the Sinai against the Israelis almost thirty years ago, and nine of every ten men that followed my orders died in less than a day,' Baris said. 'I was the lucky one – I lost only part of my right leg. I learned that day that I am far more adept at observing and advising than making actual decisions.'

'Nonsense, Ahmad.'

'As a famous American psychopathic renegade police officer once said, "A man's gotta know his limitations,"' Baris said with a smile. His love for American cop movies and westerns – the more violent the better – was well known throughout Cairo. 'I am content and secure in the knowledge that I have given good, sound advice to many government officials over the years, and I believe I have served God and made Egypt a better place for it. That is enough for me.' He paused, studying Susan carefully, then asked, 'What is it you seek, Sekhmet?'

Susan Salaam did not respond for several moments, and Baris was surprised to see a faint smile on her lips when she finally replied, 'Am I wrong for saying "I would like to see Zuwayy and al-Khan dead"?' Baris did not return the smile, so hers dimmed and her exotic eyes narrowed. 'The truth, my old friend?' Baris nodded, and she looked away and nodded as well. 'I'm happy to be alive. I'm glad I wasn't killed. And so I think that perhaps God had a reason for not wishing me dead. I feel there is something more I must do.' Susan shook her head, staring off into space as if reading a newspaper headline from a great distance. She paused, then looked at the retired general. He swallowed as he saw something ominous in her dark almond-shaped eye and full yet innocent lips. 'Yes. There is work to be done. You and my husband had plans to restore Egypt to its rightful place as leader of the Mediterranean nations and of the Arab world. I want to continue your goals.'

'My dear, the concept of a united Arab world is a dream, nothing more,' Baris said, chuckling despite the strange prickly sensation he felt on the back of his neck. 'Don't let the apparent successes of pretentious nutcases like Zuwayy or opportunistic zealots like al-Khan cloud your thinking. The people of Libya don't believe Zuwayy is a descendant of a desert king, and no modern Egyptian will ever believe a man is invested with the power of the gods to rule their land. The Pharaohs are dead, and long may it stay that way.' He touched Susan's hand, breaking her reverie, and smiled with relief when she smiled at him. 'Even though you are a thousand times lovelier than all of Hollywood's Cleopatras put together, Sekhmet, don't ever be deluded into thinking the world will tolerate an Arab empire.'

Susan's smile dimmed as she reached up and touched her eye-patch, then ran her fingers down the left side of her face and left arm, gently tracing the scars and the pain that outlined them under all the bandages. 'No one will ever think I am as beautiful as Cleopatra. Zuwayy's and al-Khan's treachery has seen to that.'

'Don't let revenge and hatred fester inside you,' Baris warned her. 'Keep a clear head. Understand?'

'Yes, General.'

'Good.' The military helicopter had a computer terminal at the communications officer's station, so Baris swiveled his chair over to his computer terminal and logged on. His usual list of daily intelligence, status, and situation reports started popping up on the screen. 'Our first task is to get you to safety. I . . .'

'I must go back to the presidential palace,' Susan repeated. 'I must bury my husband first.'

'Your life is in great danger if you go back,' Baris warned her.

'I have no choice. If the conspirators want to kill me before or during the funeral, so be it – I will become Egypt's second martyr.

101

My last duty to my husband is to help lead his nation forward beyond their grief.' She smiled at her friend. 'But I don't want you exposing yourself in a vain attempt to stop any attack if it should come. I want you out of sight, watching, as you do best. Leave me your best and most trusted aides. I think I'll be all right until after the funeral. After that . . . we will do what we must do. Let's go to Alexandria. Can you find a secure place for us there?'

'The Naval Academy on Abu Qir Bay east of Alexandria – the commandant is an old friend, and he can ensure your safety and security. It's isolated enough to keep us out of sight, but they have helicopter and fast armed patrol vessel facilities in case we must make a quick escape from Khan's goons. Your apartment is less than a kilometer away.' But as he scanned the daily reports, he came across a shocking one and read it quickly. Susan noticed his eyebrows lifting higher and higher with each sentence. 'What in hell . . . ?'

'What is it, General?'

'Some sort of base-wide emergency happening at Mersa Matrûh as we speak,' Baris replied, reading the report with growing surprise. 'Listen to this, Susan: On the night before the attack at the mosque, there was an attack against an isolated rocket base in Libya, including possible chemical and nuclear material discharge.'

'I remember. Kamal was briefed shortly after it happened. We mobilized our border forces, but otherwise did not want to make it appear we were in any way involved.'

'That's correct,' Baris said. 'A few hours later, there were a series of attacks by unidentified warplanes, presumed to be Libyan, against several civilian commercial vessels in the Mediterranean. We were told they were some kind of retaliatory attacks, the Libyans trying to find where the commandos that attacked their base came from. A total of seven lifeboats filled with sixty-three men and women evacuated from one of the ships, a Lithuanian-flagged salvage vessel, and were picked up by our guided missile frigate *El Arish* out of Mersa Matrûh.'

'That seems like a very large crew for a salvage vessel. What else? Has the crew been interrogated? Who are they?' Susan looked at the retired general and saw that his mouth had dropped open in surprise. 'General? What is it?'

'Our frigate was captured.'

'*Captured?* By the *rescued crew?*'

'This is extraordinary,' Baris exclaimed as he read. 'The rescued crew members are apparently commandos, led by three men in unusual and unidentifiable battle dress uniforms, carrying powerful but unusual weapons.'

'What is the crew complement of the frigate?'

'About two hundred sailors.'

'*Sixty* men captured *two hundred sailors* on board one of our own warships?' Susan asked incredulously. Surprise, however, quickly turned to wonderment. 'How do we know all this, General? Is someone on the crew sending secret messages? Did someone escape?'

'No, Susan – the leader of the commando unit is allowing the captain, Commander Farouk, to send these messages,' Baris replied with astonishment in his eyes and tone. 'The leader, who calls himself Castor, says that no one on the ship will be harmed and the ship will be allowed to return to Mersa Matrûh as long as we promise not to attack the ship as they approach and do not attempt to capture them.'

'Who are they? Israelis? Americans?'

'Commander Farouk believes they are Americans, but they are wearing masks and are hiding their identities well. It is apparently impossible to tell the nationality of the leaders – their voices are electronically altered.'

'Electronically altered?' Susan thought hard for a moment. Who were these soldiers? They were powerful enough to commandeer an Egyptian warship, one of the most powerful in northern Africa, but yet they couldn't hold their base of operations, a small salvage vessel. If they were terrorists or mercenaries sent to attack an Egyptian target, they were sloppy indeed. They surely would not have let the ship's captain make a call back to base.

The leader decided to trust the Egyptians not to harm them – but just to be sure, they commandeered a guided missile frigate. An interesting blend of strength and restraint, power and caution. Who was this leader? Obviously a man concerned for the safety of his men, but not afraid to use the power at his command. Obviously highly trained and skillful, but not berserkers either.

The leader's nom de guerre was 'Castor' – one of a set of twins

103

from Roman mythology. The twin gods, the Dioscuri, were the 'cosmic stabilizers,' representing darkness and light. One was a man of peace, a horse tamer; the other was a boxer, a warrior. They also protected mortals. When Pollux, the warrior, was killed during the Odyssey, Castor the man of peace made a deal with the gods – when his fellow voyagers needed a fighter, he would die so his brother could live. Susan wondered the obvious – who and where was the Pollux?

Or perhaps there was no Pollux now, and Castor the man of peace was the leader. Perhaps that's why these men didn't slash their way on board the frigate, kill the crew, and simply steal the ship. Could this Castor be convinced to transform himself into Pollux the warrior to protect mortals . . . or perhaps one mortal in particular?

'I will return to Cairo for the funeral, General,' Susan said. 'But first we will go to Mersa Matrûh to meet these commandos. Make no attempt to retake the ship, but do not allow it to leave, either.'

'You want to keep one of our own captured warships sitting off our own shore with a terrorist commando team aboard, and not do anything about it?'

'They captured it, they deserve to stay on it,' Susan said. 'Give them food, medical attention, women – anything they want or need. Just don't let them leave.' She thought for a moment, then said, 'Rather, *ask* them to stay, until I arrive.'

'Why do you want to meet with them, Sekhmet?' Baris asked. 'They could be dangerous men.'

Susan shook her head. 'I don't think so,' she said. 'In fact, they could be just what we need to take back what Khan and Zuwayy have taken from us.'

It was one of the hardest things she ever had to do in her young life: leave her husband's side to protect her own life. Now, several minutes from landing at the huge sprawling joint forces military base at Mersa Matrûh in northwestern Egypt, Susan Bailey Salaam finally had time to sort out all the horrifying events that had happened over the past several hours.

Susan had been taken away from the mosque by an army ambulance, one of several in the area. They tried to make their way back to Abdin Palace, but the streets were now blocked by protesters and rioters who had heard that Susan had been killed in the blast on the Nile, and they sped off. She was transferred to several different vehicles, and at one point dressed in a flak vest and wore a helmet as a disguise when it appeared protesters were getting too close to their vehicle. She was finally taken to Zahir Air Base in northeastern Cairo and flown out of the city in an army helicopter. The pilot broadcast that his destination was the Egyptian Naval Academy in Alexandria, but once over the Mediterranean, the helicopter dipped low to the water, out of sight of anyone on shore, then proceeded west.

No doubt about it, she thought ruefully as they began their approach for landing – it was an evacuation, out of Cairo, out of the government, out of the people's lives, fleeing for her own life. She hated the idea of being forced to run from her own home, her own people. She preferred facing her attackers, confronting them head-on, battling for her honor and legacy and that of her husband. But now she was gone. She had to disguise herself to get out of the area – they could not even trust the citizens of Cairo to protect her long enough, even in her grief, to get her safely away from such a disastrous, monstrous, unconscionable event. Even the Presidential Palace was unsafe.

What was she doing out here, hundreds of kilometers from civilization, running from her people like a thief in the night? If there were strange commandos here in Egypt, why didn't she have them brought to her in Alexandria? Something was drawing her out here. She didn't know who these men were, but something told her she had to go look for herself out here. Not for safety. Perhaps it was the desert, the idea of *hegira*, and the cleansing forces of the desert. Perhaps, like Moses and Jesus and Muhammad and thousands of others throughout history, she needed to draw spiritual strength from the wastelands.

It was about an hour before dusk when the helicopter made its approach to the huge military base. Mersa Matrûh looked more like a large industrial complex and commercial shipyard than a military base. Sprawling almost two hundred square kilometers, it was home to nearly a fifth of all of Egypt's active-duty forces. Its main assignment – not well publicized, for fear of angering its Arab neighbors – was to repel a possible invasion from Libya, as well as to secure Egypt's northern and western flanks and protect its right to freely navigate the Mediterranean Sea. Most of the base had been built by Nazi Germany and Italy during World War II, then occupied by the British until the 1952 revolution. Susan noticed the large earth stations, part of Egypt's telecommunications network, as well as the early-warning radar installation that scanned the Mediterranean and the skies to the north and west, watching and waiting for danger.

'God must have something else in store for me rather than to die in the streets of Cairo,' Susan said to General Baris as they exited the helicopter. She looked at the men arrayed before her. 'These guards . . . ?'

'Handpicked by me for your protection,' Baris said. 'On my payroll, and as loyal to me as my own brothers and sisters. Unfortunately, you have some enemies, even out here on the frontier.' He motioned to the man, obviously a high-ranking officer, who stepped over to them. 'Madame, this is Vice Marshal Sayed Ouda, commander of the western military district headquartered here.'

Ouda made a slight bow, then returned his hands casually to behind his back. He was tall, good-looking in a rough-hewn way, with a stylish mustache, carrying – of all things – a riding crop, his cap rakishly tilted to one side. 'My condolences to you,' he said simply.

'Thank you, Vice Marshal,' Susan Salaam said. She regarded him coolly for a moment, then said, 'You do not approve of me being here, do you, Vice Marshal?'

'My duty is to protect my nation and obey orders,' he said in a low monotone. He eyed General Baris suspiciously. 'I do what I must to obey the *legitimate* authorities.' Obviously he was beginning to doubt whether Baris represented any legitimate authority at all anymore in Egypt.

'I do not mean to cause you any trouble, Vice Marshal,' Susan said.

'The president is dead, Madame,' Ouda said icily, 'and his aide de camp and widow are hiding themselves on my base, far from the capital. That is not the mark of any legitimate authority I know.'

'Nonetheless, you will obey his orders as you would have obeyed President Salaam,' Susan said, 'or you may discover your value as a commander in the Egyptian armed forces to be greatly diminished.'

Ouda looked Susan up and down with a faint smile. His unspoken words were crystal clear: My value is considerably greater than yours right now. He gave her another appraising look. Susan was very familiar with that look as well: The man was momentarily forgetting she was the wife of an Egyptian president and was looking at her as just another potential sexual conquest. Ouda was obviously accustomed to doing that, no matter who else was looking on. He gave her another half-bow, half-nod and departed.

A woman in uniform quickly stepped over to them, snapped to attention, and saluted. She wore the red beret of the Republican Guards, the elite infantry soldiers assigned to protect the president and other high government officials, and she wore a small MP5 submachine gun on a combat harness on her body. She was shorter and thinner than Susan, and rather small for a soldier, but her dark eyes and firm jaw told an entirely different story.

'Madame, this is Captain Amina Shafik, formerly an infantry officer and a company commander in the Republican Guards,' General Baris said. 'She was first assigned to protect my wife seven years ago until cancer took her. She has been my personal aide since. I trust her implicitly. Captain Shafik, Madame Susan Salaam.' Shafik saluted, then snapped to parade rest. 'I have assigned her to you as your personal bodyguard. She will stay with you night and day. You must trust her judgment when it comes to your safety.'

Susan extended her hand, and the handshake confirmed Susan's observation – she was deceptively strong. 'I am pleased to meet you, Captain,' Susan said. 'Do you have a family? A husband?'

'A brother and two sisters, Madame, both emigrated to the United States,' Shafik replied. 'My parents are dead, killed by the Israelis in the Six-Day War. My husband was an officer in the Mubahath el-Dawa, killed in a terrorist bombing of the State Security Investigations headquarters by Gama'a al-Islamiyya.'

'I am sorry for your loss, Captain,' Susan said. She looked at her carefully. 'You lost a child as well, did you not, Captain?'

Shafik's eyes widened, first in surprise, then in sadness as the memories flooded back, unbidden. She nodded. 'I lost it the day I learned of the death of my husband.'

107

'It is an enormous tragedy,' Susan said. 'But you will learn to love again, and you will find a man worthy of your love. I hope you won't let your hatred prevent you from having the child you well deserve.'

'My tragedy – and my hatred – is insignificant compared to what you must feel, Madame,' Shafik said, her voice flowing with relief and gratitude.

'No tragedy – or hatred – is insignificant,' Susan said quietly. 'I assure you of that.'

'If you permit me, Madame,' Shafik said, 'I would like to personally apologize to you for the breach in discipline and procedures by the Republican Guards on the day of your husband's assassination. I have served in the Guards for almost ten years, and I have never witnessed such a flagrant dereliction of duties and responsibilities.' She removed her red beret, crushing it in her strong hands. 'I am ashamed to wear the beret.'

'Don't be, Captain – you earned the right to wear it,' Susan said. 'It was the ones who took bribes and allowed themselves to be lured away from their posts that should strip themselves of the honor of wearing it, not you.'

'Yes, Madame,' Shafik said. 'I assure you, I will do everything I can to avenge my president's, your husband's, assassination. Those who committed that deed do not deserve justice – they deserve retribution.'

Susan Salaam touched Shafik on her left cheek and nodded reassuringly. 'And they shall have it, Captain,' she said quietly but sternly. 'The killers of both our husbands shall feel our vengeance.' Shafik smiled, nodded, then snapped proudly to attention.

'We have your quarters ready, Sekhmet,' Baris said, pointing to a waiting armored staff car.

'I want to meet the commandos first.'

'Out of the question,' Baris said. 'Captain?'

'The commandos have not allowed anyone except supply vessels near the ship, Madame,' Shafik said. 'The ship is guarded continuously by at least twenty men on deck plus one of the commandos dressed in the strange combat equipment. We have made three attempts in the past two days to sneak aboard the ship and were caught every time. Our next option being considered is a massive assault.'

'I don't believe that'll be necessary,' Susan said. 'They are keeping themselves imprisoned on the ship – I see no reason to risk any lives just so we can take them off to another prison. Let's go have a talk with them.'

'The Egyptians are being extraordinarily cooperative all of a sudden, Muck,' David Luger observed. He had just entered the Combat Information Center aboard the Egyptian frigate *El Arish* and joined Patrick and several other members of the Night Stalkers, looking over charts and satellite photographs of Libya. 'The cordon around us has relaxed – they moved their patrol boats out another half-klick. Still within visual range and easily within helicopter and deck gun range, but it takes the pressure off. All their fire-control radars and jammers have shut down. They've also agreed to send more medical supplies and extra food and water for our prisoners.' He set a folder on the chart table. 'More NIRTSat photos, hot off the press.'

'Good,' Patrick acknowledged. David looked at his friend and former commanding officer with great concern. Patrick looked bone-weary, with large dark circles under his eyes, his face drawn and haggard. He still wore the Tin Man battle armor – he had taken it off for only a few moments for an inspection several hours earlier before donning it again – and he kept it and the exoskeleton, standing near the bulkhead in quick reach, plugged in and fully charged. 'Any word yet from anyone on Wendy?'

'No,' Luger replied. 'I've put in several back-channel requests for support to the Intelligence Support Agency, Muck, but our status is only a little bit better than the Libyans themselves. They don't go for freelancers, even if it's experienced operators like us. They wouldn't like us even if the White House and Pentagon were supportive – but Thorn and Goff are out gunning for us too, which makes matters even worse. Too many heads will roll if they get caught helping us.'

Patrick looked discouraged, rubbing his eyes and lowering his head wearily. 'Screw 'em,' he growled. 'Between Dr Masters's photo recon birds and UCAVs and a few soft probes by us, we'll find her.'

'If she's still alive.'

'She's alive, dammit.'

'I hear you loud and clear, Muck,' David Luger said pointedly. 'But I want to make it clear to you, at the same time, that we have no hard information that she survived the attack. The Egyptians say they found bodies, including women –'

'They never made a complete search.'

'I know – the ship went down in Libyan waters, not Egyptian waters,' Luger corrected himself. 'But it went down close enough to Egypt to examine wreckage that has drifted east. They have not found any survivors. If she somehow survived and the Libyans got her, they will keep her tightly under wraps until they're done interrogating her, and then they'll dispose of her.'

Patrick's head snapped up, and he glared at his longtime partner with pure seething anger. But he also knew what David had been through in his life – he definitely knew what he was talking about.

Fourteen years earlier, while flying their first secret mission in the modified B-52 Megafortress bomber nicknamed 'Old Dog' out of the High Technology Aerospace Weapons Center in Nevada, then-Air Force First Lieutenant and B-52 bomber navigator David Luger was left for dead at a Russian air base in eastern Siberia after they made an emergency landing. He survived and was systematically brainwashed and interrogated for years. The KGB eventually convinced Luger he was a Russian aerospace engineer, and he worked to advance the state of the art of Russian stealth warplane technology by several years. After he was rescued, it took three years of intense psychotherapy to return him to normal.

'She's alive, Dave,' Patrick said earnestly.

'You don't know that, Muck.'

'I said she's *alive!*'

'Patrick, I'm not going to argue with you,' David said. 'I will help you tear that country apart to find her. But I will not let you risk your life or any of the team's lives to go in to attempt a rescue unless we get some hard intelligence information.'

'You telling me she's not worth it, Dave?'

'Fuck you, General,' Luger snapped. 'I'm thinking like a soldier – it's about time you start doing the same. You tell me, Muck – how many lives is worth Wendy's? Yours? Three? Five? Ten? Fifty?'

'We risked a couple dozen to get you out of Fisikous in Lithuania,' Patrick said. 'I would've brought a thousand more with me if I could.'

'But you had hard intelligence on where I was,' Luger reminded him. 'Without that information, wearing that battle armor and marching into an armed fortress like Libya would be suicide even for a hundred commandos. And you know it.' Patrick's head slumped wearily again. Luger sighed heavily. 'Muck, your son needs you,' he said. 'Why don't you go home? The CV-22 can lift you off the deck tonight, the Sky Masters jet is waiting in Tel Aviv, and you can be home by tomorrow morning. We'll stay out here and keep searching.' He paused, then added, 'And you have a brother that needs to be mourned and buried too, sir.'

'I'm not leaving without her,' Patrick said resolutely. 'Dead or alive, I'm taking her home.'

'It won't happen that way, at least not right away,' Luger said softly. 'The odds are a thousand to one we'll even get any information that she was recovered, and about five thousand to one she's alive. But if she beat the odds and survived, the Libyans will keep her in complete isolation until she recovers, which could take weeks, even months. Then they'll start interrogating her. She'll be able to resist for a short time, but they'll finally break her. They won't be as scientific as the Russians. They'll break her, and then they'll discard her.'

'Dave, that's *enough*,' Patrick shouted. 'This search is going forward, and I don't give a shit how hopeless you think it is. I don't *think* she's alive – I *know* she's alive. And as long as I know she's alive, I'm going to plan to locate her and rescue her.

'To answer your question: I'll risk the lives of any man or woman who agrees to stand beside me on this mission, because I know Wendy would agree to stand beside me to rescue anyone on this team. Now, if you have any other problems with this mission or my leadership, I suggest *you* get off this ship and evacuate to Israel with the others. If you stay, you *will* obey my orders. End of discussion.'

David Luger stood and looked at Patrick carefully. Patrick returned his glare until finally Luger nodded, satisfied that Patrick had his emotional act together enough to lead the team.

At that same moment, Patrick received a beep in his subcutaneous microtransceiver; then Hal Briggs spoke: 'Patrick, supply barge coming in, one kilometer south.'

'Roger,' Patrick acknowledged. 'Use the sensors in your armor

111

to scan the supplies for weapons and explosives as they come aboard. I'll be up to relieve anyone that needs a break.'

'I could use thirty mike for relief,' Chris Wohl, stationed on the port rail scanning the north for any signs of danger, radioed. That was no exaggeration, either – Patrick had seen Wohl go for hours after taking only a twenty-minute combat catnap. He seemed able to go indefinitely with virtually no sleep.

'I'll be right up, Chris,' Patrick responded. He turned to David and said, 'Ask Commander Farouk to get a party together to unload the barge.'

'Okay,' David replied. He paused for a moment, then added, 'Sorry, Patrick. But I feel I had to tell you how I feel – I'm responsible to you and the entire team. I love Wendy. But I know what I'm talking about.'

'I know, Texas,' Patrick said. He unplugged himself from the wall outlet, reattached his exoskeleton, and put on his helmet. 'We'll find her, and then we'll all go home – together.'

'Absolutely.' Patrick nodded, then went up on deck to relieve Wohl.

Chris gave him a quick rundown on the Egyptian Navy's deployment around them. Directly in front of the *El Arish* about five kilometers away was the *Damyat,* a Knox-class frigate, turned head-on to the *El Arish* so both its 127-millimeter cannon and four fixed torpedo tubes were trained on the captured vessel. Flanking the *Damyat* were two British-built fast missile attack craft, the *Ramadan* and the *Badr,* each with one 76-millimeter gun, a twin 40-millimeter gun, and two Otomat antiship missiles trained on them. Patrick called up the tactical picture transmitted from the *El Arish*'s Combat Information Center on his electronic visor to study the rest of the deployment. A mixture of ex-Russian and ex-Chinese patrol and fast attack boats surrounded them on all sides, with the heaviest concentration of ships between them and the base. Chris also briefed him on some of the crew's activities – routine maintenance, systems checks, and cleanup details.

Patrick held out his hands. Chris Wohl deactivated the power on the hypervelocity rail gun he was holding, unplugged the datalink from the gun to his battle armor, opened the chamber to make sure none of the depleted uranium projectiles were loaded, then placed the weapon in Patrick's hands. The electro-magnetic rail gun fired nonexplosive projectiles at almost fifty thousand feet per second, powerful enough to drive the projectile through several feet of steel after flying more than three miles. Coupled with the sensors built into the Tin Man battle armor, the gun was deadly and effective to machines of all sizes, from ships to main battle tanks to aircraft.

Patrick plugged the datalink into his suit, chambered a round into the rail gun, made sure the safety was on, then reactivated it. It immediately reported 'READY' on his electronic visor. 'I relieve you, Sergeant,' he said, knowing the ex-Marine would like a formal guard post changeover.

'I stand relieved, sir,' Wohl replied. Even with the exoskeleton, he managed a salute.

'Looks pretty shitty, huh, Sarge?' he said to Chris Wohl, motioning to the Egyptian ships around them.

'Nah. We got them right where we want them, sir,' Wohl replied, and he headed toward the wheelhouse berth, the spot he liked to go when he took a break.

It looked very hopeless, Patrick thought as Wohl disappeared from view. Why in hell did I lead these men here?

Several minutes later, Luger radioed: 'Castor, we have a visitor who wants to talk with you.'

'I'm on guard duty, Texas. If you can't handle it, it'll have to wait until I'm relieved.'

'This can't wait,' Luger responded. 'It's the Egyptian national security adviser, General Baris. He wants to talk with you directly.'

'Send him up here, then.' A few minutes later, Luger escorted an older man in a business suit, along with an Egyptian naval officer and a female security guard, up on deck. Luger was carrying a metal briefcase, one that obviously belonged to the Egyptians. Patrick watched them approach with his all-aspect sensors but did not stop scanning the sea for any sign of intruders. 'General Baris? *Tasharrafna.*'

'*Es salaem alekum.* You are the one they call Castor, I presume?' Baris asked in halting but very good English. Patrick did not answer. 'I am General Ahmad Baris, retired, adviser to the president of Egypt on national security affairs. This is my aide and my bodyguard.'

113

'It is very dangerous for all of you to be here,' Patrick said, his voice disguised by the electronic voice amplifier in the battle armor. 'I assure you, the men on board this ship will not be harmed if they do exactly as I say. I intend on returning this vessel shortly, as soon as we collect enough intelligence information to proceed against the Libyans. Anything else?'

'*Aywa, insha'allah,*' Baris responded. 'My friend, president, and leader of our country, Dr Kamal Ismail Salaam, along with his wife Susan, were assassinated yesterday in Cairo during celebration of the Prophet Muhammad's birthday,' Baris said. 'A suicide bomber, believed to be part of the Muslim Brotherhood.'

'Yes. I had been told about that. I'm sorry,' Patrick said woodenly. After all the death he had seen in the last twenty-four hours, the news of Salaam's death had absolutely no effect on him. 'I know President Salaam was very well respected in the United States; his wife was a veteran of the United States Air Force, I believe.'

'Yes.' Interesting comment – Baris filed that away for future use. Could this 'Castor' be a former American air force officer himself? 'Our intelligence sources believe the Muslim Brotherhood, led by Jadallah Zuwayy of Libya, was responsible for the assassination. He of course would have also ordered the attacks on vessels in international waters as well, in retaliation for the attack on his base at Samāh. May I assume that it was you and your men that conducted that raid on Samāh?'

'General Baris, I allowed you and your aide on board only to reassure you that your men and your vessel are being well taken care of, and I promise it'll stay that way until we depart, unless your men fail to follow my orders,' Patrick said sternly. 'I did not allow you to come up here and interrogate me. *Ma'as salaema,* General.'

'I am told you were conducting a search of the waters near where the *El Arish* picked up you and your men,' Baris went on. 'I assume, then, that you lost some men in the attack. I am sorry for your loss, sir.'

Patrick had to take a deep breath to talk past the lump that unexpectedly formed in his throat. 'You may speak with Commander Farouk for ten minutes, General Baris. Now go.'

'I can feel your pain, Castor,' a woman's voice said – an American woman's voice.

Despite himself, Patrick turned toward the voice, his movements accentuated and quickened by the electronically controlled exoskeleton. Baris's aide removed his service cap and sunglasses – revealing a woman, a very beautiful woman despite the fact that she wore an eye patch over her left eye. 'Texas . . .'

'I didn't know, Castor,' David Luger said, as surprised as Patrick. 'He . . . I mean, *she* was searched for weapons, not to verify gender.'

Baris turned to the woman. 'I shall be below, Madame, interviewing Commander Farouk.' He bowed slightly to the woman and departed. The security officer stayed, but moved a discreet distance away. David was unsure for a moment what to do, but decided that neither woman was any threat to Patrick. He set the metal briefcase down beside the first woman and escorted Baris below.

'Most generals don't bow to their aides and call them "madame,"' Patrick observed. 'I assume I'm speaking to Madame Susan Salaam, first lady of Egypt?'

'Yes,' Susan Bailey Salaam replied. She motioned to Amina. 'She is Captain Amina Shafik of the Republican Guards, assigned by General Baris as my bodyguard. Shall I assume that I'm speaking to the commander of the American commando team that attacked Samāh and destroyed several surface-to-surface rockets, including some with nuclear and biochem warheads?'

'What are you doing here, Mrs Salaam?'

Susan sighed, then replied, 'Surviving. What are you doing here, Castor? On some sort of crusade to rid the world of weapons of mass destruction? Or do you have some sort of special affinity with Egypt that you would risk your life and those of your team to destroy weapons that were probably not pointed at any American targets?'

'If the destruction of those missiles at Samāh helped Egypt, I'm glad,' Patrick replied. 'But I'm not going to play twenty questions with you. Go below and talk with the sailors if you want, or return to your launch.'

'You lost someone close to you, didn't you, Castor?' Susan asked. Patrick did not reply. 'Someone *very* close to you. I could tell it in your voice, even all electronically fuzzed.' Still no reply. 'You must be hot in that metal suit, Castor. Take it off. I won't hurt you, and I certainly won't report a fellow American soldier to the Egyptian authorities.' Silence. 'At least take off the helmet and let me look at you. You look like a cross between Robocop and Darth Vader – but your voice doesn't sound like either one of those characters.'

Patrick simply had no idea why he did it – he had already ordered her away, and he was on watch, and the navies of at least two countries were within a moment's notice of blowing him to hell. But Patrick hefted the big electromagnetic rail gun in his left hand, unfastened his helmet, and slipped it off.

Unaltered by the electronic visor, he could see that she was even more beautiful. She had let her hair fall to her shoulders in dark, shining cascades; her lips were full and red; her cheekbones high and striking; her neck graceful; her skin smooth and dark, adding to the allure. Her one good right eye widened in pleasant surprise as she studied his face.

'That's much better,' she said in a low but sweet voice. She couldn't believe how young and how innocent he looked – she had expected some grizzled old warhorse. He looked more like a high school teacher than a commando. He didn't look dangerous in the least, although his dark blue eyes were hard to read – this was clearly not his first mission in that getup, she decided, but he looked very much out of place in it. 'Thank you for trusting me.'

'Now you can go.'

'Won't you tell me your name? And I'll bet it's not Castor. That's your call sign, at least the one you're using on this mission. I've worked with lots of special-ops teams before. I was an intelligence officer in the Air Force – I've briefed dozens of teams from all branches of service before and after they do their thing. I know how you guys operate.'

'Mrs Salaam, you will –'

'Call me Susan. Please. With my husband gone, there will be hardly anyone I know in this hemisphere that will call me by my first name now. I'll be the Widow Salaam forever, especially around the Mediterranean.'

Patrick hesitated, his words forgotten. He nodded, averting his eyes. 'I'm sorry for your loss, Susan.'

'And I am sorry for yours,' Susan said. 'I am an American, a former Air Force officer, an Egyptian, and a widow – but I am first and foremost a woman. I can tell when someone is suffering. It is more than just a team leader who has lost men under his command in combat – you have lost someone much closer than that.'

It appeared for a moment that he was going to open up to her, but then she saw the hood go over his blue eyes again, and she knew he was not yet ready. She quickly decided to give it up. 'I am so very sorry,' she said. 'You will be permitted to stay on board this ship for as long as you like. If there is any assistance we can provide, don't hesitate to ask. The intelligence services of Egypt are at your command.'

'Are you in charge of the Egyptian government now?'

'No,' Susan replied. 'Prime Minister Kalir automatically takes control of the government upon the incapacitation or . . . or dea . . . death . . . of . . .' Suddenly, Susan broke down in tears. She half turned away from Patrick, sobbing uncontrollably. She realized it was the first time she had wept for her husband.

Susan felt strong hands on her shoulders, and she looked up and saw the armored commando holding her – he had set the big, strange-looking gun down on the deck and was holding her as tenderly as his armored hands would allow. She turned toward him and was surprised to see tears unabashedly flowing down his cheeks as well. She clutched his body, wanting more than anything to touch human flesh, and finally reached up to touch his face and his tears.

'My husband was murdered, butchered in a mosque on one of the holiest days in all of Islam,' Susan said through her sobs. 'I was beside him until I was pulled away by Zuwayy of Libya and Khalid al-Khan, the chief justice of our supreme court. I know they were in on it together. I know they conspired to kill my husband. Only al-Khan had the authority to switch the guards and get the assassins so close to Kamal. I want to see them both pay for what they've done.'

'My . . . my brother was killed in the attack on Samāh,' she heard him say through his tears. 'He sacrificed himself to destroy those missiles. Then . . . then when the Libyan warships attacked, we abandoned ship – but my wife stayed behind to launch an attack on the Libyan guided missile frigate.'

'Your *wife*?' Susan asked incredulously. 'You . . . *you lost your brother and your wife* on this mission? My God . . .'

'I believe my wife is still alive – I don't know how or why I know, but she is still alive,' Patrick said. 'I will search every square inch of Libya until I find her.' He raised his right hand and clenched his armored right hand into a fist. 'And I will kill anyone who gets in my way.'

'How . . . how horrible. How utterly horrible,' Susan breathed. She placed her fingers on his cheek to turn him toward her. 'I wish I could help you, but I can't. I don't know if I have any authority left in this country – I may be as much of a target here as you are in Libya. General Baris may be appointed as the national security adviser to the new president. If the *mullahs* take control of the government as we fear, he will not only be dismissed, but probably imprisoned or murdered. But as long as we have any authority left in Egypt, you and your men may stay aboard this vessel. But for your own safety, you should leave as soon as possible. If you need help, just ask.'

Patrick thought about Wendy, and he thought about how lonely and isolated he felt standing on this Egyptian warship in Egyptian waters, surrounded by the Egyptian navy. He had no plan, and his options were rapidly decreasing. There was nothing they could do. 'I understand,' he said. 'All we'll need is a shuttle to shore and access to a landing strip for our transport aircraft. By tonight, we'll be gone.'

'You shall have anything you need.' Susan motioned to the briefcase beside her. 'That briefcase contains data CDs of all the latest intelligence info we have on all of the Mediterranean states. Some of it is only hours old. Photos, field reports, overhead imagery, radio intercepts, everything we could gather. It should help you find your wife and your missing men.' He realized he was still grasping her shoulders, and he started to move them away, but she took his armored gauntlets and held them to her, keeping his hands on her shoulders. 'Thank you for what you've done for Egypt,' she said. 'I'm sorry for the sacrifices you've made for our country.'

'Where will you go now, Susan?'

Susan sighed. 'Go to Cairo to bury my husband.'

'I think that would be very dangerous.'

'I must,' she said. 'It's my last duty as first lady of Egypt. After that, I can start planning my own future.'

'What will you do?'

'I don't know. The United States might be the only place my husband's enemies can't touch me.' She paused, then looked at Patrick. 'And you? Will you go home as well?'

'I don't believe in leaving before the fighting's over,' Patrick replied. 'If my wife is alive, I'll find her. If she's dead, I'll make the Libyans sorry they ever decided to launch those attack planes.'

'What do you intend to do?'

'I can't hope to use overhead imagery to find her, and there are too many bases she could have been taken to,' Patrick said. 'So I'm going to go right to the source. I'm going to make Zuwayy an offer he can't refuse.' He looked at her, then added, 'Seems to me you have some fighting of your own left to do.'

'Fighting?'

'Someone killed your husband and tried to kill you, Susan,' Patrick said. He looked into her eyes deeply, carefully, as if deciding if what he was about to say was accurate; then: 'You're a soldier. No one would blame you if you got away – but something tells me it's not entirely in your nature to run.'

'What do you suggest – soldier to soldier?'

He did not contradict her guess, but looked at her carefully, with a steady stare, and replied, 'Find out who your allies and fellow soldiers are. Assemble and organize your forces, then evaluate: If your forces are superior, fight; if inferior, run, preserve your forces; if equal, stay on the move and harass the enemy.'

'Sun-Tzu. Basic combat doctrine,' Susan said with a nod and a thin smile. 'I've been a politician's wife for so long I've almost forgotten how to be a soldier. But I don't have an army, and soon I probably won't have a country. Survival seems to be the best option.' She paused. 'Perhaps I can to talk with the National Democratic Party officials, lend any support I can to our party's candidate for president. Dr Kalir, the prime minister, will certainly run. The chief justice of the Egyptian Supreme Court, Ulama al-Khan, will run as well – he is the danger, the one who wants to turn Egypt into a theocracy and align it with the Muslim Brotherhood states. He has the power to do it, too.'

'Sounds like a plan of action to me.'

'Thanks for the advice,' Susan said. She looked deeply into his eyes. 'Before you go – can you tell me your real name?'

He hesitated once again, the old security regime automatically kicking in again, but it dissolved just as quickly. It was time to start trusting someone again, he told himself.

'Patrick. Patrick McLanahan.'

'Chief petty officer? Colonel? Special agent . . . ?'

Still trying to gather intelligence, Patrick noted. She needed careful watching. 'Just Patrick.'

'It is a pleasure to meet you, Just Patrick McLanahan,' Susan said with a mind-blowing smile. She reached up to kiss him on the cheek, holding her lips there long enough for him to feel a jolt of electricity course down his spine. 'Welcome to Egypt.'

About an hour later, Salaam, Baris, and Shafik disembarked from the supply vessel. They were met on the pier by Marshal Ouda, the military district commander, who looked mad enough to chew nails. 'How dare you overrule my orders and approach my ship without my permission?' he shouted. 'Who do you think you are?'

'No one is undermining your authority, Marshal Ouda,' Susan said. 'I thought it would help to resolve the issue if I met with the terrorists themselves.'

'And were you successful?'

'Yes.'

'Then they are surrendering?'

'On the contrary – I offered them the use of the facilities here on the base for as long as they need them.'

'*Ana mish faehem!* Are you insane?' Ouda exclaimed. 'Those men are terrorists! They have taken an Egyptian warship and are threatening to kill everyone on board!'

'But they have not killed anyone, and I believe they are telling the truth when they say they will not harm our men,' Susan said. 'I do not want them harmed.'

'Who are they?'

'They are commandos, mercenaries, on a mission against the Libyan government,' Susan replied. 'They destroyed several Libyan rockets that carried chemical, biological, and nuclear weapons aimed for Egypt.'

Ouda looked surprised. 'Or so they say.'

'I believe them,' Susan said. 'I repeat, Vice Marshal, I do not want them harmed when they come ashore.'

'I must report this incident and your contact with the terrorists.'

Susan turned to General Baris and said, 'There is your superior officer. You may give your report to him.' But Susan saw the skepticism, perhaps even the outright hatred, in Ouda's eyes, and quickly concluded that Ouda would indeed report the incident – perhaps directly to Ulama Khalid al-Khan himself. 'Have quarters near the airfield prepared for them – I'm sure they will wait until nightfall to make the move. Give them anything they require.'

'This is ridiculous,' Ouda growled. 'Giving aid and comfort to terrorists!'

'They may have saved your base from complete annihilation, Vice Marshal,' Susan said. 'You should not only be welcoming them – you should be on your knees thanking them. Now get to it.' She turned away, leaving a still very angry general officer fuming behind her.

'That was most unwise, Sekhmet,' Baris said. 'You should have played that calmly, perhaps even deferentially – included him in on what the terrorists did and who they are.'

'Men like Ouda need to be talked *to*, Ahmad, not *with*.'

'Ouda is a vice marshal and one of the highest-ranking and most highly decorated officers in the armed forces, Sekhmet,' Baris reminded her. 'I'm sure he does not approve of civilians telling him what to do on his base, especially a woman. Learn to be more diplomatic, especially when on his installation, in front of his men. He can make very, very serious trouble for us, if he chooses to do so.'

'He will be a bigger fool than even I assume he is if he tries to use this incident against us,' Susan said resolutely.

'Do not underestimate him,' Baris warned. 'And I suggest you meet with him later today and explain to him exactly what you hope to accomplish by helping those men. He may be a strutting peacock, but he is a military man – if you explain the tactical situation to him, he will be more likely to play along.' He paused, looked at his friend, and said with a wry smile, 'Perhaps you can explain it to me as well.'

'Those men have weapons, and power, and abilities that I think we do not fully comprehend,' Susan Bailey Salaam said. 'As you said, soon we will have no power at all. Perhaps there is a way we can use their power to help restore a legitimate government to Egypt – or, at the very least, help us to survive.'

Chapter Three

People's Assembly Building, Cairo, Egypt
several days later

'My brothers and sisters, the danger all around us is great, and we must be strong and united,' Ulama Khalid al-Khan said in a deep, resonant voice. He was speaking before a special session of the People's Assembly, the 454-member legislative body of the Egyptian government. As ever, Khan wore traditional Arab garments, the white *jubba, quba, sirwal,* and *qalansuwa,* even though most of the rest of the members of the People's Assembly wore Western-style business suits. But it was not only his clothing but his long, angular features, his carefully trimmed beard, haunting voice, and hypnotic eyes that commanded attention from all, even those who thought of holy men such as Khan as threats to freedom in Egypt.

'Our nation, our way of life, our very *souls* are under attack,' Khan went on, his voice growing louder and more strident by the moment. 'The horrible murder of our beloved President Salaam, may he stand at the right hand of God, is vivid proof that we are not safe and secure even within our holiest shrines and most precious places of worship. The danger is everywhere, my friends. It is time for bold leadership and unity for Misr.' Khan preferred using the traditional name for his country, rather than the foreign-derived name, Egypt.

'I know many of you do not stand with me,' Khan went on. His eyes drifted toward where he knew a large congregation of his political opponents sat. 'Although our laws are based on Shari'a, the holy book, you do not feel those laws should be strictly interpreted and applied, as I and my fellow high priests do. I am not here to debate your attitudes about how to serve God. I am here to offer to you my vision for our country.

'My goal is to stop the anarchy, stop the violence, stop the corruption of our laws, our families, our companies, and our beliefs.

125

I believe those dangers emanate from two places: the Zionists and the Americans.' Several dozen legislators shook their heads and voiced their displeasure in carefully muted tones. 'Yes, you know it as well as I. Our nation has slipped into crushing recession and inflation ever since the traitor Sadat signed the so-called peace treaty with Israel. We have barely been able to hold on to the very fabric of our country. And who has come to our aid to help? The Americans, with their spies, their fat bloodsucking industrialists, their weapons of hatred and class warfare, and their corrupting cash. It is all tied together, my brothers – the Zionists weaken us, and their masters the Americans suck us deeper into their lustful, depraved ways.' More voices, some disagreeing but more of them agreeing with Khan, easily drowning out the dissenters.

'Well, I say, no more. *No more!* Allow me to place my name on the ballot in the next elections, and I promise to root out the evil in our government and our society. I promise to return Misr to the people and to God. You know the people are behind me. You cannot risk our future and alienating the will of the people by not allowing my name on the ballot. It is vital that our country begin the process of healing. With God's wisdom, strength, and strong guiding hand, I pledge to you that I will carry the banner of unity and honor for our country.'

There was a round of light, polite applause throughout the People's Assembly – most of the members knew enough to at least appear enthusiastic. There was little doubt that the Assembly would vote to approve al-Khan's candidacy; the question was, would the people of Egypt vote for him? Khan was a very shadowy character, powerful in the Egyptian mosques and in smaller, more religious communities, but not very well known or trusted in the cities. He represented a step backward for many folks in Egypt, and that did not make him very popular.

Al-Khan bowed and stepped off the dais. The Egyptian prime minister extended his hand to shake Khan's, but al-Khan simply bowed and kept his hands inside the sleeves of his robes. The prime minister awkwardly lowered his hand, ignored the gestures and whispers of disapproval from the Assembly, then stepped up to the dais. 'Thank you, Ulama al-Khan. Ladies and gentlemen of the Assembly, we will now hear from the National Democratic Party candidate, Prime Minister Dr Ahmed Kalir.'

Khalid al-Khan took his place in the front row center of the Assembly, reserved for special guests, and sat quietly while the next presenter was ushered to the dais with a round of enthusiastic applause. Dr Ahmed Kalir represented the greatest challenge to Khan's candidacy. He was an experienced politician, a wealthy and internationally recognized cardiologist and surgeon, and well respected in the cities and among the business community. Kalir had transformed the post of prime minister, allowing the common people greater access to government. Although certainly not a charismatic personality, he was well known in the capital and well respected everywhere. Kalir was definitely the man to beat.

'I am pleased to be here,' Kalir began. 'On behalf of the National Democratic Party, I thank you for this opportunity to speak.' He paused, an uncomfortably long silence, then went on: 'And on behalf of the National Democratic Party and myself, I wish to announce to the National Assembly and the people of Egypt that I am withdrawing my name as candidate for president.'

The entire National Assembly exploded into bedlam – all except Khalid al-Khan. He could not have been more pleased, although he fought hard not to show it. With the death of Kamal Salaam, Ahmed Kalir was by far the most powerful secular politician in Egypt – he was as influential and respected as al-Khan was feared. With him withdrawing his name from nomination, the road was clear for al-Khan to be elected the next president of Egypt.

And at that, Kalir looked directly at al-Khan and nodded. What was going on?

'I wish to place my support and prayers for my choice as candidate for president, the one person in all of Egypt who has the moral strength, intelligence, and vision to lead our nation forward out of this crisis and toward the peace and security we all seek,' Kalir said. Was Kalir actually endorsing him for president? al-Khan thought. This was too good to be true! 'With the blessings of Allah and the hopes and prayers of a nation, I place into nomination today the next president of Egypt . . . our first lady of Egypt, Madame Susan Bailey Salaam.'

Khan was already placing his hands on his left breast, feigning surprise at this unexpected endorsement, when he gasped in total shock. *Susan Salaam was alive?*

And then he noticed Kalir looking directly at al-Khan, the

127

accusation obvious in his face. Al-Khan had to fight to erase his surprised expression. It was a test, a stupid trick, nothing more.

And then, to al-Khan's complete surprise, Susan Salaam walked out on stage, and then there was no doubt. The entire People's Assembly fairly leapt to their feet and applauded, some even cheering and stamping their feet.

Susan Salaam walked gingerly, as if still in pain, but she did so without using crutches or a walker, just a simple wooden cane with a large, wide crook supporting her left leg. She wore an eye patch on her left eye, and the hairline on the left side of her head was higher than on the right, indicating she had lost some hair or sustained a head injury. Her hands were marred with cuts and burns; her arms and torso were covered by simple, unadorned clothing, but the burns definitely appeared to extend down her arms.

But her natural beauty was still striking, still breathtaking. Susan made no attempt to hide any of her wounds with makeup, which enhanced her beauty, her sense of pride – and her pain – even more. She embraced Ahmed Kalir and then stepped to the podium, waving to the assembly. Yes, even al-Khan had to admit, she was still beautiful, achingly so.

It took several long minutes for the cheering and applause to die down, and then she began: 'Members of the People's Assembly and fellow Egyptians, with great pride and with your support and prayers, I gladly accept the National Democratic Party's nomination for president, and on behalf of my husband, our late President Salaam, I announce that I am a candidate to be your president.'

The applause was back, even louder than before. Khalid al-Khan was stupefied. In just a few brief moments, he had gone from a close second in the election race, to the uncontested winner, to just another also-ran.

He could stand it no longer. He stood up, raised his hands, and said in a loud voice, 'Hold! *Hold!*' The assemblymen weren't responding, so Khan quickly stepped up on stage. 'A point of order!'

The Speaker of the People's Assembly hurried back to the dais. 'Order!' he shouted. 'Order!' Susan Salaam had stepped back away from the dais to allow al-Khan to speak. 'Please let Ulama al-Khan speak!'

After the assembly had quieted down, mostly in rapt attention to the looming confrontation on stage, he said, 'I am most grateful to God that Madame Salaam is alive and well. And I know that it warms our hearts and strengthens our souls for Madame Salaam to seek the same office as her dear husband, who certainly now sits at the right hand of Allah.' More applause, not for al-Khan or for Susan, but for Kamal Ismail Salaam, their slain president. How can he possibly fight a dead man? Only with the law – that's all he had left.

'But if I am not mistaken, a candidate for president of Egypt must hold a seat either in the Supreme Judicial Council or the People's Assembly,' al-Khan went on. 'As much as we honor the memory of President Salaam, as much as it would gladden our hearts to see Madame Salaam once more in the presidential palace, she cannot run for president because she does not hold a national elective office.' He turned and bowed graciously to her. 'I am sorry, my child, but it is the law.'

Finally, what appeared to be leaders of the various groups were getting together. More talking, more gesturing. Finally, several from the group of leaders began filtering up toward the speaker's seat.

This didn't look good at all. Al-Khan turned. His angry gaze caught the attention of the Speaker of the People's Assembly, Representative Jamal Gazali, a member of the National Democratic Party coalition but also the leader of the Society of God, a smaller party representing the religious conservatives in Egypt. Gazali motioned al-Khan quickly to the podium. 'What is happening here, Gazali?'

'It is of no consequence, Ulama,' Gazali replied. 'The matter will be dealt with, and all will be taken care of.'

'I asked you what is happening, Gazali.'

Gazali looked nervously up at the speaker's podium. 'There apparently is a statute still in the law that allows the wife of a legislator or other public official to take her husband's office if he dies while in office,' Gazali said. 'The law was put into effect after the War of Retribution so the government could continue functioning even if lawmakers serving in the armed forces were killed in battle –'

'Are you saying that Salaam may still become a presidential

candidate even though she is *not even Egyptian?*' al-Khan thundered.

'It is of no consequence, Minister,' Gazali said quickly. 'Salaam may have been the wife of a public official, but in peacetime the statute is symbolic, nothing more.' Gazali made some pretense of being needed on the other side of the podium and scurried away after giving the cleric another nervous bow.

But al-Khan could quickly see for himself that this was much more than symbolism – it was about to happen. A few moments later Gazali stood to address the Assembly:

'The Assembly will come to order,' the speaker ordered. When the chamber assumed some semblance of quiet, the speaker continued, 'A motion has been brought before us by the honorable senior delegate from Alexandria that any wife of a public official who dies while in office may assume her husband's office for the remainder of his term. There is considerable debate by the members on whether or not this applies to the high office of president.'

Gazali paused, then glanced at al-Khan. The deadly warning stare he received in return decided his course for him – Khalid al-Khan was too powerful a force in Egypt to be crossed.

'We note with pride and affection the love many in our country have for Madame Salaam,' Gazali went on. 'We note that Madame Salaam served Egypt well as an officer in the American air force, advising and supplying our armed forces with vital information, advice, and counsel during the conflict between Iraq and Kuwait. She has been a faithful and loving wife to our beloved president and a friend to us all. We also recognize her countless contributions to the betterment of Egyptian society, especially her patronage and support for universal education, the restoration of our ancient libraries in Alexandria, and the rescue and rehabilitation of orphaned and outcast children in our cities.

'However, we question the efficacy of this award as it applies to peacetime Egypt,' Gazali said, slowly and deliberately. 'The law was put in place to be sure our legislatures and bureaucracies continued their work even if its members were killed in battle. Although this honor has been recently applied many times, we see this as merely symbolic, an honorific, which is used as a convenience and token of honor until new elections are held. Further, this custom has never been applied to the office of president, and well it should not, for fear of eroding the importance of that high office. Another consideration, of course, is the fact that Madame Salaam was not born in Egypt, and has not yet qualified to become a naturalized citizen. Therefore, we do not consider Madame Salaam as meeting the strict standards of the law, and therefore –'

The Assembly chamber erupted into sheer bedlam. It seemed every representative was screaming and shaking their fists at Gazali. Several lawmakers even got out of their seats and attempted to rush the podium, but were turned away by uniformed security officers that appeared as if out of nowhere. No one had ever seen such an uprising in the Assembly chambers before – and certainly, Khan had never seen such a loud outpouring of emotion.

Through this chaos, Ulama al-Khan made his way off the dais and to a side hallway toward the back exits. He knew he had lost. The memory of Kamal Ismail Salaam was too powerful and Susan Salaam was almost as popular in Egypt as her husband – perhaps even more so, because of her bewitching beauty.

Several Assembly members siding with Kalir shook their fists, shouted, and even tried to grab at al-Khan as he made his way off the dais. Supreme Judiciary security officers, led by the chief of security of the Supreme Judiciary Council, Major Amr Abu Gheit, who was assigned as al-Khan's personal bodyguard, roughly pushed the protesters out of the way, even clubbing one across the head with a pistol butt.

What fools, al-Khan thought. They would actually consider physical intimidation to try to turn him aside? Several more assemblymen rushed to their colleagues' aide, but Gheit and the rest of al-Khan's bodyguards had no trouble subduing them as the presidential candidate made his way out of the chamber.

As he emerged from the chamber into the back hallway, he turned to Gheit: 'Take down the name and political party of any representative who even dared look angrily in my direction,' he ordered.

'Why? So you can have your henchmen kill them as well?'

Khan turned. There, standing before him, was Susan Salaam. Her husband's aide and national security adviser, Ahmad Baris, was standing with her. A few Assembly aides and staffers were milling about, fascinated by a confrontation between these two political rivals.

'Madame, it is good to see you alive,' Khan said evenly. Aware of the growing crowd gathering to watch them, he stepped forward to Susan as if reaching out to shake her hand, lowered his voice, and said, 'But you should not have returned to Cairo. Your life here in Egypt is finished. Go back to the United States and start a new life.'

'General Baris warned me not to return to the capital, to go into hiding until just before the funeral and to go back into hiding immediately afterward,' Salaam said, her voice loud enough for all to hear. 'But all I could think about was what happened to us at the celebration, and I knew I had to confront you directly, to see your face as I accused you directly –'

'*Accuse me?* Of what?'

'I have been able to piece together what happened that morning at the mosque. You substituted your own handpicked Judiciary guardsmen for the presidential guards that normally would have been on duty during the procession, and you gave them strict orders to always face the procession, not scan the crowd for any sign of danger. By the time the assassins were in place, it was too late for them to react to save my husband.'

'Are you suggesting that *I* had something to do with that terrible attack, Madame?' al-Khan said. 'That is purely ridiculous! Why, I was no more than five steps behind you and your husband – I could have been blown to bits as well! Why would I put myself in such harm? I even helped pull you clear of danger once I realized what was happening! You seemed prepared to throw your body in front of that bomb in a vain attempt to save your husband from his destiny. I gave you the chance to live.'

'Maybe the rumors that you wore a Kevlar bulletproof shroud under your robes are true – because bystanders farther away than you were severely injured, while you and that rat-snake Zuwayy walked away unscathed –'

'Unscathed? They told me one of my lungs had to be reinflated, and His Highness King Idris the Second of Libya suffered flashblindness and loss of hearing that still lingers! We were lucky to escape with our lives! You actually think we would have engineered such a sloppy and dangerous assassination attempt in such close quarters?'

'I think you put yourself in just enough harm so no attention would be drawn to you directly,' Salaam argued.

'You are delusional,' al-Khan said, dismissing her with an angry wave of his hand. 'I am glad to see you are alive, Madame, and I pray for you and your late husband. But I warn you, do not spread false rumors or try to discredit my good name. There are laws against such activities.'

'There are laws against subversion, conspiracy, and treason too, Khan,' Salaam said bitterly. 'But since when have you ever been concerned with the law, except when it most benefits you? You hide behind your robes and the holy Koran like a desert scorpion, hopping out into the sunlight just long enough to strike, then hide in the shadows once again and wait for your victim to die before devouring him.'

'Take great care, woman,' al-Khan warned. 'You try my patience.'

But Susan hobbled over to block his path. 'I will get you for what you did, Khan,' she hissed. 'If it takes my very last breath, I will avenge my husband's killer – you and your puppet master, Zuwayy.'

'Get out of my way, woman,' Khan ordered. His bodyguards were ready the instant he made eye contact. They had been staying back, visible but not intrusive, threatening but not imminently so, but when al-Khan motioned for them, they moved like coiled snakes. One of them grabbed for Salaam's cane, the other for her right arm.

But as fast as they moved, Susan was faster. She let the man grabbing her cane pull her toward him, then merely redirected her momentum slightly, driving the crook of the cane up into his throat. The hall echoed with the crack of his larynx, and he collapsed to the floor, clutching his shattered windpipe. Then she immediately swung the cane with her left hand and cracked it hard against her second attacker's right kneecap. Even though she heard more bone crack, the big, burly bodyguard did not go down, but twisted Susan's right wrist around and down, trying to force her to the floor.

Susan didn't resist, but simply twisted faster. The bodyguard

133

lost his grip with a howl of pain when he tried to put weight on his right leg, sinking down to his left knee, and Susan was free. She watched and waited. The second bodyguard did exactly as she thought he would: He reached inside his jacket and pulled out his side arm, a fearsome-looking Spanish-made Star Z-84 mini-submachine gun. Susan simply swung the cane as if she were making a two-wood tee shot, aiming not for the gun but the bodyguard's head. The *snap!* they heard was the left side of his jaw, and he went down hard.

A stunned Khalid al-Khan stared in amazement at the writhing men at his feet. The entire fight had lasted only seconds, but both highly trained bodyguards looked as if they might be in critical condition. 'Obviously you have done a lot more than just be the supportive wife of a president, Madame.'

Susan hefted the cane. It was just an oaken cane, but now al-Khan could see that the crook was larger, its tip was menacingly pointed, and the shaft had decorative inlays in it that obviously served to help grip the cane in defensive situations. 'A skill taught by some friends from Nevada. Weapons – and fighters – are all around you, Khan.'

'Are you insane, woman?' he breathed. 'Are you gloating? Look at what you have done! You're a madwoman! Or are you trying to live up to your ridiculous nickname, Sekhmet the Goddess of the Hunt?'

'I want you to know that you and I are enemies, Khan,' Susan said, her voice low but hard as the oak in her cane. 'I know you set up the assassination of my husband, and I know you are using your terror network to force any opposition into hiding or into silence. I know you are being funded by Zuwayy of Libya, and I know if you gain the presidency, that you will move to join the Muslim Brotherhood and force Egypt to join an alliance of terror that will cut off all Western aid and strangle our country. I will do everything in my power to stop you.' Several security officers ran up to the growing crowd just then. Both General Baris and al-Khan barked orders at them, but the chief justice of the Supreme Judiciary's voice, authority, status, and perceived threat were far more powerful than Baris's, and Salaam and Baris were roughly led away.

They were met outside by dozens of reporters and cameras,

and the security guards slinked away as Susan and Ahmad approached them. 'That was not very wise, Susan,' Baris said under his breath. 'Khan needs only the slightest excuse to have you arrested, deported – or killed.'

'I wanted to let him know that we're not done fighting,' Susan said resolutely. 'Beating up his bodyguards will be nothing compared to what I'm going to do to him on election day.' She stepped over to the reporters and bank of microphones and started answering questions:

'Yes, I attended my husband's memorial service,' Susan responded to the first question. 'Upon the advice of my husband's national security adviser, General Ahmad Baris, I attended in secret. I was also present at his interment in the family cemetery at Giza. It is a credit to General Baris and his staff that you did not know I was there. After the mourners left, I was able to perform the burial ritual.' She held up her left hand, showing a large man's ring on her middle finger as well as her engagement ring on her ring finger. 'I have Kamal's wedding ring, and he now has mine. I also placed topazes on his eyes, so he will not be blinded by the suns of heaven when he crosses over.

'Yes, I spoke with Ulama al-Khan just now. We greeted each other with warmth and relief that neither was very seriously injured from the attack. He explained his objection in the National Assembly to me very well, which I fully accept. His concern was that new elections not be clouded with any constitutional challenges during our nation's most critical time. I assured him that I will do what's best for Egypt and myself.

'Yes, of course, my husband's murderers should be hunted down, but only to be brought to justice, not retribution. This should be a time of healing, not revenge. I'm sure that's what my husband would have wanted, and I know that's what Dr Kalir and Ulama al-Khan want too.

'Yes, with the help and support of my friends in the National Democratic Party and the people of Egypt, I am a candidate for president of Egypt. Of course, my doctors will have to give their blessing as well – I am strong and determined, but I'm not foolish enough to think I know more than my doctors.

'I suffered some damage in my left eye and some burns, but I'm feeling all right, *kwaysa ilhamdu lillah, shukran*. Thank you.

135

'Yes, I believe I can work with Ulama al-Khan in a National Democratic Party-led government. The Ulama and I share many of the same beliefs: that Egypt can and must be the spiritual, moral, and philosophical leader of the Arab world and show by example the power and courage of the Arab people. My husband believed strongly in this, and I shall continue to work to make this idea a reality.

'No, I have absolutely no intentions of leaving Egypt except for brief visits abroad or in some capacity with the government.

'Yes, I still hold dual nationalities – I can't change my place of birth. But out of respect for my husband and to his countrymen, and reflecting the love I have for all Egyptians, I'm staying. I have no plans to reside in the United States or anywhere else but *Misr, insha'allah. Sabah el kher. Shukran.* Thank you all.'

General Baris and Captain Shafik escorted Susan out of the National Assembly building into a waiting car. 'I think it went pretty well, don't you, Ahmed?' she asked.

'The interview was fine,' Baris replied. 'But this is a dangerous game you're playing, Sekhmet. Men like Khan do little all day but dream up ways to defeat, humiliate, or eliminate their political opponents. Unless you want to reduce yourself to their scum-sucking level, stay away from political intrigue.'

'I have no illusions of this – Khan wants to see me dead,' Susan said. 'Khan failed to do the job before, so he will ensure it's done now.'

'And you somehow believe these American commandos will help you?' Baris asked. 'I must tell you, Sekhmet, I think it is dangerous to have those men in Egypt. We know nothing about them. The American government obviously knew nothing about them except to tell us that they are not part of the American government whatsoever. They are privateers, former military men who now work for whoever pays them.'

'Then they can work for us,' Susan said. 'We have no military behind us now. These men are skilled enough to take one of our warships – they can do a lot of harm to al-Khan's men, possibly even to the Libyans as well.'

'To what end? Do you expect them to kill al-Khan or invade Libya for you?' Baris asked. 'That's a fantasy, Sekhmet. They have obviously been paid by a very wealthy individual, company, or conglomerate to perform a task. If they don't do the assigned task, they won't get paid. As soon as they've rested and gathered some intelligence information, they'll be gone – leaving you with whatever chaos they've created. I don't think you want that.'

'What I want, General, is for Egypt to be free from murdering scum like al-Khan or terrorists like Zuwayy,' Susan said bitterly. 'I sense something in McLanahan. He is in great pain, yes – losing both his brother and his wife in so short a time must be devastating for him. If he has a child, it must make the pain even greater. But there is something else about him. I sense another conflict within him.'

'He is certainly not like the others,' Baris agreed. 'I would guess he is a trained soldier, but not necessarily a commando. And he knew of your background – specifically, he mentioned your Air Force background, with definite pride in his voice. If I had to guess, I would say he is a former American air force officer, perhaps even a high-ranking officer.'

'So if he is not a commando, perhaps he's out of his element,' Susan surmised. 'Maybe he doesn't want to be where he is, fighting for money instead of for his country.' Susan turned to Amina Shafik. 'Any information on McLanahan's background, Amina?'

'No, Madame,' Shafik responded. 'It's very unusual. My contact in the American Air Attaché's office at the American embassy in Cairo has no record of a Patrick McLanahan in the American military. Their records go back about five years.'

'Can we search any farther back?'

'Not from the Air Attaché's office,' Shafik replied. 'For that, we would need help from the Mukharbarat el-Aama.'

'The General Intelligence Staff is still loyal to me – I can get that information,' General Baris said. 'But it may take some time. Should we trust this McLanahan and his men until we find out who and what they are?'

'Should we? No – I should trust no one,' Susan said. 'But will we trust them? Yes – for now. Be sure they have all the information they need – every map, every photograph, every piece of data. Make sure they have access to any base, every unit, and every weapon system.'

Baris shook his head, then half-turned in his seat to look directly

137

into Susan's eyes. 'Listen to me, Sekhmet: Your life is in incredible danger here,' he said. 'I know you want to carry on your husband's work and avenge his death, but is running for president worth risking your life?'

'What do you suggest I do, General? Run?'

'In the United States, we have a chance to rebuild our power. We can wait for al-Khan's government to implode. The people will welcome you as a conquering hero then. You would be proclaimed president.'

'But what about the people that I would be leaving behind?' Susan asked. 'They'd be at the mercy of al-Khan and through him, Jadallah Zuwayy. I won't abandon the people of Egypt to save myself.'

'The people of Egypt will survive – we have for thousands of years,' Baris said. 'I can trace my own ancestry back seventeen hundred years, Sekhmet. A dozen different empires, dictators, and religious oligarchies have occupied our nation. We Egyptians have an annoying way of surviving men like al-Khan.'

'That doesn't mean the innocent should suffer because the next despot or conqueror feels it's time to move in,' Susan said.

'The Egyptian people won't be entirely innocent,' Baris said. 'Khan will be voted in by an overwhelming majority, even if Prime Minister Kalir decides to run again. Should not the people be allowed to choose their own government, their own fate?'

'No one should be permitted to rule by force, intimidation, fear – or murder,' Susan said bitterly.

'Even if al-Khan is a murderer, the people of Egypt will still choose by whom they will be ruled. Whether Khan is the president or not, people will follow him because they choose to do so.' Baris lowered his head sadly. 'You may hate me for saying so, Sekhmet, but the reason al-Khan survives – and your husband, my friend, did not – is because the people *want* a man like him as president.'

'Wha . . . what did you say, General?'

'I said, the people get the leaders they want, my friend,' Baris said. 'Your husband was a great man, a great statesman, a hero to Egypt. He helped put this nation back in touch with the rest of the world and ended the isolation and ostracism we have been facing for fifty years. But men like al-Khan survive, and many say he has more power, *much* more power, than Kamal Ismail Salaam ever had. Khan preaches power, Sekhmet, not coopera- tion. He preaches leadership. Kamal wanted Egypt to join the community of nations, especially the Western nations. Khan sur- vives, and will become president, because people like what he says.'

'Even if he gets his power by murder, death, and betrayal?'

'Betrayal to you is another man's patriotism, Sekhmet,' Baris said. 'Murder and death to you is justice, vengeance, action, and destiny to another. Which is right? Which is wrong? I suppose it depends on your point of view.'

'I can't believe you're saying this, Ahmad,' Susan retorted, her eyes wide in surprise. 'Killing my husband, the president of Egypt, was not justice. Conspiring to align Egypt with a bunch of mur- derous anarchists like Zuwayy and the Muslim Brotherhood is not patriotism.'

'Not to you, it isn't,' Baris said. 'Not to me. But to twenty million Egyptians, fifteen million Libyans, five million Sudanese – yes. To over half the Egyptian military forces, al-Khan is a hero for killing your husband. To half of the Saudi royal family, to three-quarters of the Lebanese, to most of the Syrians, Zuwayy is a liberator, the sword of Allah.'

'How is that possible?' Susan asked incredulously. 'How can that be true? Don't all those people realize how dangerous he is? Can't they see Zuwayy's crazy? He thinks he's descended from an ancient Libyan king. He's nothing but a goofball – a mur- dering, thieving goofball!'

'You're not listening, Sekhmet!' Baris said with a smile, like a patient teacher who is watching realization dawning on a prom- ising student. 'You're not paying attention. It *doesn't matter* what you think or what you *know* – it's what the people *believe*. Look back through your own country's history, Susan. Everyone believed John Kennedy was the so-called prince of Camelot, and then were disillusioned because you later found out he was a womanizing adolescent privileged politician who knew little except what his brother Robert and his "Kitchen Cabinet" told him. You know much of Egyptian and Middle East history – do you truly believe the western European kings organized the Crusades to liberate the Holy Land from the infidels? Do you

139

believe Alexander the Great sought to unify the kingdoms of eastern Europe?'

'So it's all propaganda? It's all illusion?'

'Of course it's all illusion,' Baris said. 'The only thing that is real is the law – but there are many, many things more powerful that the law. Image. Perception. Emotion. Fear. Anger. Hate. Love. Control these things, and you control all.'

Susan shook her head in confusion. 'Why are you telling me this, General?' she asked in a low, strained voice. 'Why? Are you telling me that my husband died for nothing more than a dream, an illusion?'

'Because I'm trying to explain men like Zuwayy and al-Khan to you, Sekhmet,' Baris said. 'Your husband died because he was strong in his heart, but perhaps not strong enough in his mind. He believed in something he could never, ever have. Now it's time for you to choose what you want, Sekhmet. Choose.'

Tripoli, United Kingdom of Libya
a short time later

'Yes, I said Susan Salaam. She's *alive!*' Khalid al-Khan hissed in the cellular phone. 'I thought I was seeing a ghost when she walked out on stage! And she's crazy! She actually attacked and seriously wounded some of my men – nearly killed them with a *walking cane!*'

'A walking cane, eh?' Jadallah Zuwayy of Libya chuckled. He was relaxing in his office, flipping through reports and paperwork with several of his advisers. 'I think you need to hire better body-guards, my friend.'

'She's accusing *me* of trying to kill her!'

'Calm yourself, Ulama. Let her rant and beat up on your body-guards – it makes her look all the more unstable.'

'Unstable? *She's running for president of Egypt,* Highness!'

Zuwayy froze, then sat bolt upright in his chair. 'Running for president? How is that possible, Khalid? She's not an Egyptian! She's not even a naturalized Egyptian citizen!'

'The law allows it,' Khan said. 'The law actually says that she

140

assumes the office of her husband if he dies in office – the law was amended in this case to allow her to run for the office.'

'How in the world can you allow that to happen? What kind of lawmakers do you have out there?'

'She is immensely popular here, Highness,' Khan said. 'Even after being hit by that explosion, she is still beautiful.'

'You Egyptians sound like the Italians sometimes – beauty is enough to become a great politician, eh?'

'This is not a joke, Highness,' Khan said. 'The polls already show Salaam twenty points ahead, and she has not raised one penny or made one speech yet!'

'All right, all right,' Zuwayy responded. 'Listen to me, Khalid. Most of this fight is yours – Libya cannot become involved in Egyptian elections. You command considerable power in Egypt, especially in the outlying areas and with conservatives. Use that power. Rally your supporters. You also hold a high position, both in government and in your citizens' personal and spiritual lives – use that power as well. Don't just beat Salaam – *destroy* her. You can do it, Khalid. If necessary, get some secular advisers and help them design a campaign for you – don't rely on a bunch of clerics to fight a battle in an arena they know nothing about.' Zuwayy paused for a few moments; then: 'I may be able to help stir some things up in other areas, Khalid. But it is your fight. Fight to win.'

Zuwayy cut off the call by angrily throwing the receiver back on its hook. He shook his head, deep in thought. 'Khan is such a weakling, it's amazing he's even strong enough to venture outside his own bedroom by himself, let alone run for public office,' he said to no one in particular. 'Whining and bleating like a lost sheep because the wife of his political adversary is still breathing – deplorable.' But he ordered his aide to dismiss his other advisers and staffers with a wave of his hand.

When his office was cleared, he looked at his military chief of staff, General Tahir Fazani, and his Secretary of Arab Unity, Juma Mahmud Hijazi. 'What if the lovely Mrs Salaam does win the election?' he asked.

'Khan will retain his post as chief justice of the Supreme Judiciary,' Hijazi said. 'He's almost as powerful as the president. Little will change.'

141

'Salaam will certainly want to form even closer relations with the West than her husband,' Fazani said. 'That means more foreign military presence, more military ties, more foreign investment. Libya will be squeezed out of any development deals.' He glanced at Hijazi, then added, 'So will our secret benefactor.'

'I am still opposed to making any more deals with Kazakov, Jadallah,' Hijazi said. The two men in Zuwayy's office were fellow officers in the Libyan military who helped Zuwayy overthrow Qadhafi to take over the government – they were two of the few in all of Libya who could call Zuwayy by his real name, and still only in private. 'The man's in protective custody by the World Court, for God's sake. This could all be an elaborate ruse to implicate us. Remember, he's ratted out half the organized-crime leaders in Europe in just the past year. Maybe we're next.'

'I still say, let's take all the weapons Kazakov can put into our hands,' Fazani said, 'and blast the Egyptian military to hell right now. They may have American weapons, but they don't have any more power or support than they ever had. We have historic claims to the Salimah oil fields – let's just move in, wipe out the Western and ignorant Turkish roustabouts, and take over the entire Libyan Desert region of Egypt. We can lay claim to everything west of thirty east longitude and everything south of twenty-five degrees latitude, and I think we can hold it easily. Our forces in Sudan already have the region surrounded – it would be easy. We can pump oil and send it to Libya for six months, maybe a year, before the West starts to threaten retaliation. Then we keep the proceeds, destroy the wells, and get out.'

'It won't work, Tahir,' Zuwayy said. 'What if we do occupy those fields? No one will buy one drop of oil we pump after we invade Egypt.'

'There is always a market for crude, Jadallah,' Fazani said. 'If nothing else, we threaten to dump it on the world market if no one buys it at market price. Dozens of nations, including the West, will buy it at cut-rate prices just for the chance to store it and resell it at higher prices later, and the OPEC countries will buy it just to prop up oil prices. Once we make peace with Egypt, pay some measly reparations, and maybe even take our cut of the profits and move to South America or Southeast Asia, the West will be happy to deal with us again – they'll make a deal with Satan himself to get at all the oil we'll pump from Salimah.'

'You tired of running the Libyan military, Tahir?' Zuwayy asked with a smile.

'Jadallah, I give you all the credit in the world for engineering this scam,' Fazani said. 'It was a stroke of pure genius, coming up with the whole Sanusi thing. Most of the folks in Libya and a good portion of the world bought it. But we're not in it to rule the damned country – we're in it for the money, remember? Libya pumps five billion dollars' worth of oil out of the desert a year. If we can siphon off even ten percent for ourselves, we'll be set up for the rest of our lives. Why do we want to stick around after that?'

'Because if we can take the Salimah oil fields, we can take twice as much,' Zuwayy said.

'I'm all for that, Jadallah,' Fazani said, 'but I'd be just as happy splitting a five-hundred-million-dollar take. I can't water-ski behind more than one megayacht anyway. Besides, how much of those billion dollars do we need to split with Kazakov? He's got a reputation for killing off all his partners. I'd rather get out while we're still alive to enjoy the money.'

'Don't worry about it,' Zuwayy said. 'We've got our escape plan ready to go – that's the mistake Qadhafi made, believing he really was some big-shot Arab desert chieftain. If we need to implement the escape plan, we won't hesitate. Until then, we press on with our plans.'

Supreme Judiciary, Cairo, Egypt
that same time

'"Defeat her" – easy for you to say,' Ulama Khalid al-Khan murmured. He hung up the phone and held his head in his hands. 'How do you defeat a ghost? Scare her away?'

'Sir?' Major Amr Abu Gheit, Khan's bodyguard and chief of the Supreme Judiciary security forces, asked. He waited for a few moments, then asked, 'Can I get something for you, sir?'

'Nothing,' Khan responded. 'Nothing – except perhaps Salaam's head.'

'I can get that for you, sir,' Gheit said with an evil smile. 'Just give me immunity from prosecution, and I'll do it tonight.'

'Tempting, but not quite yet,' Khan said. 'What are the pretty Mrs Salaam's whereabouts, anyway?'

'Last report had Mrs Salaam and General Baris in National Democratic Party headquarters, meeting with district political chairmen and major supporters to organize her election campaign,' Gheit reported, reading from a notebook. 'We have a list of those supporters. Wiretaps, surveillance, and financial investigations can begin on all of them as soon as you wish.'

'Very well. Get them moving,' Khan said. 'And if you can't find the information you need, invent it.'

'Yes, sir,' Gheit said. He continued glancing at the report. 'This is interesting, sir: It is reported from interviews with the flight crew that Mrs Salaam had flown in to the People's Assembly meeting from Mersa Matrûh military base in the west.'

'Mersa Matrûh? What was she doing there?'

'It is apparently where she evacuated to after the assassination, sir,' Gheit said. He read on, shaking his head as he did so. 'There is no mention of it in here.'

'Mention of what? What are you muttering about, Major?'

'There was some sort of emergency at Mersa Matrûh days ago – the base commander, Vice Marshal Ouda, reported that there was some sort of incident, a mutiny or some other violent action, aboard one of his ships,' Gheit replied.

'Major, that does not concern me,' Khan said.

'If I may, sir, I will contact Vice Marshal Ouda and see if he has anything to report on Salaam or Baris's presence there,' Gheit said. Khan dismissed him with a wave of his hand, and he departed, leaving Khan wringing his hands and shaking his head at his desk. But Gheit excitedly returned several minutes later. 'Holiness . . . !'

'What is it now, Major?'

'I have Vice Marshal Ouda on the line,' Gheit said. 'He has something incredible to report. Salaam and Baris were indeed there – and so were some unidentified foreign commandos. Salaam and Baris spoke to them, after which they offered the use of base facilities and other assistance.'

'*What?*' Khan exclaimed. 'What commandos? Who were they?'

144

'It is not known, sir – but Ouda thinks they are Americans.'

'*American commandos are on one of our bases?*' Khan exploded. 'Who authorized this? Why wasn't I notified? Why wasn't anyone in Cairo notified?'

'General Baris ordered Ouda not to report it,' Gheit replied. 'Baris is still national security adviser and Ouda's superior officer.'

'Not for long,' Khan said angrily. 'Issue an order to the Ministry of Defense, stating that the Supreme Judiciary dismisses Baris from his post immediately in the interest of national security. He is suspected of masterminding the assassination of President Salaam and inciting a military coup. Have him arrested and Mrs Salaam arrested as well. . .' Then he thought better of the political ramifications of that and said, 'Better yet, have her taken into protective custody. Do it right now.' Khan picked up the telephone. 'This is Ulama al-Khan, chief justice of the Supreme Judiciary. Is this Vice Marshal Ouda?'

'Yes, Holiness.'

'You will tell me everything you know about what has gone on out there, Vice Marshal, and you will do it *quickly,*' Khan ordered.

He did – and Khan couldn't believe what he heard. 'They are still here, Holiness,' Ouda concluded. 'They have virtual free run of my base, thanks to General Baris. He has ordered my intelligence directorate to turn over the latest intelligence information on hundreds of military sites in Libya. They fly aircraft in and out of here almost hourly, everything from light jets to medium transports. These are the same men who commandeered one of my warships! How dare Salaam and Baris give them all that material and then harbor them on *my* base without even consulting me?'

'Baris and Salaam gave them classified information?' Khan couldn't believe what he was hearing.

'Yes, Holiness. The latest information we have. Mountains of it! Most of the data dealt with Libyan defenses and installations –'

'Anything on Egyptian installations?'

'Some, Holiness. Overhead photos of some of our bases, easily obtainable commercially.'

'But are they classified photos?'

'We classify all photos we obtain for three months, sir.'

'Then Salaam and Baris gave the Americans classified information?'

'Well, technically, the photos are not —'

'Yes or no, Ouda?'

'Yes, Holiness. We classified the photos "Confidential," but only because —'

'It doesn't matter,' Khan said. 'General Baris violated the law by turning over classified information to foreign nationals. You will do everything you can to stop those men, Vice Marshal. They are a threat to Egypt and to our peace and security. Use every man and woman on your base, or get more men — I don't care if you take every soldier in your district, but you will not allow those men to leave. And if Salaam or Baris returns to your base, you will place them both into custody. Do you understand?'

Khan didn't wait for Ouda to respond, but hung up the phone. 'Major! Get in here!' he shouted. When Gheit returned, he said, 'Get the king of Libya on the phone immediately — and have Salaam and Baris found and arrested immediately!'

Tonopah Test Range, Nevada
that same time

The security checks and identification procedures took unusually longer than normal for one simple reason: None of the security officers or their US Air Force supervisors had ever processed a security clearance on a nine-year-old before. But Kelsey Duffield kept her amused, sincere smile and bubbly personality despite all the probes, pat-downs, questions, and the double and triple takes as they proceeded past the several layers of security.

Helping occupy Kelsey's attention was one of the female security guards, who identified herself only as Sandy, a small but very beautiful woman appropriately dressed in sand-colored battle dress uniform, web harness, desert-weight boots, desert hat and aviator sunglasses, and carrying an Uzi submachine gun. Accompanying Sandy was her partner, one of the largest Doberman Pinschers Kelsey had ever seen. It was lean, muscular, angular, and lithe in every movement it made. Its face never changed expression, but it was soon evident that the dog's demeanor could be judged by the position of its long, regal, pointed, cropped ears: When the ears were pointed straight up and motionless it was locked onto its prey; when they swiveled around like radar dishes it was hunting, searching; and when the ears were down, it was sorry for not paying attention.

Kelsey saw the big dog and instantly fell in love. When she tried to go over to it, the big dog's ears drooped, and its little stubby docked tail actually seemed to wag, but Sandy motioned her away. 'Stay away, little girl,' she said sternly.

'But why?' Kelsey asked.

'We call her the Alpha Bitch,' Jon offered. Sandy made a scolding expression toward him, and he smiled back. 'Not Sandy; the dog, Sasha. She was trained by the best military working dog school in the world – right here at Tonopah. She is the most pro-tective dog I've ever seen – I think she'd kill anyone who tried to lay on hand on Sandy. I've seen her in training: She can climb a two-story-tall vertical ladder, drag a two-hundred-pound man, and open doors with her jaws. I've also seen that dog eat – she devours two cans of dog food in two bites.' He smiled at Sandy again and quipped, 'Still can't find a date yet, eh, Sandy?' The guard said nothing, only smiled evilly. Kelsey waved good-bye to Sasha as they proceeded on, and Sasha seemed to be disappointed she was leaving.

With Kelsey was her mother, Cheryl, being escorted by Jon and Helen Masters. Although Cheryl was patient throughout the several-hours-long process, at the end of it all her patience was definitely wearing thin. 'Is all this security absolutely necessary?' she asked as they finally cleared the last checkpoint and walked inside the facility toward one of the large steel hangars.

'You should know better than to ask, Cheryl,' Helen responded.

'But we have Top Secret clearances . . .'

'That's just for *you*,' Helen explained. 'These procedures are for this *area* – it's different. There is another set of security proce-dures once we actually get to the specific *project* – they won't be as difficult as those were, but you will have to submit to them as well, each and every time. The procedures change depending on which area we're going to and which projects are active, so they might be easier or harder next time –'

147

'Harder?'

'This isn't even the worst of it,' Jon added. 'Hangar Seven-Alpha's classification is only Secret. If you want to go to the Top Secret areas, it'll be an extra hour. Heck, we've gone through three hours of in-processing just to pick up a can of soda because the ice chest was in the wrong lab.'

'How do you get any work done?'

'You get used to it,' Helen said. 'You just budget your time accordingly. You learn not to come out here unless you've lined up an entire day or more of work, and you stay until the work gets done. We sleep out here all the time. You ask why we invest in the best computers, why we buy two or three systems when we only need one, and don't use leased equipment – this is part of the reason. Getting a service tech to come out here would be impossible, and it takes even longer to get clearance for a piece of electronic equipment to come in here than it does a person – every diode, microchip, and printed circuit board has to be checked for bugs before it comes in here.'

'This is insane,' Cheryl muttered. 'We've been involved with many classified projects before, and I've never seen security procedures this tight.'

'Getting a briefing or giving a talk on a classified program is one thing,' Jon said. 'Actually building a weapon system that won't officially *exist* for another five years is another.'

'This is like going to Disneyland,' Kelsey exclaimed happily.

'I love your attitude, kiddo,' Jon said. Her excitement and glee, Jon had to admit, were infectious.

The partnership deal between Jon, Helen, the shareholders of Sky Masters Inc, and Sierra Vistas Partners went through quickly and without any major glitches, once Jon was convinced it was the best for all – thanks to Kelsey. Jon and Helen Masters instantly became multimillionaires, not just on paper but in reality. The price for that newfound liquidity was twofold – having a lot of strange people working around the administration areas, and dealing with a whole new attitude from the board of directors, who overnight went from having virtually no power in the company to having the critical swing vote in every decision in the entire company. They didn't *ask* for information anymore – they *demanded* it. Memos flew, phone calls followed, and the staff was kept hopping keeping up with requests for updates from directors and their attorneys and accountants.

Most of Jon's day was filled with bringing Kelsey up to date on all of Sky Masters Inc's projects and programs, a chore that Jon actually found beneficial. Since very few engineers at the company could match Jon's intelligence and innovation, Jon rarely talked to others about his projects – when he needed input or help, he usually had to spend more time explaining what he was trying to do. Not so with Kelsey. She listened intently, rarely took notes, could speed-read a page of engineering data in just a few seconds, and always asked intelligent, relevant questions – not just on the basic science, but on future applications or future directions to push the research. Jon found that explaining a project to Kelsey actually helped him rethink the problems and discover a new approach to solving a dilemma or impasse.

Today was the most exciting day for Kelsey – actually going out to the flight line to see some aircraft. Cheryl's only reason for going along, other than the fact she wanted to be with her daughter as much as possible, was that she had spent so long getting her special Top Secret security clearance that she thought she'd better use it. Now she was regretting that decision. They had flown the company jet from Arkansas to Tonopah Municipal Airport, and then loaded up into a company Suburban for the drive out to the Tonopah Test Range, sixty miles to the southeast along narrow, winding, cracked roads.

'I thought we were going out to Groom Lake,' Cheryl said perturbedly.

'Not likely,' Jon said. 'Heck, it took *me* a year to go out there – and I designed a lot of the stuff they were testing out there! Helen is one of the senior engineers at the company and has been for years, and she's *still* never been there! As rough as you might think the security is here, it's nothing compared to . . . well, out there.' It was obvious Jon was uncomfortable even *saying* the words 'Groom Lake.' 'Security is not just a procedure out there, or part of the cost of doing business – it's a way of life.'

'So how did that Soviet spy make it in there?' Cheryl asked. 'How did –?'

Jon suddenly turned, stepped right in front of Cheryl until he was just inches from her, and held up a finger right in front of

149

her face. 'Cheryl,' he began, his voice quiet but deadly serious. His eyes were affixed directly on hers, and it shocked and surprised her. 'You have got to learn something right here and right now: We don't talk about stuff like that. No one does. Not here, not at the company, not anywhere, not anytime, to no one. *No one.*'

'It's no secret, Jon –'

'Cheryl, listen . . .'

'Jon, I heard all about it at a bar in Nashville, Tennessee, during a space technology conference,' Cheryl Duffield said with a nervous smile. 'Why, I even heard –'

'Cheryl!' Jon interjected – it was the most emotion he had ever displayed in front of anyone before. 'Listen, Cheryl, you have got to learn something – security is not something to be taken lightly around here or most anywhere in the company. To call these guys "sticklers" for security would be a gross understatement. A company that gets a reputation for lax security gets aced out of every single contract competition – ask Northrop, ask British Aerospace, ask any of a dozen excellent companies that had one little breach. It doesn't matter how good your product is – they'll blackball you in a heartbeat.'

He pointed to a tiny white box on the side of a hangar several dozen yards away. 'This place is totally wired for sound – I should know, because I designed most of the systems they use here. We are constantly being scanned for bugs, weapons, recording devices, explosives, stolen components, tracers, communications equipment, chemicals, microwaves – you name it.

'Every word you or I say is recorded and electronically transcribed and analyzed, and any keywords found in the transcript sends a security flag all the way up to FBI, CIA, DIA, and a dozen other government and military security and intelligence agencies in Washington for follow-up,' he went on. 'You say the word "Soviet," "bar," and "Nashville" in a sentence, and in two days the FBI will have launched an entire investigation of you, all your acquaintances, all the circumstances surrounding your presence at that bar in Nashville, and any other permutation of those words they can think of – and believe me, you'll be shocked at the shit they'll come up with.'

'Jon, don't you think you're exaggerating just a little?' Cheryl asked with an exasperated smile. 'I've been involved with some of the most sensitive and intensive security systems out there too, and I've never heard of any of that stuff. And why would they be scanning employees out here in the open for things they just got through checking us for at the entrance? And besides . . .' Just then, Jon put his head down and muttered something under his breath. 'What did you say, Jon?'

Moments later they heard, *'Hands in the air, all of you!'* Cheryl turned and saw a soldier in strange pixilated black, silver, and gray fatigues and helmet aiming an M-16 assault rifle at them from the corner of a building. The strange outfit made him blend in extraordinarily well with the buildings and the shadows at the same time.

'What in the world are you doing? How dare you!'

'I said, *hands in the air!*' the soldier shouted again.

Jon and Helen raised their hands high. Cheryl grabbed Kelsey as another soldier appeared and aimed his weapon as well. Kelsey giggled and raised her arms too. 'Cheryl, I *strongly* advise you to do as they say, *right now,*' Helen said. She turned to her husband, wilted inside when she saw his 'I-told-you-so' smile, and asked perturbedly, 'Jon, *what* did you say?'

'I said, 'Cheryl, are those bombs under your bra there?''

'Oh, my God,' Helen moaned. 'This is not going to be pretty.'

It wasn't. Three hours later, including over one hour being individually interrogated and debriefed by security personnel and another two hours going through the original searches, ID checks, and scans all over again – including more of the same astounded expressions and whispered comments about the nine-year-old, as if it was the first time they had ever seen her – the four were right back to where they were before, walking toward the large sand-colored Hangar 7A.

'I don't think that was very funny, Dr Masters,' Cheryl finally said.

'It wasn't meant to be funny, Cheryl,' Jon said. 'But it's hard to impress upon anyone how strict security is around here unless they experience it for themselves. Besides, I'll bet you've never been strip-searched before – it'll make you really watch your p's and q's from now on, not just in here but everywhere.'

'Jon, this is not funny. Those security people strip-searched and X-rayed my *daughter.*'

'It's not over, Cheryl – in fact, it's only begun,' Jon said, his voice turning serious again. 'Your life will not be your own until what you're about to see, and every piece of technology associated with it in any way, has been declassified for at least five years. And we're only going into the Secret area – if you go into the Top Secret or higher areas, you, your entire family, and all your known associates will be under constant scrutiny until you all die – plus five years. It's the way it is from now on.'

They entered the big hangar, submitted – more humbly this time – to yet another battery of checks and searches, and then proceeded inside. Two dark gray military aircraft filled the hangar; several smaller aircraft and air-launched weapons were on the hangar floor, all closely guarded by Air Force and company security guards, watching not only the hardware and the visitors but one another as well.

'Here they are, ladies – Sky Masters Inc's latest air combat projects, in advanced R and D or initial deployment,' Jon said proudly. 'The little ones first.' He stepped over to the first weapon. 'This is the FlightHawk, our multi-purpose unmanned combat air vehicle. He can do anything a combat aircraft can do – dogfighting, bombing, reconnaissance, minelaying, anything – and do it completely autonomously.

'This is Wolverine, smaller, faster, and much more maneuverable than FlightHawk, primarily designed for standoff attack missions against multiple heavily defended targets – it can out-maneuver even a Patriot missile. It has three weapon sections where it can carry a variety of payloads, including thermium nitrate explosive, developed by us, which has ten times the explosive power of TNT by weight. It also uses imaging infrared seeker and millimeter-wave radar for terminal guidance and re-attacks. This is Anaconda, our hypersonic long-range air-to-air missile.

'Over there, with all the extra guards around it, is Lancelot, our air-launched near-space weapon,' Jon went on. 'It has a three-stage throttleable solid-rocket motor that gives it a range of over three hundred miles in a ballistic flight path or over one hundred miles in altitude in an antisatellite attack profile. They have extra guards because of Lancelot's warhead: It carries the plasma-yield warhead. It's most effective above thirty thousand feet, which makes it a perfect antiballistic missile and antisatellite weapon, but we can get a one-quarter- to one-half-kiloton-equivalent yield even at sea level. At higher altitudes, the plasma field created by the explosion is electronically selectable in both yield and size – at maximum yield it can destroy a target twice the size of the International Space Station, and at maximum size it can disrupt the flight path of incoming nuclear warheads spread out over four hundred thousand cubic miles of space. The plasma field does not just destroy a target: It converts it into a state of matter that exists in nature for only billionths of a second – or in the center of a sun.

'All of these weapons are designed to be carried by our combat aircraft, but they can be fitted to be carried by just about any combat-coded aircraft – even transport planes. You probably saw our DC-10 test aircraft outside – we can carry up to three FlightHawks or six Wolverines on board, and we can refit just about any cargo-category aircraft to launch them. The Lancelot, of course, has been deployed in the Air Reserve Forces and is fielded by the One-Eleventh Bombardment Wing, which is based here for now but will soon be based up in Battle Mountain Air Force Base here in Nevada.'

He then moved over to the first warplane. 'This is one of our EB-1C Vampire battleships. As you know, it's a highly modified B-1B Lancer strategic bomber. It can still carry all of the Air Force's strategic and tactical air weapons, along with all of our new weapons. It's faster, stealthier, and has longer range and greater warload than the active-duty or Reserve Forces models. It uses laser radar arrays for targeting and terrain-following – it is fully air-to-air capable and can even attack satellites in low-Earth orbit with Anacondas or Lancelots. We have six modified right now out of a planned twelve-plane force, all coming from the B-1B fleet once assigned to the Air Reserve forces.'

Kelsey Duffield had already stepped over to the second plane – she was gently touching it, running the very tips of her fingers across its smooth ebony surface as if it were a skittish young colt. Watching her carefully, she noticed, was the security guard Sandy, with Sasha the red Doberman right beside her. 'This must be Dragon,' she said. 'It's very pretty.'

153

'Right, Kelsey,' Jon said proudly. 'Our newest and best project – the AL-52 Dragon airborne laser anti-ballistic missile weapon system. We modified a B-52 H-model Stratofortress bomber to carry a zero-point-seven-five-megawatt diode-pumped solid-state laser, along with laser radar arrays for detection and tracking. I call it our newest system, but it's actually been in the works for eight years. We were part of the original competition for the Air Force's Airborne Laser.'

'You just lost out to Boeing, TRW, and their 747 variant,' Cheryl reminded him.

'We didn't "lose out" – Boeing just had a more aggressive marketing strategy,' Jon said defensively. 'We spent a tenth of what they did on marketing and almost won it.'

The new bomb doors of the AL-52 Dragon extended halfway up the side of the fuselage, exposing the entire bomb bay and mid-fuselage space, and Kelsey looked up inside the open doors. There were four large curved devices, the laser generators, on each side of the fuselage. Forward of the generators was a large stainless-steel container, the laser oscillator, with a large steel tube coming from the chamber forward along the inside center of the fuselage. Behind the laser generators were the capacitors that stored enough power to 'flash' the diodes to produce a pulse of laser light. 'Beautiful,' she said in a tiny voice. 'Just beautiful. You did such a good job with those laser generators, Jon. They're so small, but you can get about fifty thousand kilowatts out of each one, right?'

'That's right. We can push it probably to two hundred each, but we don't have enough generating power on board.'

'It looks like we can fit a few more laser modules in there if we make smaller capacitors.'

Jon liked it when Kelsey said 'we' – it was that exciting to work with her. He almost hated to say anything negative around her for fear of discouraging or distracting her – it sometimes seemed as if she was talented enough to cure a rainy day. 'Doesn't really matter – we just don't have enough power on board to make a bigger laser.'

'Can't we put more generators on board?'

'We've got as many as we can hold,' Jon said. 'We're maxed out on capacitor size too – it just generates too much heat to increase the size any more.'

She continued to examine the intricate SSL components, carefully but with sheer, unabashed awe in her eyes. She paused again at the laser oscillator unit, forward of the laser generators. 'This is what you use to combine and channel the laser light?' she asked.

'The Faraday oscillator,' Jon said. He stepped over to the young girl, studying her eyes as she looked at the device. It was as big as the eight laser generators combined, taking up a huge amount of space inside the fuselage.

Jon had not been with Kelsey Duffield that much since her dad's company became one-third partners in Sky Masters Inc. But Jon had quickly learned one very interesting thing: Kelsey's eyes were truly windows into her extraordinary brain. He could look at her eyes and see the calculations, the engineering, the mechanics, and the physics coming alive, almost as clear as a computer printout. He tried to guess what she was looking at, figure out what she was studying so intently, and then try to out-guess her. It was not an easy task – but it was a constant challenge for him, trying to at least match her lightning-quick mind, and he loved the mental exercise.

That's why he was so disappointed when she moved on. He thought she figured something out about the oscillator. It was easily the clunkiest and most low-tech component of the SSL – basically just a big airless can with mirrors in it and a big lens in front. The laser light coming from the generators was directed into the collimator and bounced back and forth and rotated around between liquid-cooled mirrors in the oscillator. When the light was at the precise wavelength and all of the light waves were in perfect alignment, the lens allowed the light to escape out the front to the argon-filled waveguide, which channeled the laser energy to the deformable mirror in the nose turret.

'What are you thinking about, Kelsey?' Jon asked.

'Energy,' the girl replied.

'What about it?'

'How much we need, how much we have.'

'Relatively speaking, not very much,' Jon replied. 'We added just one alternator and one generator to the basic B-52 electrical system to power the laser. Four three-hundred-amp engine-driven alternators, each one supplying power in a separate circuit to four

155

essential AC buses and two emergency AC buses. Four twenty-kilowatt engine-driven generators supplying power to two DC essential buses and one emergency DC bus. Backup power is four engine-driven hydraulically powered alternators and generators, which power only the essential A and emergency A buses.'

'Generators and alternators, huh?' Kelsey asked.

'This is an airplane, Kelsey, not a spaceship. What do you want on board – fuel cells? A nuclear reactor?' She looked at him with a silent 'Why not?' expression. 'You want to put a nuclear reactor on board a B-52?'

'You have one, don't you?'

'A nuclear reactor? Are you craz—?' But then he stopped – he was doing that a lot, as if the ideas that flooded his brain used so much energy that he was unable to budget enough brainpower to move his lips. 'We . . . we can't do that!' He didn't sound too convincing, even to himself.

'Sure you can. We've had megawatt-power generators smaller than my mommy's car for years.'

'Sure – fission reactors.'

'Right.'

'Well, you can't put a nuclear reactor aboard an aircraft!'

'Why not?'

'Why not? It's . . . it's . . .' Jon couldn't think of a reason why right away. 'Because . . . because no one wants a plane with a nuclear reactor flying over their homes, that's why.'

'I guess,' Kelsey said. 'We've had ships with nuclear reactors sailing past our homes for a long time – but an airplane is different, I guess.' She continued to study the inner plumbing of the fuselage. 'But the LADAR is a diode-pumped solid-state laser, right?'

'Sure. But it's only one-tenth the power of the SSL – not enough to destroy a ballistic missile at the ranges we want to engage at.'

'But if we had more power?'

'The smallest diode-pumped laser in the one-megawatt range that I know of is the size of a living room, and it has its own transformer farm to power it.'

Kelsey looked up at the B-52 bomber. 'This plane is a lot bigger than a living room, Jon,' she said with a grin.

'We can't do that kind of engineering with . . .' But he stopped

156

– again – as his mind began to race. 'I wonder . . . if we used a different pumping system . . . ?'

Kelsey turned around and pointed to the Lancelot missile. 'We can take your plasma-yield warhead,' Kelsey said, 'and use it to pump the laser.'

'Pump a laser with . . . with *plasma?*' Jon gasped. 'I . . . I've never heard of that before.'

'You thought of it years ago, Jon,' Kelsey said. 'I read about it in one of the magazine articles you wrote. You were going to use lasers to create a plasma field – Lawrence Livermore built their inertial confinement plasma generator based on your ideas – and then you talked about the feasibility of using a plasma discharge to pump a laser. The system would have generated its own power and its own fuel – a virtually unlimited power supply. Why don't we do it? Take similar SSL arrays you use for the laser radar. You have four arrays on the Dragon. How many laser emitters in each array?'

'Three hundred and forty.'

'Oh, boy,' Kelsey cooed happily. 'We shoot the lasers into an inertial confinement chamber loaded up with deuterium and tritium fuel pellets and then channel the plasma field into the laser generator. What was the power level of the one they built at Lawrence Livermore?'

'Fifty trillion watts for a billionth of a second,' Jon said breathlessly. 'That's fifty thousand watts per second. We need at least seven hundred and fifty thousand.' His eyes darted aimlessly as he started to fill in details in his mind. 'But that's using only *one* ion generator . . .'

'And a solid-state ion generator is much smaller than your diode laser pumps,' Kelsey said. 'How many can we fit in the Dragon?'

'Hundreds,' Jon said. 'No . . . thousands. One generator of neodymium disks could have over a thousand in it alone. We could fit . . . we could fit over a dozen generators in a B-52. Over ten thousand ion generators, pumped by a plasma field . . . my God, Kelsey, we're talking about a *ten-million-watt laser!*'

'That's two million watts per second,' Kelsey said proudly. 'Almost double the size of the Air Force's chemical laser.'

'My God,' Jon muttered. 'A plasma-pumped solid-state laser – on board an aircraft. Incredible! Why didn't I think of that?'

'You did, remember?' Kelsey giggled.

'The plasma-yield warhead . . . can we confine the fusion reaction to the laser chamber?' Jon started mumbling to himself, the others forgotten. 'How much power will we need for that?' It was several moments later before he realized that Kelsey was holding a school notebook up to him – with preliminary figures already calculated. 'Kelsey!'

'I don't know all the details on your plasma-yield warhead, Jon,' she said, 'and I need to look at the schematics of the oscillator and laser generators. But a plasma field of this approximate size and of this density will need only this much laser power for the inertial confinement process in the fusion chamber, and then will require approximately this much power in the magnetic field to channel the plasma to the laser generator. I think we can do it.'

'You *think* you can do it? Kelsey, *you've just done it!* This is it!' Jon exclaimed breathlessly, looking at the formulas with ever-widening eyes. 'This is the answer! I can take this to the engineering department and have them start building the fusion chambers right away! We've got so much work to do – reconfiguring test article number two, getting the engineering going . . .' To Jon's great surprise, Kelsey started heading for the door. 'Kelsey? Anything wrong? Where are you going?'

'To the bathroom,' she replied matter-of-factly. 'I can help with the engineering after I get done.'

'Well,' Helen remarked with a smile, *'that's* certainly something you don't hear every day from a world-class engineer.'

At that moment, Jon's secure cell phone beeped. He looked at the caller's ID number, smiled broadly, then punched in a descrambling code. 'Patrick!' he said happily. 'Is that you?'

'Hi, Jon,' Patrick McLanahan said. Kelsey and Cheryl Duffield looked on with great interest as they heard the name of the man they most wanted to meet at Sky Masters.

'How are you? Any news about Wendy?'

'Not yet, I'm afraid,' Patrick replied. 'Are you secure?'

'I'm here with our new partners,' Jon said.

'Then buzz me once you're by yourself.'

'I can't do that, Patrick,' Jon said. 'They're our full partners now – they've got to be told about what we're doing. They have the proper clearances. I have no choice.'

Patrick paused for a long moment; then: 'All right, Jon. We're going to turn up the heat a little. I need some gadgets to fly a mission.'

'You got it,' Jon replied. 'Just tell me where, when, and how much.'

'What about your new partners?'

'I said I have to tell them – I didn't say they had a vote,' Jon said. 'Don't worry about it. Whatever you want, you get, as long as it helps bring back Wendy.'

'It will either help bring her home – or punish the ones that took her,' Patrick said. 'I'll transmit the order of battle to you in a few minutes. They'll need to launch within the next sixteen hours.'

'I've had the crews standing by ever since this went down,' Jon said. 'Everything will be ready. If your . . . benefactor can keep the feds off our back while we generate, it'll be much better for us.'

'Getting a lot of heat out there?'

'Ever since the new partnership deal, we've been getting shit on . . .' Jon looked sheepishly at the Duffields and shrugged an apology. Cheryl Duffield looked mad enough to scold him for the rest of the day; Kelsey just giggled. 'Yes, we've been getting a lot of attention – from everyone.'

'Our benefactor should be heading off most of the heat,' Patrick said. 'Hang in there.'

'We'll do whatever we need to do to get Wendy back. You just watch yourself. We're praying for you.'

'Thanks, Jon.'

'Good luck, Patrick,' Jon said. 'We'll be ready. Count on it.' He closed up the phone.

'Was that General McLanahan?' Cheryl Duffield asked. Jon nodded as he opened the phone again and dialed a number. 'Where is he? What's going on?'

'I'll explain everything on the way back to Blytheville,' Jon replied. On the cell phone, Jon said, 'Paul? Listen, we're expecting – You got it already? Good. Any problems . . . ? Excellent. We're heading back now. We should be there in four hours.' He hung up the phone, then made another call to the flight crew of the corporate jet, then to the driver of their car waiting to take them back to Tonopah Municipal.

'Kelsey? *Where is Kelsey?*' Cheryl asked. The sound sent chills through everyone – especially through Sandy, the security guard . . .

. . . because it wasn't until just then that she noticed that Sasha wasn't right beside her. 'Sasha!' she shouted. *'Aspetta! Fermi!'*

They found the two of them moments later – sitting in front of each other, with Kelsey leaning up against one of the AL-52 Dragon's huge main landing gear tires. 'Kelsey!' Cheryl Duffield shouted. 'Get away from that dog!'

'But she's nice, Mom. . .'

'Don't move, little girl,' Sandy said. 'Sasha, *basta! Adesso!'* Despite her commands, however, the dog stayed right with Kelsey. 'I don't understand this. . .'

'I think the dog likes Kelsey – and not as a snack, either,' Jon said with a smile. 'Don't take it personally – your dog didn't rip a stranger to shreds.' Kelsey gave Sasha a big hug and a tickle on its head between its flattened, contented-looking ears before she was slowly, carefully taken away by her mother, and Sasha was led away with a string of sharp admonitions in Italian from Sandy.

Once they were back in the Suburban on the ninety-minute ride back to the airport, Cheryl Duffield finally asked in between a flurry of cell phone calls, 'Okay, what's going on, Jon? Who's going to launch what?'

He looked at her, then at Kelsey, with a little apprehension. He then shrugged. 'I promised I'd tell you everything at the appropriate time – I guess this is it,' he said. And he started explaining. The explanation continued well past the ride to the airport – in fact, it continued well after takeoff. Kelsey listened to each and every word, sitting impassively, her little hands folded on her lap as usual.

Cheryl Duffield, however, was not as patient. 'Do you mean to tell me, Dr Masters,' she finally stormed after Jon had finished his explanation, 'that Sky Masters Inc has been involving itself with unsanctioned, illegal military missions all over the world? You have been investigated and are currently under surveillance by the FBI because of these activities? And – let me get this perfectly straight – your vice president in charge of research, General Patrick McLanahan, is *right now* planning an operation in Libya, and you are going to help him – by sending an aircraft loaded

160

up with experimental cruise missiles and launching them against Libya?'

'Cheryl, that's not the *half* of it,' Jon said in response.

'This is outrageous! This is . . . this is *unacceptable!*' she thundered. 'You didn't reveal one bit of this in days of contract negotiations! This is fraud! This is criminal! This is a major breach of contract! We will not be a part of it!'

'Cheryl, I warned you each and every day of our negotiations that we are involved in things that you might not want to be part of,' Jon said earnestly. 'You looked at our books. You interviewed our personnel. . .'

'All except the McLanahans – they were the ones we wanted to talk with! Now we see why – they were busy blowing up missile bases in Libya!'

'We couldn't tell you anything until your security clearances came through, and by then it was too late – the operation was already under way,' Helen said.

'We will not stand by and watch our company be destroyed by this . . . this lunacy!' Cheryl shouted angrily. 'You didn't answer to a board of directors when you started this wild escapade – but you have one now, and they have the power to oust you, the McLanahans, and everyone else involved in this crazy scheme right out of the company. And that's exactly what I want to see done!'

Jon was still busy on the telephone, coordinating launch activities with his Blytheville headquarters. He ignored Cheryl Duffield until there was a lengthy pause on the other end; then: 'Cheryl, I don't really care what you're going to do – go cry to the shareholders, sue us, close us down. I don't care. But I'm going to do everything in my power to support the McLanahans and the team out there in Egypt. I'll do as much as I can for as long as I can. In less than ten hours, our planes will be airborne. In twelve hours, it'll all be over – either we'll be successful, or folks will die. Either way, it won't matter what you say or do. You can't stop it.'

'Oh, I will stop you, Dr Masters,' Cheryl retorted. 'Maybe not this time, but after this day, you won't be able to order a pizza, let alone an air strike. I guarantee it.' And she got up and disgustedly walked off to the front of the aircraft. As she moved forward she half-turned, waiting for Kelsey to join her.

161

Their two gazes met. Cheryl saw something in her daughter's eyes, a request or a plea: Whatever it was, Cheryl recognized it. She obviously didn't like it, but she accepted it. She shook her head, her lips taut, and continued forward.

'Mommy's pretty mad,' Kelsey said.

'I'm sorry about all this, Dr Duffield,' Helen said. 'We had no choice but to keep this information from you. Too many lives are at stake.'

'The McLanahans – are they in danger?' Kelsey asked.

Helen looked at Jon. He looked at Kelsey, wondering whether or not to answer. Most times, it was so difficult to remember that Kelsey Duffield was still a nine-year-old and not just a world-class, superintelligent, fully adult thinker. He always wanted to treat her as an adult, a peer – but most times he usually ended up treating her like a smart little sister. That time, Jon realized, was just about past.

He told his caller that he would get back to them, hung up the phone, and then looked seriously at Kelsey. 'Yes, Kelsey – the McLanahans are in terrible danger,' he said. 'In fact, Wendy McLanahan is missing, and General McLanahan's brother Paul is dead.' Kelsey's eyes widened in fear, becoming shiny with tears, but she said nothing. 'General McL – Patrick, is trying to force the Libyans to turn Wendy over to him.'

'What will he do?' Kelsey asked.

'He is going to attack some key military targets inside Libya, places that are vital to Libya's defenses,' Jon replied. 'All he has to help him are two men, Hal Briggs and Chris Wohl, with Tin Man battle armor; some soldiers, one or two aircraft . . . and us. The Libyans have over one hundred thousand troops, a very big air force, and nuclear, chemical, and biological weapons.'

'What will you do?'

'Patrick wants me to launch several Wolverine and FlightHawk missiles against targets in Libya,' Jon replied. 'Once the targets are destroyed, he'll be able to fly in and attack more vital targets from the ground. He plans on attacking more and more targets in Libya until the president of Libya turns over Wendy and the others. We'll launch two attack planes, twelve hours apart.'

'What if Wendy is dead?' Kelsey asked, her face drawn with fear.

'I don't know,' Jon replied. 'I hope Patrick will come home. He has a little boy, you know – his name is Bradley. He hasn't seen Bradley in a long time.'

To Jon's complete surprise, Kelsey Duffield started to cry. It was the first time he had ever seen her display any emotions at all, let alone such utter sadness. But then another completely unexpected thing happened: Jon Masters reached over and hugged the little girl. For several long moments, the two stayed in each other's arms. Her weeping got more intense, deeper, and for a moment Jon didn't know if he could maintain his composure – before he realized that tears were running down his cheeks too. Helen put her arms around her husband, and they shared that terrible moment together – the first time in their short but close relationship that they shared anything more than business together.

After a while, the little girl's weeping subsided but they stayed in their siblinglike embrace. Finally, Jon asked, 'Are you going to be okay, Kelsey?'

'I think so,' Kelsey replied, sniffing. She was silent for a moment; then: 'Jon?'

'Yes?'

She sniffed away a tear again, still holding Jon Masters tightly, and asked, 'What warheads are you going to put on the cruise missiles?'

'W . . . what?'

'What are you going to arm those Wolverines and FlightHawks with?' the sad little girl asked. Slowly but surely, Jon could hear the familiar business-like steel returning to her voice as she added, 'I have some ideas that might help . . .'

Chapter Four

Over the Mediterranean Sea, off the coast of Libya
the next afternoon

The flight had originated from Arkansas International Airport, Blytheville, Arkansas. The crew had filed an ordinary IFR flight plan with the FAA, with Bangor, Maine, as its destination and McDonnell Douglas DC-10 as its aircraft type. About twenty minutes before reaching Bangor, with unusually good weather all across the northeast United States, the crew descended below eighteen thousand feet, canceled its Instrument Flight Rules flight plan, and elected to proceed using Visual Flight Rules. The handoff was routine. Once the flight descended below three thousand feet it disappeared off radar, lost in the ground clutter of the White Mountains of eastern New Hampshire. As far as American air traffic controllers were concerned, it was a successful and completely routine trip. They did not check to see if the flight made it to Bangor, nor were they required to do so.

In fact, the aircraft never descended at all. The crew was able to electronically alter the Mode C altitude readout of its air traffic control radio transponder, making the controllers think it had descended for landing. The controllers never had a 'skin paint,' or hard radar return, on the aircraft – they were relying only on the transponder to get the aircraft's position. The aircraft actually stayed at thirty-nine thousand feet, heading eastward on a great circle route to take it over the north Atlantic Ocean.

Once the transponder was turned off, the aircraft became invisible – because it was not really a DC-10, but a modified US Air Force B-52H Stratofortress bomber nicknamed the EB-52 Megafortress, owned and operated by Sky Masters Inc as a government research and testing aircraft, designed as a stealth technologies demonstration aircraft. Its skin and major structural components were made of composite fibersteel, not metal, covered with radar-absorbent materials; instead of a large cruciform radar-

167

hungry tail, its control surfaces were smaller, swept backward, and radically tilted in a low V-shape to minimize radar reflections. Even though the aircraft weighed nearly half a million pounds and its wingspan was longer than the Wright Brothers' first airplane flight, it had the radar cross-section of a bird.

A few hours later, the Megafortress rendezvoused with a real Sky Masters Inc DC-10 aircraft that was modified for aerial refueling. Within half an hour, the B-52 was fully topped off with fuel. With the DC-10 in loose formation, the B-52 made its way across the north Atlantic, using bursts of its Laser Radar system to be sure it was well out of visual range of other aircraft. The DC-10 was on a standard over-water flight plan, en route to Glasgow, Scotland. About an hour prior to landing, the B-52 again hooked up and filled its tanks from the DC-10. The big converted airliner headed immediately for landing in Scotland – it was now dangerously low on fuel, even though a conventional DC-10 can make the trip across to Europe easily with plenty of fuel reserves. Its stealth wingman had nearly sucked it dry.

The EB-52 continued right across Europe, overflying countries without clearance. The reason was simple: No conventional radars could see it, so no one knew it was up there. It flew across a dozen western and central European nations without a hint of its presence. Even in crowded airspace, it was able to keep its distance so no other aircraft could see it, changing altitudes or maneuvering far enough away to keep out of sight.

John 'Bud' Franken, Commander, US Navy, Retired, thoroughly enjoyed the danger of what they were doing. As the aircraft commander aboard the Sky Masters test bed aircraft, he had seen his company's planes do some amazing things – but even when the EB-52 was doing nothing but flying straight and level nearly seven miles above the Earth, it was still amazing. Franken was a former US Navy test pilot and test squadron commander, and he had flown in every Navy aircraft design, both operational and ones that never made it past 'black' status, over the past twenty years – but he was truly awestruck by the EB-52.

In his soul he would always be a Navy fighter pilot, but his heart now belonged to the experimental EB-52 Megafortress.

His mission commander, sitting in the right seat across the wide cockpit, was as young as Franken was old, as operationally inexperienced as the pilot was combat-tested. Twenty-five-year-old Lindsey Reeves was simply a natural-born systems wizard. It didn't matter if the system was a complex, high-tech flying battleship like the EB-52 Megafortress or her pride and joy – a 1956 Aston-Martin DB4 GT Sanction I convertible, which she restored herself, including rebuilding the engine – she could look at it, experiment with it for a few minutes, and instantly figure out how it worked. Sky Masters Inc's worldwide team of head-hunters had recruited her at the age of sixteen at a county science fair in her hometown of Madison, Wisconsin, where she had won the competition by modifying a radio receiver to pick up Global Positioning Satellite navigation signals – at a time when GPS was still a classified military program.

Franken was a systems guy too – you had to be to fly the Megafortress. It was so different from all other aircraft that it was best to let the computers do the flying, watch the computers like a hawk, and be ready to take over if they rolled over and died. But Lindsey was from another dimension when it came to machines. She wasn't much of a flier – she got airsick at the slightest hint of turbulence and used almost every non-narcotic airsickness remedy known, from wristbands to ginger tablets, to help her get through it. But when it was time to go into action, she was ready – usually.

'Three minutes to low-level entry point,' Lindsey reported. She had two overhead air vents blowing cold air on her face, plus she was breathing pure oxygen to try to settle her stomach. 'All birds reporting ready.'

'Then try to relax a little, Lindsey,' Franken suggested. 'Take off the gloves and loosen your fingers.' Lindsey always wore gloves – she said it was easier to find them that way in case she needed something to throw up in. 'You're too tense.'

'I've never flown into . . . into combat before,' she murmured.

'The exercises we do back in the ranges are much more intense than we'll see here,' Franken assured her. 'You're a good crew dog, Linds. Relax and take it easy.'

'Okay,' Lindsey said. But it was no use – a few moments later, she was holding a barf bag at the ready. She was nervous, Franken thought – usually within three minutes time-to-go, she was fine.

'Give me the leg brief, Linds,' Franken said.

169

'I don't feel so good . . .'

'The leg brief, MC,' he ordered sternly. 'Right now.'

The voice got her attention, and the discipline and routine got her mind off her churning stomach. 'First heading one-nine-five, leg time twelve minutes fifteen seconds, auto TF descent,' Lindsey recited. 'Level-off altitude two thousand feet . . . set and verified. The SA-10 site at SAM is our first threat. I've got only air traffic control search radars up now.'

At the initial point, Franken issued voice commands to the EB-52 Megafortress's flight computer, and the big aircraft responded – it started a ten-thousand-foot-per-minute descent, automatically retarding the throttles to keep the airspeed under the red line. All he had to do was monitor the computers, keep up with his ears as the cabin pressurization changed, and watch out for floating objects as the fast descent created some negative Gs, almost like being weightless. Franken kept an eye on Lindsey – if she was going to hurl, it would be now. But she was wearing her combat face now, and nothing would interfere with it – he hoped.

The pilot's side of the instrument panel had three sixteen-color multifunction displays (MFDs) that showed the route of flight, flight instruments, engine instruments, and system status readouts; Franken could switch between the displays with simple voice commands. Three more MFDs in the center instrument panel had fuel, electrical, hydraulic, pneumatic, threat, and weapon status readouts, with conventional backup instruments and gauges underneath. The mission commander's instrument panel was dominated by a supercockpit display, a huge one-by-two-foot computer screen that showed a variety of information, all selected by the mission commander and controlled by voice commands or by a trackball on the right side. Two more MFDs on either side of the supercockpit display showed systems readouts and warning messages.

Their course was depicted on Lindsey's display as a roadway, with the road as the computer-recommended altitude. Symbols showed known and detected threats and obstacles. Two large upside-down green cones either side of course represented the search radars in eastern Libya, with the 'roadway' threading precisely between and underneath the edges of the cones; more cones represented Egyptian and naval search radars. Colored symbols all along the Libyan coastline represented the location of known antiaircraft threat sites, but so far none were active.

'Our first threat is an SA-10 site, two o'clock, forty miles,' Lindsey reported. 'We should be underneath it in five minutes. We've got two Egyptian Roland sites at eleven o'clock – search radars only. We should be outside detection range. Egypt also has a Patriot site at extreme range, nine o'clock, fifty miles – we should be well clear. No fighters detected yet. LADAR coming on – our course is clear so far. We might have Libyan fighters at three o'clock, seventy miles – they're moving pretty fast, but they don't have radars on so we can't identify yet.' Lindsey kept up a constant litany of reports and observations. Although Franken had all that information right in front of him as well, it was reassuring to hear Lindsey reciting it all – two pairs of eyes scanning the instruments was always better than one, especially when the action got hot and heavy.

The computer-generated 'road' started to rise up to meet the aircraft depiction on their navigation displays, so both crew members monitored the level-off carefully. They performed a fast terrain-following system check, verified that everything was working normally. They were over water right now, forty miles off the Libyan coast. The Libyan coastal air defense sites were all around them, but right now they were quiet – no radar emissions at all.

'Want to step it down, Bud?' Lindsey asked.

Franken studied the threat display. They knew the position of the nearest SA-10 site – it just wasn't transmitting yet. At two thousand feet, they were right at the edge of lethal coverage at this range. They could descend well below the missile's engagement envelope, but then risk being heard from the ground. Only government and military aircraft were allowed to fly at night over Libya, and a big plane like a B-52 flying low to the ground well away from an airport would certainly attract attention. 'Let's leave it here for now,' Franken replied. 'We'll give it a few minutes and then –'

Suddenly a female voice from the threat warning receiver spoke: *'Caution, search radar in acquisition mode, nine o'clock, thirty-seven miles, Patriot SAM.'*

'The Egyptian Patriot got us,' Lindsey said. 'If the Libyans detect the Patriot system fired up, they'll fire up their own radars.'

'Stepping down,' Franken said. He hit the voice command button on his control stick: 'Set clearance plane to one thousand.'

'*Clearance plane set one thousand feet, pitch mode auto TF,*' the flight control computer responded. Just then the computer reported, '*Warning, Patriot SAM tracking, nine o'clock, thirty-six miles . . . Patriot SAM acquisition mode . . . warning, Patriot SAM tracking, nine o'clock, thirty-five miles . . .*'

'Darn it, he got us, he locked on,' Lindsey reported. 'Let's step it down to five hundred feet.'

'*Caution, Patriot SAM acquisition mode . . .*' But that brief lock-on, just three or four seconds, was all it took for the Libyan air defense sites to be alerted. '*Caution, SA-10 SAM at ten o'clock, thirty miles, acquisition mode . . . warning, SA-10 SAM height-finder at ten o'clock, thirty miles . . .*'

'Trackbreakers active,' Lindsey verified. 'Let's take it down to two hundred.'

'I didn't expect to be flying hard TF so far out,' Franken said. 'Here we go.' He issued commands, and the big bomber rumbled down until it was two hundred feet above the Mediterranean Sea.

'*SA-10 SAM in acquisition mode,*' the computer reported.

'He knows we're out here, but he can't find us . . . yet,' Franken said. 'Linds, where are those fighters you saw earlier?'

Reeves activated the laser radar for a few seconds. 'They're on their way now,' she said. 'Three aircraft headed our way at six hundred thirty knots, twenty-nine thousand feet. Less than six minutes out. No identification yet.'

'Not exactly burning up the program here, are we?' Franken deadpanned. 'So much for the stealthy approach. We might end up fighting our way in.' There was no response from Lindsey – and when Franken turned to find out why, he noticed Lindsey vomiting into her barf bag. He reached across and grasped her shoulder. 'You okay, Linds?'

Her eyes were wet with tears – obvious even in the dim red glow of the EB-52's cockpit. 'I . . . I don't know,' she said weakly. 'I'm . . .'

'I need you, Linds. I can't do this without you.'

'I'm so scared,' she cried. 'My stomach . . . I don't know if I can do this.'

'Lindsey . . .' He waited a few moments while she retched in her bag again; her trembling fingers dropped the bag somewhere on the center console. She was so rattled that she couldn't refasten her oxygen mask. 'Lindsey, listen to me –'

'*Warning, airborne search radar in acquisition, three o'clock, forty-seven miles, MiG-25,*' the threat computer reported.

'I . . . I can't do this,' Lindsey sobbed. 'I'm sorry, I can't –'

'Listen to me, Lindsey – listen to me!' Franken shouted. 'If we turn around, the Libyans will chase us all the way across the Mediterranean Sea. When we run out of missiles, they'll shoot us down. We might make it out – but our guys on the ground probably won't. We have to keep going. Do you understand?'

'I don't know if I can.'

'You have to!' Franken said. 'There are three guys on the ground who won't stand a chance unless we help. But I can't do this alone, not even with the computers.' He grasped her shoulder tightly and shook it. 'You've got to hang in there, Linds. Just think of this as a simulator ride – a very, very intense simulator ride. Okay?'

It didn't look good at all. Lindsey's head lolled back and forth, slowly at first, then faster, as if she was looking for something. She started to pull off her left flying glove. 'Here,' Franken said. 'Go to town – and then let's get to work.' He pulled off his right glove and passed it to her. She barely got it up to her face before the torrent quickly filled the black Nomex glove. Franken couldn't believe that tiny little stomach of hers still had anything left in it to regurgitate.

Reeves was hunched down, her head almost between her knees, her hands holding on to the eyebrow panel for support, as if she was going to puke right on the deck – Franken thought she might pass out. But to his relief, Lindsey pulled her oxygen mask up to her face, fumbled and finally snapped the bayonet clip in place, then took several deep breaths of pure oxygen. Her right hand disappeared onto the right console, and soon her super-cockpit display started dancing as the displays changed with ever-increasing speed.

'Scorpions are ready,' Lindsey reported weakly.

'How about you, kiddo?'

'I'm hungry,' she said. 'Let's do our thing so we can go home and get a couple burgers.'

'*Warning, airborne search radar tracking, three o'clock, thirty miles, MiG-25,*' the computer reported.

'The weapons pylons are making our radar cross-section as big as a friggin' barn,' Franken said. 'Looks like we're going to pop some Scorpions after all.' The AIM-120C Scorpion air-to-air missile was the Megafortress's main defensive weapon – a radar-guided supersonic missile capable of hitting enemy fighters as far as thirty miles away. The EB-52 carried four on each wing, mounted on launch rails attached to the sides of the weapon pylons.

'Let's step it down to COLA,' Lindsey suggested. 'Maybe he won't want to come down that low.'

'Roger. He we go. Hold on to your lunch.'

'My lunch is long gone,' Lindsey shot back. Franken shoved the throttles to full military power and ordered the computer to COLA mode. COLA, or computer-generated lowest altitude, used both the terrain and cultural data in the terrain-following computer and combined it with occasional bursts from the laser radar and air data information to compute the absolute lowest altitude the EB-52 bomber could fly, depending on airspeed, terrain, obstructions, and flight performance. The faster the bomber flew, the more aggressively the autopilot would hug the ground – literally flying at treetop level if it could. Over water, the computer could take the bomber right down to fifty feet above the surface of the water – only a very tall sailboat mast could stop them.

'Threat report,' Lindsey asked.

'*MiG-25 tracking four o'clock, twenty miles, altitude ten thousand feet,*' the computer reported.

'They're trying to get on our tail,' Franken said. 'Let's do it, Linds. Ready?'

Reeves froze for a few long moments, then looked over at Franken. 'Let's do it,' she repeated. She pressed the voice command button. 'Attack MiG-25,' she spoke.

'*Attack MiG-25, stop attack,*' the computer responded, offering her the command that would stop the attack. When she did not respond within three seconds, the computer said, '*Launch commit Scorpion*

174

right pylon.' There was a slight rumble from the right wing and then a streak of light from Lindsey's windscreen. The AIM-120 Scorpion missile flew an 'over-the-shoulder' launch profile, arcing over the EB-52, then back toward the Libyan MiGs. The laser radar array automatically activated for two seconds, updating the Scorpion's autopilot with the fighters' flight path. The missile climbed above the MiGs, then descended rapidly toward the spot where the missile predicted the MiGs would be at impact. Ten seconds before impact, the LADAR flashed on again, updating the missile's autopilot for the last time. Five seconds before impact, the Scorpion's own radar activated and locked onto the lead MiG-25 fighter.

That was the first indication – an immediate 'MISSILE LOCK' warning – the Libyan pilots got that they were under attack.

The wingmen did exactly what they were supposed to do, executing a textbook formation breakaway, climbing and turning away from each other and giving their leader room to maneuver. But the lead pilot – concentrating on the attack, just moments away from firing his first radar-guided missiles – didn't react fast enough, or didn't believe the indication, or chose to ignore it, hoping for a lucky break, the two-in-three chance that the attack was against one of his wingmen.

The thirty-seven-pound shaped warhead detonated like a shotgun blast a fraction of a second before the missile hit the MiG right above and to the left of the starboard engine nacelle. The MiG-25's heavy steel hull, reinforced with titanium – the MiG-25 was designed to fly at nearly three times the speed of sound – deflected most of the energy of the blast. But the missile still had enough punch to crack the fuselage, rip open the fuselage fuel tank, and smack the starboard engine. Running at one hundred percent power, the engines didn't need much of a hit. The engine's turbine blades, knocked out of their precisely engineered high-speed orbits, shot through the engine case like atomic particles flying into space after a nuclear explosion; the extreme heat from the engines ignited the fuel from the ruptured fuel tank, causing a fire. The MiG-25 pilot had only seconds to react – but again, he was concentrating too hard on his quarry to pay attention to the warning lights, telling him he had only a few heartbeats to punch out – before the MiG blew itself into a ball of fire and spun into the Mediterranean Sea.

'Good going, kiddo,' Franken said flatly – killing someone was never cause for celebration, even if it meant saving your own skin. 'You got him.'

'Thanks,' Lindsey said – then promptly whipped off her oxygen mask, lowered her head between her knees, and vomited on the deck.

The two remaining MiGs spent several minutes rejoining – they were obviously spooked by the unexpected threat warning and having to do an evasive maneuver so low to the ground at night – and then several more minutes trying to locate their leader. By the time they resumed the search for the EB-52, it had changed headings and proceeded on course to its target area.

Within a few minutes, the picture had changed considerably. Where before it was relatively quiet, now it seemed every air defense radar in both Libya and Egypt was up and operating. Lindsey kept busy steering the Megafortress around a variety of antiaircraft weapon systems, and every few minutes a fighter radar would sweep past them. They were forced to stay at low altitude to avoid all the threats.

'Headbanger, this is Stalker One, say status,' Patrick McLanahan radioed.

'We're sixty seconds to initial point, Stalker,' Franken responded on the secure satellite command channel. Thankfully Lindsey was feeling all right now, because Franken had now run out of flying gloves – he hoped he wouldn't have to eject now. 'We were chased by Libyan MiGs a while ago, but we're clear. Unfortunately every air defense site in eastern Libya and western Egypt is looking for us, and both sides are on full alert. We had to go low and stay low, so our time in the box will be much less. I estimate only twelve minutes until we bingo. Sorry, Stalker.'

'No sweat, Headbanger,' Patrick replied. 'I don't plan on staying very long anyway. We're in position and ready for some fireworks. We're glad you're here.'

'Glad to help, Stalkers. Watch the skies. Headbanger clear.'

The Libyan town of Jaghbub was located one hundred and twenty miles south of Tobruk. Jaghbub was an oasis fed by an occasionally dry river, which for most of its two thousand years of history never had more than a few hundred persons living there. But the area was one of the best farming regions in the northern Sahara, with many different types of fruits, vegetables, and nut trees in abundance, and travelers and nomads going across northern Africa found Jaghbub to be a rich and inviting place to stop and rest before continuing their trek across the wastelands. It had therefore developed over the centuries as a crossroads of many different nationalities, religious sects, political identities, and schools of thought from all over the known world.

So when an obscure descendant of the Prophet Muhammad was forced to flee his home in Fez, Morocco, by French colonists in the early nineteenth century, he escaped across the burning sands of the northern Sahara desert, following the ancient nomadic routes over fifteen hundred miles back toward the holy land, and came upon this little oasis. There he found a home for his own particular style of Islam. Instead of the wild, untamed 'whirling dervish' being practiced in many Islamic sects, this holy man, who called himself Sayyid Muhammad ibn 'Ali as-Sanusi, preached a return to strict Muslim practices – abstinence, prayer, and strict adherence to the words of the prophet in the Koran. He built a mosque, then a university, and finally a fortress on the banks of the little river, and the holy city of Jaghbub was born.

For the next one hundred and forty years, Jaghbub was the birthplace of some of the most powerful and revered kings of Africa. The Sanusi dynasty became the lords of northern Africa and the ghosts of vengeance of the Sahara. They ruled the oases with an iron fist, tempered with justice through the laws of Islam. Travelers and pilgrims from any nation were welcome and treated with extraordinary kindness and generosity; anyone who preyed on a traveler or pilgrim was punished with equally extraordinary swiftness and cruelty, usually by being buried up to the chin in the sand outside an oasis where insects and vultures could pick at the robber's head for a day or two.

They were never conquered. Despite invasions from the French, British, Turks, Italians, Germans, and Americans, the Sanusi dynasty survived and prospered. On December 24, 1951, Sayyid al-Hasan ibn 'Abdullah as-Sanusi, the fourth Grand Sanusi and the first to be chosen amir of each of the three kingdoms of Libya, proclaimed the independence of Libya from post-World War II

177

British rule and himself ruler of the United Kingdom of Libya. The Sanusi family moved the capital of their new kingdom to Tripoli, keeping the family stronghold at Jaghbub as a retreat and family mosque; soon, Jaghbub became a destination for Muslim pilgrims from all over the world who visited and prayed at the tombs of the great nomadic kings of early Libya.

The newly independent kingdom survived mostly by borrowing money from its Arab neighbors and the United Nations, until British geologists discovered oil in the desert southeast of Tripoli in 1958. Virtually overnight, Libya became one of the richest and most strategically vital countries in the world, almost on a par with Egypt and its famous Suez Canal. First the British, and then the Americans, built some of their largest and most important overseas military bases in Libya, all to ensure the delivery of the seemingly endless supply of oil being pumped from its deserts. With its newfound wealth, the king of Libya improved the cities, built large and modern ports and rail lines, improved education and health care, and made Libya an attractive destination for people and investors from all over the world. Once again, travelers and pilgrims were welcomed and protected by the as-Sanusi family.

All that changed in September of 1969, when a group of young army officers led by Muammar Qadhafi staged a bloodless coup against the monarchy. The king himself was out of the country, recovering from eye surgery in Turkey. He abdicated and named his second son Muhammad heir to the throne; the rest of the family fled the palace. The family retreated to Jaghbub, thinking that even Qadhafi would never dare violate a sacred mosque or try to destroy the Muslim university.

When Qadhafi's rule became more bloodthirsty, violent, and repressive, and Libya was distancing itself not just from the West but from many of its Arab neighbors, the people began to call for a return of the Sanusi dynasty to rule Libya as a constitutional monarchy. Jaghbub started to become the symbol of the once and future Libya, the root of Libya's past greatness and the source of leadership of the new Libya, should the military dictatorship fail or be overturned.

Crown Prince Sayyid Muhammad ibn al-Hasan as-Sanusi of Libya was welcomed into the capitals of many countries, and he made it clear that, with the right support from outside his country as well as within, he would assume the throne once again. Muhammad was born in 1962, the king's second son. Officially he, like most of the Sanusi men before him, was born in the holy sanctuary at the Great Mosque at Jaghbub – in reality, Muhammad was born at the American base hospital at Wheelus Air Force Base, which had far better medical equipment and medical professionals than at Jaghbub. His family had learned their lesson from the birth of the first son, al-Mahdi, who really was born at Jaghbub but had suffered dehydration and circulation problems during delivery.

Muhammad began his schooling at the Royal Military Academy in Tripoli at the age of four and learned the basics, the Libyan 'Five "R"s' – reading, writing, arithmetic, religion, and riding – with extraordinary speed. Although his future, chosen by his father, was as a religious scholar and teacher, his real love was the military. He loved hearing stories of his grandfather, a general in the Turkish Army when Libya was still part of the Ottoman Empire, harassing the Third Reich's Field Marshal Erwin Rommel's Panzers all across the Sahara. But he soon realized that tanks in the present day, like horses in World War II, were obsolete – a strong air force was the best way to secure a nation as large as Libya, on a continent as large as Africa.

After the military coup in 1969, Muhammad attended elementary and high school classes conducted at the university in Jaghbub, then was accepted to Harvard University in 1980 and graduated in 1983 with a double major in political science and international relations. He was admitted to Harvard Law School in 1983 and was the first foreign first-year student ever named as an editor of the prestigious *Harvard Law Review*.

But Muammar Qadhafi wasn't done with the as-Sanusi family – he needed a scapegoat, and they were perfect targets. Qadhafi had suffered an embarrassing defeat in a brief war with former ally Egypt in 1977; he failed in his attempt to occupy neighboring Chad and Sudan; he failed in his attempt to support his friend Idi Amin in Uganda; and he suffered an embarrassing loss of four Libyan MiG-25 fighters when they tangled with two US Navy F-14 Tomcat fighter planes defying Qadhafi's 'Line of Death' over the Gulf of Sidra. There had already been several assassination attempts against Qadhafi, and there was a brief but violent military uprising in Tobruk, organized and funded by the deposed

King Idris and his newly formed Sanusi Brotherhood. Qadhafi charged the Sanusis with sedition, treason, and inciting revolution – all crimes punishable by death. In 1984, Qadhafi ordered the entire as-Sanusi family arrested, the Jaghbub university closed, and the tombs of the Sanusi kings opened, destroyed, and the remains thrown out into the desert.

But he knew it would be too politically costly to turn the Sanusis into martyrs, so he allowed them all to escape. The king himself remained in Istanbul; the other family members fled, mostly to Egypt or Saudi Arabia, never to return. Once they were out of the country, though, Qadhafi pursued them relentlessly. His assassination squads fanned out over most of Europe and Africa, under orders to kill all Libyans who refused to return to Libya – and the Sanusis were at the top of their lists. The Crown Prince first met his family in Egypt and publicly denounced the desecration of the Sanusi tombs; when being public exiles in Egypt became too dangerous, the family scattered.

The historic buildings, mosque, tombs, and university at Jaghbub lay baking in the hot Saharan sun, virtually unused. The university was turned into a military headquarters; the fortress was turned into a winter palace for Qadhafi and a convenient but isolated place to hold propaganda events. To cover up the desecration of the holy place, the river that fed the oasis was dammed, flooding the plain and covering up all traces of the destroyed historic buildings and tombs. It appeared as if the legacy of the kings of Libya was at an end.

But another ambitious, treacherous Libyan army officer resurrected the memories of the as-Sanusi kings of Libya – but for all the wrong reasons. Jadallah Salem Zuwayy was an officer assigned to a Special Forces unit at Jaghbub in the early 1990s. When Qadhafi Lake – the lake covering the Sanusi tombs – was low one extraordinarily hot summer, he was able to view the ruins of the tombs of the Sanusi kings that lay exposed in the mud from the low water level. Although he and his officers were forbidden to go near the tombs, he went anyway – but even after he was discovered, the fear of retribution from Qadhafi was so strong that no one dared bring him up on charges. That fear of the Sanusi dynasty is what inspired Zuwayy to begin his claim as a descendant of the Sanusi line.

It was easily researched: Sayyid al-Hasan as-Sanusi, the first king of united Libya, had six sons and three daughters. Actually, the records showed only five sons, but the Sanusi kings usually had three or more wives, and they adopted many children, so why couldn't there be a sixth – or seventh, for that matter? The second son, Muhammad, was appointed the heir apparent. The entire family fled the country after the desecration of the tombs at Jaghbub – all, went the new story, except Jadallah, the youngest son of King Idris. Instead of fleeing, Jadallah decided to join Qadhafi's army, not only to study his weaknesses but also to learn from him how to be a leader in the modern world.

The real Idris the Second, Muhammad, hadn't been heard from since 1992, when he became King Idris the Second upon the death of his father in Istanbul. From his hiding place – no one knew for certain where it was – he had proclaimed a Libyan constitutional monarchy in exile, formed a Royal War Council, and was raising money and building an army. Rumors spread like wildfire: Some said he was a spy for the American Central Intelligence Agency, for the British MI6, or for the Israeli Mossad. Most knew he was the leader of the Sanusi Brotherhood, a secret counter-assassination group, hunting and killing first Qadhafi's, then Zuwayy's assassins worldwide on behalf of his family and all exiled Libyans. Others claimed he had been assassinated, or just deep in hiding, probably in South America. In any case, he or his followers hadn't been heard from in years.

He was a coward, or so the story went – it was Jadallah who had the courage to dare to try to retake the government of Libya from Qadhafi. As an officer at Jaghbub, Jadallah secretly preserved 'his' family's heritage and assembled his army, and from his ancestral home launched the attack on Tripoli that eventually brought Qadhafi down. Although Muhammad as-Sanusi was in reality the second king of Libya, Jadallah Zuwayy proclaimed himself the true King Idris the Second and chieftain of the Sanusi Brotherhood.

It was a ridiculous story. The most superficial examination of official records showed Zuwayy's real birthplace and lineage – he was definitely no Sanusi. There was ample evidence that King Idris had only five sons, not six; Zuwayy's concocted evidence was disproved immediately. But Zuwayy stuck to his story, and eventually the people of Libya accepted it. He turned Jaghbub back into a holy city and announced the reincarnation of the United Kingdom of Libya, to the delight of the people of Libya and the amused relief of most of the rest of the world. He then went about having all the Arab history books changed to reflect his fictional lineage.

In fact, Jadallah Zuwayy, the self-appointed and totally fictional king of Libya, hated Jaghbub. Yes, it was beautiful and fertile. But it was well within artillery range of Egyptian forces, just fifteen miles away. Although he had built a modern stronghold there, with the most modern air defense network surrounding it and a force of ten thousand troops and a couple hundred armor, artillery, and mechanized infantry pieces in place, it was still over a hundred miles from civilization and reinforcements, and could be easily overrun or infiltrated. But its weaknesses made it a good hideout. No military forces would ever touch Jaghbub, especially the Great Mosque, for fear of scorn by the rest of the Muslim world – it was considered as holy a shrine as Mecca or Medina. And it was far enough away from the Mediterranean coast to give him ample warning of an attack or invasion from the sea.

It was Zuwayy's alternate headquarters, his safest hiding place in all of Libya – and the entrance to his preferred escape route, should his plans fail and his little self-conceived revolution dissolve. It was an easily concealed flight from there to Sudan, Yemen, then Saudi Arabia or Syria, all of whom might give him safe passage or asylum. Besides, occasionally he would do a prayer service or celebration at Jaghbub, televised throughout the Arab world, and the people of Libya would delight in seeing the historic mosque and Green Palace in use once again.

The mosque and the Green Palace, the home of the as-Sanusi kings, were located inside a sixty-acre ancient sun-dried brick walled fortress. The original three-meter-high walls were heightened an extra four meters, reinforced with steel, and topped with motion detector probes, with a catwalk on the inside and guardposts installed every ten meters around the perimeter. The original wooden gate was reinforced with Kevlar and steel, with an extra set of electrically operated steel antitank doors inside. Along with the mosque and the palace, there was a small security building, an eight-horse stable and barn, a covered riding arena with bleacher seats, and a short equestrian show-jumping course. North of the compound out as far as two kilometers, antitank and antipersonnel mines were laid across the open desert. Guards patrolled the oasis and the area to the south, and more guards patrolled by boat on Lake Jaghbub.

The military base was located to the west and south, spread out over several hundred acres, including an airfield large enough to accommodate light to medium transport planes. The entire area was defended by radar, numerous antiaircraft artillery batteries, roving patrols with man-portable SA-7 antiaircraft missiles, and a wide variety of low- and medium-altitude-capable mobile surface-to-air missile systems, including several SA-6, SA-8, SA-9, and SA-13 units deployed in random patrols over two hundred square miles around Jaghbub. The Libyan army practiced artillery and mortar fire missions in the desert beyond the airfield.

There was at least one squadron of attack helicopters stationed at the air base, including ex-Soviet Mil Mi-24 heavy helicopter gunships and French-made SA342 Gazelle light helicopter gunships, and one full armored battalion with ex-Soviet main battle tanks and armored personnel carriers. The base was considered too close to the Egyptian border to station a large number of fixed-wing combat aircraft there, but a few ground attack and air defense aircraft played a 'shell game,' hiding in one of a dozen reinforced concrete shelters located on the base. There was even a road-mobile Scud missile battalion located there, with a dozen SS-1 Scud missiles deployed all over the region at presurveyed launch points, ready to strike at preprogrammed targets in Egypt, Chad, Kenya, or Ethiopia, or targets of opportunity passed along by reconnaissance forces.

The Egyptian intelligence data Patrick had received from Susan Salaam and Ahmad Baris gave precise details on all of this – and all had been passed along to Patrick's mission planners in Blytheville. Now the Night Stalkers were on the attack.

The EB-52 made the turn at the bomb run initial point. Most threats were several miles ahead or far behind them, so Franken and Reeves risked a slight climb to two thousand feet above the desert just as the computer began the first launch countdown. 'Computer counting down,' Lindsey reported. 'Release switches to "CONSENT."'

Franken made sure his red-guarded switch was up and the switch inside was up. In this highly automated digital cockpit, he noted with a trace of humor, it was always amusing that Patrick McLanahan and the other designers always kept these Cold War-era 'two-man control' switches in place. Both switches had to be set to release a weapon. It was of course possible for one person to activate both switches – but the idea was for one of two persons to overrule the other if the need arose. Some things – some mind-sets – never change.

At zero, the port-side FlightHawk detached itself from its wing pylon and fell two hundred feet while it unfolded its wings and flight controls and started up its small turbojet engine. Once it had stabilized itself, it began a climb to its patrol altitude. A minute later, the second FlightHawk launched as well. Both unmanned combat aircraft carried air-to-air weapons, long-range surveillance sensors, and electronic jammers and decoys, all to protect the Megafortress while it was in the target area. At the flight planned point, the Megafortress started a right turn in its racetrack orbit area, which allowed the FlightHawks time to fly into their patrol positions east and west of the racetrack.

'Computer started the countdown to bomb bay weapon release,' Lindsey reported several minutes later. 'FlightHawks are on patrol and ready.'

'Get ready, Linds,' Franken said. 'We might be getting busy again.'

She hurriedly took a big sip of water from a plastic bottle. 'Then I better get something in my stomach to barf up,' she said. But judging by the way she said it, Franken was sure she would be ready if things started to heat up again.

When the computer counted down to ten seconds, the forward portion of the EB-52's bomb bay doors swung open and a Wolverine cruise missile dropped free, followed by seven more in twelve-second intervals. The Wolverine missiles resembled fat surfboards, with a small turbojet engine in the tail. They had no wings or flight-control surfaces, but used mission-adaptive skin technology to reshape the entire missile body to create lift and steer itself with far greater speed and precision than conventional flight controls.

Each Wolverine missile had four weapon sections, including

three bomb bays and a fourth weapon section right behind the sensor section in the nose. Using an inertial navigation system updated by satellite navigation, the Wolverine missiles flew to preprogrammed bomb run initial points, then activated infrared and millimeter-wave radar sensors, looking for targets. Their small size and low profile meant they were almost invisible to the air defense radars surrounding them – but they were all able to detect, analyze, classify, and lock onto the radars themselves.

The Wolverine missiles then worked together with the FlightHawks to analyze and correlate the radar transmissions and then locate the associated missile launchers. The radar units for most air defense units were set up far away from the missile launcher so antiradar missile attacks would not destroy the missiles or launchers; they were usually connected by some sort of electronic link, usually a microwave system or cable. Many times the enemy would set up decoy radar transmitters, hoping the antiradar weapons would go after the decoys. But the FlightHawks were able to determine from the type of radar detected what kind of air defense system it was, and if it had a remote launcher setup it would listen for the data transmission between the radar unit and the missile launch unit in a surface-to-air missile battery, compute the location of the launcher, and pass its location to the Wolverine missiles. In this way, their weapons wouldn't be wasted on nonlethal radars or on decoys.

Six of the Wolverine missiles were programmed for SEAD, or suppression of enemy air defenses. As they flew over each air defense weapon site they detected, they scattered cluster bombs across the missile launchers. Each of the Wolverine's three bomb bays held seventy-two one-pound high-explosive fragmentary bomblets, which covered an area of about thirty thousand square feet with shrapnel. If a Wolverine attacked a particularly lethal SAM site but the FlightHawks determined that the site was still active, it would command the Wolverine to turn around and re-attack the target. Once all three bomb bays were empty, each surviving Wolverine missile would perform a suicide dive into a fourth target, where an internal two-hundred-pound high-explosive warhead would destroy one last target and hopefully all remnants of the missile itself.

The remaining two Wolverines were programmed to hunt

down vehicles instead of antiaircraft sites. Instead of bomblets, they carried devices called sensor-fuzed weapons, or SFWs. There were eight SFW canisters per bomb bay in the Wolverine. When the infrared sensor in the Wolverine's nose detected large vehicles nearby, it flew toward them and ejected two SFW canisters overhead. The canisters floated down on small parachutes, spinning as they descended. As they spun, tiny heat-seeking sensors spotted the location of vehicles on the ground. At a precise altitude above the ground, the canisters exploded, sending dozens of one-pound slugs of molten copper at the vehicles. The copper slug was like a sabot round from a tank or artillery piece – the hypervelocity slug was powerful enough to punch through three inches of solid steel. Once inside a vehicle, however, the slug cooled enough where it couldn't penetrate the other side – so the slug simply exploded and spattered inside, creating thousands of tiny white-hot copper bullets that shredded anything in its path in the blink of an eye. Like the other Wolverines, these tank-killing cruise missiles located, attacked, and reattacked targets until all of their SFWs were expended; then they suicide-dived into preprogrammed targets – one into the base command post, the other into a communications building.

Hal Briggs marveled at the intelligence information they received from the Egyptians – it was all up to date and incredibly detailed. As he scanned the area with his battle armor's electronic sensors, the satellite datalink connecting him with the temporary headquarters at Mersa Matrûh filled in details of what the sensors picked up – guard posts, boundaries of minefields, fence positions, even locations of doghouses and latrines were pointed out. He was kneeling just to the north of the minefield, scanning the compound, when suddenly he heard a ripple of explosions.

'Nike, looks like our little buddies are on the job,' Hal radioed on the secure command satellite network. He heard several secondary explosions as a Wolverine cluster bomb attack destroyed a pair of SA-10 antiaircraft missiles, sending a balloon of fire into the night sky. The Libyans began firing antiaircraft artillery into the sky, tracers arcing everywhere, but judging by the wild, random sweep of the tracers across the sky, it didn't appear as if they were locked onto any of the Wolverines yet. 'What's it look like to you?'

'Why do you ask me these things, sir? You can see everything I see.' Chris Wohl was stationed on the south side of the military compound, keeping watch on the main access road between the military base area and the Jaghbub compound.

'Relax, Sarge. It looks quiet out here.'

'That's because you've got five hundred mines between you and the bad guys,' Wohl said. 'I've got two T-55 tanks less than a hundred meters away from me. This looks pretty damned suspicious to me, sir – the Libyans look like they're on full alert.'

'I don't blame them – we're only fifteen miles from the Egyptian border.' Just then they heard three beeps come over their communications network. 'Here we go, guys.'

Briggs raised and adjusted a device that looked like a small, fat mortar launcher. He double-checked the settings on the mount, armed it, and then used his boot thrusters to jet-jump away from the area. Thirty seconds later, the launcher activated, shooting a projectile with a one-thousand-foot-long piece of half-inch-thick rope behind it. As the rope reached its full length, the projectile detached itself, and the rope sailed through the sky, eventually fluttering gently to the sand in a wavy snakelike pattern. Ten seconds later, the rope – which was actually a detonatorlike cord – automatically exploded.

The shock of the explosion caused every mine within a hundred feet either side of the detonator rope to explode, creating an incredible light show across the desert as an entire three hundred thousand cubic feet of sand simultaneously blew into the sky. The vibrations and shock waves rushing across the desert set off even more mines in a spectacular ripple pattern, like waves from a rock thrown into a still lake.

'Yeah, baby, *yeah*!' Briggs exclaimed as the rolling explosions washed over him like a brief but violent minihurricane. 'Talk to me, honey!'

'Don't get yourself shot while you're patting yourself on the ass, sir,' Wohl said.

'Hey, you got the job I wanted – just make sure you don't miss.'

'I've got this job for one reason, sir – I *never* miss,' Wohl said. At that, he hefted a huge rifle that looked like a cross between a big Barrett .50-caliber BMG sniper rifle and something out of a science-fiction movie. The weapon was plugged into his belt with a short fiber-optic data cable, and with a simple voice command it was activated and Wohl started searching for targets.

It did not take long. Vehicles started rolling out of a security building inside the tall fence less than a minute after the explosions in the minefield. The first out was an armored car with only two men in it, probably officers; Wohl let it pass. His intended targets: the two ex-Soviet T-55 tanks sitting near the entrance, both small, fast, and still powerful despite their age, following closely behind the armored car.

Wohl didn't want to wait until the first one cleared the gate, so he had it in the electronic sights of the big gun as soon as he saw it move out. About ten meters before it reached the gate, Wohl pressed the trigger. Silently, with the recoil electromagnetically dampened out, a sausage-sized depleted-uranium projectile weighing about three pounds shot out from the muzzle of the electromagnetic rail gun at over twenty thousand feet per second. There were no explosives in the projectile – its effectiveness was in mass times velocity, pure momentum. In about a second, the sabot round hit the tank in the right side just below upper track level. It pierced the thick outer hull and passed completely through the tank's diesel engine and transmission and out the other side without losing more than twenty percent of its velocity. The projectile didn't even begin a ballistic flight path for another two miles, and it finally buried itself thirty feet diagonally in the sand after flying more than five miles.

For a few seconds, it appeared as if Wohl had missed – there was nothing at all to indicate that the tank had been hit except it had stopped suddenly and one track drive sprocket and drive shaft was sliced into pieces. But inside, the tank's engine was disintegrating with incredible speed and destructive force. It was as if a hundred parts inside the engine, instantly dislodged from their bearings and mounts, simply decided to fly apart at the same instant. The big diesel engine simply split apart and became a deadly cloud of shrapnel, killing the four crewmen inside instantly. The T-55's gun turret popped off the top of the tank like a champagne cork, spinning twenty feet in the air before landing against the fence. Smoke and flames spewed out the opening like an upside-down rocket engine.

Wohl immediately targeted the second T-55, and seconds later it too was a burning mass of metal, blocking the base entrance. Wohl jet-jumped twenty yards east, retreating to a spot where he could fire inside the base. He sent one projectile into the security building through the front door, hoping to take out some communications equipment. But he was only waiting for his real target.

It came less than five minutes later: an Italian-made Agusta A109 VIP transport helicopter, escorted by a Mil Mi-8 transport helicopter. Their intelligence information was right on: The Agusta was Libyan president Zuwayy's personal helicopter, and the Mi-8 carried his security staff, twelve heavily armed Republican Guard troopers. Wohl didn't have to lead either helicopter with the rail gun at such short range: one shot each, and both helicopters came down hard.

But by now security forces and infantrymen had started streaming out of the base, and they were even starting to walk automatic weapons fire in his direction – time to leave. 'Nike is evacuating,' he radioed.

'Taurus is on the move too,' Hal Briggs reported. 'Let's get the hell out of Dodge.'

Wohl turned to leave – but before he could use his thrusters to jump away, suddenly the sand around him disappeared in a blinding cloud of fire. Out of nowhere, a third T-55 tank had raced around the two stricken tanks, located Wohl's hiding place, and had opened fire with a 101-millimeter round that exploded just a few feet away – if he had been hit by the round, at this range, it might have killed him. Wohl was blasted off his feet and thrown twenty feet in the air.

'Taurus . . . Taurus . . .' The blast had stunned Wohl – he could make his arms and legs move, but he couldn't get his legs under him well enough to run or jump away. He could hear the T-55 moving closer, and he desperately tried to crawl behind a sand dune or into a ditch – anything to avoid a direct hit by a tank shell. Alarms were ringing in his suit – most of the energy in his suit was already gone.

No answer. Briggs was already gone. Even if he heard him, he couldn't get back in time.

Wohl could now feel the T-55's treads moving closer. He picked up the electromagnetic rail gun, hoping to get one last shot off – but it was already a tangle of broken parts in his hands. The hypervelocity rail gun rounds were nonexplosive – he couldn't even fashion a grenade or smoke screen out of the now-useless rounds. His electronic stun-bolts were useless against a tank, and even if he was confronted by infantrymen, he might have one or two bolts left before his power drained out completely.

Crap. In his entire military career, he hadn't gotten more than a scratch or a few minor cuts and bruises in combat – unless he was dealing with the Tin Man battle armor. Every time he had anything to do with it, the damned suit had managed to bite him in the ass. This time, he had relied on it too long. The one weakness in the suit is that you started to believe you were invulnerable, and that's when you got into trouble, getting too cocky and getting into worse and worse scrapes.

The Libyan tank sounded as if it was right beside him. Wohl pulled himself up with his arms, but he still couldn't get his legs to work. He commanded his jump-jets to fire – hopefully they would blast him away from the area, giving him a precious few moments to hide or get to his feet, but the thrusters weren't responding – all he got was a power level warning message. He frantically tried to issue override commands, to use the last bit of 'housekeeping' power in the suit to fire the thrusters, but the computer ignored his commands. Damn machine . . .

A big white searchlight on the tank blinded him. Wohl could now see the muzzle of the T-55's big main gun trained on him, less than thirty yards away. Would they actually use the main gun on him? Wouldn't they realize it would blow him into tiny pieces, like a double-barreled shotgun blast a few inches away from a little bird sitting on a fence? They probably weren't looking for prisoners at this point . . .

Wohl saw the bright flash of light from the tank. 'Hal . . . ,' he muttered weakly, for the last time. 'Hal, help me.'

Strange, but he didn't expect to hear the noise or feel the heat from the blast, but he did. Would he see the round flying out and striking him as well? Or would they just use the thirty-millimeter cannon on him, save some ammo? Then there was an impossibly loud, impossibly bright flash of light and a deafening roar, and it was all over . . .

. . . except it wasn't over. Wohl realized a few moments later that the burst of light he saw wasn't the main gun going off, or even its coaxial machine gun – it was the tank itself. Then he heard the faint whine overhead, and he knew what happened: the first burst of light he saw was a sensor-fuzed weapon canister dropped from a Wolverine attack missile going off, followed moments later by the T-55 tank exploding as the SFW's copper slugs blasted it apart.

A few moments later, Wohl was able to roll and crawl away from the fierce heat and flames shooting from the T-55. He tried again to get to his feet when he felt his body levitated off the ground as if he suddenly weighed as much as a handful of sand. What the hell . . . ?

'You all right, Sarge?' Hal Briggs asked. His exoskeleton made it as easy to lift him up as a child lifting a stuffed toy.

'Jesus, sir,' Wohl retorted, 'didn't you ever hear of checking the wounded over before lifting them up like that? You ever hear of spinal injuries, concussions, broken bones?'

'You were trying to get to your feet already – I figured I couldn't do any more harm,' Briggs said. 'Sheesh – maybe I should just gently set you down again and let Zuwayy's boys give you a hand when you're feeling better.'

'Just shut up and let's get out of here, sir,' Wohl said. He extended a thin cable from his backpack and plugged it into Briggs's backpack, and immediately he could send and receive datalink information and reactivate his suit's environmental controls. The 'buddy power' also reactivated Wohl's exoskeleton, allowing him to walk on his own again. 'Let's go. This way.'

'You needed me,' Hal said.

'What?'

'You needed me. You called my name – my real name, not my rank or "sir." I think that's the first time you ever did that.'

'Don't let it go to your head, sir,' Wohl said. 'I thought I was dead – I was desperate. Now let's get out of here.'

191

As Wohl reached around Briggs's shoulder to support himself as Briggs carried him away, the big ex-Marine patted his partner's shoulder with an armored hand. Briggs knew he couldn't say 'thank you' any more sincerely.

As they were instructed and trained, the Republican Guard security forces entered Zuwayy's private apartment without knocking – but they did not dare to go more than a step inside. 'Your Highness, there is an emergency,' the officer in charge shouted.

A few moments later, Colonel Osama Mekkawi, chief of security of the Republican Guards and Zuwayy's personal bodyguard, dashed into the room, hurriedly buttoning his uniform tunic. He pushed past the security guards. 'Don't just stand here gawking! Get out of here and secure the hallways and escape tunnel for our departure!' Mekkawi shouted. He went to the door of Zuwayy's bedchamber. It was locked. With a thrill of panic, he drew his side arm, stepped back, then kicked the door open.

Jadallah Zuwayy was sitting upright in his bed, startled out of a deep sleep. Curled around him were two young girls, members of Zuwayy's equestrian staff, the younger no more than thirteen or fourteen years old. Mekkawi learned long ago not to look or act shocked at anything he saw or heard coming from Zuwayy's bedchamber. 'Highness, there's an emergency,' Mekkawi shouted. The younger girl began to whine for her mother; the older one, still half asleep, began kissing Zuwayy's face. 'You must evacuate.'

Zuwayy practically stomped the younger girl in his haste to get out of bed, and he hastily put on a pair of trousers, robe, and sandals, the two girls forgotten. Mekkawi escorted Zuwayy outside to the evacuation route; a guard stayed behind, guarding the apartment door to make it appear as if the room was still occupied.

'What is happening?' Zuwayy asked.

'We are under attack, Your Majesty,' Mekkawi said breathlessly. 'Action in the minefield – several hundred square meters of minefields exploded, probably a mine-clearing operation, in preparation for attack. Then cluster bomb and missile attacks against antiaircraft emplacements and armored vehicles all across the base. Could be a prelude to a large invasion force. We must evacuate.'

'Who could it be?'

'With firepower like that? Israelis or Americans, I'd guess.'

'How in hell could such a force get that close without being detected?'

'Perhaps it is a stealth bomber attack, Highness,' Mekkawi said. 'It is not important now. We must get you to safety. I will ask you to wait in the Great Mosque until your transports arrive, then we will evacuate you to a safe location immediately.'

Mekkawi escorted Zuwayy down into the basement of the palace; in a storage room filled with old furniture, he pressed a hidden switch. A secret door swung open on electrically activated pistons. The door led to an escape tunnel. They passed one security checkpoint along the two-hundred-meter tunnel, then climbed a spiral staircase. They emerged in a janitor's room in the Great Mosque. Zuwayy was escorted to a rectory, and the guards were posted outside. The rectory, inside the mosque, was believed to be immune from attack from almost any nation in the world, even the Americans. This one had been specially modified to protect its occupants from chemical, biological, and even low levels of nuclear weapons, and the walls had enough armor in them to withstand a forty-millimeter rocket-propelled grenade.

Mekkawi placed a satchel with a shoulder strap on a desk and opened it. He withdrew a nuclear/chemical/biological agent detector from the bag and activated it. 'You remember how to don your protective mask and hood, Highness?' Mekkawi asked. Zuwayy nodded, his lips taut with fear. 'Good. If the alarm goes off, you will have about thirty seconds to do so. Take your time and do it correctly, and you'll be all right. There is the mask, a weapon, atropine injectors, a first-aid kit, and other items in this bag – don't hesitate to use any of it. The helicopter will be here within three minutes to take you into hiding. I recommend the alternate command center at Sawknah; if it's a general attack, we can coordinate all our forces better from there.'

'If it's a general attack, I don't want to wait until I arrive in Sawknah – I want a full rocket barrage started against all Area A targets,' Zuwayy said angrily. 'Then scramble all alert bombers and commence the follow-on attacks against both A and B targets. Understood?'

193

'I will need to issue those orders by coded radio from my office, Highness.'

'Then go. I will wait here.'

'Very well, Majesty. I have guards posted outside both entrances if you require anything.'

'All I require are the heads of anyone who dared attack this facility!' Zuwayy shouted. 'Go!' Mekkawi dashed off.

Zuwayy sat at the desk and picked up the chemical warfare mask. He saw his fingers starting to tremble. He had donned one of these many times in the past, of course – all Libyan Special Forces troops were very proficient in their use, because every unit had chemical and biological weapons in their arsenals – but he was so nervous right now that he doubted if . . .

'*Es salaam alekum*, Captain Zuwayy.'

Zuwayy nearly jumped out of his skin – he leapt to his feet, nearly stumbling backward over his chair. There, standing before the desk just a few meters away, was a strange figure in some sort of futuristic costume. He could not see a face, or eyes – the figure was wearing a full-face helmet with large bug-eyed visors. He carried no weapons. '*Bolis! Bolis! Ilha'uni! Ilha'uni!*' he screamed, his voiced as high-pitched and trembling as those of the young girls he had just finished raping.

To their credit, both guards stationed outside the two doors to the rectory burst in immediately – unfortunately, they didn't think about calling out an alarm before they did. One had a radio in one hand and a pistol in the other; the other guard had his rifle at the ready. Both were immediately stunned off their feet by a blast of lightning from the stranger's shoulders. The stranger dragged the guards inside the rectory, secured the doors, then stepped toward Zuwayy.

Zuwayy reached into the satchel, pulled out a Spanish Star Z84 autopistol, cocked it, and opened fire at full auto from less than five meters away. The figure flinched and made a half-step backward but did not go down. Another bolt of electricity made Zuwayy cry out in pain. The Z84 felt as if it was a live two-hundred-volt wire, and he dropped it with a scream. '*Who the hell are you?*' Zuwayy shouted, half in pain, half in sheer terror.

The strange figure said nothing. Zuwayy was about to repeat

his demand when the figure responded in an electronically synthesized voice, 'I am called Castor, Zuwayy. I am the instrument of your death.' Zuwayy was surprised to hear the electronic voice speaking Arabic.

'You can't kill me. I am the king of united Libya. This is my country, and we are standing on holy ground.'

A bolt of electricity made Zuwayy stagger to his knees. The figure stepped forward. 'You are no king, and this is not your country. You are an impostor and a murderer. Judgment has been passed. You are found guilty of murder. Your sentence is death. It shall be carried out immediately.'

Mekkawi trotted through the escape tunnel, through the storage room, and into his security office. One of his officers, alerted earlier, already had the joint operations command center in Tripoli on the line. While Mekkawi was talking to the senior controller, receiving a force status report and issuing Zuwayy's orders, the duty officer received a radio message: 'Sir, the king's helicopters have been shot down!'

'My God . . . ,' he gasped. He thought quickly. Zuwayy was in grave danger – it could be a matter of minutes before the area was invaded – or destroyed. 'I want the best helicopter available, any kind, fueled and ready to fly as soon as we arrive on the flight line!' Mekkawi shouted. 'And I want an armored personnel carrier brought around to take the king to the base. Hurry!' He turned back to the secure telephone: 'You heard me, Major. The king has ordered that all Area A targets be attacked immediately if there is any indication that a general attack is under way. . . Yes, with all available rocket and air forces designated to strike Area A targets, including special-weapons forces. He has also ordered that sorties be generated immediately for follow-on attacks on Area B targets on his command . . . yes, stand by for authentication.' Mekkawi pulled out a decoding document from a chain around his neck, quickly computed the code using the formula plus the current date and time, then read it to the senior controller. 'I also want . . .'

'Sir!'

'What the hell is it? I'm on the line to headquarters.'

'Look!'

Mekkawi turned to a bank of security monitors.

'The security camera to the rectory in the mosque – it is off!'

'*What*?' Mekkawi grabbed the phone, but it was dead. He dropped the phone and drew his side arm. 'Have all available palace security forces converge on the mosque and cover all exits, and I mean *now*!'

'Muck, it's me,' Hal Briggs radioed via their secure command channel. 'We're waiting for you at the exfil point. Check your datalink, brother. We're showing lots of troops on the move, heading your way. Bug out immediately!'

'Roger,' Patrick replied. It was too late, Patrick realized. The plan was to kidnap Zuwayy and hold him until all the prisoners were set free – unfortunately, it didn't look as if he'd be able to get him out of Jaghbub. 'I want Plan B set in motion, Hal. T minus two minutes.'

'You haven't got two minutes, Muck.'

'Two minutes,' Patrick said, and he terminated the connection.

'*You can't kill me!*' Zuwayy screamed, half out of terror but hoping someone outside would hear him. 'What have I done to you?'

In response, Patrick picked Zuwayy up, carried him outside, then jet-jumped up to the roof of the rectory, beside the green dome of the Great Mosque. Patrick held Zuwayy up by his bed-clothes in one hand, turning him so he faced west, toward the military base.

It was a spectacular sight. Over and over again, strings of explosions rippled across the ground as the Wolverine cluster bomb attacks continued. Antiaircraft artillery fire continued, with tracers streaking across the sky like incandescent snakes. Occasionally there was a large secondary explosion as the last of the Wolverine missiles suicide-dived into their last targets. Burning tanks, trucks, and buildings lit the night sky everywhere, like dozens of camp fires. Men were shouting, calling out, screaming and firing in confusion.

'Sixty seconds, Muck,' Briggs radioed.

Patrick glanced to the northwest, following the datalink-generated cues displayed in his electronic visor. The Sky Masters EB-52 was right on time, coming in at medium altitude – now that the Wolverines had destroyed all of the area defenses, it could climb higher to stay away from the surviving optically guided antiaircraft artillery units still operating.

'I am going to destroy your military base, Zuwayy,' Patrick said in his computer-synthesized voice. A microphone was picking up Zuwayy's voice, broadcasting it via satellite back to Mersa Matrûh, where it was instantly translated by computer; Patrick's voice was similarly translated from English to Arabic the same way. 'You will watch it all burn. And then I am going to destroy you.'

'Whoever you are, I have powerful friends, and I have money,' Zuwayy said. 'Spare my life, and I'll pay you. Ten million dollars. A hundred million dollars. You don't have to kill me. We can make a deal.'

This last statement intrigued Patrick. 'Who are your friends?'

'Powerful international arms merchants and black marketers,' Zuwayy said. 'Let me go and I'll tell you everything.'

'Talk or you die.'

'Thirty seconds, Patrick. You've got heavy armored vehicles on their way to you. Best way out is to the east. Move it.'

'Talk!' Patrick shouted. 'This is your last chance.'

'He is a Russian,' Zuwayy shouted. 'He has access to nuclear weapons, missiles, aircraft, oil, anything you want. Just let me live and it's all yours.'

It couldn't be, Patrick thought. It was impossible. The Turks convicted him of murder and crimes against the state. He got the death penalty – and in Turkey, there was no appeal process. He was supposed to have been executed months ago. . .

'Ten TG, Muck,' Briggs warned him. 'Find a place in the shade and hold on.'

Eight miles to the north, the EB-52 Megafortress opened the aft portion of its bomb bay doors, and one by one four bombs dropped from a rotary launcher exactly twelve seconds apart. These were GBU-28F JDAMs, or joint direct attack munitions – two-thousand-pound gravity bombs guided by satellite navigation signals that could glide as far as ten miles and still hit their targets with great accuracy. But instead of simple high-explosive warheads, these bombs were fuel-air explosives – the most devastating non-nuclear weapon devised. At a precise altitude above the ground, the bombs split open, releasing a large cloud of vapor.

197

The vapor mixed with oxygen in the air to form a highly explosive gas. At the right moment, three small incendiary bomblets ejected into the gas cloud were ignited.

The resulting explosion of each JDAM was equivalent to a hundred tons of TNT, creating a fireball a half-mile in diameter and a shock wave that crushed everything above ground for a mile in every direction. Spaced exactly two miles apart, the four fuel-air explosive bombs created a blinding wall of fire over the Jaghbub airfield. Detonated on the mostly uninhabited west side of the airfield, the fireballs themselves did relatively little damage – but the tremendous overpressure caused by the explosion overturned vehicles, blew out windows, burned wooden buildings, and scorched the sand black all across the reservation, right to the walls of the Green Palace and the Great Mosque where Patrick stood with his captive.

Zuwayy screamed as the huge wall of fire blossomed out toward him, but his screams were drowned out by the roar of rushing fire and burning air. The overpressure that roiled over them was like a one-second superhurricane, tossing Zuwayy around like a puppet. Patrick kept him facing into the rushing wall of sand and red-hot wind until the air, now needing to fill in the vacuum created by the burnt air near the fireballs, reversed direction and rushed back outward.

Patrick jumped down off the roof of the rectory, went back inside, and tossed Zuwayy on the floor. All of Zuwayy's hair on his face, head, and the back of his hands had burnt off, replaced by a beard and hair made of gray ash. He found a pitcher of water on the desk and dumped it on Zuwayy's face to keep him from passing out. 'Can you hear me, Zuwayy?' Patrick asked. Zuwayy was trembling so hard that Patrick thought he might be having a seizure. 'Answer me, you coward! Can you hear me?'

'Yes . . . yes, I can hear you,' Zuwayy cried. 'Don't kill me, please, don't kill me!'

'You have one chance to live, Zuwayy,' Patrick said in Arabic. 'You captured some prisoners off some vessels your military forces sank . . .'

'I know nothing of this! What are you accusing me of? This is not –'

Patrick silenced him with another shot of electricity. 'Be quiet,

Zuwayy. There is no doubt that your forces attacked those vessels – the only question now is whether or not you will die for doing so.'

'Do not kill me! Do not kill me!' Zuwayy bleated. 'What do you want? Tell me!'

'You will turn them over to the Egyptians immediately,' Patrick said. 'If they are not delivered within twelve hours, I will hunt you down and execute you before the entire world. And if any of them are harmed in any way, I will find you and crush you like an insect.' The stranger hammered the desk in the rectory with a gloved fist, and the heavy cedar-and-burl desktop smashed into pieces as if a wrecking ball was dropped on it. 'I will burn your houses, destroy your bunkers, tap into your computer systems, and wipe out everything you own. Twelve hours. I'll be waiting. If they are not returned, you die.' To punctuate his order, Patrick reached down, took Zuwayy's nose between two fingers, and crushed it. Blood spurted everywhere, and Zuwayy howled in pain. The figure departed through the door to the mosque itself.

Moments later, Mekkawi returned through the secret tunnel entrance, his side arm in his hands, followed by three heavily armed soldiers. 'Highness, there have been more attacks. I have relayed your orders –' He stopped in sheer horror when he saw Zuwayy lying on the floor, his hair burnt off, blood covering his face and chest. *'My God, what happened!'* He was going to call for the outside guards, but then he saw them, lying on the ground, still twitching from the voltage discharging through their bodies.

'Find out . . . find out . . .'

'Find out what, Highness?'

'Find out where the prisoners that were captured off the vessels sunk in the Mediterranean are,' Zuwayy gasped, blood flowing from his mouth and shattered nose. 'Find them all, alive or dead; round them up, and get them ready to move out of the country. Truck them . . . no, bus them . . . no, fly them . . . oh hell, *just get them out of my country immediately!* I don't want one hair on their heads touched. Contact that peacock Khan in Egypt and tell him to get ready to pick up those prisoners.'

'Prisoners? Khan? Who did this to you, sir . . . ?'

'Just do it,' Zuwayy cried, spitting blood. Mekkawi helped him up. 'Do it *now*!' Zuwayy found a liquor bottle, poured, and downed a glass, his hands shaking uncontrollably.

Akranes, Iceland
a short time later

'What in hell is going on out there, Zuwayy?' Pavel Kazakov asked angrily on the secure phone. This time, Kazakov put the call on the speakerphone, so his aide Ivana Vasilyeva could hear how the great 'king' of Libya bleated and whined like a sheep being led to slaughter. Kazakov knew how Vasilyeva, a former commando and trained intelligence officer in the Russian army, hated weak men – Jadallah Zuwayy, the man who claimed to be a descendant of Arab kings, would infuriate her. 'Why are you calling me now?'

'Hey, Kazakov, this was your idea to begin with!' Jadallah Zuwayy retorted. 'This is *your* fault!'

'*My* fault?'

'It was your suggestion to retaliate against the commandos that attacked Samāh,' Zuwayy said. 'That's what I did. They somehow found out where I was, broke into my sanctuary, and threatened to kill me! He smashed my nose! He threatened to kill me, my entire family, break into my computers, and destroy my military bases.'

'They sound like extremely powerful, efficient, and well-informed commandos,' Kazakov commented dryly. I could use an entire battalion of them, he said to himself. Something that Zuwayy said nagged at his brain . . . 'Or your soldiers need more security training.'

'How could he have found out where I was? That information is top secret!'

'Zuwayy, the entire world knows about your pleasure palace in Jaghbub,' Kazakov said. 'They know that it is the entrance to your escape route if there is ever a coup against you; they know it is where you bring young girls for whatever perverted pleasure you get out of screwing children. Besides, Jaghbub is less than forty kilometers from the Egyptian border – any good special-operations team can get in and out of the area in mere hours. You ought to try a security back-trace on yourself some time,

200

Zuwayy – you might be surprised to learn some of the things anyone can find out about you if they tried.'

'This is outrageous!'

'Just shut up, Zuwayy,' Kazakov said. 'Nothing has changed. You should have just killed all those captives, then set a trap for those commandos when they returned to finish you off. You should never have turned them over to the Egyptians. At least you had the brains to turn them over to Khan and not to Salaam.'

'That commando said he was going to kill me if I didn't turn them over to the Egyptians,' Zuwayy said. 'He got into the sanctuary so easy, I didn't –'

'Hold it,' Kazakov interrupted him. 'You said, "that commando." Do you mean to say there was *only one commando*?'

'I told you there was only one!'

'But you said a minefield and your military base were also hit.'

'They were, but only one commando got into my sanctuary,' Zuwayy said. 'He neutralized the guards and was waiting for me when I –'

'He "neutralized" the guards? How? Did he kill them?'

'No. He had no weapons – he didn't even touch them.'

Kazakov nearly choked on the cognac he was sipping. He rose slowly to his feet, his throat suddenly dry, his ears ringing. It couldn't be, he thought wildly. No, it *couldn't* be . . . !

'Did you hear me, Kazakov?'

'This commando – he was wearing a black outfit, a full helmet with large eyeholes, and a slim backpack? Did he paralyze you with an electric shock that traveled from electrodes on his shoulders to you, without projectiles or wires?'

'Yes! How did you know?'

'Because I have been hunting him and his team down for the past year,' Kazakov said. 'These commandos are Americans. I do not believe they are government operatives – I believe they are privately organized. They fund their organization by shaking down their targets for money or weapons.'

'How do you know so much about them?' Kazakov was about to tell him not to ask stupid questions, but Zuwayy came up with the answer by himself moments later: 'So you've encountered this group before, eh? Perhaps they are the reason you were captured and brought to trial in The Hague?'

201

'Zuwayy . . .'

'And perhaps this private organization got part of its funding from you, eh, *tovarisch*?' Zuwayy asked, laughing. '*On dal yimu pa pizde mishalkay*? Did you get your ass handed to you by them? Now that I think about it, he did seem to know about you.'

'Listen to me, you ignorant goat-fucker,' Kazakov snarled, 'you can make fun of me all you want, but if we don't stop these commandos, they'll destroy all of us. You were lucky they just broke your nose and blew up your base – they could have just as easily carried you out of Libya and destroyed your whole fucking capital!'

'What are you going to do, Kazakov?'

'I am going to find those Americans,' Kazakov said, 'and I'm going to capture them somehow. I'll learn all the secrets about who they are and all the secrets about their weapons and technology – and then I'm going to roast each and every one of them on a spit in my living-room fireplace.' He paused for a long time, turning the few details he knew over and over and over again in his mind; then 'First your missile base at Samāh is attacked by an obviously high-tech force; then, your armed residence at Jaghbub is attacked by an equally effective high-tech force. The commando asks that all the detainees from your attack out in the Mediterranean Sea be released. That means that the same commandos were involved in both the attack on Samāh and Jaghbub – and that you probably had some of their comrades in custody.'

'Obviously. *Na huya eta mn'e nuzhna*? So what?'

'You idiot – you might have had the men that attacked your base,' Kazakov said. 'I want details, Zuwayy. I want to know everything you know about these attacks, both on Samāh and Jaghbub, and I want to know everything your military forces learned before, during, and after you attacked those vessels out in the Mediterranean Sea.'

'I can tell you almost everything,' Zuwayy said. 'Especially the last part – the part of the incident where some of our planes were shot down.'

'Some Libyan attack planes . . . *shot down*? By whom?'

'By the men firing missiles from one of the ships.'

'*Firing missiles!* And you've been sitting on this information all this time! Which ship, damn you?'

'The Lithuanian salvage ship,' Zuwayy said. 'We recovered eleven men and one woman from the water.'

'It was them. I know it,' Kazakov said. 'They invaded your country to force you to release those prisoners.'

'I will blast them to hell,' Zuwayy said. 'Khan thinks he has them surrounded. I will –'

'What did you say, Zuwayy?' Kazakov thundered. '*What did you say?*'

'I received a call from Ulama Khalid al-Khan, the chief justice of the Egyptian Supreme Judiciary,' Zuwayy said. 'He claims that Susan Salaam and General Ahmad Baris aided and abetted a group of soldiers believed to be American comm—' He stopped, his throat completely dry, as he finally made the connection in his head. 'Oh, my God . . .'

'You knew this?' Kazakov screamed into the phone. 'You knew those commandos were on that base?'

'*I have been attacked!*' Zuwayy shouted, not quite knowing what else to say. 'I didn't know these were the men you sought. I didn't realize –'

'Are those commandos still in Egypt?' Kazakov interjected.

'I believe Khan is holding them at Mersa Matrûh.'

'Tell him not to let them leave under any circumstances,' Kazakov said. 'They must stay in Mersa Matrûh. Tell Khan that you will deliver the prisoners there – that should keep the commandos in place. And you will detain all of those prisoners that have the slightest appearance of being Americans. Do not send them along with the others.'

'And then what do we do?'

'This is what you will do, Zuwayy,' Kazakov said. 'You will do exactly as I tell you to do, and you had better not slip up, or I will see to it that a lot more than your damned nose is smashed.'

'You will not speak to me this way!' Zuwayy shouted. 'I am the king of united Libya –!'

'Zuwayy, the quicker you get that fiction out of your head, the better we will all be,' Kazakov interjected. 'You are nothing but a second-rate army officer who deceived, murdered, and bribed your way into the presidential palace. It was a brilliant scheme

– until you actually started to believe the shit you were feeding your fellow Libyans. Now, you are nothing. Even Qadhafi had a better reputation than you do right now – before you had your men put a bullet in his eye and string him up from the flagpole in broad daylight. You had him and his family pleading for their lives on your living room floor, and you still didn't have the guts to pull the trigger yourself.

'Now, I will tell you what to do, and by God you had better do this mission right this time, or I'll see to it that you end up like your so-called "ancestors" – your bones will be tossed out into the desert as vulture food.' Kazakov outlined the targets he wanted struck and the way he wanted it done. Afterward, the line went dead.

Pavel Kazakov nearly turned over his entire desk in sheer fury. 'That incompetent ass!' he shouted. 'I want him, dead, dead, *dead*! I want his friends dead, his mistresses dead, and I want it public, messy, and I want it done *now*!'

Ivana Vasilyeva appeared – again – as if she was going to have another orgasm. She was a good aide and a fierce lover, Kazakov thought, but how could anyone with the kind of psychosexual dysfunctions that she had rise so far in the Russian army?

'Send me,' Vasilyeva breathed. 'Send me to Libya. I can get close to this peacock. I will pull his feathers for you – one by one, slowly and painfully – and then cook him for you.'

But Kazakov wasn't paying attention to Vasilyeva's psychotic panting right now – his mind was occupied with trying to figure out who was attacking Libya.

It had to be the Tin Man organization, the same ones that had destroyed his Russian oil empire, Metyorgaz, and captured him. Kazakov's sources said most likely it was a private group, not government, with access to the latest high-tech military hardware. Well, they needed access to not just a few guns and futuristic body armor with jets in the boots to destroy two Libyan military bases – they needed access to large precision-guided bombs and the heavy, long-range aircraft to deliver them.

Mersa Matrûh was the key. Zuwayy suspected they might be operating from there – if they were, he could track them down, follow them, and find a way to destroy them.

'Yes . . . yes, I think you would do very nicely,' Kazakov said to Vasilyeva. 'You shall leave immediately.' But finally her orgasmic rush was too much for him to bear, and he reached out for her hard, sexy body. 'Well,' he said with a smile as she began to unbutton her blouse, 'perhaps not *immediately*.'

Chapter Five

Mersa Matrûh Joint Military Base, Egypt
a few hours later

Patrick McLanahan stared blankly at the computer image, flipping back and forth through stills of several FlightHawk overhead photographs downloaded from the latest surveillance flights. He was sitting in a small, un-air-conditioned but secure little semi-underground building in an isolated part of the Egyptian military base set aside for them by General Baris. Their facilities were spartan, but they had access to Egyptian communications and intelligence information via computer, also courtesy of Baris.

Since returning from his infiltration at Jaghbub, Patrick had been reviewing each and every minute of aerial reconnaissance from the stealthy unmanned reconnaissance aircraft flying over Libya. The strain was definitely showing. Patrick didn't know if he was eventually just going to totally collapse or end up throwing the computer against a wall in disgust. But he felt that the conflict was drawing to an end. Zuwayy *had* to release the prisoners now . . . he *had* to.

'Hey, man,' Hal Briggs said softly, 'let me and the sergeant take a look through those images. You go take a nap.' Patrick ignored him. 'You hearing me okay, Muck?'

'I heard you,' Patrick said, rubbing his eyes wearily. 'But I want to go over the last batch of images, the ones of daybreak over that Libyan naval base where Wendy was probably taken . . .'

'There's at least three bases she could have been taken to in the past twelve hours, Muck,' Briggs pointed out. 'Or she could still be on one of the ships.' Left unsaid was the other obvious possibility – Wendy was not in Libyan custody at all. 'We've got trained guys waiting to look at those pictures. Why not let them do their jobs?'

'I gave them a job to do – plan a nighttime infiltration of those three military medical facilities,' Patrick said irritably. 'But we need to target the most likely one, because once we go in, the Libyans will be alerted.' He looked angrily at Hal and added, 'And I asked you to check on the aircraft and the weapons, Hal.'

'The sergeant is on it,' Briggs responded. 'But he asked me to talk to you . . .'

'I'm not stopping this, Hal,' Patrick said, his irritation quickly growing into anger. 'We've got eight hours until sunset. We need a target in that amount of time so we have enough time to brief the infiltration, extraction, and exfiltration, then launch and –'

'Obviously the entire Libyan armed forces are on full alert.'

'I know that, Hal.'

'If you did, Muck, you'd be suspending plans to go in until the situation stabilizes,' Hal said seriously. 'C'mon, man, think about it.'

'Hal, just do what I ask you to do, all right? Get the team and the aircraft ready to go.'

Briggs finally relented – arguing with him was not doing any good. 'All right, Patrick, we'll press on – for now.' He ignored Patrick's warning glare. 'But listen to me, man – it won't do anyone any good if you're dead on your feet. Take sixty minutes, Muck. Get some rest. I'll look at the imagery myself, and I'll have one of the guys double-check it. If there's any evidence that Wendy was taken to any of those facilities, we'll plan an entry to take a look. You might be overlooking something if you're too tired to check each image carefully.'

'I'm not too tired, Hal,' Patrick told him. But he again rubbed his eyes wearily, and he found he had to fight to keep them open. He nodded and got to his feet. 'Okay, buddy. I'll go take a nap. Wake me if you find anything.'

'Just get some rest. We'll handle everything.'

Patrick, David, and Hal shared a room right beside the mission planning room, but this was the first time Patrick had been there since the Egyptian military made room for them. Someone had laid out his gear on a small shelf beside the bed, and Patrick found himself eager to shave, brush his teeth, and scrub his body for the first time in what seemed like weeks. After he was done, he felt a hundred percent better. He told himself to be sure to take at least five minutes out to do this every day – it wouldn't look good for the other team members to see the team leader looking like crap. It was a quick and simple thing to do, but it –

And that's when he noticed Paul's gear, stacked in the corner of the room – a lone green duffel bag with a yellow tag on the canvas handles that read, 'P. McL.' – Paul McLanahan.

Dammit, Paul, why were you here? Why are any of us here? Just to fight a battle for some oil executives? Was it worth the pain, the suffering, and the death? Who would understand? Anyone? No one?

His head was a jumble of thoughts and emotions, all fighting for attention, analysis. But somehow, through it all, a woman's voice told him to lie still, to put all violent thoughts out of his head. There would be plenty of time for planning the next battle, the voice said – now was the time for sleep. Rest was as much a part of fighting a war as the bomb run, the voice wisely said, and she was right.

Patrick didn't know how long he had been asleep, but he awoke gently and felt completely rested. He felt as if he could take on the entire world. The room was quiet, and even the adjacent planning rooms had only routine noises. There were things to do, he thought, and now he felt as if he could do them. He opened his eyes . . .

. . . and found Susan Bailey Salaam sitting on the bed beside him. She smiled at him, her eyes sparkling, her hair shimmering in the dim light. Patrick immediately sat up. Susan placed a hand on his chest as if to tell him to stay put, but he got up anyway. 'Mrs Salaam, what are you doing here?'

'She's been here for the last hour and a half, Muck,' David Luger said. He was standing casually in the doorway of their room, but with a look of concern on his face.

'An hour and a half?' Patrick asked incredulously. He could scarcely believe he could sleep that long with everything that was going on. 'Everything all right?'

'Mrs Salaam wants to talk with you,' Luger said. 'I'll be in the command post.' He turned and departed, but not before giving Susan an inquisitive, concerned look.

'Your officers have been standing guard over us the entire time,' Susan said to Patrick. 'They are very loyal to you.'

'You should have waited outside.'

'You looked restless. I thought I could help.'

'That was your voice I heard?'

Susan nodded. 'Feeling better?'

'Yes.' He sat up and swung his legs around to the floor, expecting her to stand to let him get up. But she didn't move, and he found himself face-to-face with her. She glanced at his lips invitingly, looked deeply into his eyes, then averted her eyes and let them roam across his broad chest and thick shoulders. The only sport Patrick ever excelled at was weight lifting, a sport that was solitary, much like the man himself. He had been doing it for many years, and it showed. He lingered there for a moment, trying to decide what she was doing, then got up and pulled a clean T-shirt from his duffel bag and pulled it on. 'Let's go outside to the command center where we can talk, Susan.'

'I need to talk with you in private first,' she said. He nodded, deciding to stand right there, but after a short, awkward silence, he returned and sat beside her on the bed. 'I spoke with your officers outside while I was waiting. I still don't know Taurus's real name; it's obvious you and Mr Luger are very close.' Patrick did not respond. 'I gave them the very latest information we have on both the Libyan naval vessels that searched the site where your ship was sunk.'

'Thank you. I'm sure it'll all be very useful.'

'Judging by the information they requested and the information they reviewed after I arrived, I'd guess you were planning a soft probe on either the Tobruk joint operations center or the Darnah naval base,' Susan said.

'I must be sure to remind my team members that you used to be an intelligence officer,' Patrick said with a wry smile.

'And you have obviously been trained to not offer any information to anyone, even in casual conversation.'

'We're eight thousand miles from home, at a strange military base – there's nothing casual about this situation.'

'Are you ever going to trust me, Patrick?' Susan asked.

'Would it upset you if I said "no"?'

'Yes, it would,' Susan replied. It was obvious to her that he didn't care if it upset her or not. She paused for a moment, then said, 'Going in to either Darnah or Tobruk even in normal day-to-day circumstances would be very, very dangerous. Both bases are massively armed fortresses, especially for Anglos but even for Arabs. But our intelligence information tells us both bases are at the absolute highest readiness stages, just short of all-out wartime conditions. I strongly advise you not to plan to go in there unless you have your target – I'm sorry, I should say, your *wife* – located first. Or unless you have some massive firepower lining up behind you to support a soft probe that could turn hot in a matter of moments.'

Her inquisitive eyes told Patrick she was still fishing for information – he was glad for the rest, because he needed to stay sharp to avoid giving this beautiful, captivating, disarming woman any good intelligence data. 'I know that, Susan,' Patrick said. 'But I'm counting on the combat operations to help screen our movements in a soft probe. You know as well as I do that security measures sometimes get curtailed when moving men and equipment is the most important thing.'

'It's risky.'

'She's worth the risk.'

'I didn't mean to imply she wasn't,' Susan said. 'But if you're discovered, even if you can fight your way out, your entire operation is finished – they will kill your wife and erect an impenetrable wall around every military and government base, building, or office. All you will have left . . . is retribution. Will that be enough for you?'

'I don't intend to let that happen.'

'With all due respect, Patrick, that's a pretty bad attitude,' Susan said directly. 'Think about it for a moment. What if you did nothing? What if you did no probe at all, so your team never risked discovery? Your wife is probably in a Libyan medical facility badly injured, probably unconscious and unable to speak, so they will wait until she regains consciousness, which means you still have time to plan, locate her precisely, and wait for the perfect opportunity.

'If she is conscious, they may try to interrogate her. That could take days, perhaps weeks. If she talks, they will keep her alive to extract every bit of information from her. That still gives you time.'

For the first time, Patrick reconsidered his plan. Susan was absolutely correct: There was nothing to be gained by going in now. War could break out any moment between Libya and Egypt, or just about anywhere in northern Africa, and Patrick and his team would be right in the middle of it.

But holding back and waiting would put him no closer to rescuing Wendy. It didn't matter what Libya was planning against Egypt, or if war would break out any time – for him, the most important thing was finding and rescuing Wendy.

'Thank you for your advice, Susan,' Patrick said. 'I'll take it into serious consideration.'

Susan Bailey stood, stepped toward Patrick, and touched his shoulder. 'What has happened to you, your wife, and your men is already a horrible tragedy,' she said, 'but please don't compound the tragedy by launching off on an impossible mission against overwhelming odds for an objective that you cannot define.'

Patrick nodded, then opened up the door. 'Dave.' Luger appeared within seconds – obviously he was standing very close by. 'Please escort Mrs Salaam outside.'

Susan looked into Patrick's eyes once more, but his deep-blue eyes were even more dark and inscrutable than before – he might as well have been wearing the strange high-tech helmet right now. She left without another word.

Patrick put on his flight suit and flying boots and went into the command center, where he met up with Hal Briggs. 'Glad you got some shut-eye, Muck,' he said. He motioned to a stack of CD-ROM disks inside an open metal briefcase. 'Mrs Salaam brought over tons of intel for us – some of it's only a few hours old. I doubt if even the US government has this data.' He looked at Patrick closely. His longtime friend was staring at the doorway where Susan Salaam had just exited. 'What'd she have to say, Patrick?'

'Same as you – don't try going into Libya.'

'Well, then I'll give her credit for more than being a drop-dead stone fox,' Briggs quipped. 'What are you going to do?'

Patrick picked up a few of the CD-ROMs and looked at their index labels. He chose a couple of them and headed for the portable computer terminals. 'I'm going to do a little target study,' he said.

'What does she want with us, Muck?' Hal asked.

'Same thing that the Central African Petroleum Partners want – to fight and die for them,' Patrick replied. 'I don't know if she wants revenge for her husband's assassination, or something else – but I've got my own agenda first.'

'It appears that Zuwayy has ignored our warning,' Patrick McLanahan said grimly as he began the briefing a few hours later, 'so we're going to put the strike plans in motion in about two hours.'

His entire group of Night Stalkers were inside the semi-underground bunker reserved for them by Susan Bailey Salaam and General Baris, south of the airfield in an isolated part of the sprawling Egyptian joint forces base. Patrick was wearing his battle armor with the helmet on the table nearby, the power pack and electromagnetic rail gun plugged in and ready to go in just a few moments. He was definitely ready for battle.

'The primary target area will be the command-and-control center at Benina, ten miles east of Benghazi,' Patrick went on. 'It is located at a Libyan air force base, with a large mix of Russian and French fighters and transports based there, plus antiaircraft systems of all sizes. Our target is the air operations center.' He displayed a high-resolution image of the air base, with one building outlined with a red triangle. 'This building is the headquarters of Libyan air combat operations in the eastern half of the country, and it is also an alternate national military command center. It forms the junction of all communications from the eastern half of the country to Tripoli.

'The attack will commence with a flight of three Wolverine cruise missiles, launched from over the Med,' Patrick continued. 'They will spread out and perform a coordinated multiaxis attack on the air defenses north of the city of Benina. Each Wolverine will attack three air defense sites with cluster munitions, followed by "suicide" attacks on the air traffic control radar site, the northern security headquarters here, and the southern security headquarters, here.

'The main attack will follow thirty seconds later – a flight of three more Wolverine cruise missiles. They will use a flight path cleared for them by the preceding Wolverine suppression attacks, but they will be programmed to divert if necessary to avoid any air defense sites missed or pop-up threats not targeted by the first flight.' He switched slides to a close-up of a small cluster of buildings on the northeast side of the large two-runway airfield. 'This is the Benina Command Center, headquarters of Libya's Eastern Joint Operations Center and Eastern Air Defense Sector. The heart of the facility is two stories underground, protected by twelve-inch reinforced concrete on each floor.

'Each Wolverine will carry two different warheads: a deep-target penetrating warhead using a rocket-propelled one-thousand-pound warhead, followed by a one-thousand-pound thermium nitrate high-explosive warhead. Each Wolverine will travel a different flight path but will be programmed to hit the same spot; each missile will perform a pop-up push-over maneuver to drive the first warhead down through the roof to the subfloors, followed by the thermium detonation. The weapons should have no problems going through each level to the command center level, even if they put armor in we don't know about.

'As you know, the thermium warhead has the explosive power of five tons of TNT,' Patrick went on, 'so if the FlightHawk can determine if the target has been destroyed, we may divert the other Wolverines, probably the third one, to a secondary target, which is the military communications facility at Benina. If we need a tertiary target, we'll switch to the combination petroleum-fired power plant and desalination plant just east of Benghazi – that should turn out the lights and shut off the taps in Benghazi for quite some time.'

Patrick displayed another map, this one of northwestern Egypt. Hal Briggs noted that Patrick's briefing was cool, calm, professional, and well under control. He had seen Patrick give countless reports and briefings over the fourteen years he had known him, and despite everything that had happened to him and everything they were facing now, he seemed like the same emotionless all-business guy he'd always known. Yet in a way, this mission was much different: Although Patrick planned this mission as a strike against a very-high-value military target, Hal reminded himself, it was still a *punitive* strike – Patrick was simply lashing out at the Libyans. That was not like him at all.

'We'll position ourselves at three principal border crossings in western Egypt – Salûm, Arasiyah, and Shiyah,' Patrick went on.

216

'We'll have Egyptian Mi-8 and Chinook CH-47 helicopters with us, enough to take at least fifty survivors with us, along with Egyptian security forces and some of our own commandos. In case the prisoners are turned over after the attacks commence, we'll be ready to take them or go in and rescue them if the Libyans have a change of heart. If the prisoners show up any-where along the border, the other helicopters can respond to help. Questions?'

The telephone in the briefing room rang; all heads turned, because they knew that the Charge of Quarters would not allow any calls through during a briefing unless it was absolutely urgent. David Luger picked it up immediately; he listened, then snapped his fingers at the television set bolted in one corner of the room. 'CQ says turn on the TV right now,' Luger said.

Patrick couldn't believe his eyes. There, on Egyptian national TV, was Ulama Khalid al-Khan, giving a press conference. The caption at the bottom of the screen, written in both Arabic and English, read 'LIBYAN PRISONERS RELEASED TO EGYPT.'

'The men were rescued from the Mediterranean Sea by the Libyan Navy,' Khan was saying, replying to a reporter's question. 'I have no details as to why or how their ships were sunk. The Libyan government detained the survivors until their identities could be verified – apparently there were some survivors whose identities or even their nationalities could not be verified, so it took longer than usual. But once all of the survivors were iden-tified and questioned on the incident, King Idris of the United Kingdom of Libya ordered their release. He requested that I assist in providing transportation and medical care for the survivors, and I immediately agreed. He asked me to assist in processing the survivors and seeing to their care and repatriation.

'Yes, there are casualties,' Khan said, replying to another ques-tion. 'Several dozen men were fatally injured in the incident. In addition, several men were injured while being detained by the kingdom of Libya, apparently because they refused both to reveal their identities and also to cooperate with Libyan authorities. They were suspected of engineering the attacks on friendly, neutral shipping in the Mediterranean. When they resisted while in deten-tion, they were dealt with harshly, as any detainee who lashes out at his rescuers deserves.'

'Yeah? Let's have a look at some of those "resisters,"' Hal Briggs scoffed. 'I'll bet the Libyans tortured the hell out of them.' He saw Chris Wohl glaring at him disapprovingly – it wasn't until then that he realized with horrified embarrassment that Wendy and some of the Night Stalkers might be some of the ones killed while in captivity. He looked at Patrick with a silent apology, but Patrick's attention was riveted on the television.

'Despite the unfortunate loss of life, the incident is now at an end, thanks to the king of United Libya,' Khan went on. 'The prisoners will be taken to a location where they will receive medical care and then released. This spirit of cooperation between Libya and Egypt also paves the way for further talks between our two countries in other matters, such as the cessation of attacks against suspected terrorist training centers in southern Egypt and Chad, and the resumption of talks aimed at bringing more coop- eration in planning mutual petroleum production contracts.'

The interoffice phone rang again, and Luger answered it right away again. This time, he looked panicked as he slammed the phone down. 'The Egyptian base commander, Vice Marshal Ouda, is outside the compound with a force about the size of an armored company. He wants to talk with you upstairs, on the liaison freq.'

Patrick donned his helmet, unplugged his fully charged battle armor, and went upstairs to the front of their half-underground concrete facility. From the topmost security room, Patrick could look outside without being seen. There was a twelve-foot-high fence surrounding their building, topped with razor wire, about fifty feet away. The military district commander's armored vehicle and several dozen light tanks and heavy armored personnel car- riers were stationed outside the gate, weapons trained inside. More tanks and armored vehicles were spread out all along the perimeter – the Night Stalkers were suddenly sealed up tight.

'Dave, we got trouble,' Patrick radioed to Luger. 'We got a company of armor outside the fence. They're not coming through the fence, but they've got us surrounded pretty well.'

'I can have a FlightHawk and a couple Wolverines with SFWs overhead in about four hours,' Luger said. 'We'll have to repro- gram the weapons from the Benina strike, but that'll only take a few minutes.'

Patrick thought quickly; then: 'Find a safe orbit area for the

Megafortress and the tanker,' Patrick said, 'and have them stand by as long as possible. We're just hours away from getting our guys back – I don't want to do anything to piss off the Egyptians now. But I want the strike aircraft available in case we have any trouble getting our folks out.'

'We've only got one refueling aircraft available,' Luger reminded him, 'and it's been on the go for two days straight. If we send the Megafortresses into holding orbits, that means less fuel for the strike package, less fuel reserves for the tanker, and more flying hours. Those guys will be wiped.'

'That can't be helped,' Patrick said. 'We've got to fly those planes hard until our guys are rescued. The tankers will just have to keep cycling as best they can. Contact Martindale and see if he can get us some more tanker support.'

'Okay,' David said. 'Remember, we have that escape tunnel we found as a backup.' In the first few hours after occupying the bunker, which was an old security outpost protecting the southern part of the base, the Night Stalkers found an emergency escape tunnel, which ran several hundred meters west. 'I'll send some guys out to check to see if Ouda is covering it.'

'Roger,' Patrick said. 'Cancel the strike meeting and have everyone get ready to bug out – we might have to move in a hurry.' He switched to the Egyptian liaison radio frequency: 'Vice Marshal Ouda, this is Castor,' he said in his battle armor's radio. His battle armor's communications computer made the translation from English to Arabic and back again for him. 'We have heard about the prisoner exchange between Libya and Egypt. We will not interfere. Once our men are returned to us, we will depart.'

'The prisoner exchange will take place tomorrow morning,' Ouda said via the computer datalink translation. 'You are to stay here. No one will be allowed to leave this compound.'

'Where will the prisoners be taken?'

'Here, by bus,' Ouda replied. 'They will be in-processed, identified, examined by doctors, and questioned first. Then the Egyptian government will contact representatives from the various governments who will be allowed to take their citizens with them. The airfield will be available for their use if needed. The government of Egypt is doing everything we can to facilitate this exchange – we do not want you or your men to interfere.'

'We will not interfere,' Patrick said. 'I request permission to allow one of my men to accompany the foreign government representatives to see the prisoners.'

'Denied,' Ouda said quickly. 'Not one of you is allowed to leave. If you try to leave, I will order my men to attack.'

'Very well. We will comply with your orders, sir. I wish to speak with Mrs Salaam or General Baris.'

'They are not available.'

Patrick could hear Ouda's real voice underneath the electronic translation, and his skin instantly tingled – there was something ominous about the way he said that. 'Very well, sir. We will stay. Please ask Mrs Salaam or General Baris to contact me immediately when they return to the base.' Ouda made no reply before the connection was broken.

Patrick returned to the briefing room downstairs. 'There's something else going on here,' he told everyone assembled there. 'I think Salaam and Baris are either dead or under arrest, and Vice Marshal Ouda sounded to me like he thought they were already dead, or soon would be.'

'Maybe part of the deal to release the captives was to eliminate Salaam and Baris,' Hal Briggs said.

'Or maybe Khan found out that she's been helping us, and he's convinced the military that they're traitors,' David Luger said.

'In any case, I think our days remaining here are down to hours – maybe only minutes,' Patrick said. Just then, Chris Wohl, in full battle armor and exoskeleton, entered the room with one of the Night Stalkers. 'Did you check the emergency tunnel and exit, Master Sergeant?'

'Yes, sir,' Wohl replied. 'No guards on the other side. The closest Egyptian forces are about two hundred meters away, facing toward the compound – we'll exit behind them. More units are inbound – I think they have another armored company almost in place.'

'It's hard for me to believe they've forgotten about that tunnel,' Hal Briggs said. 'Not guarding that exit could be a ruse. If they catch us sneaking out, it could give them an excuse to attack us.'

'They don't need an excuse,' Patrick said. 'If we've lost our patrons and if they want us, they'll go in and get us. We need to be gone by then.' To Wohl, Patrick said, 'Get your men together and evacuate the compound, Sarge.' He referred to a map on the wall of the base. 'Assemble here, at this oil well complex south; then we'll disperse and go to exfiltration points. If the oil well complex is not secure, we'll head southwest toward these oil well complexes and disperse. Avoid contact with the Egyptian military if possible, but avoid capture at all costs. Questions?'

'Are you coming with us, sir?'

'I'll stay here, just in case Ouda wants to talk – I want him to think we're still here,' Patrick said.

'How many men do you want here with you?'

'Zero,' Patrick said. 'Everyone else will depart and go to the exfiltration points.'

'I don't think that's wise, sir.'

'Chris, I think the Egyptians are no longer our friends,' Patrick said. 'I think they'll come for us first thing in the morning, when they've built up their forces to maximum. But I still don't want to get into a firefight with the Egyptians. I can stall them until you are safe.' Wohl nodded. 'Get moving.' Wohl barked an order, and the Night Stalkers got on their feet and headed out to get their gear and evacuate.

Hal Briggs and David Luger stayed behind. 'What are you thinking about, Muck?' Luger asked. 'Why stay?'

'I'm afraid that if Khan or Ouda have Wendy and the others, they'll use them to get to us,' Patrick said. 'If we bug out completely, they'll hold them hostage to get us back.'

'So you intend on staying here and getting captured?'

'It's the only thing I can think of to keep all our bases covered,' Patrick said. 'But I need you guys out so we can organize a rescue. When they realize you guys have disappeared, they'll be less likely to hurt us – they know what you can do.'

Hal Briggs shook his head. 'I sure hope you know what you're doing, Muck,' he said. He held out a hand, and Patrick shook it. 'We'll stay in touch. Keep your head down.'

'That's what I do best.'

'Since when?' Luger asked with a smile. He shook hands with his long-time partner. 'I don't want to lose another McLanahan, my friend. When it's time to get out, give us a call, and we'll come in and help get you out.'

'I'll be right behind you. Now get moving.' He and Briggs headed for the tunnel. 'Hal?'

'Yeah?'

'Set some mines on that emergency exit after you get clear,' Patrick ordered. 'If the Egyptians try to come in that way, I want it sealed.'

'You got it. Be careful.'

The Pentagon, Washington, DC
that same time

Director of Central Intelligence Douglas Morgan entered Secretary of Defense Goff's office, holding a thin imagery file marked 'CONFIDENTIAL.' He held it up, a questioning look in his eyes. 'Here's the data you asked for,' he said. 'What's up?'

'Our friends might be at it again,' Goff said, waving him to a seat. Already seated at the meeting area in front of Goff's desk was Joint Chiefs of Staff chairman General Richard Venti. 'The general has some data to show us, but he needed your latest overheads to nail it down. What did you find?'

'Satellite imagery from over North Africa,' Morgan explained. 'Infrared detectors picked up four large blasts in eastern Libya last night. They were first classified as oil derrick fires. But their location was right over a small Libyan military base called Jaghbub, mostly used as a border security outpost and a security base for one of the Libyan president's retreats – sort of Libya's answer to Camp David.'

'I'm familiar with Jaghbub, General,' Goff said. 'What happened there?'

'We got some overhead shots of the area, and analysts say there was an air strike against that base,' Morgan responded. 'Precision guided attacks against air defense sites, communications, security, and even pinpoint attacks against armor.'

'Interesting.'

'This is even more interesting – the Libyan president, Zuwayy, was there at the time.'

'Really? Did they get him?'

'Doesn't appear so,' Morgan said. 'We have been tracking

222

aircraft coming and going from there ever since the attack, and we think we tracked a helicopter convoy leave there for Tripoli shortly after the attack. Shortly thereafter, Libyan state television announced a terrorist attack on Jaghbub, accusing the Egyptians and Israelis of attacking a Muslim holy place. The reports claim Zuwayy is safe, but we haven't seen him yet. Our guess is he got out but may be injured.'

Goff shook his head, then nodded to Venti. 'Tell him what your boys found, Richard.'

'About an hour after those fires broke out,' Venti said, 'a Navy Hawkeye over the Med is tracking a flight that took off from Athens bound for Shannon, Ireland. Pretty routine stuff, except the plane's not exactly on course for Shannon – he's flying basically westbound, over the Med, instead of getting a clearance direct. But he's following his filed international flight plan, he's on time and on course – no problem. The Navy is watching him. Soon, he's slowing down – way down. He's lost about a hundred knots. We call up the guy and ask if there's a problem, and he says no, they're just doing some engine performance data checks where they have to retard throttles. It's weird, doing stuff like that over water far from home – the aircraft is based in North Las Vegas, Nevada – but it's no big deal.

'We happened to have a couple Tomcats on patrol nearby, so we vector them over and do a silent join-up on the guy to make sure he's okay. They got a picture of the plane with the F-14's telescopic FLIR.' Venti opened another briefing folder and showed it to Morgan.

It was a very fine, detailed picture of an EB-52 Megafortress bomber being refueled behind a DC-10 aircraft.

'Oh, shit,' Morgan muttered. 'Is that one of Sky Masters Inc's modified B-52s?'

'That's it,' Venti said. 'And we checked the N-number of the DC-10 – it's a Sky Masters launch aircraft also, modified for aerial refueling.' He handed Morgan another photo, this one an even more extreme close-up. 'Look under the wings.'

'Weapon pylons?'

Venti handed him a magnifying glass. 'What else do you see?'

Morgan studied the photo, then whistled. 'Missiles on rails on the sides of the pylons.' He studied another photograph, shaking his head. 'One missing on the right pylon.'

223

'Presumably expended,' Secretary Goff said perturbedly. 'Libya claims in its broadcast that some of their aircraft were shot down during the attack too.'

'Were your Navy guys able to track that bomber?'

'They lost it,' Venti said. 'When the bomber was done refueling, they must have fired up their radar again, spotted the fighters, and evaded them. We have no idea where they went. With the stealth capabilities of that aircraft, they could fly right over Washington, DC, and we'd never know it.'

'Pretty circumstantial evidence,' Morgan pointed out. 'We don't have any actual evidence that the Megafortress bombed Libya, or that the Night Stalkers had anything to do with it.'

'This isn't a court of law – yet,' Goff said angrily. 'But I don't need a warrant to search a Sky Masters installation – they're federal contractors working on classified government programs, which means we can walk in on them anytime.'

'Let me play devil's advocate,' Morgan said with a smile, 'and ask – why not let these guys do their thing? They obviously uncovered something in Libya with that attack on Samāh – Libya was definitely storing weapons of mass destruction there, and was probably getting ready to use them – and they probably uncovered something in Jaghbub, too. The US government is not in any way involved in this, and that's for real: We're not avowing any knowledge of the Night Stalkers or their activities – we're not directing them in any way, shape, or fashion. They're terrorists as far as we know, but we have no legal reason to pursue them.'

'I am not going to let a bunch of Lone Rangers fly an intercontinental bomber from American shores and bomb another country with explosives big enough to show up on a satellite as a *nuclear explosion* and let them get away with it,' Secretary Goff said angrily. 'They're going to start a war in north Africa before this is over, and I don't care how deniable they are, we're responsible if we don't try to stop them.'

'You going to run this by the boss first?'

'Sky Masters is a Department of Defense contractor – that means I'm responsible for their activities,' Goff said. 'I'm going to start my investigation, and I'm going to use all my enforcement authority to find out what they're up to. In addition, the Night

Stalkers are under federal indictment as well – if we uncover evidence that Sky Masters is aiding them, I can and I *will* shut them down.' He looked at General Venti. 'Any way we can find that bomber again?'

'We know the tanker's profile,' Venti said. 'Basically, the Night Stalkers are doing an en route air refueling rendezvous, with the tanker flying a long, slow anchor route – they're obviously very well coordinated and in constant secure contact. They'll probably stay over the Med, although they can certainly do the refueling over Europe – they'd be worried about being spotted visually. We just intercept any aircraft matching that refueling profile. It'll keep our Navy guys hopping, but I think we can do it.'

'Can you find the bomber before it links up with the tanker?'

'That'll be tougher,' Venti said. 'The Megafortress is pretty stealthy – we'd have to get in pretty close before the fighters' radar will be able to lock on, well inside the bomber's laser radar detection range. If they see us hanging around, they'll just bug out.'

'That's what I want, then,' Goff said resolutely after a few moments' thought. 'If the tanker guys are in such good contact with the bomber, they'll tell the bomber to get out as soon as we intercept the tanker. I assume McLanahan has some kind of contingency plan in place, an alternate landing location somewhere in the region – they'll have to abort their attack run and head right for it. They'll be out of the fight.'

Venti looked at Morgan quizzically, then nodded. 'I'll give the order, sir,' he said.

'I'll ask you one more time, Bob – you sure you want to chase McLanahan and his boys out of there?' Intelligence Director Morgan asked. 'They may be cowboys, but at least they're fighting on our side.'

'They're not cowboys – they're wild dogs,' Goff said. 'They need to be put away in cages.'

On the Libya-Egypt border
that same time

Traffic at the As-Sallum border crossing between Egypt and Libya was always busy, both because of the number of persons crossing

225

the border – thousands of Libyans flocked to Egypt every week on three-day visas to go shopping, buy food, enjoy Egypt's superior beach resorts, or to get better medical treatment – and because of the tight security. Even before the current conflict with Libya, Egypt maintained strict security at the border crossing – today, it was even tighter. Every vehicle was searched, every person was photographed and questioned, every truck was unloaded and thoroughly searched.

That's why it was so unusual to see an unmarked limousine, three buses, and a refrigerated truck being waved through the crossing without so much as one customs officer peeking inside.

The convoy was met by an Egyptian army escort and driven off at very high speed another two hundred kilometers east to Mersa Matrûh Joint Military Base. The vehicles were driven inside a government warehouse facility, where over a hundred soldiers, clerks, doctors, translators, and medical examiners were waiting. A military officer went on board the buses and explained to those inside what was about to happen.

One by one, the individuals on board the buses were taken off. Most were suffering from a variety of injuries, mostly burns to the upper half of the body and head injuries of all kinds – the result of trying to swim through or surfacing through spilled-oil fires on the Mediterranean Sea. Many had to be helped off; about two dozen were taken off the third bus by stretcher, some unconscious. Clerks, nurses, and doctors with interpreters were on hand, steering the men and women to interview examination cubicles.

The refrigerated truck was driven to a separate area of the warehouse, closed off from the main section. Six autopsy tables had been set up, with forensic pathologists and medical examiners waiting to begin their work. One by one, light gray body bags were carried out of the truck. Each body bag had a plastic bag with various records inside. A clerk took the paperwork, then escorted the body to an examination table, where video cameras were rolling, recording everything. While dictating into an overhead microphone, the medical examiner unzipped the bag and began his work.

It was not the examiners' job to ascertain cause of death – their main task was gathering enough information to assist in identification. But most times the cause of death was plainly –

226

and painfully – obvious. Most of the forty-nine corpses had died of blast trauma or fire from exploding ordnance or systems on board their vessel when the Libyan air force attacked. Severed body parts were sometimes simply thrown into a body bag, often without any real attempt to try to match the parts by gender or race. Many suffered no injuries from blast trauma or fire – they obviously died from wounds inflicted by gunshots at very close range, blunt-force trauma, knife wounds, crushed throats, slashed arteries, mutilated genitalia, or burn marks all over the bodies.

It was obvious they had been tortured to death by their captors after being rescued from the sea.

In all, eight female corpses were examined. They were not exempt from the torture the others endured.

A few hours after the examinations began, a helicopter landed at a helipad outside the warehouse facility, and a group of government officials, surrounded by bodyguards, were quickly taken directly from the helicopter to a waiting limousine and then directly to the warehouse. On his orders, a special corridor had been erected from cubicle dividers with one-way mirrors installed that allowed anyone walking inside the corridor to look out but no one to look in.

Ulama Khalid al-Khan, wearing a military garrison cap and sunglasses to hide his identity even though he was safe from any outside scrutiny, could not believe what he was looking at. The stench was horrific – he wanted to put a cloth up to his nose to block the smell of these tortured, bloody, unwashed bodies, but he dared not show any weakness in front of the soldiers escorting him. The corridor took him and his aide, Major Amr Abu Gheit, into the makeshift morgue, where he was able to view several of the corpses, and he had to struggle to keep his stomach from turning inside out. Finally, he was escorted out of the warehouse complex and into a separate office.

'What . . . what in *hell* was that?' Khan gasped.

'One hundred and twenty-nine persons recovered by the Libyans from the Mediterranean Sea after their ships were attacked, sir,' Major Gheit responded. It was obvious that even the veteran warrior could barely stomach the sight himself. He handed Khan a list of the survivors. 'Forty-nine fatalities,

227

including nine women. Fifty-six others severely injured, some critically. They are almost done with the identification process.'

'Were . . . were some of those men *tortured*?'

'Obviously the Libyan military wanted information out of them,' Baris said. 'The king of Libya explained that the attacks were in retaliation for the commando attack on their missile base.'

'Damned brutal animals,' Khan muttered, taking a sip of water to try to settle his stomach. 'I've never seen men mutilated like that.'

'There are only nine Egyptians in the group, and they were working as crew members on someone else's ship, not an Egyptian flagged vessel,' Gheit said. 'Why would Zuwayy want to turn them over to you?'

'He dumped those men and women on our doorstep, leaving us to clean up *his* mess,' Khan said disgustedly. 'He's either trying to implicate me in this unholy mess, or he's trying to embarrass me. Either one won't work.'

'This doesn't make sense,' Gheit said. 'He must know those prisoners are going to talk about the treatment they received in Libya. Zuwayy will be vilified all over the world.'

'Well, I'm not going to play whatever game he's playing,' Khan said resolutely. 'This is insanity.' Khan waved at the door. 'Let's get out of here,' he said. 'The stench is too much for me to bear.' Gheit ordered Khan's car pulled up beside the door. When it was in place, Khan stepped outside.

Just as Khan was about to step into the car, his attention was drawn to an impossibly bright flash of light – he was surprised he noticed it in daytime, but it was that bright – somewhere very close, followed by a tremendous *BOOM!* like the loudest thunderclap ever heard. Moments later there was another flash of light, bright enough to erase shadows on the ground, followed by a second explosion. A thunderstorm in an almost cloudless sky?

Could it be some sort of attack? But there was no sign of anything wrong on the ground except a great stirring of dust and sand, like the gust front ahead of an approaching thunderstorm or sandstorm – but again, there were no clouds in the sky. He could hear screams somewhere off in the distance, but still there seemed to be nothing amiss.

'Let's get out of here,' Khan said. 'This place feels like death all of a sudden.'

Patrick, wearing full battle armor and exoskeleton, was watching TV coverage of the busloads of ex-Libyan prisoners being taken into the warehouses through his helmet-mounted visor. He stared carefully at the screen, trying to pick out even one familiar face, but the cameras were too far away and the prisoners were not in the open long enough for Patrick to recognize anyone.

The commentator made several mentions of the refrigerated trucks being driven to an adjacent warehouse – Patrick didn't want to think about what was in those vehicles. He just hoped and prayed that Wendy and his men were all right.

But another movement caught his attention: the movement of men and vehicles outside the compound. Shit, he thought, here they come. 'Hey, Texas,' he radioed.

'We see them, Muck,' David Luger responded. Patrick's electronic visor in his battle armor automatically datalinked the view to all the others wearing the Tin Man armor. 'Still think they're just going to take you into custody?'

Patrick ignored the question. 'Are you guys secure?' he asked.

'Almost,' Luger replied. The Night Stalkers had to move to a third recovery area, a set of abandoned oil rigs almost thirty miles to the southwest – most of the Egyptian army was on the move west of the base and along the coast to seal off the Libyan border. They had stolen two tracked vehicles to help their getaway across the desert. 'The closest units are about three miles behind us. We're waiting for the choppers to come after us any minute. If they do, we'll ask Headbanger Two to take them out.'

'Headbanger Two is standing by,' the aircraft commander aboard a second EB-52 Megafortress flying battleship reported. The second Megafortress had been able to refuel from the Sky Masters Inc's DC-10 tanker, but had to break off and run into southern Libya shortly thereafter because US Navy fighters from a carrier in the Mediterranean had pursued it. The DC-10 landed in Iraklion, Greece, where American and NATO authorities were questioning its crew as to why it had to make the unscheduled landing and exactly what its mission was. It had been a close call.

'We can stay on station for only about an hour before we have to head on home.'

'Copy,' Patrick said. 'What a lousy time for the feds to be on our ass.'

'Patrick, I think it's time for you to get the hell out of there,' Hal Briggs said. 'Start moving out the emergency escape. We'll vector in the Megafortress to cover you.'

'I'm going to give Ouda one more try,' Patrick said.

'He's not answering you. Better get out before they start moving in.'

'Stand by,' Patrick responded. It was his only chance to get out without a firefight – a very slim chance. 'Vice Marshal Ouda, this is Castor. Can you hear me?' Patrick called on the liaison radio channel. Outside the half-underground bunker, several of the tanks were on the move. Covering smoke began to belch from exhausts, obscuring them from sight. Patrick switched to his imaging infrared visor so he could see them. 'Several of your tanks are moving toward the fence outside our compound. It appears as if you are attacking my position. State your intentions. Can you hear me?' There was no reply – nor did he really expect one.

But that moment an alarm went off in his battle armor – a radiation alarm. Patrick quickly scanned the datalink images around him – nothing. A few moments later, another radiation alarm sounded.

'Marshal Ouda, this is Castor. Respond immediately. We are detecting radiation in the area. Levels are rising quickly – they are approaching lethal levels. Do you copy?' No answer – and now the Egyptian tanks were on the move. 'Dave, I'm outta here,' Patrick said on his command channel, and he raced for the emergency exit, careful to disarm, then rearm the booby trap at the rear entrance.

He was about to jet-jump away when the first Egyptian tank crashed through the twelve-foot-high fence surrounding the bunker. The tank was followed by several dozen Egyptian infantrymen, some carrying rocket-propelled grenades and bazookas. Patrick saw several of the tanks wheel in his direction – they had spotted him. He raised his electromagnetic rail gun, charged it, and aimed for the closest tank . . .

. . . and found the rail gun completely inoperative. It had power, but all of the electronic displays were blank. His suit's electronic visor – also blank. His defensive electronic bolts – powerless. He did a quick self-test of all his suit's systems and found everything dead. He tried to jet-jump away – but the jets were deactivated as well. His suit still had power, but everything was in reset, as if it had shut itself down to prevent an overheat or overload. He thought it would all come back, but he didn't know when or if anything had sustained any damage.

Patrick took off his helmet before he suffocated to death – the suit's environmental system had shut down too – just as the Egyptians rolled over to him. The soldiers stripped his battle armor off, handcuffed him, and took him to a security building on the other side of the base, where he was thrown into a windowless, hot room a little larger than a closet. He tried to contact someone through his subcutaneous transceiver, but there was no response. Everything looked as if it was scrambled. What in hell was going on?

Vice Marshal Sayed Ouda met with Patrick a couple hours later. He was sweating profusely, almost as much as Patrick was. 'Where are your comrades?' Ouda asked through an interpreter.

'They've escaped and are probably being airlifted out of the country,' Patrick replied.

'Why did you remain behind?'

'Because I am still here to meet up with my comrades that were captured by the Libyans, the ones that were brought here,' Patrick said. 'But we suspected we were being held here to prevent us from meeting with them. Apparently I'm right. What's going on, sir?'

'No questions from you,' Ouda said. 'You will be turned over to the Supreme Judiciary for further interrogation.'

'Turned over to Khalid al-Khan?' No response – the soldier doing the interpreting didn't look very good either. 'Where are Madame Salaam and General Baris?'

'I said . . . I said no . . . questions,' the interpreter said – and then he vomited violently on the floor right in front of Patrick, with more blood than bile gushing out. The jailer had to drag the suddenly unconscious man out. Marshal Ouda dashed out of the room as well, in such a hurry that he didn't even bother to close or lock the door behind him.

The security office was in complete bedlam. Men were rushing around shouting and yelling, some in complete, very unsoldierlike panic. Some of them were hurriedly putting on gas masks. But it didn't seem as if they were under attack. 'What's happening?' Patrick asked. 'What's wrong? Does anyone speak English?' Everyone was ignoring him. Patrick was able to find his way through a maze of corridors and up one flight of stairs and finally emerge outside . . .

. . . where he found several dozen dead Egyptian soldiers, simply lying in the road. All of them had lost a significant amount of blood through their mouths and nostrils and in some cases through their ears and eye sockets.

Patrick went back inside the security building. There, at a reception desk, a pregnant female security officer was frantically dialing a telephone. Her hands were trembling so bad, she couldn't punch the buttons. 'Can you help me?' Patrick asked her. 'Do you speak English?' She looked at him, and she seemed to understand what he was saying, but she kept trying to dial the telephone. Once she did correctly dial, she cried out in frustration as she reached a busy number or one that didn't answer. 'You speak English, don't you?' he asked.

'Yes,' the officer replied. 'Please stand away from the door and do not panic. Do not . . .' And then she wiped a rivulet of blood from her eyes, and she started to bawl.

'It's all right,' Patrick said. He didn't know what else to say. He was standing in the lobby in long underwear, barefoot, with his hands cuffed behind his back, unable to do anything. 'Just relax.'

'I cannot find my husband,' she sobbed. 'I do not know what is happening.'

'It looks like the building is being evacuated,' Patrick said. 'Why don't you report to the base hospital? Your husband will find you there.' The woman nodded, got out of her chair, then noticed Patrick was handcuffed. She went back to her desk with a handcuff key and released him. '*Shukran gazilan*,' Patrick said. 'Do you need me to drive you to the hospital?' She seemed to have trouble understanding him. He made a steering motion with his hands. '*Mustashfa?*' Patrick asked, dredging up as many Arabic words as he could. '*El is'aef? Doktor? Haelan.*'

The woman nodded, then retrieved a desert camouflage jacket someone had left on a coat hook and a set of keys from a wall keyholder. Patrick went over to open the door for her . . .

232

. . . and that's when he noticed the trail of blood coming from between her legs. The woman took Patrick's hand, nodded her thanks . . . and then her eyes rolled up into the back of her head, and she slumped to the floor, dead.

What was happening? Patrick cried to himself. Jesus, was it a chemical or biological weapon attack? He didn't have long himself if it was. He took the keys from the woman's dead fingers, slipped on the jacket, then went back inside the security building. After twenty minutes of searching, he found his battle armor, exoskeleton, backpack unit, and helmet, and headed outside. After a five-minute search of the parking lot, he found the right vehicle and drove off.

What he saw on that drive was unimaginable horror – dead bodies everywhere. He saw vehicles overturned, corpses still in the driver's seats. He saw armored vehicles and tanks crashed into buildings and gates with corpses hanging out of them as if they tried to climb out just as they died. There were burning, crashed helicopters dotting the flight-line access road, fires everywhere – even dead vultures and other desert animals lying everywhere. It was like a scene in some kind of horror movie. As far as he could see, across the runway and toward the main base area, he could see signs of slow, painful death. He . . .

Patrick gasped. The base . . . the base where Wendy, the other Night Stalkers, and the other prisoners had been taken. My God!

He tried the car radio: It was working, but it was silent – not static, just a silence, as if the announcer's microphone was left open. But if the car and the radio worked, maybe his battle armor did too! He stopped the car and dragged all his gear out of the trunk. Sure enough, the outside status lights were green – the power pack and computer were working. As quickly as he could, Patrick climbed into the suit and powered it up. It was working again! He put on the helmet and secured the entire system . . .

. . . and then learned what had happened: radiation alarms were going off. There had been an intense release of gamma and neutron radiation in the past several hours. Although the radiation levels now were high – he would have to get out of the area within thirty minutes or risk getting seriously sick – they had been a thousand times higher not long ago.

A neutron bomb. It had to be. Someone had set off a neutron

233

bomb on the base. Everyone within a mile of the explosion would be dead within hours, and everyone within two miles would get sick from radiation poisoning. The neutron bomb – a conventional hydrogen bomb without its uranium-238 jacket – was designed to kill humans but leave vehicles and buildings intact.

Wendy . . .

So the Libyans couldn't release the prisoners, Patrick thought grimly. It was impossible. The news report said some of the prisoners were tortured. The Libyans couldn't allow the world to see that. So they planted a nuclear device into one of the buses and set it to go off just as the prisoners were being off-loaded. All of the evidence of what they had done would be wiped clean. They would of course deny they had anything to do with the nuclear detonation.

Wendy . . . my God, Wendy . . .

Zuwayy was going to pay for this, Patrick vowed. He was going to die, brutally and messily. He was going to rip his beating heart out of his chest and rub it in his face.

The air felt electrified, as if every movement of his body caused thousands of static electric shocks that were growing in intensity. Patrick knew that if he stuck around much longer, the shocks would eventually kill him.

Patrick reluctantly turned his back on what was once Egypt's largest military base outside Cairo and headed southwest, towards a rendezvous with his men. As he drove, he felt nothing – no anger, no weariness, no hatred, and no sadness. The battle had been fought, and he had lost.

Chapter Six

White House Situation Room, Washington, DC
a few hours later

The detailed briefing had just concluded, and the men and women present sat in stunned silence as the room lights were brought back up. The Air Force intelligence officer that gave the briefing was dismissed, leaving behind the members of President Thomas Nathaniel Thorn's 'National Security Council.' Although the Thorn administration did not have a formal NSC, Thorn met with Vice President Lester Busick, Secretary of Defense Robert Goff, Secretary of State Edward Kercheval, Director of Central Intelligence Douglas R. Morgan, and Chairman of the Joint Chiefs of Staff General Richard Venti to discuss any military developments.

'Damned brutal attack,' Secretary of Defense Robert Goff remarked. In his mid-fifties, with a round face and compact frame, Goff was normally energetic and animated, even jovial – but the briefing he had just received left his features cold, hard, and angry. 'What kind of a sick bastard does this?'

'Someone who obviously did not want to leave any traces of evidence behind,' Vice President Lester Busick offered. He turned to General Venti. 'What did our reconnaissance folks report, General?'

'Space Command recorded the explosion from geosynchronous satellite infrared sensors,' Venti explained. 'Based on radiation and photon levels, the Command is estimating between a point-five- and two-kiloton device – a so-called "backpack" nuke, probably from a nuclear artillery round or torpedo warhead. It appears to have been an enhanced radiation device, what we call a neutron bomb – designed to kill humans but leave buildings and vehicles intact. Probably fired from a small artillery piece or large mortar mounted in a truck. It did its work very, very effectively.'

'Radiation? Fallout?'

'None, sir,' Venti replied. 'Enhanced radiation devices leave no fallout, and the radiation is present for only a few seconds at most. But the damage to human cells is massive. Within a mile of ground zero, death occurs within twelve hours; within two miles, death can occur within twenty-four hours. It would take twenty feet of earth or twelve inches of steel to block the radiation enough to survive.'

Thorn was leaning forward in his seat, elbows on the table, his lips hidden behind his interlaced fingers. His advisers were accustomed to talking among themselves, as if the President of the United States were not even in the room, while he processed what he heard and combined it with his unique insights, intelligence, military experience, and philosophies to come up with a plan of action. After several moments of listening, he looked at his Director of Central Intelligence, Douglas R. Morgan. 'What's been the region's general response, Robert?'

'General alert of active-duty Egyptian military and paramilitary forces along the Libyan-Egyptian border − that's it,' Morgan responded, flipping through his briefing notes. 'No counterattacks or mobilizations. Israel has already been on heightened alert status. I believe everyone simply considers this to be a terrorist attack, not a general attack.'

'Although I'd expect a general attack to take place at any time,' Secretary Goff said, 'and we can't rule out the use of nuclear weapons − full-yield fission weapons − by the Libyans again.'

'All of our forces in the Med are on heightened alert, sir,' Venti added. 'Securing ships at sea was accomplished very quickly, and the ships are positioning themselves to assist other vessels. We're hoping it won't be a killer. We're ready in case the Libyans try to take a shot at our ships or launch a rocket attack against Israel or Europe.'

The President nodded, then turned to his secretary of state. 'Ed? Reaction from local politicians, neighboring countries, and organizations?'

'The streets of Alexandria and Cairo are practically deserted, sir − looks like most folks expect more attacks in the cities,' Secretary of State Edward Kercheval replied. Kercheval was not a Jeffersonian Party member, as was the President and the rest of his cabinet officers, but was considered a highly respected and valuable addition to the President's inner circle of advisers – even though he disagreed more with his boss than agreed with him. 'Immediate and heated condemnation of the attack by Dr Ahmed Kalir, the prime minister of Egypt and the leader of the current majority party. Dr Kalir has requested help from the United States in fighting off an impending invasion by Libya and possibly Sudan.'

'Does that appear likely?'

All heads turned to the Director of Central Intelligence. 'Very possible – given the new information we've seen over the past several days,' Morgan replied. 'Libya has no capability to beat Egypt in a conventional conflict – Egypt has a three-to-one numerical advantage and at least a twenty-to-one technological advantage. But Egypt has no weapons of mass destruction as far as we know, and a patchwork air defense system stitched together from many countries that doesn't all work well together. If Libya decides to launch a nuclear attack against Cairo or Alexandria, it might very well succeed. Plus, several thousand Libyan troops are stationed in Sudan now – they could open up a second front against Egypt at any time.'

'As far as the rest of the Arab world, most nations are neither condemning nor endorsing the raid, except for other Muslim Brotherhood nations, which praised the raid as the beginning of the end of Western imperialism in the Arab world,' Kercheval went on. 'It appears that the leading opposition member in Egypt, Khalid al-Khan, was killed in the explosion.

'No word yet from Susan Bailey Salaam, the widow of the assassinated president, either, who is a candidate for president,' Kercheval added. 'Information has it that she might be under arrest or in hiding from Khalid al-Khan's men.'

'I thought she was killed in that attack at the mosque a couple weeks ago.'

'So did the rest of the world, Mr President,' Kercheval said. 'She suddenly turned up at a National Assembly meeting to announce her candidacy for president before being refused by the Assembly on technical grounds. She was injured but not seriously.'

'She's an American, I believe?' Thorn asked.

'Yes, sir. Ex-Air Force. Dual citizenship.'

'She'd better hightail it back here where she belongs before her husband's assassins catch up with her,' Vice President Busick idly commented. Thorn glanced at the veteran politician but said nothing.

'Recommended course of action, sir?' General Venti asked.

Thorn thought for a few moments. The 'Kitchen Cabinet' was accustomed to Thorn's seemingly disconnected way of pondering an issue – he would adopt a faraway expression, as if searching through space, for an answer. Former military men called it the 'thousand-yard stare,' but even though Thorn was ex-Army Special Forces, no one gave him that kind of credit.

Thomas Nathaniel Thorn was the first third-party candidate since Abraham Lincoln to be elected to the White House. To be elected president of the United States without a massive, well-organized political machine behind you was unusual enough – but Thorn was odder still. He was a loner, a politician who seemingly shunned crowds and the spotlight. He was rarely seen in public, although now into the third year of his term he was seen more and more on the reelection campaign trail. He worked long hours in his private study or in the Oval Office in a very hands-on but decentralized management structure. The executive branch of government was the smallest in sixty years, all carefully orchestrated by a man who used to kill for a living but was now perceived as one of the gentlest, nonconfrontational, and nonconformist commander-in-chiefs ever to occupy the White House.

As was his custom, Thorn glanced up with an unspoken request in his eyes, first to his vice president. 'Park a carrier battle group off the Libyan coast,' Busick said.

'I agree, sir,' Secretary of Defense Goff chimed in. 'One carrier battle group would just about equal the entire Libyan military's strength.' Left unspoken was the fact that an aircraft carrier battle group was just about the *only* option open to them – since one of Thomas Thorn's first acts as commander-in-chief was to bring most troops stationed overseas home. Although the United States still had basing rights in all of the North Atlantic Treaty Organization countries and still deployed overseas often for joint military exercises, no US combat forces were permanently stationed anywhere in Europe or the Middle East.

'Of course, we would condemn the attack in the United Nations, in the media, and in every appearance we made for the next few weeks,' Secretary of State Kercheval said. 'I think it would be easy to swing world public opinion against Libya. But I think moving an aircraft carrier off Libya's coast would send a pretty strong message as well – the United States thinks it is definitely in our best interests to defend Egypt.'

Thorn turned to General Venti. 'General? Who's over there?'

'The *Stennis* carrier group is cruising in the Med right now, sir,' Venti responded. 'The *Reagan* group is scheduled to join them in four days. They have a week of joint exercises planned in the Med, and then the *Stennis* was scheduled to come home. The groups have canceled their exercises and are at threat condition Delta. The *Reagan* sails with an amphibious squadron assigned – three to five ships, two thousand Marines. We also have an amphibious group assigned to the Med attached to the *Stennis* with twenty-one ships and approximately fifteen thousand Marines.'

'How far out are other forces?' Thorn asked. 'If we did have to go into Libya or Egypt in the next twenty-four hours, what other forces would we have to draw on?'

'Primary strike forces would be ship- or sub-launched cruise missiles, followed by carrier-based bombers,' Venti replied. 'Those strikes could be launched within six hours if needed and would be focusing on neutralizing air defense, surveillance, and antiship forces, softening up the beachhead in preparation for an amphibious landing. Bombers from the CONUS would then follow up and strike larger targets deeper inside Libya – infantry bases, ports, warehouses, docks, and supply lines, as well as defensive positions – concurrently with a Marine beach landing, well within twenty-four hours.

'I need a decision on whether or not to generate the nuclear forces to alert status, sir, and what targets you would like loaded up,' Venti added. 'The Peacekeepers can be reprogrammed for Libya-Sudan-Syria-Iraq target set in about two hours. The naval forces in the Med will take about a day to reprogram targets after they receive their messages – the subs take a little longer to decode valid messages. The B-2 stealth bomber fleet needs seventy-two hours to generate both squadrons, eighteen planes, to full nuclear alert status.'

Most of the President's advisers were surprised by the swiftness of the President's decision: 'I want a flight of B-2 bombers loaded up for nuclear strike sorties against Libyan, Sudanese, Syrian, and Iraqi targets,' he said. 'Then I want them launched to positive control orbits over the Med.'

'The subs and surface forces in the Med can be ready to fly nuclear sorties in half the time,' Secretary of Defense Goff pointed out.

'But then the whole world will think I'm ready to go to war,' Thorn said evenly. 'I want the carriers and subs on full alert, but I don't want them going nuclear unless this situation gets completely out of hand.'

'The rest of the strategic force, sir?'

'Get them warmed up and ready to go,' the President said. 'Russian and Chinese target sets – I think we'll have enough forces ready in the Med if it goes nuclear without the ICBMs.' General Venti nodded as he made notes to himself. 'What kind of reconnaissance do we have in place over the theater, General?'

'Strategic and theater recon is by satellite,' Venti replied. 'We usually fill in with U-2 spy planes and carrier-based unmanned reconnaissance aircraft when requested.'

'You said "usually"?' Thorn asked. 'I take it in this current political climate that Egypt is not allowing us to use their bases or fly freely through their airspace?'

'Yes, sir,' Secretary of State Kercheval said. 'Egypt has currently suspended overflight privileges for American military aircraft. Because of the upcoming elections and because of the confusing situation over the area now, the Egyptian Foreign Ministry says that no overflights by military aircraft or landing privileges by combat-coded aircraft of any kind will be allowed – only civil transport and humanitarian missions permitted.'

'When did this happen?' Busick asked.

'Just last night our time,' Kercheval said. 'Shortly after it was announced that those prisoners would be taken to Egypt. Their ministry claims they don't want to accidentally shoot down any of our aircraft.'

'Bullshit,' Busick snarled. 'It's that Muslim Brotherhood thing. Khalid Khan wanted to be elected and align Egypt with the Muslim Brotherhood, so he cut our military access in Egypt. Whole lot of good that did him.'

'Egypt is an important friend of the United States, a moderate Arab nation, and one of the most powerful nations on the African continent,' Robert Goff said emphatically. 'It's also one of the most geopolitically and strategically important countries on the planet, for reasons almost too numerous to list. Whatever affects Egypt will eventually affect Europe and North America. I feel it's important to defend Egypt with everything we've got.'

'I agree, Mr President,' Kercheval chimed in. 'Quite frankly, sir, the Libyan action, although horrific in the loss of life and the use of nuclear weapons, was relatively minor. We still have a chance to prevent them from attempting an invasion of Egypt or widening the conflict.'

'I agree with Secretaries Goff and Kercheval, sir,' General Venti said. 'The Libyan attack hasn't destabilized the situation in North Africa – yet. We need to get in there and tell the world that we won't tolerate any more actions like this.'

Vice President Busick waited for the President to respond; when he didn't, he turned to him and said in a low voice, 'I'm afraid I agree with your advisers here, Thomas. I know you don't go for things like this, but I'd like to slap Libya down hard. If you don't want to go in after Zuwayy and kick his ass for using nuclear weapons, at least park the Sixth Fleet right outside his front door and make our displeasure clear.' He paused, then added, 'And I know you're thinking of a second term. This would be a good time to exercise your military muscle. Libya is a pushover. If there's a shooting war, it'll be over quickly.'

The President nodded that he understood the veteran politician's view, then quizzically glanced at Doug Morgan. 'I have a feeling you have something else that might influence my decision, Doug,' he said.

Morgan produced another briefing folder, sighed, then opened it. 'I'm afraid I do, sir,' he began. 'I think our friends the Night Stalkers might be involved in this Libya-Egypt conflict.'

'Oh, for chrissakes . . . ,' Busick moaned. 'Those bastards are going to get their butts kicked one of these days.'

'I think that might have already happened, sir,' Morgan said. 'I already reported on the unexplained attacks on that Libyan missile base where chemical weapons and possibly nuclear materials were detected. We thought it was the Israelis, and then

243

Egyptian special forces – we still have no concrete evidence of either. I also reported that the Libyans attacked several ships in the Mediterranean Sea following that attack, apparently in retaliation or perhaps looking for the commando team's base of operations. The identities of all the ships were verified – two Greek, Italian, French, Moroccan, and a Lithuanian vessel, all sunk or heavily damaged. The Egyptian navy rescued crew members from four of the six ships, including over sixty men and women from the last ship that was attacked – the Lithuanian salvage vessel.'

'Salvage vessel?' the President asked. '*Lithuanian* salvage vessel?'

'Yes, sir,' Morgan said. He could tell the President had been doing his homework – he recognized the clues immediately.

'Don't tell me,' the President said. 'The so-called survivors of the Lithuanian ship captured a helicopter right off the deck of an Egyptian warship and spirit off into the darkness.'

'Worse than that – I think the survivors *captured the entire Egyptian warship*.'

'*What!*'

'We intercepted some interesting radio traffic between one of the Egyptian frigates and their military base at Mersa Matrûh,' Morgan went on. 'At first we thought a little mutiny had broken out between some rival factions on the ship. But then it occurred to us that someone else other than the crew had seized the ship. A couple days later, the vessel returned to port and everything else was back to normal.'

'And you think the guys that seized this frigate were Martindale's crew?' Venti asked.

'It fits,' the President said. 'Operating off a salvage ship – just like an Intelligence Support Agency cell, which a lot of those Night Stalkers once were. Martindale would certainly have the ability to get one of his ships flagged by Lithuania – he practically saved that country himself when the Russians attacked. And blowing up a Libyan missile base – that's signature Martindale; or, more accurately, McLanahan. Doug, did you . . . ?'

'Ask about McLanahan? Yes, sir. We requested a report from the FBI, who still have Sky Masters under special surveillance.' Morgan turned to another page in his report. 'General

McLanahan, his wife, Colonel Luger, and Colonel Briggs are not at the Sky Masters facility in Arkansas.'

'Doesn't mean they were involved in the Libyan attack,' the President said.

'Mr President, I'll bet you my Orange Bowl box seats they're involved – up to their eyeballs,' Vice President Busick exclaimed heatedly. 'They have opportunity, and they certainly have the means. Are any of them traveling overseas?'

'Yes . . .'

'You see!' Busick exclaimed. 'I'm sorry, Mr President, but I'm getting sick and tired of that bunch of wanna-be heroes creating a mess and then fading off into the sunset, letting someone else clean up their messes afterward.'

Thorn raised a hand to his vice president, silently informing him that his point of view was clearly understood and asking him to tone it down, then turned back to Morgan. 'You mentioned something about them getting their butts kicked, Doug,' he said. 'What else do you have?'

'Another piece of the puzzle – but a corner piece, I think,' Morgan said. 'The remains of one Paul McLanahan were reported by customs agents in New Jersey being flown in from Tel Aviv by a funeral director based in Sacramento, California. The FBI's preliminary investigation confirms that Mr McLanahan was involved in a suicide bomber attack in Rehoval, Israel, ten days ago. He was a guest at the Hilton Tel Aviv Hotel, checked in the day before. Airline tickets, visas, guided tour schedule – all checks. He was there on vacation.'

'Baloney!' Busick exclaimed. 'It's either the most incredible coincidence I've ever heard, or it's a lie, a cover-up. Paul McLanahan is one of the Night Stalkers – hell, he's their main guy, next to his brother Patrick and former president Martindale himself. Martindale could have easily created the fake hotel registration, airline tickets, even police reports. McLanahan and the Night Stalkers are in Libya. I know it. He got killed in that raid on the Libyan missile base, and I'll bet the Night Stalkers are still in the region, in Egypt or Israel, getting ready to finish the job – or grab some payback.'

'So if the Libyans thought the Egyptians engineered that raid, the attack in Egypt could've been retaliation,' Kercheval said. 'If

245

this thing goes hot on us, McLanahan and Martindale could be responsible for igniting a major war in the Med.'

'You know what it is, don't you?' Busick asked angrily. 'It's Sky Masters Inc. and Jon Masters. He's supplying the Night Stalkers with the weapons they need to do these damned secret missions. Those are weapons *we* funded. That high-tech combat armor, the aircraft, the weapons – he's supplying them all for this private little mercenary army of Martindale's.'

'We should slap Sky Masters with sanctions for their support of those nutcases,' Kercheval exclaimed. 'We should just shut them down, once and for all. And the Justice Department needs to conduct an investigation of Kevin Martindale. He can't be allowed to continue organizing private military operations all over the world. If Justice can't do anything, maybe the press should be told about this. . .'

'That's already in the works,' Robert Goff said. 'Some of our Navy interceptors caught up with one of Masters's research aircraft – refueling a modified B-52 bomber over the Mediterranean Sea.'

'*What*?'

'I'm afraid we have photos – positive proof,' Goff said. 'It appears they had expended weapons too. It's still circumstantial evidence, but it's pretty convincing to me. We have Masters's refueling plane in Greece right now, questioning the crew, after we think they had rendezvoused again with a Megafortress bomber last night. The bomber got away both times – it's too stealthy to track except up very close, and it doesn't let us get close enough.'

'Are those guys crazy?' Busick exclaimed. 'Are they *trying* to start a war?'

'Martindale is not doing anything illegal, at least not in the United States,' General Venti interjected.

'But we can refuse to shield him against foreign indictments,' Kercheval shot back. 'Russia, China, North Korea, Iran, Iraq, Libya, Syria, and a half-dozen other nations have all pressed criminal charges against Martindale for his activities –'

'*Alleged* activities.'

'Call it what you want, General – you and I both know he's involved,' Kercheval said. 'We can threaten to not block extradition.'

'We are *not* going to turn over a former president of the United States to any foreign country,' Busick said. 'That's crazy. Martindale will never believe our threat. But we can sure as hell bust McLanahan and his men.'

'Let's stick with the problem at hand, shall we?' Kercheval asked. 'We need some kind of consensus about what in the hell to do about Libya.'

All eyes turned toward Thomas Thorn. He considered it for a few more moments; then: 'Have the *Reagan* and *Stennis* groups proceed with their planned exercises,' he said. 'No changes whatsoever in their plans – in fact, I want Pentagon briefers to start including a few details of the exercise to the press, just so everyone knows we're not adjusting the exercise to threaten Libya.'

'Sir, are you *sure* don't want to put any additional military pressure on Libya?' Goff asked incredulously. He was accustomed to the various surprises served up by this very new and certainly different commander-in-chief, but he still couldn't control his reaction when he made such unexpected decisions. 'Mr President, I'd like to prepare a briefing regarding Egypt's importance to –'

'Save it for now, Robert,' Thorn said. 'Gentlemen, I need to hear just one thing before I make the decision to commit American troops against Libya: that the people of Egypt want the help of the United States. From what you've said, that hasn't happened.'

'That's not true, Mr President,' Kercheval said. 'We've had calls from the prime minister, from major opposition groups, from leaders in the Pan-African Leadership Council . . .'

'That's not good enough,' the President said. 'You say that Khan, the chief justice of their supreme court, might have been involved in the Salaam assassination – and then you tell me that he was the front-runner in the national election? This tells me that the people of Egypt condone and even embrace these actions.'

'Maybe they were too scared of Khan to resist him, sir.'

'I don't believe that's possible,' the President said. 'We've seen too many cases of common people toppling dictatorships, and we've seen too many cases of common people embracing dictatorships – not because they were coerced into doing so, but because they liked having a strongman in charge. If that's what the people choose, they can have it – and everything that goes along with it. Egypt is a progressive country. It currently has a free press, allows free expression of ideas, and easy immigration.'

'Mr President, certainly, you can't believe –?'

'I most certainly do, Edward,' the President said. 'If Egypt wants our help, they need to prove to me that they really want our help – we will not impose our ideals on them, no matter how much we distrust Libya.' He turned to Goff and Venti and went on: 'I want the theater and naval commanders fully briefed on the situation in Libya, I want our forces in the Med, the Red Sea, the Gulf of Aden, and the Persian Gulf on the highest state of alert, and I want contingency plans drawn up for air strikes against Libyan forces that move against Egypt. But I am not going to threaten Libya or come to the aid of Egypt unless the people of Egypt elect a president that wants to cooperate and work with us.'

They outlined what they would discuss with the media, including a few items to be leaked by 'unnamed sources' in the White House and Pentagon, and then the meeting broke up. Thomas Thorn went upstairs to the residence to see what the family was up to and visit with the kids who weren't in school, and then he entered his bedroom and shut the door behind him. The children and his wife all knew not to disturb him now.

Thomas Thorn first learned meditation in the US Army Sniper School at Fort Benning, Georgia, where he trained as a sniper himself in order to be a commander of a Special Forces Group. To tell the truth, Thorn was not the best shot in the world, and he wondered if he could cut it. But he soon learned that being a sharpshooter was only twenty percent of being a sniper – the mental struggles and challenges of stalking and shooting a living target were the hard part. Snipers had to learn how to move without being detected, sometimes within mere feet of the enemy, and they had to learn to detect a target out of camouflage or deep in cover. They had to have perfect eyesight and exceptional infantry and outdoorsman skills, but most of all, they had to have the mental discipline required to inflict quick, catastrophic, and 'one shot, one kill' finality to a pursuit. Thorn soon learned that mental discipline – what he called 'mental quietude' – was the most important qualification.

Not everyone at Benning used meditation, but it worked for

Thomas Thorn. Meditation helped him relax, helped him rejuvenate his body and mind, and it helped him concentrate, focus, and clarify his task and objective. Some likened it to a catnap but, properly done, it was the exact opposite – it was a recharger, a rejuvenator. It served Thomas Thorn well after he left the US Army – he had meditated for twenty minutes, twice a day, every single day since he received his mantra and learned how to do it properly.

It took only moments for Thorn to slip into his higher state of consciousness, and then the journey began. The reason Thomas Thorn never took vacations, rarely visited Camp David, played no sports other than T-ball with his children, and had no hobbies, was that he took a 'vacation' twice a day when he slipped into a transcendental state. Arriving at that level was like stepping off a supersonic jet and arriving at a different place every time.

But it was not such a journey this time. Instead of traveling himself in a different world, dimension, or time, he was a spectator this time, watching events happen. That was unusual – certainly not impossible or unheard of, since the soul has no beginning and no end – but why couldn't he watch it as well as experience it?

He awoke with a start – also not an usual occurrence. He glanced at his watch and realized with relief that his meditation lasted almost exactly twenty minutes, as it should have. So why did he feel so odd?

He knew why he felt that way – he felt it for a long time now, ever since the Turkey-Ukraine-Russia conflict over the Black Sea, ever since the raid against Pavel Kazakov's base in Romania. He knew what was happening.

'Patrick,' he spoke.

**Munkhafad al-Qattarah Lowlands,
thirty-two miles southwest of Mersa Matrûh, Egypt
that same time**

The gas had run out, both in their vehicles and in the men themselves. Patrick and the rest of the Night Stalkers had taken shelter in yet another complex of oil wells – these appeared to be bombed out rather than run dry. They provided minimal cover: Chris Wohl had the men dig foxholes in the burning sand to conceal themselves as much as possible and wait for rescue.

They were all exhausted, physically, mentally, and emotionally. Patrick told them about the detonation over Mersa Matrûh. They had received no other reports from anyone – the electromagnetic pulse from the nuclear device had electrified the atmosphere so badly that no satellite transmissions could get in or out . . .

'Patrick.'

Or so he thought – apparently now the satellite transceivers implanted in their bodies were up and running again.

He recognized the voice immediately, of course – and his next move was also immediate: 'Cancel Thorn to Patrick.' And the voice went silent.

It was the one thing that kept Patrick and the other Night Stalkers out of prison after their first series of raids the year before: They were still tied into the subcutaneous microtransceiver system they had received while working at the Air Force's High Technology Aerospace Weapons Center in Nevada – and the President of the United States got one too, a tiny rivet-sized wireless biotransceiver injected into a shoulder, powered by a radioisotope power supply worn as an anklet. The satellite transceiver allowed global communications, tracking, biofunction monitoring, and data transmission, although the user could selectively cut off individual functions.

This was the first time the President of the United States had activated his transceiver – and it startled Patrick completely. But what surprised him even more was to hear: 'Patrick. Talk to me.' Even though Patrick had instructed the transceiver satellite server to cut out the President, he was still coming through!

'What is it, Mr President?' Patrick finally responded.

'I'm sorry about Paul,' Thorn said. The transmission was scratchy, but the emotion in the President's voice was still evident, still genuine. 'I know you loved him, and that it hurt you to have him go into battle with you.'

Patrick immediately recognized the subtle query – he was hunting for information – but Patrick didn't have the energy to try to resist an interrogation right now. 'Someone had to go in and stop the Libyans,' he responded. 'You won't do it.'

'What else happened, Patrick?' Thorn asked. 'Why didn't you come home with your brother?' No reply. The President's eyes narrowed, thinking hard – and then they widened in absolute horror. 'My God, not *Wendy*. Was she caught in the attack on your ship? Was she . . . oh, no . . . was she one of the prisoners sent to Mersa Matrûh? Oh God, Patrick . . .'

'Mr President, soldiers are resting here, preparing for battle,' Patrick said woodenly. 'You know the old saying – lead, follow, or get the hell out of the way.'

'And you think Kevin Martindale is your leader?'

Patrick had to close his eyes against the pain of the dart thrust through his heart. '*Damn you,* Thorn!' he cried against clenched teeth. The other Night Stalkers turned toward him, but no one approached – they seemed to instantly know whom he was talking with. Patrick knew that, again, Thomas Thorn the hippie-dippie president had cut right to the heart of the matter.

Patrick didn't believe in this fight. They were fighting for money, and that was not a reason to kill and die. Worse, he had accepted the assignment, even though he had not only the power but the *responsibility* to refuse it. Even worse than that – he had allowed his wife and his younger brother to follow him. Now one was dead, and the other was missing and probably dead in the nuclear explosion at Mersa Matrûh. He would burn in hell for all eternity for what he had done – and he knew it, and Thorn knew it too.

'I'm sorry, Patrick.'

'You have access to the same information we do!' Patrick cried out. 'You know what's going on out here! And yet you decided to do nothing! I did it because there's a battle that needs to be fought over here, Thorn! What are you waiting for?'

'I hope one day you'll understand why,' Thorn replied. 'I'm still not going to do anything, not unless the people of Egypt want our help.'

'What about leadership, Thorn?' Patrick retorted angrily. 'What about justice and freedom and the strong protecting the weak? Basic stuff we both learned in kindergarten! How about believing in something and standing up for it?'

'That's exactly what I'm doing, Patrick,' Thorn said gently. 'Tell me: What do you believe in? You are out there in Egypt or Israel planning more death and destruction – tell me, General, what is it you believe in now?'

'Go to hell, Thorn!'

'General, I want you to come home – right now.'

'Why do you keep on calling me "General," Thorn? You fired me, remember? You involuntarily retired me.'

'Take care of the proper things first,' Thorn patiently went on. 'Bring your soldiers home – they're tired, you're tired, and the situation there is far too desperate for you to continue. Hold your son, bury your brother, mourn your wife, console your mother and your sisters, and try to explain to them what's going on. Then come to the White House, and we'll talk.'

'Trouble, Patrick,' Hal Briggs called out.

Patrick turned and saw a rising cloud of dust on the horizon to the east – heavy vehicles, quickly heading their way. The Egyptian border patrols had finally caught up to them. 'We're pressing on,' Patrick said aloud, not to Briggs but to Thorn, and he cut the connection. This time Thorn did not override it.

What were they doing here? Patrick asked himself for at least the hundredth time in the past three days. What was the objective? Spy on the Libyans, find out if they had any designs against the Egyptian oil fields – well, that question was answered now, wasn't it? Did Paul sacrifice his life for nothing? So what if they found out that Libya had chemical, biological, or even nuclear surface-to-surface missiles ready to launch? Any smart defense planner in Egypt, Israel, Nigeria, Ethiopia, Algeria, Greece, or Italy would already assume that and be planning a counterstrike or retaliatory strike.

Just closing his eyes seemed to take away some of the pain. Paul was dead – and he was not even buried yet, still on his way back home to Sacramento for burial beside their father. Wendy was missing, probably dead. How was he going to tell her family? How in hell was he supposed to explain it to their son? Your mother won't be coming home, son. Should he tell her she was in heaven watching over him? Should he tell him about war, about fighting, about death? How do you tell a four-year-old about something like that?

He watched a vision of his life with Wendy Tork play in his mind's eye, from the time he first met her at Barksdale Air Force

Base in Louisiana during the US Air Force's Strategic Air Command Bomb Competition Symposium over twenty years earlier. She was a young and talented electronics engineer; he was a young hotshot B-52G Stratofortress bombardier who had just helped his unit win the coveted Fairchild Trophy for the second year in a row, along with a long string of other trophies and awards. The old saying 'opposites attract' was true only with magnets – Patrick and Wendy were as alike as could be, and they became almost inseparable from that moment on.

They had been shot at, shot up, shot down, and they did their fair share of shooting. They had flown all over the world together, sharing adventures as well as themselves. Of all the dangers they had faced together, having a baby was their most dangerous – and most joyous – moment. But even after young Bradley James McLanahan arrived in the world and Patrick was unceremoniously, involuntarily retired from the US Air Force, Wendy would not – *could* not – leave her husband's side when he went off to battle.

Now, that dedication may have destroyed her.

The vision playing in Patrick's mind shifted from past memories to possible futures, and none of them were pleasant. Patrick believed that reality was nothing more than a state of consciousness: Reality was whatever he decided it would be. But as hard as he tried, his mind couldn't play an image of a successful rescue or escape. He saw Wendy first being manhandled, isolated, imprisoned, even tortured; then he saw her incinerated in the fireball at Mersa Matrûh. It was too horrible to comprehend.

'Patrick?'

His focus snapped back to the present. His armor's sensors were inoperative – he visually estimated their range at around two miles, well within main gun range. 'Any contact with Headbanger?' Patrick asked.

'No,' Dave Luger replied. 'EMP still has all communications shut down.'

'Won't the crew see the Egyptians coming after us and launch the Wolverines?' Hal Briggs asked.

'They should – if their gear survived the blast, if our datalink is still active, and if the Wolverines can fly through the EMP,' Patrick said. 'It should all work, but it doesn't. I just spoke with

President Thorn, but we can't raise the Megafortress – the EMP is really screwing up transmissions.'

'What did Thorn want?'

'For us to come home and bury our dead,' Patrick said. Unfortunately, they might be among the dead soon. 'Master Sergeant, any advice?'

'We first send the men out as fast as possible away from the area,' Chris Wohl said. 'Then we take out as many of the big tanks as we can and engage the other threats as best we can.'

'Do it,' Patrick said. Wohl immediately ordered the Night Stalkers to retreat west. But no sooner had they started off than someone yelled, 'Sir! Tanks behind us, coming in fast!'

Patrick turned, and his blood ran cold – another line of heavy armor, this one smaller than the line to the east but coming on twice as fast, had appeared as if from nowhere. A company-sized force must have managed to speed across the desert and surround them. Before he could react, some of the small tanks to the west opened fire with their main guns.

'*Take cover!*' he shouted. 'Chris, Hal, take the tanks to the east! I'll take the ones to the west!' But even as he swung his electromagnetic rail gun west to attack the newcomers, he knew he was too late – he could hear the shells whistling closer and closer . . .

. . . but they didn't hit their position – instead, the shells started impacting near the Egyptian tanks. Their accuracy wasn't that great, but it didn't seem to matter: The Egyptian tanks took immediate evasive action, and Patrick could see the gun barrels elevating and turning, changing targets to the oncoming, unidentified vehicles to the west.

Whoever they are, Patrick thought, they're on our side, at least for the moment. He swung his rail gun back to the east. The targeting sensors weren't operable, but at this close range it didn't seem to matter. The newcomers created lots of smoke and confusion; Chris, Hal, and Patrick hit a few of them with the hypervelocity projectiles, and that's all it took. The remaining Egyptian tanks reversed direction and scattered. The Night Stalkers immediately turned their attention to the newcomers from the west.

With the threat from the Egyptian tanks over for now, the newcomers raised a large flag from the lead vehicle. It was a green banner trimmed in gold with a strange and unidentifiable crest on it, with crowns on top and a crown atop a circle ringed with nine stars with a crescent and star inside. 'Who are they?' Hal Briggs asked. 'Turks? Algerians?'

The newcomers moved in swiftly. They had a collection of all sorts of vehicles, from aged M60 tanks to Russian BMPs to Humvees to Jeeps, armed with an even wider variety of weapons: heavy cannons, machine guns of all sizes, even older ex-Soviet antitank rockets and antiaircraft missiles. Their uniforms didn't help identification either: They wore everything from Bedouin robes to World War II-era Nazi-style desert uniforms to American 'chocolate chip' desert cammos.

'What do you want to do, sir?' Chris Wohl asked.

Patrick hesitated, but only for a moment: 'Lower your weapons.'

'Are you *absolutely* sure, sir?' Wohl hated the idea of lowering his weapon while anyone, especially unidentified hostiles, had theirs aimed at him or his men.

'Do it, Master Sergeant,' Patrick said. Patrick lowered his rail gun to port arms but did not shut it down. The others did likewise.

The scene looked like something from a bad remake of the TV show *The Rat Patrol*. As soon as the convoy of vehicles reached the oil wells, several of them jumped off their vehicles and motioned for them to drop their weapons and raise their hands. Their personal weapons were a mix of hardware from half the world's arms manufacturers spanning four or five decades. 'I'm not surrendering to these guys, sir,' Wohl warned Patrick in a low voice. 'Do something, or I will.'

'You Americans?' one of the men who stepped out of the lead Humvee said. He had an Egyptian accent, but it was very slight – he could've been an Arab convenience-store clerk from Boston. 'Who are you guys?'

'We're escapees,' David Luger said. 'We were detainees at Mersa Matrûh.'

'You're very well armed for escapees,' the stranger said. He looked over at Patrick and the others in their Tin Man battle armor. 'Very well equipped – more like attackers than escapees.' He motioned to Patrick. 'If I didn't know better, I'd say those

255

were electromagnetic weapons that fire hypervelocity projectiles.'

'What?' Luger was completely surprised, and he showed it. 'How do you know about hypervelocity weapons?'

'You think because I live in the desert I don't know about such things?' the man asked. 'I read *Popular Science* and *Aviation Week & Space Technology*. I read about the exoskeleton your friends over there are wearing in the London *Times*. I didn't know they actually came out with something, though. Very interesting.'

'Who are you?'

'It appears we're not doing names today,' the stranger said, 'so I don't have an answer for you now. What I do require of you is to put your weapons down on the ground and raise your hands.'

'That will not happen,' Chris Wohl said.

'By the sound of it, I think you must be the noncommissioned officer in charge of this team,' the stranger said. Patrick noticed then how young the man was under his black Kevlar helmet wrapped with a white turban, chocolate-chip battle dress uniform, green Nomex flying gloves, and thick-soled heavy-tread knee-high tanker boots. When he moved, Patrick actually noticed a black shirt underneath his BDUs, with a white shirt underneath that made it appear as if he were wearing a cleric's collar. 'But you will be silent now. I am in command of this area, and you are the trespassers.' He turned to Luger, shook his head. 'And you, sir, are not the commander of this force.' He looked over to the others. 'I will speak to him now.'

Patrick stepped forward. 'What do you mean, you are in command of this area? We're in Egypt.'

The man turned, and Patrick noticed a smile on his youthful face. 'I assume I am addressing the infamous Castor. Finally.'

'You are very astute, sir,' Patrick said. 'Who are you?'

'Since we are now talking in code words, I am called *Dabbur* – the wasp,' the stranger said. 'We are called the *Hubub* – the sand storm. And this is my desert. It has been so for nearly two hundred years. We have protected it for that long. It is not about lines on a map or governments.'

'Your intelligence system is effective – Your Highness.' The man smiled, which made him look even younger than he looked at first. He issued a command in Arabic, and his men lowered their weapons.

'Who is he, Muck?' Hal Briggs asked.

'His Royal Highness, Sayyid Muhammad ibn al-Hasan as-Sanusi, the true king of Libya,' Patrick said. The man smiled, shouldered his weapon, and bowed in thanks for the recognition and proper address. 'The sword of vengeance of the Sahara and leader of the "Sandstorm," the Sanusi Brotherhood.'

'You got it,' Muhammad as-Sanusi said. 'And who are you – other than trouble of the first magnitude around here?'

'Friends – as long as you don't align yourself with Jadallah Zuwayy.'

'You mean my "sixth brother," Jadallah the Brave, the protector of Islam and the savior of the people of Libya? Give me a break,' Sanusi said disgustedly. He took off his helmet and poured water from a canteen on his face. He had a thin, triangular face, wide eyes, and a ready smile, even while deriding someone. 'But what pisses me off even more is that the people of Libya really bought his bucket of bullshit.' He looked carefully at Patrick, then nodded. 'You know my good "brother," then? So I assume you're the devil robot that nearly destroyed Jaghbub and scared the living shit out of him?'

'Maybe. How do you know about that?'

'Zuwayy's men blabbed it all over open channels all last night – you couldn't shut it off,' Sanusi said. 'I think your impromptu nose job improved his looks. And of course, we saw your fireworks show from twenty miles away. Very impressive. Some of my radar outposts picked up traces of an aircraft still orbiting west of here – your air support, I gather?'

'We came close to taking out your men here with our air support.'

'Unless you have EMP-proof radios, I doubt it,' Sanusi said dryly. 'We lost contact with all our patrols the instant that device went off. God in heaven, I always suspected Zuwayy had nukes, but I never thought he'd be stupid enough to actually use them.'

'You don't talk like an Arab, Your Highness.'

'Oh, I can talk Arab just fine when I need to,' Sanusi said. 'But I've lived in the States for the past five years, and I picked up the lingo pretty well.' He held out his canteen to Patrick. 'Can you drink water through that thing?'

'Yes,' Patrick said – but then he disconnected his helmet, pulled

257

it off, and accepted the canteen. 'But I prefer not to.' He grimaced at the canteen.

'Don't worry – it's purified,' Sanusi said. 'I've lived in the States too long to drink the local water, especially from the oases. I may be the sword of vengeance of the Sahara, but the worst my stomach can handle is LA tap water. My men can drink month-old camel piss dug out of a hole in the desert if they had to, but not me. I've got plenty of purification tablets in there.' Patrick took a deep swig, then handed it back. 'What's your name?'

'McLanahan. Patrick McLanahan.'

'Good Irish name,' Sanusi said. 'Who are you guys? Where do you get all that firepower? US Army Special Forces? Delta Force? Navy SEALs?'

'None of the above.'

'Ah. Some supersecret commando job, contracted by the CIA or something,' Sanusi said, taking a drink. When Patrick did not reply, Sanusi merely shrugged. 'My men will find out eventually. We have spies everywhere, and neither the Egyptians nor the Libyans can keep a secret – they all think once you get out into the desert, no one can hear you. I heard a report that the lovely Mrs Salaam and General Baris had been meeting with some special infantry teams at Mersa Matrûh – I assume that's you. Good thing you got out when you did.'

'Some of our guys were not so lucky.'

'The prisoner exchange,' Sanusi said, nodding. 'I heard. I'm sorry, Patrick. So it was you guys in on that raid at Samāh that started this whole mess.'

'We didn't start it – but we mean to finish it,' Patrick said ominously.

'I'm sure you guys are tough – and you're going to have to be, to go up against Zuwayy and his troops,' Sanusi said. 'They've got some mean-looking shit all of a sudden – new Russian weapons, armor, rockets, aircraft, the works, hundreds of millions of dollars' worth. Zuwayy's either been investing some of the money he and his cronies have been ripping off from the Libyan treasury and buying weapons on the international arms market with it, or he's got a wealthy new Russian sponsor.'

That last comment set off nightmarish explosions in Patrick's head, but he ignored the warning bells for the moment. 'We could use your help to get back to Cairo.'

'Cairo? What in hell do you want to go back there for?' Sanusi asked in surprise. 'I thought you said you were escapees from Mersa Matrûh.'

'We were being held there during the prisoner exchange so we wouldn't interfere.'

'Oh really? You sure it wasn't so they'd be sure to fry you just like your friends?' Sanusi noticed Patrick's face blanch and harden to stone, and he put a hand on Patrick's shoulder. 'I'm sorry, McLanahan. You lost some of your men in that explosion, I know.'

Even though Patrick was beginning to trust this man, he still did not feel like elaborating. 'Egypt is wide open for attack. We can help stop Zuwayy until the rest of the world organizes a defense against him.'

'What makes you think they will?' Sanusi asked. 'Who will lead them – Thomas Nathaniel Thorn, the so-called leader of the free world? He's too busy having séances so he can communicate with the spirit of Thomas Jefferson.

'Patrick, no one cares about Libya or Egypt – all they care about is the oil,' Muhammad Sanusi said. 'It's been that way since the Brits discovered oil here. The world will deal with anyone who will sell oil to them – they don't care if it's Salaam, Zuwayy, Khan, or Bozo the Clown. And when the oil runs out, the world will turn its back on this entire continent. All Arabs know the score, Patrick – I'm surprised you don't. Do you really believe you're here fighting for justice or to protect the weak? You're here because of the oil – how to get it, how to keep it coming. I don't care who your employer or commander is – you're here because of the oil. Am I right, my friend?'

Patrick didn't answer – he didn't have to. King Idris the Second, the true king of Libya, nodded knowingly. 'You want to fight for Susan Bailey Salaam? Well, I don't blame you – she is definitely one hot babe, even after taking one in the face in Cairo.' He paused for a moment; then: 'Sure is lucky she survived that blast, wasn't it?' Patrick said nothing – he couldn't, because he didn't know anything about her or the incident at the mosque. 'You're sure you want to do this?'

'I'm sure.'

'Okay. But I still contend: Why go back to Cairo? That's where the action's going to be soon. Either Zuwayy will chew it to pieces with his army, or it'll collapse under the pressure of its own loss of identity. Why would you, an American, hang around for that?'

'You gotta fight for something.'

'Sure you do. Home, family, God. I'm out here in the Sahara with my men instead of back at The Resort at Squaw Creek up in Lake Tahoe or my three-bedroom suite that my buddy Mohammed al Fayed owns at the Hotel Bel Air because Qadhafi chased my family out of our own country, and Zuwayy is busy raping what's left.' Then he stopped and looked knowingly at Patrick. 'Unless you've already lost those things – then you fight for whatever captures your heart – or your soul. Has Susan Bailey Salaam done that for you, Mr McLanahan?' Patrick did not – *could* not – answer.

Muhammad as-Sanusi looked carefully at Patrick; then, apparently noticing something in the man's face, he smiled and winked. 'Man, you are one out-of-place dude,' he said. 'I'm not sure exactly *where* you're supposed to be, but it is *not* here in the desert, wearing metal pajamas and carrying a Buck Rogers space gun.' Again, Patrick couldn't respond. 'Whatever. I still think it would be suicidal for you and your men to go back to Cairo or anywhere in Egypt. But I have the perfect place. If you agree to work with me and my soldiers, I'll bring you there and you guys can set up and work there.'

'Where is this place?'

'Not far. About a half-day drive, assuming we don't run into any patrols.' He looked at Chris and Hal, still in their battle armor, smiled that boyish smile again, then added, 'But I think we can probably handle any patrols we run across out here. Let's go.'

'You have a base right on the Egyptian-Libyan border that's secure from Zuwayy and his troops?'

'I didn't until today,' Sanusi said with a chuckle. '*Min fadlak*. Let's go.'

They hadn't moved far before alarms started going off in the Tin Man battle armor. 'Radiation warning, Muck,' Hal Briggs reported.

'How convenient – radiation detectors in that armor,' Sanusi said to Briggs. 'You must tell me all about that system. My men and I might be in the market for a few dozen.' He turned to Patrick. 'The Libyans are broadcasting that the Zionists set off an American nuclear device at Jaghbub,' he said, 'to kill Zuwayy. Did you have such a device?'

'You know we didn't,' Patrick replied.

Sanusi just smiled. 'But all of Libya and most of the world believe this is so,' Sanusi said. 'It'll make Libya's next move easier to justify.'

'The invasion of Egypt?'

'Well, I think that's pretty obvious,' Sanusi said. 'The question for you is: What's the objective?'

'You said it yourself: oil.'

'Libya has oil. Lots of it.'

'Then Libya either wants more, or it wants to control what it doesn't have – or destroy it.'

Sanusi smiled. 'I think I know where you belong now, Mr McLanahan – or is it General McLanahan? It's still not out here in the desert, though.'

Soon the effects of the electromagnetic pulse in the atmosphere from the explosion at Mersa Matrûh were subsiding, and shortly after that, they started receiving position data. 'We're only twenty miles from Jaghbub,' Patrick pointed out.

'Correct.'

'The radiation levels are getting higher,' Briggs said. 'They'll reach danger levels soon.'

'The radiation levels are high enough to affect normal radio communications,' Sanusi said. 'If a Libyan patrol doesn't have radiation detectors – and by now, all of them do – the disruption of radio communications would get their attention.' Patrick wondered why Sanusi would bother to offer that unusual detail.

By the time they were within five miles of Jaghbub, the radiation levels had reached danger levels. From here they could see the base – and there was no doubt that the base had suffered a tremendous attack. The sand was scorched black, like the ruins of Mersa Matrûh; armored vehicles, buildings, helicopters, and all sorts of objects, most unidentifiable, lay bent and smoldering. Bodies, charred black and burned almost to the skeleton, could be seen scattered everywhere, along with the carcasses of vultures and other desert scavengers who tried to feed off them. The

261

Libyans had erected signs on every road and path, warning in Arabic and English to stay away from the area because of deadly radiation. Obviously many Libyans had ignored the warning, because they could see abandoned Libyan armored vehicles everywhere – they imagined they were filled with the bloated, rotting corpses of radiation-poisoned soldiers.

'My ancestral home,' Sanusi said, 'or at least what remains of it after Qadhafi and Zuwayy desecrated and perverted it.'

'I'm sorry it's been destroyed,' Patrick said.

'You should be – you did most of it, at least to the base,' Sanusi said. He smiled, nodded, then added, 'Nah, don't be sorry. The base was an abomination to the spirit of my ancestors. They created a place of worship and a place of learning here – Qaddafi and Zuwayy turned it into an armed fortress and a den of sin. You only did what I've wanted the power to do – flatten it. Come on.'

'You're going *there?*'

'Of course,' Sanusi said. Some of his men dismounted to examine the new armored vehicles; shots rang out, indicating that some half-dead soldiers were being dispatched by Sanusi's men. But then, to Patrick's surprise, the soldiers started up the vehicle and drove it off – not away from the base, but *toward* it!

'Patrick . . .'

'It's okay – I get it now,' Patrick said. Muhammad Sanusi just smiled and nodded as they continued on.

As they got closer to the carnage that was once the holy Islamic town of Jaghbub, the details became clearer: Some of the corpses were real, but most of them were faked plaster or wooden mannequins. Some of the armored vehicles had been destroyed not from a nuclear blast but by regular antitank or RPG rounds or by the Wolverine cruise missile's Sensor-Fuzed Weapon rounds blowing through the weaker upper hull. The blackness surrounding the base was dark sand, gravel, or charcoal, not the vaporized remains of buildings. 'You *faked* a nuclear blast here?' Hal Briggs asked incredulously.

'It wasn't hard to do after what you guys did here,' Sanusi said. 'The base had been pretty much evacuated by morning – we cleaned up a few security patrols, captured a bunch of good equipment, blew up several thousand pounds of high explosives and ammunition for realism, and used the dead and destroyed vehicles to create the look of a decimated base.'

'And the radiation . . . ?'

'Some captured medical radioisotopes, scattered along the roads and paths. Not enough to be picked up by a radiation-detecting aircraft or satellite, but plenty to be picked up by ground-based sensors. You don't need much if you got the rumor mill going properly – start spreading rumors by radio and teletype that there's been a nuclear detonation in the desert, and bad news travels real fast.'

'So all the messages and reports about an American nuclear attack . . . ?'

'Provided by us,' Sanusi said. 'Complete with pictures, eyewitness accounts, sensor data, even some soldiers suffering radiation sickness. Combined with what's happened at Mersa Matrûh, folks will believe anything now.'

'Eventually the army will send in troops to secure this base,' Chris Wohl said. 'You can't fool them forever.'

'We'll be out of here before they get brave enough to send someone with more brains, Sergeant,' Sanusi said. 'But I think the action will be starting elsewhere, and they'll hold off on investigating Jaghbub for a while.'

'Why do you think that?'

'Because I'll be the one starting the action,' Sanusi said with a smile. 'And now, with your help, we'll make an even bigger splash.'

They drove out to the flight line, where the burned-out hulks of several helicopters and one large jet, about the size of a Boeing 727, sat. The runway was lined with dozens of bomb craters – there didn't appear to be more than one or two hundred feet of usable pavement anywhere. But Patrick already figured that Sanusi and his men were masters at concealment and camouflage. 'Okay, Your Majesty – how did you do it?'

'A little sand, a little wood – it won't stand up to closer scrutiny, but visually, they look real enough,' Sanusi replied. 'A couple men can sweep them off to the side in a few minutes, and it takes less than an hour to put them all back in.' He stopped his Humvee. 'Your attack destroyed most of the buildings and facilities above ground, but not all of them – and best of all, the POL storage is intact.'

'It is?'

'The army put most of the petroleum storage underground, so your big explosive didn't destroy it,' Sanusi explained. 'The fuel farm your bombs blew up was the old tanks. The underground tanks were topped off, too – there's probably one hundred thousand gallons of jet fuel down there, ready to go. Maybe more. All his weapons are underground, too – bombs, missiles, rockets, guns, rifles, and ammunition from seven-millimeter to fifty-seven-millimeter. I would need a thousand men to help me haul it all away.' He looked at Patrick. 'And I'll trade it all for some help.'

'What do you want us to do?'

'Stop Zuwayy and whoever's behind this sudden military buildup of his,' Sanusi said. 'Zuwayy's got something up his sleeve, and he's getting some big-time financing to do it. I'm only irritating him right now – but you could really put the hurt on him. I assume that because you were still in the vicinity of the base you didn't use all your resources here – I'm convinced you can destroy any base, any military site, in Libya or Egypt.'

Just then, Patrick heard, 'Tin Man, this is Headbanger.'

'Go ahead, Headbanger.'

'Thank God we got you, sir,' George 'Zero' Tanaka, the pilot aboard the EB-52 Megafortress bomber, said. 'We were just about to bug out for an emergency landing strip. What's your situation?'

'We're secure,' Patrick reported. 'What's your status?'

'We're a few minutes past bingo for the secondary recovery base,' Tanaka said. Patrick knew that the secondary recovery base for the EB-52 was an isolated abandoned air base near Vol'vata, in the extreme southern tip of Israel – no support, no fuel, just a relatively safe piece of concrete on which to set a two-hundred-thousand-pound plane and wait for help. It was also their last planned emergency recovery base – any other emergency strips they might use from here on out would be in Egypt, Libya, Sudan, or Algeria – or they would ditch in the Mediterranean Sea or Red Sea. 'We lost our tanker support. Got any instructions for us?'

The question, Patrick thought, was rather moot now. Patrick knew he shouldn't trust anyone, especially a Libyan, but Muhammad as-Sanusi was different – or so he hoped.

264

'Yes, I have instructions,' Patrick said. 'Get a fix on my location – you'll find a seven-thousand-foot concrete airstrip here. We have fuel, possibly weapons, some support equipment.'

There were a few moments of silence as the Megafortress crew plotted his location; then: 'Ahh . . . verify this location, sir?' Tanaka asked.

'The location is accurate: Jaghbub, Libya.'

'And you are secure?'

'Affirmative.'

'Then you wouldn't mind telling me the nickname of the base where we launched from.'

Their conversation was on a secure satellite link, but Patrick was still pleased that the Megafortress crew thought of a code phrase to use that only a few folks would know; plus, by saying a nickname, if Patrick was under duress, he could make up any name without arousing suspicion. 'Hooterville,' Patrick replied, giving the nickname the B-52 crews once used for Blytheville Air Force Base in rural northeastern Arkansas.

'Good copy, Tin Man,' Tanaka replied. 'We'll see you shortly.'

Patrick turned to Muhammad as-Sanusi and extended a hand. 'You've got yourself a deal, Your Majesty,' he said. 'My first plane will be here in a few minutes.'

Sanusi issued orders in Arabic, and most of his men raced off in their vehicles. 'My men will have the runway, taxiways, and hangars cleared away for your aircraft immediately,' he said. He shook Patrick's armored hand. 'Welcome to Jaghbub, United Kingdom of Libya. *Ahlan wa sahlan, es salaam alekum.* You are most welcome.' He looked at Patrick's gloved hand, touching the strange BERP fabric and composite exoskeleton with wonder. 'I have *got* to get me a few of these!' he said with glee.

Hūn, United Kingdom of Libya
several hours later

Shortly after the 1986 American air attacks, the late Libyan dictator Colonel Muammar Qadhafi built a complex called *Ginayna* – 'the Garden' – under the streets of the town of Hūn. Ginayna was actually an immense complex of underground tunnels, shelters, alternate command posts, and military storage facilities, extending out several dozen kilometers around the city. Despite its size, it was possible to reach any point of Ginayna from anywhere on foot within an hour. When fully staffed – as it was right now – Ginayna housed over thirty thousand persons.

The complex – five stories underground, shielded by six layers of Kevlar and steel and with its own power generator and air scrubbers, was meant to protect Qadhafi and his personal protection forces in case of another massive attack. It was said that Ginayna was the Doomsday shelter – since a very large majority of the personnel staffing it were women, it was said that Qadhafi planned to repopulate Libya with the personnel housed within Ginayna.

Jadallah Zuwayy considered Ginayna his primary residence. It was craziness to live anywhere else. He was surrounded by plenty of security, they were safe from most all bombs and missiles – the complex was considered strong enough to withstand anything except a direct hit by a nuclear weapon – and there were plenty of escape routes out of there. Sure, he lived like a rodent – but better to be a live rodent than a dead king.

Ginayna was broken into sections controlled by the various branches of the armed services, but Zuwayy stayed mostly in the section reserved as the operational headquarters of the Revolutionary Guard. This was Zuwayy's personal protection force; five thousand men and women, equipped with the best weapons and afforded the best training of all the Libyan armed forces. The main corps of the Revolutionary Guard was the Praetorian Guard, the unit charged with protection of Zuwayy himself, as opposed to all of the king's residences and offices.

It was the only unit in all of Libya that Zuwayy would trust with this particular group.

Thirteen men and one woman – that was all that was left of all the persons taken from the Mediterranean Sea during the air attacks on the ships suspected of staging the raid on the missile base at Samāh. They were taken and separated from the others for one reason only: They looked, spoke, or behaved like Americans. And of the group, the most important and the most intriguing one was the woman.

She was hanging, naked, from manacles bolted to a concrete wall. Her strength had given out days ago – she was no longer able to support herself except for a few brief hours every day, so her wrists were blackened and the flesh had been scraped almost to the bone. Her hair was thin and falling out from dehydration; her ribs protruded so far that they appeared as if they would likely pop right through her skin.

Zuwayy thought she had been very pretty, once. Not anymore.

The lights were turned on as he stepped into the cell. The one lightbulb was like a red-hot poker to the woman's eyes, but she could not shield them. 'Any more information, Sergeant?' Zuwayy asked.

'No, Your Highness,' the jailer responded. 'Her response to all questions is "Help me, please." No names, no other information.'

Zuwayy examined her. The interrogators had tried every possible combination of physical torture, drugs, deprivation, and disorientation to try to break her. He was impressed. 'Very strong, very tough young woman,' he said. He was surprised when she opened her eyes and moved unsteadily to her feet. 'I see you are awake. How are you feeling today, miss?'

'Help me, please,' she muttered through swollen, cracked lips. 'Please, sir, help me.'

'I will be glad to help you,' Zuwayy said. 'All you have to do is tell me your name.'

'Help me. Please.'

'You don't need to resist,' Zuwayy said. 'Your comrades have told us everything about you. You were responsible for infiltrating and attacking a Libyan military base, then escaping via helicopter to your ship. We know everything. We know you are American commandos, on a secret mission to inspect and, if necessary, destroy our military weapons. You might as well talk. If you do, we will treat you like a combatant instead of a spy and afford you treatment under the Geneva Conventions. Do you know what that means?'

'Please, Your Highness . . . please, help me, I beg you . . .'

'I see you recognize who I am? Good! I can guarantee you much better treatment, everything to which a captured combatant is entitled – food, water, clothing, medical attention, and contact with the International Red Cross.'

267

'Please . . . help . . .'

'But under the Geneva Conventions, as you know, you must first tell me your name, rank, serial number, and date of birth,' Zuwayy went on. 'We'll start with your name. That is not a violation of your oath as an American soldier. It is not a national secret. You won't be disgraced or prosecuted by your government, I assure you. Most of your comrades have already told me this information, and that's why they are no longer in here with you – they are being fed, they have seen a doctor, and they have even filled out their Red Cross contact cards.'

'Please, Your Highness . . . please, help me, I beg you . . .'

This was getting nowhere, he thought – the same mindless imprinted resistance babble for days on end. 'Where is that band she was wearing?' Zuwayy asked.

The guard brought it to him. 'We have determined it is some kind of power source,' the guard said. 'We searched her body and found this.' He showed Zuwayy a device about the size of a tack. 'It is some kind of transceiver. We checked it; it is deactivated. It may have been some sort of locator, perhaps even a communications device.'

'Did the others have it?'

'No, Highness. She could be valuable. . .'

'Or she could be a real danger,' Zuwayy said. 'If she was missing, she'd be just another casualty – but here, she could destroy us if they found out she was alive.'

'Torture doesn't seem to be working, Highness,' the guard said. 'Maybe we should try nursing her back to health. We can always eliminate her later.'

'Perhaps . . .'

'Help me . . . please, Highness, help me . . . I beg you . . .'

Zuwayy reared back and slapped her across the face with the back of his left hand. There was no blood – her face, in fact most of her extremities, had long ago lost the ability to bleed. 'Stop begging to me, bitch! You disgust me, you weak sniveling American whore! What is your job onboard your ship – servicing the real warriors, the real soldiers? Are you the unit's traveling whore? Why are we even bothering with this one? We won't learn any information from prostitutes. Throw her disease-infected body into the trash with the other garbage.'

'Please . . . please, help me . . .'

'Your name, whore,' Zuwayy snarled. 'All I want is your name. First name, last name, it doesn't matter. Is keeping that useless bit of information from us worth risking your life? When was the last time you felt your fingers? When was the last time you had a drink of water? We will give you proper medical care and start treating you like a human being and an American soldier instead of a stupid American cocksucker if you will only tell us your name.' No response. She looked as if she might pass out – she was beginning to slump against her chains again. 'One last time, bitch – your name. Right now.' Again, no response.

She is strong, Zuwayy thought. But they were wasting too much time with her. She was a novelty because she was a woman – one of the few captured – but it was too risky keeping a woman imprisoned in a place like this. 'Has she made any contact with any of the others?' Zuwayy asked the jailer. 'Talking, tap code, hand signs, anything?'

'No, Highness. When they were together, they did not even look at each other. They never tried to communicate.'

Very well trained indeed. He examined her face once more. Her eyes were ready to roll back into her head; her tongue was swollen and almost black; and blood was seeping from her eyes, ears, and mouth. 'Get rid of her,' Zuwayy said. 'She's practically dead already. Bury her in the desert. The last thing we need is for her to be caught in here like this. Make it quick, and make it untraceable. I want to see the others.'

Zuwayy was almost out of the cell when he heard her mutter behind him – and it didn't sound like 'Help me, please' this time. He turned and went back to her. She had completely slumped against her chains now. He grabbed her hair and yanked her head up. 'What did you say, bitch? Repeat! What did you say?' She muttered something unintelligible. He put his ear as close as he dared to her lips. 'Speak up! What did you say?'

Through her cracked lips and swollen tongue, he heard her utter, 'M . . . Mc . . . McLanahan,' jut before she passed out again.

Jaghbub, Libya
several hours later

It was hard, steamy, sweaty work – no other way to describe it; and there was no other way to do it except virtually by hand. At first Patrick McLanahan spelled the flight crew in the cockpit while the plane was being refueled – they had to use water pumps and fire hoses to get the fuel out of the underground storage tanks, and then gravity-feed it into each of the Megafortress's twelve fuel tanks. Patrick kept one engine running through the entire refueling just in case they came under attack and he had to start all the other engines, but he acknowledged to himself that there was almost no chance of getting the Megafortress off the ground unless they had at least twenty minutes' warning. But in about a day, the EB-52 Megafortress bomber was fully fueled.

King Idris the Second of Libya, Muhammad as-Sanusi, was nowhere to be seen until dawn, out on patrol all night with his 'Sandstorm' desert warriors. The effects of the electromagnetic pulse had subsided, so Sanusi could maintain radio contact with his men while taking a closer look at Mersa Matrûh. 'The destruction is total, my friend,' he told Patrick after he returned, putting a hand on Patrick's sweat-bathed shoulder. 'The dead are everywhere – it is the most horrible sight I've ever seen. I know you told me it would be safe to go there, that the radiation dissipates almost immediately, but my men refused to go near the place, and I chose not to force them. I am truly sorry, McLanahan. Very sorry.' Patrick nodded – he was beyond feeling sorrow or despair. Once the Megafortress touched down on Jaghbub's runway, he was all business again. 'Very cool bird you have here, Mr McLanahan,' he said. 'Unreal.'

'Thanks.'

'So you will be departing soon?'

'I assume that the Libyans will start getting curious about Jaghbub and send a force down from Tobruk or Benghazi to investigate,' Patrick said. 'I'll bet scouts are already on the way. The bomber needs to be gone by then. We can have a special-operations aircraft meet us here tonight to get us out of the country.'

270

'Well, we're as ready as we can be,' Sanusi said. 'My men picked up some shoulder-fired antiaircraft missiles from their underground arsenal, and we've taken them out so we might have a chance of tagging an attack helicopter or two before it gets close enough to lob a missile in on us.'

Patrick didn't like hearing that. 'What will you do, Your Highness?'

'I need enough time to cart the weapons away, that's all,' Sanusi said. 'I've called for all the men I can muster, but they won't start filtering in for several hours. Once they get here, I'll load up as many weapons and as much fuel as I can carry, then head off to our desert bases. But we know Zuwayy's scouts will be back here before long – like you said, they could be here tomorrow morning, or even tonight.' He paused, then nodded at the EB-52 Megafortress. 'We sure could use your little toy there to help us hold off the heavies.'

It was risky – too risky. The EB-52 had enough fuel to make it to Scotland, where a Sky Masters Inc DC-10 launch/tanker aircraft could meet them to refuel and take them back to the States. Jon Masters used to have secret deals with the British government to use their facilities in emergencies – perhaps that still held true. Bottom line: They had a pretty good chance of making it out of here if they got out tonight.

But Patrick also knew that angry Libyan soldiers could surround Muhammad Sanusi and his men any minute now. He couldn't just leave these guys to their fate. He spoke: 'Patrick to Luger.'

'Go ahead, Muck,' David Luger responded. Sanusi shook his head and again silently marveled at the technology these Americans possessed.

'Let's get the Megafortress uploaded with target information for Zillah Air Base and Al-Jawf Rocket Base,' Patrick said. 'We'll have to use the intel we got from the Egyptians.'

'It's several days old, and a lot of shit has happened since then,' Luger pointed out.

'I don't think we have any choice,' Patrick said. 'Time's running out. We need to . . .' Just then Sanusi received a frantic call on his portable radio. 'Stand by, Dave.'

'I'm afraid time may have run out already,' Sanusi said. 'My

271

scouts reported a convoy of four tanks and five armored personnel carriers heading south. They're about forty kilometers north of here, coming fast. They have also seen several helicopter patrols heading this way, but they have lost contact.'

'Low-level helicopters – could be attackers,' Patrick said. 'Dave, let's get the Megafortress ready to launch. Me, Chris, and Hal will have to go out with the king and his men and see what we can do, but if the helicopters get past us, the Megafortress will fight better in the air.'

The Sanusi Brotherhood 'Sandstorm' warriors raced across the desert at full throttle in their jeeps and Humvees, leaping up and over sand dunes and gullies at more than sixty miles an hour. If they encountered a minefield, Patrick was sure they'd never set any mines off because they hardly touched earth at all. They passed the remains of one Mil Mi-8 helicopter gunship, downed by one of the warriors with a Stinger shoulder-fired missile; a few kilometers away, they found the remains of the warriors and their vehicle, blasted apart into a twisted hunk of burning metal and human tissue.

'Sorry about your men, Your Highness,' Chris Wohl offered over the roar of their speeding vehicle. 'They took on a gunship and defeated it.'

'I wish I could say that their death made a difference, or that they will find peace in God's hands as a reward,' Muhammad as-Sanusi said. 'All I can tell their families and their fellow warriors is that they died trying to win back a kingdom we all believe in so much. All the others can hope for is the chance that their death might rally others to our cause. We shall see.'

They proceeded another few miles until they met up with one of the Sanusi Brotherhood patrols on a slight rise, about two miles west of the Tobruk-Jaghbub highway. From there they crawled over to the edge of the rise, where they could see the oncoming Libyan scouts approaching, now about five miles away.

'I think I found the one thing this battle armor doesn't do very well – you can't fight very well on sand,' Hal Briggs observed. 'You sure as hell can't crawl around with it, and the thrusters don't work very well unless you find a patch of hard-packed sand.'

272

'All true – that's why we can't fight like the king does,' Patrick said. 'Your Highness, I recommend you stay in hiding and keep an eye out for newcomers or anyone who tries to escape. We'll engage – *our* way.'

'We could use a few of those tanks and armored personnel carriers, Tor,' Sanusi said, using his new nickname for Patrick in his battle armor, 'Tor,' meaning 'bull.' 'Try not to destroy all of them, my friend.' Patrick nodded and moved off. Patrick had Hal circle around to cross over to the east side of the highway, keeping Chris on the west side. Patrick took the middle – the highway itself.

The line of Libyan armor was following the highway but staying well off it, spread out about a mile either side of the highway. The armored vehicles stayed on the road – they were wheeled, not tracked – with gunners at the ready in the cupolas. The armored vehicles had AT-2 antitank missiles fitted out on the front of the vehicles along with a fifty-seven-millimeter rapid-fire cannon and a 12.7-millimeter machine gun for the commander; the tanks were ex-Russian T-60s with one-hundred-ten-millimeter main guns. They were not moving very quickly – they were probably playing it cautious after losing contact with their helicopter gunship.

The commander of the lead armored vehicle was surprised to see a lone figure standing in the middle of the highway when he crested the slight rise in the highway. He was standing right there, not moving or attempting to get away or hide. He might have been a hitchhiker – except for the weird head-to-toe outfit he wore. Both armored personnel carriers' fifty-seven-millimeter cannons trained on the solitary figure as they approached, but the stranger did not move.

'*Wa'if hena,*' the lead APC commander ordered. The stranger was dressed unlike anyone he had ever seen. It resembled a chemical warfare exposure suit, which is why he ordered his column to halt – if there were biochem weapons around, he didn't want to go charging in blindly. 'What in hell does he think he's doing?'

'What kind of uniform is that?' the other commander radioed in response. 'Could it be one of our men, maybe a survivor from Jaghbub? Maybe that's a protective suit he's wearing. Who else would be stupid enough to be walking right up to an armored patrol unarmed in the middle of the day?'

'Ordinarily I'd say yes – but we just lost contact with one of our scout helicopters, which means everyone's an enemy until we find out otherwise. Stay back: I'll go have a chat with him. Everyone else, stay alert.' He ordered his men to dismount. Eight heavily armed Libyan soldiers ran out of the back of the APC and took up defensive positions on either side of the highway. The lead APC then began to roll forward toward the stranger.

The APC hadn't gone fifty feet when suddenly two tanks, one on either side of the highway, disappeared in a ball of fire – the dismounts heard only a faint *plink* sound, and then the tanks exploded. The soldiers had just enough time to dive for cover in the depression on the side of the highway before they were showered with burning debris. Huge gushes of fire fed from ruptured fuel tanks poured across the desert floor, and the dismounts got to their feet in a hurry and retreated back toward the remaining APCs, firing in the general direction from where those projectiles came from.

'Attention, Libyan soldiers,' he said through his electronic synthesizer and translation system. 'I am Castor. I order all of you to surrender immediately. Do not traverse your gun turrets or you will be destroyed.'

'The east tank's turret is moving toward you,' Briggs reported.

'Kill it,' Patrick said. Briggs fired a hypervelocity round into the tank, and it blew even more spectacularly than the first two. That's all it took – one by one, the Libyan soldiers popped hatches and started climbing out of the tanks, hands upraised. 'Your Highness, the Libyans are surrendering,' Patrick radioed to Sanusi. 'You can move –'

The helicopter came out of nowhere, popping over the sand dunes only a few feet above the desert floor – a Mil Mi-24 attack helicopter, fully configured for combat with a four-barreled 12.7-millimeter remote-controlled cannon in the nose and two stubby wing pylons filled with a variety of rocket pods, bombs, and missiles. It was firing its machine guns almost as soon as it popped into sight.

Hal Briggs's position was hit first, and the gunner's aim was perfect. The hail of bullets from the gunship was like a massive swarm of fifty-caliber bees – they were beginning to sting, and after enough stings, they could kill. 'Mother*fucker!*' Hal Briggs cursed. 'That bastard got my rail gun. Chris has the only one left.'

The Libyan soldiers cheered and dashed back into their vehicles, ready to resume the fight. Chris Wohl turned and aimed his rail gun at the retreating helicopter gunship – but at that moment, another Mi-24 appeared from the east, no more than fifty feet above the desert, and launched a salvo of rockets at Wohl's position, while the gunner started hammering at Patrick with the steerable cannons.

The gunner swung his cannon away from Patrick after only a quarter-second burst, choosing to concentrate fire on the armed stranger and assuming Patrick would go down under the barrage of gunfire. That gave Patrick his chance. As the Mi-24 cruised over the highway, Patrick used his thrusters and leaped at it. He landed on the left side of the helicopter right between the gunner and pilot's cupolas. Patrick drove his left hand through the bow in the pilot's forward windscreen, drove his left foot through the gunner's left window, then punched through the pilot's left window with his right fist.

The pilot screamed. Patrick grabbed the pilot's throat with his armored right hand. *'Wa'if! Awiz aruh hena, ala tul!'* he said over the roar of the huge rotor overhead through his electronic translator. 'Stop and land it right here.' The Mi-24's flight engineer, seated right behind the pilot in a small jump seat, tried to pull Patrick's hand off his pilot's neck – Patrick finally knocked him out with a bolt of electricity from his shoulder-mounted electrodes. Threatened with having his throat crushed, the Libyan pilot set the big gunship down, and Patrick knocked him out too with an electric shock.

Meanwhile, Chris Wohl rolled to his feet and checked over his rail gun – still operational. He was going to line up on the second Mi-24, which was wheeling back around for another pass. 'Sarge! The tank!' He saw that the Libyan tank's crew members had almost reached the entry hatch. He fired one shot that blew the driver's upper torso apart, spattering the entire top of the tank with blood and gore. The other tankers froze and raised their hands in surrender.

Hal Briggs tried to make a jump for the road, but his thrusters wouldn't push into the sand, and he could only jump a few feet into the air. But suddenly, behind him, Muhammad Sanusi's Humvee roared toward him. Without slowing, Sanusi steered right for Hal. With perfect timing, Hal jetted up just before the Humvee reached him, and Hal landed on the Humvee's hard top. He clutched onto the roof as the Humvee roared toward the highway. Just before reaching the highway, Hal jetted off the roof and landed on the easternmost armored personnel carrier just as the last man was climbing aboard. He took command of the 12.7-millimeter machine gun on the commander's cupola, swung it around, hit and killed one APC commander who was covering his men, then raked machine-gun fire over the heads of the other APCs beside him until the crews froze with their hands in the air.

The second Mi-24 was coming around again. Wohl turned to fire at it, but the rail gun was out of commission, damaged in the rocket attack. The Mi-24 attack helicopter's steerable cannon lined up on Sanusi's Humvee. Hal fired from the commandeered Libyan APC, but the Mi-24's armor was too strong and the bullets had no effect. 'Chris! Tag that son of a bitch!' But he saw in his own electronic visors that their last rail gun was out of commission. 'Look out!'

Suddenly, a small explosion erupted on the right side of the Mi-24. Another of Sanusi's Sandstorm warriors in what looked like a World War II-vintage jeep had fired an RPG round at the helicopter, missing the tail rotor and cockpit and hitting only the heavily armored side. The Mi-24 wheeled in an impossibly tight right turn and fired a rocket salvo, and at that range the attack was devastating. The jeep exploded in a twisted, burning hunk of metal. Hal continued to fire on the Mi-24, hoping that his shells would hit something vital, but he couldn't tell if he was hitting anything at all.

Then he saw Sanusi's Humvee stop, and Muhammad as-Sanusi himself climbed out, went into the back of the vehicle, and emerged with a man-portable Stinger missile system. But the Mi-24 pilot saw him at the same time, and he wheeled the helicopter left to line up on him – the nose cannon was already leading into the turn. *'Sanusi! Take cover!'* Briggs shouted.

But Sanusi stood his ground. With his men firing rifles at the oncoming helicopter, the king stood calmly, his feet together, and hefted the Stinger to his right shoulder. He activated the battery, powered on the unit, then pulled a lever with his right thumb, uncovering the missile's seeker head. The Mi-24's cannon started firing long before the pilot finished the turn, and at less than a mile away, he couldn't miss. The shells made a rooster tail of sand race across the desert, headed right for Sanusi. The ripple of sand reached the king just as Sanusi pulled the launch trigger and sent the Stinger blasting out of the launch tube.

The missile exploded on the Mi-24 gunship's left engine intake, and the force of the explosion followed by the complete destruction of the left engine caused the Mi-24's main rotor to fly off in a cloud of fire. The helicopter plunged straight forward into the desert floor, then flipped upside down on its back before exploding less than a hundred meters from where the king of united Libya stood.

It was as if everyone, including the Libyan soldiers, were stunned motionless as they saw the sand and dust settle and King Idris the Second still standing, holding the Stinger launcher triumphantly in one hand, laughing loudly as the smoke and debris from the wrecked helicopter gunship wafted near him – but it was as if even the smoke and flames dared not touch him. His men cheered as they rolled up to cover him, but Zuwayy's soldiers did not try to run or fight – instead, moments later, they joined in the cheering.

'Pretty good shooting, Your Highness,' Patrick said as he and the other Night Stalkers joined him a few moments later.

'Shukran gazilan,' Sanusi replied. He looked at the other Mi-24 gunship and nodded happily. 'Pretty good piece of flying yourself, Mr McLanahan.' Sanusi's men were already taking possession of the vehicles that were still intact – one T-60 tank, four armored personnel carriers, and a Mil Mi-24 helicopter gunship.

To Patrick's surprise, Sanusi's men and a good number of the Libyan soldiers were greeting each other like long-lost brothers – the Libyan soldiers were tearing off insignia and patches that had anything to do with Zuwayy's regime, and Sanusi's men were giving the defecting soldiers imperial insignia to wear. Moments later, they were all lined up before the king and each individually swore loyalty to him in front of the others. They all did so

277

without one moment's hesitation. The two surviving officers refused to swear loyalty to the true king of united Libya – and were executed on the spot by a knife thrust to the heart, by their own men.

'Turns out most of these men were from the same town, west of Tripoli,' Sanusi said several minutes later after he rejoined Patrick and the other Night Stalkers. 'They are based at Al-Jawf. They were sent out to investigate the reports of nuclear weapons and possible hostile military presence at Jaghbub. They believe that if they made contact with any enemy forces Jaghbub was going to be attacked by attack helicopters and bombers from Zillah or rockets from Al-Jawf.'

'Strange that the Libyans haven't sent more troops, Your Highness,' Hal Briggs observed as the day wore on. 'They lost three attack helicopters and a light armor scout platoon – I thought they'd be a bit more curious as to why.'

'They didn't lose them,' Sanusi replied with a smile. 'The platoon has checked in every hour on the half hour, as ordered. The platoon is continuing their search of Jaghbub. They have encountered heavier-than-expected radiation levels, however, and are advising against sending any more forces toward the town.' He was pleased at Briggs's smile.

'Clever, sir. But you realize that won't last long.'

'We have extended the fiction another day or two, I think,' Sanusi acknowledged. 'But soon the platoon will be relieved, and that's when Zuwayy will strike with force.'

'That's why we need to attack,' Patrick said. 'Let's get back to Jaghbub and get our planes in the air.'

Chapter Seven

Outside Zillah Air Base, central Libya
that night

'Grumble Twelve, this is Lion Seven at checkpoint two-nine-three.'

Dead on course. With all the activity around the base as the division got ready to go to war with the Egyptians, it was a relief to have a helicopter crew where it was supposed to be, especially at night. 'Acknowledged, Lion Seven,' the Libyan air defense radio operator replied. 'Radar contact, four-eight kilometers bull's-eye. Verify altitude.'

'Altitude four hundred.'

Checked – right on course and altitude, although he was very late checking in. If only all the army aviation guys did it this well, the air defense operator thought, his job would be a lot easier. 'Acknowledged. Descend to two hundred meters on course. Are you a single ship?'

'Affirmative, Lion Seven.'

The commander of the S-300 surface-to-air missile site stood behind the radar station and optronics officer's station, listening in. He narrowed his eyes in thought. 'He is very late – almost outside the code change time limit,' he said, verbalizing his thoughts to the backs of his crew's heads. Radio and identification codes were changed daily, and deployed units had to return to receive new ones within three hours of the changeover time or risk getting shot down without warning. 'Does his transponder check?' he asked his radio operator.

'Yes, sir.'

Something still didn't feel right. The commander keyed his command channel radio button: 'Lion Seven, are you single ship tonight?'

'Affirmative.'

'Where are your wingmen?'

281

'One unit is *daeyikh*,' the pilot of the inbound helicopter reported. That meant it had been destroyed. 'The other unit has stayed behind to assist. We are returning for a code change.'

'Acknowledged,' the commander said. That was standard procedure: Perhaps an officer aboard the undamaged helicopter had returned with this crew to pick up new decoding documents, because no aircraft could approach Zillah, especially at night but any time under this wartime posture, without a valid transponder code.

The S-300 commander, situated thirty kilometers northeast of Zillah, had already alerted his battery and the two flanking missile batteries of the approaching helicopter five minutes ago when it popped up on radar. The S-300 air defense system, one of the best all-altitude long-range surface-to-air missile systems in the world, had managed to pick up the low-flying helicopter ninety kilometers away even though it was only four hundred meters above the desert – the S-300's powerful multiscan radar could pick up aircraft as low as thirty meters' altitude or as high as thirty thousand meters and as far as three hundred kilometers away.

There were only three security ingress routes into Zillah, and they changed daily. All flight crews were required to cross a route entry point and then fly a designated ingress track until positive visual contact was made. The S-300 system also employed a powerful target-tracking low-light telescope, normally used in high-radar-jamming environments or when the radar was down, but was used routinely for aircraft identification. While the aircraft stayed on course, the S-300 optronics operator could easily locate and track it. Each aircraft had an identifying infrared-fluorescent code stripe on its nose and sides to aid in long-range identification; the stripes were changed on a random basis, usually once every week.

The commander stood over the primary radar engagement officer and his assistant, frowning at his own confusing thoughts. While the radio operator verified the authentication codes, the radar officers checked the transponder identification codes, which showed up on the radar screen along with the target's speed, altitude, and call sign. Everything checked okay. So why was he so nervous about this inbound?

'Air defense alert,' the commander said suddenly. He looked at his watch, then made a note in his log. 'All units, prepare to repel airborne attackers. This is not an exercise.'

His crew members turned to look at their commander in surprise, then snapped their necks around, frantically checking their indicators and screens for any sign of an intruder, something they missed. There was nothing. But they responded anyway: the deputy pressed a button on his control panel, which sounded a Klaxon throughout the battery that an attack was imminent; reload crews began making preparations to load another four-round missile rack onto the transporter-erector-launchers; and a warning was sent out to all aircraft and all air defense units in the region, warning of an impending attack.

The brigade command phone rang almost immediately: 'Lieutenant, what do you have?' the air defense brigade commander asked.

'Inbound Mi-24 attack helicopter, Lion Seven, sir.'

'Does he authenticate?'

'His codes are almost invalid, but as of right now, he has been verified.'

'Any other targets?'

'No, sir.'

'Then why did you issue the air defense warning, Lieutenant?'

The commander swallowed but did not otherwise hesitate: 'Sir, Lion Seven left his wingman behind, even though he reported another wingman destroyed. All of our aviation units understand the importance of returning to base to be issued up-to-date authentication documents – they must do so unless they are actively engaging the enemy.'

The brigade commander hesitated. The lieutenant was a prior noncommissioned aviation officer, well experienced in both air defense and aviation procedures – at least, the lieutenant hoped the brigade commander remembered.

But it came down to only one thing, which the brigade commander pointed out moments later: 'That's not a violation of procedures or a cause for issuing a general air defense warning. So . . . you're saying you have a hunch, is that it, Lieutenant?'

'Yes, sir.'

'Well, you're allowed all the hunches you like, Lieutenant –

it'll keep the men on their toes,' the brigade commander said after another lengthy, agonizing pause. 'But may I remind you that your battery will have to reposition to another location after the alert is over, so your men will be up all night.'

'I am aware of that, sir.' Once the missile batteries turned on their radars, spy planes and satellites could map their location easily, so it was important to move the missiles and radars around to make it more difficult for the enemy to find and target their radars. Fortunately, the S-300 missile system was very easy to relocate – it took less than a half hour to set up again after finding a suitable spot. The units were moved several times a week – no more than a few hundred meters, but far enough where garbage pits, latrines, and launcher anchor points had to be redug each time out of the desert. That was usually the hardest part, and the aspect of the move that caused the most grumbling.

'Very well.' The lieutenant was one of the best battery commanders in the entire brigade. The lieutenant started out as a conscript after dropping out of high school at the age of fifteen. By the age of eighteen, he had accepted a regular enlistment, and just two years after that was made a noncommissioned officer. Being prior enlisted himself, he could handle his enlisted men, conscripts, and noncommissioned officers just fine. 'Report your threat assessment and engagement to the brigade operations officer immediately after you've called off the alert.' There were a few clacks in the net; then, on the brigade-wide channel, the lieutenant heard, 'All units, all units, Twelve has issued a general air defense warning for the brigade. Report and correlate all contacts now. This is Brigade, out.'

'My God, what in hell is going on here?' Greg 'Gonzo' Wickland, the mission commander aboard the EB-52 Megafortress, exclaimed. They had just launched from Jaghbub and had no sooner turned southbound on course than the entire Libyan air defense network seemed to light up all at once. 'SA-10, SA-11, SA-5s – every theater and tactical air defense radar is on the air all of a sudden.'

'Sanusi's men didn't make it,' the aircraft commander, George 'Zero' Tanaka, surmised. 'The Libyans probably shot down the Mi-24, and that alerted the whole country.'

284

'What do we do?'

'We press on,' Tanaka said. 'The Hind helicopter was just a feint – we can still go in on our own.'

Wickland shook his head. 'This is crazy, Zero,' he said. 'We've got the gas to get us all the way to Iceland – why didn't he just order us to head west and link up with a tanker to send us home? We're loaded down with crappy Russian bombs and missiles that probably won't work; we're surrounded by bad guys; and this isn't even our damned fight!'

'Just button it, will you, Gonzo?'

'I'm serious here, man!' Wickland shouted. 'What are we doing here? I'm an engineer, for Chrissakes! I've never been in the military! My job is designing and testing weapons and attack systems and writing software, not dropping bombs on Libyans who want nothing more than to shoot my ass off! I want to –'

'Gonzo, I don't give a shit what you want,' Tanaka interrupted. 'Just keep the computers humming and shut your pie-hole.'

'Sure, go ahead – bitch at me. You're the ex-Air Force war hero – you get off on this shit, not me. It's McLanahan who's going to get our asses shot off! I didn't come out here to . . .'

'Wickland, I said, *shut the fuck up*,' Tanaka said. 'You knew exactly where we were going and what we were going to do, when we briefed this mission. You knew we were going to attack Libya, refuel and rearm, then attack again. You took the money, bought your Mercedes and your big house in Memphis, and got your big stock options. Now you gotta earn your money. So just fly the plane, keep those computers going and that nav system up tight, and *shut up*.'

Wickland seemed to shrivel up just then. He sat upright in his ejection seat, seemingly oblivious to all the new air defense warnings popping up on their threat display. Tanaka looked over at him, and after a few moments realized that the guy was just plain scared. Tanaka, a twenty-one-year veteran of the US Air Force and retired lieutenant colonel, with over five thousand hours in about nine different tactical fighter and bomber aircraft, instantly felt sorry for him. Combat was just another phase of flight for Tanaka. The simulators they flew back at Sky Masters Inc's headquarters in Blytheville were a hundred times more hectic and

285

every bit as realistic as the real thing – Tanaka thought it was excellent preparation for these operational missions, so much so that he felt ultra-prepared for almost every Megafortress flight. He never realized that the other, less experienced guys might not think that way. Wickland was an engineer, a designer, not a combat aircrewman.

'Listen, Gonzo,' Tanaka said, 'I'm sorry. I know you're scared. . .'

'I'm not scared.'

'Okay. That's fine. I just want you to do your job –'

'I'm *going* to do my job, George.'

'Good. I know you will. Just think of this as just another sim ride. We're wringing out a new weapon code, that's all, nothing to it.'

But as soon as Tanaka uttered those words, he knew they didn't ring true.

'I'm sorry, Greg,' Tanaka went on. 'We're not in the sim. We're not wringing out a new software program. This is the real thing. The missile that we fail to defeat or we don't see will kill us, not just crash the IPL or freeze the sim. I know you didn't sign up with the company to go to war. And I know you agreed to do this mission on the ground – but now we're in the air, and we're surrounded by about nine hostile SAM systems that will shoot us out of the sky the instant they get a lock on us, and you're having second thoughts.' He paused, looking at Wickland, who said nothing. 'Am I right?'

'Zero . . .'

'It's okay, Gonzo,' Tanaka said. 'We use these call signs and dress up in cool flight suits and pretend we're Tom Cruise and Anthony Edwards in *Top Gun*, but the truth is hammering us in the head right now – that we're in deep shit, that we could die any second up here; and if we do, no one will know what the hell we're doing up here. We'll be dead, and that's all.' Wickland remained silent, but he turned to his aircraft commander, his chest inflating and deflating as if he was having trouble breathing all of a sudden.

'Gonzo, we don't have to do this if you don't want to,' Tanaka said. 'This is the general's fight, not ours. We're the crew members aboard this plane, but we're not sworn to fight and die for whoever the company is doing all this for. We signed a contract to fly planes for Sky Masters Inc, not get our asses shot at by a thousand Libyan SAMs. So if you want to break out of here, we will.'

Wickland's mouth opened in surprise. 'You will?'

'Damn straight,' Tanaka said. 'I realize we're not in this to save our country. We're doing this because we like flying planes and building cool weapon systems and watching them work. So if you say so, I'll call the general right now and tell him we're aborting the mission.'

'*You will?*' Wickland repeated, stunned.

'I said I would,' Tanaka said. 'We'll climb out, avoid all the SAMs and intercept radars, get out over open ocean away from all other air traffic, head toward the Scotland refueling anchor, and call for gas to take us home or land at our facility at Glasgow or Lossiemouth.'

'We'll catch hell for doing that . . .'

'The company can't do dick to us, Gonzo. They can't fire us, they can't dock our pay, and they can't sue us.'

'What about the guys on the ground?'

'If they're smart, they'll bug out shortly after we do,' Tanaka said. 'I'll let them know exactly what we're doing, and why.' That made Wickland swallow hard – he was scared of dying, obviously, but also scared of being thought of as a coward by his cohorts. 'Like I said, Gonzo, this is the general's fight, not ours. I'm flying this mission because I happen to believe that we're doing something good, something right – and besides, I like flying this kickass plane into battle, *real* battle. But I respect your wishes, too – we do this together. So what do you say?'

Wickland looked at his supercockpit display, automatically entering commands or adjusting settings. He turned to Tanaka, opened his mouth as if to say something, then turned back to his console.

'Gonzo? What's it going to be?'

The mission commander shrugged. He was called the 'mission commander,' but truthfully he didn't feel like a commander of anything. All he wanted to do was build and test cutting-edge neural network computer systems. He didn't want to go to war. Still . . .

'Let's keep going,' he heard himself say. 'I spent four hours getting the interface to work between those hunks of junk in our bomb bay – now I want to see if they'll work.'

'Sounds like a plan to me,' Tanaka said. 'Let's plot a course around as many of these SAMs as we can, then make our way to the initial point on time.' He was pleased to see Wickland immediately start punching the supercockpit display's touchscreen and speaking computer commands – he was back in the lab or in the sim, where he really belonged. Whatever it took to get his head where it needed to be . . .

'We've got two SA-10s, one just nine miles east of the IP, the other forty miles west-northwest,' Wickland reported. 'Looks like they moved them since this morning when those Libyans scouted them.'

'The target run will put us just inside lethal range of the second SAM after we're IP inbound, and he'll be alerted if we have to fire on the first site,' Tanaka said. 'What's the computer say?'

'It says let's get the fuck out of here, go home, and have a beer,' Wickland quipped. He turned to Tanaka, smiled, and corrected himself, saying, 'Nah, that was me – but I'll do what the computer says: descend to computer-generated lowest altitude, replot the IP to bypass the first SAM, and attack the second SAM with one antiradar missile. It'll take the first SAM at least thirty seconds to acquire us, and by that time we'll be just a few seconds out of detection range and within a minute of flying out of lethal range. We save one antiradar missile for later.' He punched up instructions on the touchscreen. 'Center up on the bug to the new IP. I've got COLA terrain-following mode selected, minimum safe altitude is on the barber pole.'

'Roger, MC,' Tanaka said. Yep, he thought happily, he's back. 'Here we go.'

'Grumble, this is Lion Seven,' the Mi-24 pilot radioed. 'I copy you have declared an air defense emergency. Do you need us to reverse course and re-enter the security approach? We are five minutes from bingo fuel, and we have wounded on board. We must land immediately. Over.'

The S-300 battery commander had a decision to make. The proper procedure was to kick all aircraft out of the airspace and have them reenter the restricted area, usually on a different ingress route to be sure they were familiar with all the routes, not just the one they filed for. But this guy was bingo fuel, and he obviously saw some kind of action.

Well, the lieutenant thought, all that wasn't his fault. That hot prickly sensation was still hammering away on the back of his neck – no time to ignore it now. 'Adem Seven, reverse course and reenter through checkpoint one-one-nine at three hundred meters.'

He heard the pilot radio a muttered *'Insha'allah,'* which in this case probably more closely meant 'Who do you think you are, God?' rather than 'If God wills it.' But the pilot responded curtly, 'Roger, Grumble Twelve. Reversing course.'

'He sounded pretty mad, sir,' the radar operator observed.

'If he runs out of fuel and crashes, I'll take the blame for it,' the lieutenant said. 'But as long as we follow procedures, we can't be faulted too badly. Clear your screens and report.'

The radar operators switched their radar briefly from short-range tracking and identification to long-range search. The short-range tracking gave altitude information and more precise tracking information, but sacrificed range, so the radar had to be manually reset for longer-range scans on occasion. The Mi-24 helicopter briefly disappeared from the radar display when the mode was changed. 'Radar is clear, sir.'

'Very well. Continue tracking Seven to the ingress point.'

'Yes, sir.'

'Comm, ask him his fuel state again. If we need to, we'll have to coordinate an off-base refueling.'

'Yes, sir.' He turned to his radios; the lieutenant lit a cigarette while they worked. But moments later: 'Sir, no reply from Lion Seven!'

The creepy-crawling sensation on the back of the lieutenant's neck was raging now; he crushed the cigarette out with a stamp of a foot. 'Radar . . . ?'

'He just disappeared off the scope, sir,' the radar operator reported. 'I had his transponder signal and primary target just a moment ago – now it's gone.'

'Any ELTs?'

The radio operator switched his intercom panel – and sure enough, they heard a *pingpingpingping!* signal on the international

289

emergency frequency. The ELT, or emergency locator transmitter, activated automatically upon impact if the helicopter crashed.

'Shit,' the lieutenant cursed, 'he crashed. I thought he said he was bingo fuel – he should've had at least a thirty-minute reserve. Those hot dog helo pilots would rather kill themselves than admit they screwed up and stretched their fuel past safe tolerances. Give me a bearing to the signal, notify Units Ten and Nine and have them triangulate his position, then send it to Brigade to organize an immediate rescue.' He picked up the command phone. 'Brigade, Twelve.'

'Go ahead.'

'Sir, we have lost contact with Lion Seven. We are picking up an ELT; he may have crashed. He reported he was low on fuel, but he first reported that he . . .'

'Sir, unidentified fast-moving aircraft inbound, range thirty-five kilometers and closing!'

'Release all batteries!' the lieutenant shouted, still with his finger on the phone's call switch. He threw the phone into its cradle. 'Release batteries and fire!' He looked at the radar screen – it was a hopeless jumble of streaks, dots, swirls, and radiating electrical noise.

'We are being jammed, sir! Heavy jamming, all frequencies!'

'Switch to optronic control, search along the last known bearing. Switch the radar to short-scan multifrequency to simulate missile guidance uplink – let's see if he switches his jammers to counter the uplink. Where's the optronic crew? Report, dammit!'

'Optronics crew searching along predicted flight path . . . Sir, optronic crew has detected a fast-moving target!'

'Match bearings and reacquire in medium-scan mode!'

'Target reacquired . . . target locked in medium-scan mode.'

It was a crapshoot after this: time for the missile to fly to its target minus ten seconds, the minimum amount of time it took to lock on with the more precise short-range scan, then transmit the uplink data to guide the missile to its target. No time for guessing now . . . 'Release batteries and launch two.'

The deputy commander hit the 'LAUNCH' alarm, flipped a switch guard, and then reached down inside the switch to a covered button underneath. Moving the switch set off another alarm in the command cab; the lieutenant silenced the horn with a commander's 'pickle switch' that he held in his left hand, which issued a consent command to the launch controller.

Outside, at a launcher two hundred meters away, a three-thousand-pound missile popped out of its launch tube from a slug of compressed nitrogen. The missile flew straight up for about seventy feet before the solid-rocket booster ignited, quickly accelerating the missile to well over five times the speed of sound.

'Twenty seconds to impact.' Three seconds later, they heard a second loud blast from outside – the second 5V55K missile had popped out of its launch tube and was following the first on its way to the target. 'Second missile away . . . fifteen seconds to impact.'

'Stand by to switch to narrow-beam mode . . . now.'

The engagement officer switched radar modes. 'Target acquired in narrow-scan mode . . . target locked, sir! Ten seconds to –'

Suddenly the entire command vehicle violently rocked on its eight wheels. The India/Juliett-band radar of the S-300 was carried aboard the same semi-trailer truck as the command unit. The lights flickered, then went out completely. Moments later, a second object struck the vehicle, harder than the first. A burst of fire erupted from the control console. 'Evacuate! Now!' the lieutenant shouted. The crew members ran outside just as thick black smoke began billowing out of the command cab.

As the command crew assembled outside, the lieutenant quickly determined the cause of the double explosion – a Mil Mi-24 attack helicopter, just a few kilometers away, was firing guided antitank missiles at the S-300 battery. He realized then that the Mi-24 hadn't crashed – it had just ducked down below the S-300's radar coverage, cruised in, and attacked. It was flying perhaps ten meters above the desert, flying at just thirty or forty kilometers an hour, slowly and carefully picking its targets. Occasionally a blast of machine-gun fire erupted from its nose cannon, followed by a streak of fire as its laser-guided missiles sped off their launch rails and hit home.

In seconds, it was over – and the entire S-300 battery, eight launchers and a control/radar vehicle, had been destroyed, and the Mi-24 helicopter simply disappeared into the night sky. Soon, only the sounds of burning vehicles and screaming men could be heard.

King Sayyid Muhammad ibn al-Hasan as-Sanusi, on board the Mi-24 helicopter in the flight engineer's station, patted the pilot on the shoulders, then turned to the radio console at the engineer's station behind the cockpit. 'Headbanger, Headbanger, this is Lion,' he radioed. 'Target Alpha is down, repeat, Alpha is down. Commence your run.'

At that moment, he saw a long trail of fire coming from the direction of Zillah Air Base. The bombers were on their way.

He hoped to hell the Megafortress could stop them.

'LADAR coming on . . . now,' Greg Wickland reported. Seconds later: 'LADAR standby.' The image frozen in his wide-screen supercockpit display was almost as clear as a sixteen-color photograph. What he saw horrified him: 'The bombers – they're gone.'

'Oh, shit,' George 'Zero' Tanaka muttered. He strained to take a look at the supercockpit display. 'Looks like two planes still on the base, getting ready for takeoff.'

'Fighters,' Wickland said. 'MiG-23s. Must be the last of the bombers' air cover.' He flashed the LADAR on and off several times so he could keep watch on the fighters, taking a laser snapshot and then rolling and turning the three-dimensional image to pick up as much detail as possible. Soon he could see them rolling down the runway – the LADAR even detected their afterburner plumes. 'Looks like they're heading north – not toward us.' He turned to his aircraft commander. 'Our mission was to try to destroy the bombers or crater the runway so the bombers couldn't launch. We missed them. What do we do now? There's no use attacking the base if the bombers are gone.' His eyes grew wide with fear as he started to guess what Tanaka had in mind: 'You're not thinking of *going after the bombers,* are you?'

'It's our only chance of stopping them.'

'We've only got eight air-to-air missiles,' Wickland reminded his AC – not just for Tanaka's benefit, but also to assure himself of how dangerous this plan really was. The EB-52 Megafortress carried eight radar-guided AIM-120 Scorpion missiles in stealthy external weapon pods, along with four AGM-88 HARMs (high-speed antiradar missiles). Internally, the EB-52 carried a rotary launcher with eight AGM-154 JSOW (joint standoff weapons), which were satellite- and imaging-infrared-guided thousand-pound glide bombs that could be targeted by the laser radar and attack computers; plus another rotary launcher with eight Wolverine powered 'brilliant' cruise missiles, which could locate and attack their own targets. 'It's crazy. I think we ought to –'

'Listen, Wickland,' Tanaka interrupted angrily, 'right now, I don't care what you think.' He dropped his oxygen mask and looked at his mission commander with pure anger. 'I asked you before we entered hostile airspace if you wanted to do this, and you said "press on." Now we've stirred up the hornet's nest, we've got friendlies on the ground directly in harm's way, and we are *not* going to back down now.'

'But you said –'

'I know what I said, and I was right – this wasn't our fight, and this is not our country,' Tanaka said. 'But we're committed. Do you understand that, Wickland? The time to back out was twenty minutes ago before Sanusi's forces entered defended airspace, or even five minutes ago before we started jamming the Libyan SAM sites. Now we're in the middle of the shit, and I'm not just turning around and going home. So you'd better do your job and do it damn well, or I won't wait to be blown up by a SAM – *I'll* put a bullet up your ass myself. Now give me a heading to those planes.'

Wickland silently did what he was ordered to do. The MiG-23 fighters turned east-northeast, and Tanaka rolled in about thirty miles behind them to follow. Less than fifteen minutes later, they detected another flight of aircraft: three Tupolev-22 supersonic bombers, heading northeast toward the Gulf of Sidra. 'There they are,' Tanaka said. He began to push the throttles up until they were in full military power.

'What are you doing?' Wickland asked.

'We've got to nail those guys before the fighters join up,' Tanaka said. 'Those are Tupolev-22s – they're just as fast as the MiGs. Once they join up, they'll accelerate to attack speed, and we'll never catch them.'

Wickland was silent, but Tanaka could sense the fear in his

body as they quickly closed in. 'Eight miles to go . . . seven miles, coming up on max missile range,' he said. 'Six miles . . . five . . . the bombers will still get away. . .'

'At this point, we'll just have to hope we take the tail-end Charlie fighters out – maybe the bombers will break up once they find out their fighters are gone,' Tanaka said.

'We're in max range.' Wickland quickly touched the super-cockpit display and spoke: 'Attack target.'

'Attack MiG-23 Scorpion, stop attack,' the computer responded. Moments later, the first AIM-120 air-to-air missile shot out of the starboard external weapon pod and streaked off into the darkness.

But the MiGs must have sensed something was wrong, or maybe one of the pilots was checking his six, because the MiG-23 fighters suddenly peeled away from the formation, dropped decoy flares, climbed rapidly, then reversed direction. Seconds later, they heard a high-pitched *DEEDLE DEEDLE DEEDLE!* warning and a female computerized voice announcing, *'Warning, fighter search radar, MiG-23, eleven o'clock, sixteen miles,'* followed immediately by a fast-paced *DEEDLEDEEDLEDEEDLE!* and *'Warning, fighter radar lock, MiG-23, eleven o'clock, high, fifteen miles.'*

'The Scorpion broke lock,' Wickland said. At that moment the second MiG-23 turned sharply right, and the two Tu-22 bombers accelerated and rapidly descended. 'The second fighter is coming at us, and the bombers are getting away!' Wickland cried.

Tanaka hit his voice command button: 'Evasive action! Configure for terrain following!' he spoke. Immediately the flight computer responded to the voice command, nosing the EB-52 bomber over in a hard twenty-degree nose-down dive. Tanaka kept the power in, diving right to max airspeed – the throttles automatically pulled themselves back to keep from exceeding the airframe's design speed. 'Where are those fighters, dammit?'

'Got 'em!' Wickland shouted. 'Closest one is coming around to our nine o'clock. The nearest bomber is at our one o'clock, thirty-two miles.' He touched the icon for the Tu-22 bomber, then hit his voice command stud: 'Attack priority,' Wickland told the attack computer.

'Target out of range,' the computer responded.

'We know the bomber's heading for Jaghbub,' Tanaka said. 'We'll head over that way and bushwhack him.' He turned the bomber farther to the northeast, cutting off the corner of the route to try to head the Libyan bombers off.

'Warning, MiG-23, seven o'clock, eleven miles, high.'

The Megafortress was now down at three hundred feet above the desert, flying at nearly full military power at four hundred and twenty knots airspeed. 'I think we're losing the MiGs,' Wickland said. 'They're trying to get a shot off from up high.'

'Warning, MiG-23, six o'clock, eight miles, high.'

'If he stays high, he'll try a radar shot any second,' Tanaka guessed. 'If he follows us down, he'll try a heater next.'

'Then let's see if we can make him stay up high,' Wickland said. To the attack computer, he said, 'Deploy towed array.'

From a fairing in the tail of the bomber, a small aerodynamic cylindrical object extended out in the bomber's slipstream on an armored fiber-optic cable, quickly going out three hundred feet from the tail. The object was a transmitter that could broadcast a variety of signals – radar jamming, spoofing, noise, heat, or laser signals. When the array was extended, Wickland called up a program on the defensive system and activated it.

On board the Libyan MiG-23, the pilot's radar warning receivers started to go crazy – it was as if an entire squadron of American F-15 fighters was closing in on him. As he was wondering why he didn't see them coming, suddenly the radar warning receiver told him every one of the F-15s was launching missiles at him!

He *knew* it couldn't be true – there were no F-15s in the middle of Libya. But he could not ignore the warnings. The pilot immediately dropped radar and missile-decoying chaff and flares and executed a tight left break to escape what he believed were a dozen AIM-7 Sparrow missiles heading toward him.

The second MiG-23 did the same, breaking in the opposite direction – but not before he fired an R-60 heat-seeking missile from less than six miles away.

'Warning, missile launch, MiG-23, five o'clock, six miles,' the computer's female voice calmly reported. But as it reported the attack, it was already responding. The towed array instantly began transmitting infrared energy signals, making the heat-seeking missiles think they were pursuing a huge heat source the size of a house. Seconds later, the computer ejected decoy devices that emitted hot points of infrared energy that drifted down and away from the Megafortress, then shut off the infrared energy signal from the towed array. When the R-60 missile was able to pick up a target again, after being dazzled by the huge heat source, all it saw was the tiny, hot, slow-moving dot of the high-tech decoy – too inviting a target to ignore. The first R-60 missiles plowed into the decoy two miles behind the Megafortress, safely out of range.

With the decoy destroyed, the second R-60 missile fired by the MiG-23 veered back toward the Megafortress. It was too close to be decoyed by the towed array again, so another defensive system acti-vated: the active laser defensive system. Directed by the EB-52's laser radar, a large helium-argon laser mounted in a fairing atop the Megafortress fired beams of laser light at the oncoming R-60 missile. After a few seconds, the missile's seeker head was blinded by the laser's intense heat and light, and the missile could no longer track.

'We got it!' Wickland shouted. 'We –!'

Just then, they heard a fast-paced *DEEDLEDEEDLEDEEDLE!* warning tone and the computerized voice say calmly, *'Warning, radar missile launch MiG-23 R-24.'* The first MiG-23 had turned around, locked onto the EB-52, and had taken a shot with a radar-guided missile, then a second one.

'Take defensive action,' Tanaka told the computer. The computer was way ahead of its human commander: It immediately ejected decoy devices from the left ejection chambers, tiny winged canis-ters that had several times the radar cross-section and infrared sig-nature of the largest aircraft in the world – then threw the EB-52 bomber into a steep right bank. The defensive systems in the EB-52 Megafortress bomber were completely automatic: The tiny decoys made invitingly large targets, and with the bomber in a tight turn, the decoys were all alone in space, dangling themselves in front of the Libyan missiles. Along with the decoys, the Megafortress emitted jamming signals to the MiG-23's India-band radar that pre-vented the radar from tracking any other targets but the decoy.

With the power and airspeed already up, the bomber was able to sustain a tight ninety-degree bank turn for several long seconds, crushing both crew members into their seats with unexpectedly heavy G-forces. Both crew members caught a glimpse of one bright explosion out the left window – one of the missiles had exploded less than a hundred yards off their left wingtip. The second R-24 radar-guided missile was handled by the active laser defensive system – it took only a few seconds for the laser to completely blind the second missile, and it continued on straight ahead and harmlessly exploded on the desert floor below.

But after its tight defensive break, the Megafortress was dangerously slow. Tanaka rolled the big bomber out of its tight turn, keeping the power in full military power and the nose pointed down to try to quickly regain lost airspeed. The first Libyan MiG-23 had overshot the EB-52 – but the second MiG-23, which had stayed down low to maintain contact, was now in perfect attack position, directly behind the Megafortress. It closed in almost at the speed of sound in seconds. *'Warning, bandit six o'clock, four miles, MiG-23,'* the computer warned. *'Warning, MiG-23 six o'clock, three miles . . . warning, missile launch detected . . .'*

The Megafortress's next defensive weapon automatically activated: the Stinger airmine system. Instead of the fifty-caliber or thirty-millimeter machine guns in earlier B-52 bombers, the EB-52 Megafortress carried a fifty-millimeter cannon that fired small LADAR-guided rockets. With a range of about three miles, the tiny rockets were steered toward incoming enemy aircraft or missiles and then detonated ahead of them, creating a cloud of titanium flak that could shred jet engines with ease. The crew heard a *poof! poof! poof!* sound far behind them and a hard jolt every few seconds as the small rockets were launched. The MiG-23 that stayed down low flew through a cloud of tungsten pellets that shredded the cockpit canopy and engine; the pilot punched out just before his fighter started to spin out of control.

'Tail's clear, Zero!' Wickland crowed. 'The MiG up high looks like he's staying up there trying to find us.'

'Where are those bombers?' Tanaka asked.

Wickland expanded out his display. 'Eleven o'clock, forty miles. Three fast-movers, low. They're within fifty miles of Jaghbub, going almost six hundred knots. I'm not sure if we can catch them. They'll be over the base in five minutes.'

'Nike, this is Headbanger,' Tanaka radioed to Chris Wohl.

'Go.'

'You've got three inbounds, ETE five minutes. We can't catch them unless you can get them to turn around.'

*   *   *

297

Wohl turned to Hal Briggs. 'Sir, we need a distraction for those bombers,' he said. 'What do they have in storage?'

'Just about anything you want,' Hal said. 'I'll be right back.' Briggs jet-jumped out toward the underground weapon-storage area. He came back a few minutes later carrying a twin-barreled 12.7-millimeter truck-mounted antiaircraft gun and a large metal box of ammunition. He jet-jumped to an isolated area about two miles west of the airfield, as far away as possible from the underground shelters where Sanusi's men were taking cover. 'This what you had in mind, Sarge?'

'It's about time, sir,' Wohl said. He was already scanning the sky with his battle armor's sensors for the incoming bombers. 'Get ready.'

'Nike, one minute out. We're still just out of missile range.'

Hal Briggs had to work fast with an unfamiliar weapon, trying to quickly get the ammunition belt fed into the feeder. Normally the action was engaged electrically in the gun, but luckily Briggs found a manual crank that he used to wind a spindle that would fire the first round – after that, gas from the cartridges should initiate the action.

'What are you doing over there, sir?' Wohl called out.

'Hey, you try and load this thing.' In a second Wohl dashed over to him, gave Briggs his electromagnetic rail gun, and started unfeeding the backwards-looped ammunition belt. 'Now we're talking!' Briggs shouted as he hefted the big high-tech weapon.

'Just don't miss, sir – we're running out of projectiles,' Wohl growled.

'Oh, pul-*leese*.' Briggs plugged in the data cable to his belt, charged the weapon, raised it, and followed the cues in his helmet-mounted electronic visor. His visor gave him a complete status readout – Wohl was right, only two projectiles remaining. 'Never bagged a bomber before – this'll be fun.'

'Fifteen seconds.'

'I see it!' Briggs shouted. The Tupolev-22 bomber was coming in straight and level, about a thousand feet above ground, at six hundred knots on the dot – the target was small, fast, and low. The aiming system in the battle armor wasn't a lead-computing sight – this was going to be a thousand-in-one shot. Briggs fired at two miles out, just as he saw a stick of bombs drop from the bomb bay. 'Take cover!' he shouted. 'Bombs away!'

The streak of burning air from the projectile passed in front of the bomber's nose by several hundred feet – he had led the target too much.

The bomber dropped a stick of six five-thousand-pound napalm canisters that created a tremendous wall of fire and a wave of heat that nearly pushed both of them over. The intent was obvious – he was marking the target area for the second bomber.

Briggs whirled around and aimed. The first bomber was in a steep climbing right turn in full afterburner – a perfect profile. This time, the streak of superheated air passed right through the forward section of the Tupolev-22's fuselage. Just when Briggs thought he might have missed it again, a tongue of flame spat out from the left engine compartment. The Tu-22 twisted unnaturally to the left, its nose moving higher into the sky. Both afterburners winked out – Briggs could now see it through only the rail gun's electronic sights. The bomber seemed to hang in midair, like a big graceful eagle climbing on a thermal – then there were four puffs of light and smoke as all four crew members ejected, and the bomber did a tail-side straight down and crashed into the desert just north of the minefield.

Meanwhile, Chris Wohl had finally loaded the dual antiaircraft cannon. He held the gun up in his left hand by its mounting pedestal, held the ammunition can in his right hand, then swiveled to the west and scanned the sky, looking for the oncoming bombers. Suddenly, Wohl started firing into the sky. The big antiaircraft gun bucked and shook, but thanks to Wohl's exoskeleton, he was able to keep the weapon fairly steady. Every twelfth shell from the can was a tracer round, and as he swept the sky to the west, he created a snakelike wave of light in the sky. The ammunition was gone in a few seconds; Wohl dropped the gun and the ammo can, and both he and Briggs jet-jumped away from that spot – they knew what was going to happen next . . .

The second Tu-22 bomber veered hard to the south, away from the tracers – but the third bomber came in hard and fast and laid down a stick of thirty or forty five-hundred-pound high-explosive bombs, right on the spot where Briggs and Wohl had been positioned. The incredible pounding from the bombs knocked both men off their feet, and it seemed like dirt, dust, sand, and all sorts of debris rained down on them for at least the next ten minutes. Their battle armor's power was almost depleted by that time – but they survived the attack.

The third bomber stayed low and accelerated straight ahead without using afterburners, as it was supposed to do in a defended area, so it was able to escape. But the second Tu-22 that did the hard bank turned away from the airfield – right into the waiting missile range of the Megafortress's AIM-120 missiles. Wickland dispatched it quickly with one Scorpion missile.

'You guys all right back there?' Tanaka asked.

'Everyone's in one piece,' Briggs said, 'and they didn't hit the airfield, so I think we're still in business. Where did that third bomber go?'

'He's bugging out – probably wondering where his two wingmen went,' Tanaka said. 'We're going to head back and finish the job on Zillah, then see if there's anything we can hit at Al-Jawf. Keep your heads down. Headbanger clear.'

Wickland pressed the attack at Zillah Air Base thirty minutes later by firing one antiradar missile first at the airfield surveillance radar at Zillah Air Base, then at another unexpected SA-10 mobile surface-to-air missile site that had just activated its radar, both from high altitude. After defending themselves from the SAM sites, Wickland used the laser radar and took second-long snapshots of the base, magnifying and enhancing the images until he could identify them as precisely as possible, then designated specific targets and loaded their coordinates into the AGM-154 Joint Standoff Weapons. Once the target coordinates were entered, the attack computer loaded a released track into the autopilot.

The attack computer automatically opened the bomb doors and started releasing weapons when the bomber reached the release track. The AGM-154 JSOW did not need to be at a precise weapon-release point – at high altitude, they could glide unpowered for up to forty miles and fly to their targets with uncanny accuracy. Four of the six JSOWs were programmed for Zillah's main runway, cratering it enough so no heavy or high-performance aircraft could use it. For the other four targets, Wickland switched on an imaging-infrared sensor in the weapon's nose as it got closer to its target, and if the weapon was off-course he could lock it onto their exact impact points – a building they suspected as the base command post and communications center, the fuel farm, a power plant, and the surveillance radar facility at the base of the control tower. The one-thousand-pound high-explosive warheads made short work of all targets – Zillah Air Base was effectively shut down with just eight well-placed hits.

The EB-52 then headed toward Al-Jawf, three hundred miles to the southeast. Attack procedures for the Wolverine cruise missiles were much different from those of the other precision-guided weapons: They didn't need any procedures. Each missile was programmed with a large set of targets in memory, and the missiles were simply released when about fifty miles from the target area. Wickland used the laser radar to try to spot targets and designate final impact points for the missiles, but the Wolverines liked it best when they were on their own. They used millimeter-wave radars to search for targets; then they would fly over the targets and drop either anti-armor CBU-97 sensor-fuzed weapons or CBU-87 combined effects munitions on light armor or other vehicles. The missiles would continue their search for targets, even turning around and reattacking if they found they missed a target. Then, before the missile's jet fuel ran out, the missile would either find a building or use a designated target sent to it from the Megafortress and fly into it, destroying the target with a two-hundred-pound high-explosive warhead.

With no air defenses detected, Tanaka and Wickland were able to orbit the area, taking LADAR snapshots of the base, looking for targets to direct the Wolverines, releasing the cruise missiles one every three to five minutes so each had plenty of time to find new targets that might present themselves. Aircraft parking areas, helipads, large vehicle parking areas, fuel storage areas, and weapon storage bunkers were favorite targets for the Wolverines' cluster munitions and sensor-fuzed weapons.

Wickland picked out buildings that looked like headquarters buildings, barracks, security buildings, and hangars for the terminal targets – but what he was really looking for was the rocket storage sheds, or even some surface-to-surface rockets themselves. According to the soldiers who joined Sanusi's Sandstorm warriors, the rockets at Al-Jawf were housed in long half-underground sheds. When it was time for deployment, trucks would hook up to the rocket transporter-erector-launchers and tow them to presurveyed launch points. They could be moved in a matter of minutes, and readied for launch in about a half hour after arriving at the launch point.

But twenty minutes after starting the attack, Wickland was disappointed. 'Not one rocket anywhere,' he said. 'I didn't even see the storage sheds. Maybe they were one of the other buildings I attacked, but I didn't see anything that looked like it housed a Scud-sized rocket.'

Tanaka checked the fuel readouts and the strategic planning chart on one of his multifunction displays. The display showed the position and fuel status of their support aircraft, the Sky Masters Inc DC-10, proceeding from Scotland to the refueling anchor over the Mediterranean Sea. The fuel status of both the tanker and the Megafortress were represented as large circles – as long as the circles overlapped, they could rendezvous. But the edges of the circles were getting closer and closer – they couldn't wait any longer.

'Castor, this is Headbanger.'

'I see it, guys,' Patrick McLanahan said. He was able via datalink to look at the same strategic chart as the flight crew – and in fact he had been looking at that very display. 'You're about fifteen minutes to bingo with the tanker.'

'Sorry we couldn't get those rockets for you.'

'Maybe you did get them – we won't know until we go in there and check. You did a good job, guys. Have a good trip home.'

'Roger that. Good luck down there. Headbanger out.'

Patrick met the Mi-24 attack helicopter as it settled in for a landing at one of the many helipads at the airfield near Jaghbub. He removed his helmet as Muhammad as-Sanusi climbed out of the helicopter and approached him. 'It is good to see you, my friend,' Sanusi said, embracing him warmly. 'And it is good to see this place still in one piece.'

'Two bombers got in, but they dropped well short of the airfield,' Patrick explained. 'No damage, no casualties on our side.'

'And your bomber is heading home?'

'He is a few minutes from rendezvousing with a tanker aircraft as we speak.'

'Too bad. I would have liked to learn more about that plane's capabilities.'

'We struck targets in Zillah and Al-Jawf,' Patrick said. 'The runway appears to have been cratered nicely, so the bombers and fighters there should've had to move to Surt Air Base. We struck several targets at Al-Jawf, but we can't be sure we hit any rockets. I'm afraid that threat still exists.'

'But you have given us precious time to finish capturing the weapons stored here,' Sanusi said. 'By tomorrow afternoon, we should be long gone, with several million dollars' worth of weapons – enough to keep our little army going another few months. Thanks to you, my friend.'

They heard the sounds of an approaching heavy helicopter, and a few moments later a CV-22 Pave Hammer tilt-rotor aircraft settled in for a landing. Patrick extended his hand, and Sanusi took it. 'I wish you luck, Your Highness,' he said. 'I don't know what's going to happen, but I was glad to be on your side.'

'You are a good man and a fine leader, Mr McLanahan,' Sanusi said. 'I am sorry about your wife; I hope God protects her. You will go home now to see your son, I presume?'

'Yes. But I have a little unfinished business in Alexandria first.'

'You do not seem to be the vengeful type to me.'

'I really don't know who or what I am anymore, Your Highness.'

'I think I do – and I like what I see. I hope your superiors see it the same as I.' Sanusi looked carefully at Patrick, then said with a faint smile, 'I have a feeling we'll be seeing each other again, sir. I hope it is in happier times.'

'I hope you're right, Your Highness,' Patrick said. 'But I don't think so.'

Abu Qir, Alexandria, Egypt
that same time

From the seventeenth-floor high-rise apartment, one of the best high-rise condominiums in all of Egypt, Susan Bailey Salaam had an extraordinary view of Alexandria. From her living-room balcony she could see west all the way to the Corniche and Fort Qayt Bay, built on the site of the Pharos, the four-hundred-foot-tall lighthouse that was one of the seven wonders of the ancient world. From her bedroom, she could see all the way down Abu Qir Bay, the mouth of the Nile, and at night even see the glow of Cairo far on the southern horizon.

That evening, Susan was standing on the living-room balcony, smoking a cigarette and letting the cool Mediterranean breezes wash over her. Inside, General Ahmad Baris was inside, sorting and organizing sheaves of documents. He was having a difficult time keeping her attention.

'The death toll at Mersa Matrûh is . . . is enormous, Sekhmet,' Baris said tonelessly when he joined Susan on the balcony a few minutes later. 'They fear over eleven thousand perished in the attack. The entire Ramses Corps has been destroyed, and the Amun Fleet lost almost fifty percent of its men and ships, with the fatalities increasing by the hour.'

'Bastards,' she replied woodenly. 'How dare they lay waste to our nation like this?'

'The weapon that detonated at Mersa Matrûh was an enhanced-radiation thermonuclear device with an estimated yield of one to two kilotons, or one to two thousand *tons* of TNT. Everything within two kilometers was hit with a massive dose of radiation that killed them within a few hours, slowly and painfully. I'm sorry.

'In addition, Libyan and Sudanese ground forces have crossed our southern border and have surrounded the entire Salimah complex,' Baris went on. 'They are obviously ready to stage an attack on the Salimah oil fields, probably within the next few days.'

'Why haven't we searched for survivors at Mersa Matrûh yet?' Susan asked. 'Maybe Patrick is alive.'

Aha, Ahmad Baris thought, it was Patrick McLanahan and his commandos that were occupying her mind. Could he be occupying her heart as well . . . ? 'Are you all right, Sekhmet?'

'Fine . . . just fine.' She went over and sat down on the sofa.

Captain Shafik answered the phone in Susan Bailey Salaam's home office. Her eyes grew wide with surprise, and she gave the phone to General Ahmad Baris – and moments later, his eyes grew wide with shock as well. 'What is it, General?' Susan asked, returning to the living room.

'I just heard from my sources in the Ministry of Defense. Two bases in Libya have just been struck from the air.'

'*What?* Which ones? Which bases?'

'Zillah and Al-Jawf. Reports say that a number of Libyan aircraft were also shot down,' Baris went on.

'The Americans . . . ?'

'Dr Kalir has been in contact with the American embassy, and they insist that no American forces are involved.'

'Could it have been some of our air forces?'

'All Egyptian military air forces have been dispersed and brought in toward Cairo to protect the capital,' Baris said. 'But in any case, we don't have that kind of firepower, unless we massed every aircraft in our entire arsenal. Planning an operation of that magnitude would take weeks.'

It was Patrick, she thought. It had to be. He must be alive! But where did he get the support? Where were his air forces? They couldn't possibly be in Egypt – Baris would have known about that. Certainly not in Libya. Israel? Offshore in the Mediterranean Sea somewhere? He might be able to sneak in one large 'baby' aircraft carrier into the area without anyone knowing, but would that carry enough firepower to destroy *two* Libyan military bases? Impossible . . . or was it?

'Could it have been McLanahan and his men, General?'

'They must have died in the nuclear explosion,' Baris replied. 'The bunker they were based in was guarded by troops day and night, and all of those troops were killed by the radiation.'

'But they were underground . . .'

'The radiation kills humans even in bomb shelters,' Baris explained. 'Besides, they were just high-tech infantry forces – even with their fancy suits of armor, they could not have destroyed two Libyan military bases in one night. Only a few nations have that kind of firepower – the United States, Russia, maybe Germany, perhaps Israel. But we certainly should have known something was going to happen. It had to be in retaliation for the explosion at Mersa Matrûh – but who could have done it, and why would they not have consulted us?' Susan did not answer. Her eyes were darting back and forth, as if examining the scene of a terrible traffic accident just moments after the crash.

'What are you thinking about, child?'

'Nothing . . . nothing,' Susan Bailey Salaam said absently. 'Thank you for the information. I need some rest now. Is there anything else?'

'Only to ask you once again – what do you want to do, here, in Egypt?' Baris asked, stepping over and standing beside her. 'We are officially in protective custody, by order of the Supreme Judiciary, but I assure you, we can leave anytime we please – my friends in the Ministry of Defense and the Intelligence Bureau will see to that. The security forces of the Supreme Judiciary are nothing more than Khalid al-Khan's hired goons, easily brushed aside. I have access to aircraft, safe houses, visas, and many friends overseas, especially in the United States.'

'I . . . I don't know, General,' Susan said. 'I don't want to leave Egypt now, at a time like this, with Libya threatening our very existence almost every day.'

'Why? What are you concerned about, Sekhmet? Our nation is strong, despite Libya's aggression. They never had enough strength to destroy Egypt militarily, with or without nuclear weapons. We will survive.' He paused, looking carefully at Susan; then: 'Or are you concerned more about how you might be looked upon by the people of Egypt if you left?'

'Are you saying that because I'm American, I needn't be concerned about Egypt?' Susan retorted. 'I've lived here for many years, General. I speak Arabic. I consider myself an Egyptian. Are you saying that I'm only concerned about myself and not Egypt?'

'Of course not, Sekhmet,' Baris said. 'What I'm concerned about is that you might put yourself in grave danger by staying, in some misguided notion that you need to stay because this is where your husband is buried . . . or, yes, because you may think that the people's memory of your late husband or yourself might be tarnished if you left now. Your loyalty for our country is inspiring, Susan, but you are not safe here.'

'What if I were president?'

Finally, the truth comes out, Baris thought – this was the secret she had kept to herself all this time. 'Being president will not relieve you of the danger you faced from Khalid al-Khan and the Muslim Brotherhood,' Baris reminded her. 'You will always be the wife of their political adversary, the wife of the man that Khan conspired to murder in order to form his ideal Islamic government. In fact, I believe you will face even greater dangers, greater pressures.

'The real struggles will be political. You and the National Democratic Party will be blamed for every wrong, every deficiency, and every failure. You will be accused of impeding progress and delivering privileged information to enemies of the state and to anarchists. There are many citizens and government officials who agreed with Khan and were happy to see your husband assassinated – and would happily do the same to you. Your enemies will know your every move – if they want to ambush you, they'll know exactly when and where you'll be at all times. You are putting yourself in the lion's jaws, Susan. Why?'

'Because I feel I can do more inside the government than outside,' Susan replied. 'As simply the widow of a dead president or leader of the opposition, I create nothing but background noise. Let me trade on my name and by being a widow. Maybe I can do some good.'

Baris studied his young friend for a few moments. Her words sounded determined, conclusive, and decisive – but he still felt uneasy, uncertain. What else was wrong? What wasn't he noticing?

'I suggest you leave Egypt,' Baris said evenly. 'Once in Italy, or England, or the United States, you can get on all the talk shows and news programs and talk about your vision of Egypt. You can raise money, attract attention to your ideas, and gather support. If you try to do it now, with the nation in chaos and the Libyans threatening to blow the entire country into atoms, your voice will be lost in the cries of confusion and fear – not to mention your life will be in terrible danger, just because of who you are.' He took her hands. 'Think about it, my friend. I am only concerned for your safety now – Egypt can wait, for a little while.'

'I'll think about it.'

'Good.' He kissed her hands, smiled warmly at her, and then departed.

Khalid al-Khan was dead. The government was disorganized, frightened. Egypt was in grave danger. She had to do something. . .

Tripoli, United Kingdom of Libya
that same time

'They can't pin this on me,' Jadallah Zuwayy said proudly. 'An entire military base destroyed, and they have no idea who did it to them. God, I wish I could have seen it for myself.' Beside him, General Tahir Fazani, his military chief of staff, and Juma Mahmud Hijazi, his foreign minister, looked on with disbelief and fear . . .

. . . but mostly they were trying to decide how to get out of this predicament with their skins still attached to their bodies. 'Jadallah, let's not celebrate just yet,' Juma Hijazi, the Libyan foreign minister, said. 'Egypt and the entire world are going to be on high alert after that weapon went off at Mersa Matrûh.'

'Our plan to take the Salimah oil fields is still on schedule,' Zuwayy said. 'We still have almost fifty thousand troops surrounding Salimah, plus another twenty thousand Sudanese mercenaries. We can send in every piece of air defense equipment we own to protect them. Once we move in, we can wire the place with explosives and threaten to blow it up unless we make a deal for coproduction rights.'

'Just a couple months is all we need,' Fazani said. 'Once we have the first shot of cash in our hands, we head for Malaysia or some island in Indonesia and relax.'

'Or we can get the hell out *now*,' Hijazi said. 'Damn it, Jadallah, we've got more money than Bill Gates tucked away in secret bank accounts all over the world – why are we staying here acting like targets? Let's get the hell out.'

'I can't leave!' Zuwayy retorted. 'I am the king of united Libya! I am the head of the Muslim Brotherhood! I can't run! I am the leader of a quarter of a billion Muslims around the world . . .'

'Jadallah, give it up, will you?' Fazani interjected. 'You are not a fucking king, and the Muslim Brotherhood would gladly turn you over to Kazakov or Salaam or anyone else for the right amount of cash.'

'I say let's end it – right now,' Hijazi insisted. 'Let's get out while the getting's good.'

'If you want to go so badly, go,' Zuwayy said morosely.

Hijazi had thought about doing exactly that, and he had spoken about it at length with Fazani. But they needed Zuwayy – not because of any misguided sense of loyalty, but because only Zuwayy had the bank account numbers and access codes they needed to tap into the full range of money they had stolen from the Libyan government's oil revenues. As the mastermind of their operation, Zuwayy had all the codes – Fazani and Hijazi had only the codes for their own accounts. If they simply ran, Zuwayy would eventually hunt them down, slaughter them, and keep all the money.

'We're in this together, Jadallah,' Hijazi lied. 'We stay together.' Together – until they got the codes from Zuwayy, at which time they would jettison his ass and be done with his delusions of grandeur. 'Tahir, let's take another look at the military forces we have remaining – I think we should beef up security here in Tripoli and around our headquarters first, then see how many troops we can commit to Salimah.' Fazani was more than happy to comply – and if it turned out that they needed all available troops to secure Tripoli and all of their secret headquarters and shelters, so be it. No one was anxious to march out into the open and have a cluster bomb dropped on them anyway.

While Zuwayy and Fazani worked to reallocate troops in the wake of the nuclear detonation at Mersa Matrûh, Hijazi went to the outer office to have a cigarette and clear his head. The situation was becoming desperate, he thought. He had to try to convince Jadallah to escape. But if he wouldn't, Hijazi thought, he might have to hire his own strongmen to kidnap Zuwayy and force him to turn over the bank account numbers and access codes. He wasn't going to wait much longer for him to –

'Excuse me, Minister,' Zuwayy's private secretary said, interrupting his thoughts. 'There is an urgent phone call for His Highness.'

'Take a message.'

'Sir, the caller is Madame Susan Bailey Salaam of Egypt.'

Salaam? What was she calling for? 'Send the call to my office immediately. I'll take it there.' He thought quickly, then added,

'And if the king or General Fazani want to know where I am, tell them I'm dealing with the Egyptians – don't tell them who called.'

'Yes, Minister.'

Hijazi fairly ran down the hallway of the presidential palace to his office, then closed the door behind him. He took a shot of whiskey first to calm himself, then lifted the receiver. 'This is the Minister of Arab Unity,' he said in his most officious tone. 'To whom am I speaking, please?'

'This is Susan Bailey Salaam, Mr Hijazi,' Susan Bailey replied. 'Do you need more proof of my identity?'

'That depends on what you have to say to me, Madame,' Hijazi said. 'What do you want?'

'I wish to end this war between us,' Salaam said. 'I wish for the violence and destruction to end. We have both suffered greatly in the past few days. It is time to make peace.'

'What are you talking about, Madame?'

'I'm talking about the attack on Jaghbub last night, Minister.'

Hijazi's mouth dropped open, and he had to struggle to maintain his composure. 'What do you know of this, Salaam?'

'I know everything. I know about the attacks on Zillah and Al-Jawf tonight, too.'

'Hold,' Hijazi said. He frantically punched the call from Salaam on hold, then hit the button to the outer office. 'Put in a call to the commander of Zillah Air Base, and I want him on the line *now*.'

Hijazi was on hold for over three minutes. Then: 'This is Colonel Harb speaking.'

'This is Minister of Arab Unity Hijazi, Colonel, speaking from His Majesty's residence. I have been informed of an attack tonight on your base. What is happening?' There was a long, maddening pause. *'Colonel!'*

'The attack ended only minutes ago, Minister –'

'What attack?'

'We . . . we don't know any details, sir,' Harb stammered. 'We were hit by antiradar missiles first, and then our runway was bombed. We've lost several fighters and two bombers.'

'Who did this?'

'We don't know, sir. . . Can you please hold, sir? I have casualty reports coming in, please –'

Hijazi hung up. It was true . . . God, it was true. He didn't need to call Al-Jawf to know that it was hit too. It didn't matter that he didn't know what the damage was; enemy aircraft had invaded Libya only minutes ago, and Susan Bailey Salaam had told him about it – *before his own military did!*

Hijazi's head was tingling with confusion as he punched the line button on the phone: 'I thought you weren't coming back, Minister.'

'How . . . how in hell did you know about this, Salaam? Did you order these attacks? *Did you?*'

'No, I did not – but I know that more attacks are forthcoming, unless Zuwayy or Idris or whatever he calls himself negotiates with me.'

'Is Egypt involved in the attack on our bases, Madame?'

'No. But I control the ones that are. If you wish the attacks to stop, you must deal with me right away. I know you have only a few hours left before the deadline.'

'I'm listening, Madame.'

'The attacks are a retaliation for prisoners your naval forces captured in the Mediterranean Sea, meant to force Zuwayy to surrender them.'

'Then tell me where the terrorists and bombers are, Madame Salaam. Turn them over to the king for justice, and we will withdraw our forces.'

'I suggest you withdraw those forces today, Minister, or they'll be destroyed. And once we have destroyed your invasion force in both Libya and Sudan, we'll destroy your palaces and headquarters in Tripoli. In time, we'll level every government and military structure in your entire nation.'

'With what air force? I don't know who has done these attacks, but they are not Egyptian military forces. Who did you have sex with to get access to such weapons, Mrs Salaam? It couldn't have been the American president, Thomas Thorn – everyone knows he has no balls. What new American comrades have you been sleeping with lately?'

'We'll see how glib you are after they're done bombing Tripoli, Minister.'

This was going nowhere, Hijazi thought – better see what she has in mind quickly, before she hangs up. 'So what do you propose, Madame Salaam?' Hijazi asked.

'You will announce a ceasefire agreement has been reached in secret negotiations between the king and myself, acting as a representative of the Egyptian government.'

'You are not the Egyptian government.'

'For your sake, you had better hope I will be,' Susan Salaam said. 'You will not be able to negotiate a thing with Prime Minister Kalir or anyone else in our government after you have attacked us with nuclear weapons. Again, I am your only hope.'

'You have to do better than that, Mrs Salaam,' Hijazi said sternly. 'You are asking for everything, and are not giving anything in return.'

'You have nothing that belongs to you, and you have everything to lose,' Salaam said. 'How many more bases do you think we need to bomb before the people start losing confidence in their so-called king? Or perhaps all it will take is one raid on Tripoli?'

'Libya wants part of the Salimah oil production rights,' Hijazi said. 'Libya has nearly one hundred thousand workers fully qualified and ready to work, but they will not be hired by your Western cartel.'

'Libya's past record in dealing with its neighbors in coproduction deals has not been very encouraging,' Salaam said. 'Usually such coproduction deals end up being invasions. Besides, your government insists Libyan oil workers get higher-than-average wages; and in the past Qadhafi has insisted on sending troops to "protect" the workers. Egypt will not allow that.'

'What do you give the Central African Petroleum Partners to take your oil? Twenty percent? Thirty? Forty? More? Much more than Libyan workers ask for, I'm sure.'

'So I see – this is all about the oil, is it, Minister?' Susan asked. 'Not about the Muslim Brotherhood, or religion, or faith, or Arab unity – it's about the damned oil.'

'Your country, and mine, would be nothing without the "damned oil,"' Hijazi said. 'Don't pretend that you don't realize this. Turn the tables the other way, Salaam – what if it was Libya who had the largest oil reserves in Africa sitting beneath your feet, and you have sixty percent unemployment, but your neighbor hires Europeans and Asians and even Anglos to work the fields? I think you and your husband would be spouting a lot more about Arab unity and Arab cooperation, instead of back-stabbing and fucking their neighbors just for more money.'

'And don't try to pretend that you give a rat's ass about those sixty percent unemployed souls in Libya or Egypt or anywhere else – all you care about is yourselves, you and Zuwayy and Fazani,' Susan shot back. 'You want the oil revenues. You've been stealing money hand over fist from the Libyan treasury since the moment you marched into the presidential palace in Tripoli. But you're taking as much as you possibly can from your own oil fields, so now you want a piece of Salimah. You found some wealthy partner to finance you. He gives you money to buy weapons. But Zuwayy is too stupid to hold on to those weapons, and now he's completely fucked everything up for you. Now you're in danger of losing everything – your cushy little ministry, your private bank accounts, and your fat expense accounts.'

'You think you're so smart, Salaam? As smart as your husband?' Hijazi asked derisively. 'Tell me what your husband's legacy will be. He sells the largest oil fields in Africa to a bunch of nonbelievers. Do you think Egyptians will praise him for that a hundred years from now?

'Your husband was a traitor to his people, and you know it. Ask your pal General Baris. Ask any Egyptian who fought over a lifetime to try to repel the outsiders, the Jews and the British and the Americans. The Arabs in North Africa have been struggling for three generations to benefit from the natural wealth of their own homelands, like the Persian Gulf Arabs have done, and your husband negates it all with one stroke of a pen. He made a deal with Qadhafi and then Zuwayy to coproduce those oil fields, and then he backed out and signed with a fat cat Western oil cartel. He spat on his fellow Arabs. He should have gone through with the deal –'

'Why? So you could have marched your troops in to try to take over?'

'So he could have led a new generation of Arabs, a new generation that is hungering for a leader,' Hijazi said. 'Instead, he did what all the other scum-sucking Western-loving traitors do – he sold out, sold out his own people. He'll be hated for a century. Your husband created clowns like Zuwayy, Salaam.'

'What in hell are you talking about?'

'You know exactly what I'm talking about,' Hijazi retorted. 'Kamal Ismail Salaam was hailed for years as the new Nasser, the new leader of the pan-Arab world. But he did what Sadat and Mubarak did – they sold out to the Jews and the Westerners for cash. The Arab world was begging for a leader, and Salaam abdicated. When Zuwayy became Idris the Second, everyone knew he wasn't a king – but they accepted him anyway. Why the hell do you think that is, Madame?' No response.

'Do you think Libyans are stupid? Do you think we're that gullible?' Hijazi went on. 'We're not stupid, and we're not gullible – not any more than the Germans were before the rise of Adolf Hitler. Libyans were searching for a leader. We would have gladly accepted Kamal Salaam – yes, even an Egyptian, just as many of us accepted Gamal Abdel Nasser. Instead, Salaam turned his back on us. We embraced the first figure that showed any sort of leadership, who showed any amount of sympathy to the plight of the Arabs – Jadallah Zuwayy. He may be a psychopath, but he's also smart – he did his homework. He knew that Libya was thirsting for a leader, even a monarch, after the mess Muammar Qadhafi left. He adopted the whole Sanusi king thing because he knew Libya needed a king, a leader. He could have called himself Jesus Christ, and Libya would've followed him.

'So you want to hide behind the Americans and their high-tech toys?' Hijazi went on. 'I've got a prediction for you, Madame President – you'll end up with a suicide bomber in your face too, just like your husband. And you know what's even more ironic? The most moronic, the most comical, the stupidest one of us all, Jadallah Zuwayy, will still be in power, calling himself a king. We'll be dead, and he'll still be sodomizing his country – and the people will gladly bend over and let him do it, because he chose to be an *Arab*. You know it, and I know it.'

There was silence on the phone. Hijazi was going to ask if Salaam had hung up, when she said, 'If you try to touch Salimah with your army or with any of your Nubian goons, I'll blow you and your pretender king into the Red Sea.'

'Tough words – from an Arab hiding behind American bombs and missiles.'

'You will withdraw those forces from the border areas immediately,' Salaam demanded, 'and you will deactivate all remaining rockets, artillery, and aircraft stationed within two hundred kilometers of the border. Otherwise, I will destroy them all.'

'You dare to try to negotiate with a gun pointed to my head, woman? Who the hell do you think you are?'

'I will be the new president of Egypt, sir, thanks to Zuwayy's lunacy,' Susan Bailey Salaam said. 'I also will be the instrument of your destruction if you do not comply – and then I will still become president, and I will crush whatever is left of your so-called king and his corrupt, morally bankrupt partners. Think carefully, Minister – but not too long. My warriors have itchy trigger fingers.'

This time, Hijazi hesitated. This was an opportunity to get out of this whole mess intact – and perhaps come out a little ahead, if Salaam was willing to discuss the Salimah coproduction deal again.

'I will speak with His Highness about this, Madame,' Hijazi replied. 'But I need some assurance to take to him. You will agree not to stage any more attacks on our bases, and you will agree to open negotiations with the Central African Petroleum Partners to hire more Libyan workers. Otherwise, Madame, we are still at war – and we will use the last of our military might to destroy Salimah and render it useless to anyone for fifty years. It is you who have forced us into this desperate situation, Madame – but you can end it too.'

'We will not fly any more missions over Libya unless we are attacked,' Salaam said, 'if you promise, in writing, to withdraw all your artillery, rockets, and aircraft beyond two hundred kilometers from the border.'

'While your forces stand ready right at the border? Unacceptable.'

'We will pull our forces back as well.'

'And the Americans?' Hijazi had no idea that it was the Americans actually performing the bombing raids on Samāh, Jaghbub, and now Zillah and Al-Jawf, but it was a logical guess.

'All bombers will be pulled out,' Salaam responded.

It wasn't what she said, but *how* she said it – it was the Americans, all right. Hijazi was positive of it. 'And of Salimah?'

Salaam paused for several long moments; then: 'I will agree to immediately propose legislation that will create a worker's visa program to allow Libyan and Sudanese laborers to enter the country so that they may apply for work in Salimah. Then I will –'

'Not good enough. The Western cartel must increase hiring of qualified laborers from Libya and decrease hiring of Asian, European, and Western laborers. And Libya must be able to become a partner in the consortium.'

'That is up to the partnership.'

'Egypt is a partner – or is it?'

'Of course it is.'

'We do not seek a majority – only a rightful share of African natural resources. We shall pay for the right of admission, of course – say, for a one-third share.'

'Egypt will retain majority ownership in the partnership,' Salaam said after another long pause. 'But Egypt will grant one-third of its share in the partnership to Libya, but only under the condition that Libya buys twenty-five percent of the cartel's shares. Then Egypt's share of the partnership will be forty percent, and Libya and the cartel's share will each be thirty.'

'Agreed. And as far as Libyan laborers at Salimah . . . ?'

'*Arab* laborers must exceed the number of other nationalities in Salimah,' Salaam said. 'I will not give preferential treatment to any nationality. It's about time we are all referred to as "Arabs."'

'A wise judgment, Madame. This includes supervisory and management positions.'

'Including management and supervisors.'

'Equal pay, equal housing, equal benefits – no forced segregation, no discrimination in jobs or locations. Full access to all government entitlements.'

'Agreed.'

'And the Muslim Brotherhood.'

'Minister . . .'

'His Highness will ask. I must tell him something.'

Another pause; then: 'I will not oppose or block legislation or debate on the subject of membership into the Muslim Brotherhood in the People's Assembly, and I will allow Brotherhood officials to obtain temporary visas so that they may enter the country to meet with our lawmakers and government officials to discuss membership. But I promise, I will slam the door shut again if I learn that the Brotherhood tries to organize antigovernment movements within Egypt, or they try to funnel weapons or money to any antigovernment organizations within Egypt.'

'This I cannot guarantee.'

'Then our negotiations are ended. I will allow open, free debate on the subject of Brotherhood membership, Minister, but I will not tolerate sedition or conspiracy. We'll let the people decide, without bribes or payoffs.'

Hijazi paused. They were certainly not going to negotiate every last detail – the important point here was that Susan Bailey Salaam was talking, negotiating, not threatening. Hijazi at first thought that perhaps she didn't have those American forces under her command anymore, that maybe all this was a bluff – but now was not the time to think about that either. A turning point was happening. He could either seize it, or let it slip out of his fingers.

'Very well, Madame. All this is subject to further negotiation, a written agreement, and His Highness's concurrence,' Hijazi reminded her.

'Our deal will also have to be ratified by our People's Assembly,' Salaam said. 'And it of course presupposes that I will be given authority to negotiate anything with Libya.'

'Of course. I understand.'

'I have a demand, Minister,' Salaam said.

'I thought you said we have nothing to offer you, Madame.'

'This you will do, or all our negotiations cease immediately and we go back to war.'

'Another ultimatum? How unskilled you are at negotiations, Madame. But please, proceed anyway.'

'Zuwayy, you, General Fazani, and the entire Libyan government will endorse and support me as the next president of Egypt,' Susan Bailey Salaam said.

'*What?* We . . . *endorse* you?'

'Not only you personally and as representatives of your government, but the king as leader of the Muslim Brotherhood,' Salaam went on. 'A full and public endorsement, without any reservation. I require an endorsement from all the other leaders of the Muslim Brotherhood as well.'

'If you want their endorsement, Madame, ask them yourself.'

'If Zuwayy is indeed the leader of the Muslim Brotherhood, then his word should be all that's required to give me what I want,' Salaam said. 'If the Brotherhood is nothing more than a paper tiger, then this is a good opportunity for me to find out before I give any further support for it.'

'I . . . I cannot go in front of Zuwayy. . . I mean, His Highness, and ask him to throw all his support behind the person who attacked his holy city.'

'You will do it, or Libya does not get its partnership in Salimah, your workers stay in your country and fester in their poverty, and the Muslim Brotherhood starts to look on you and your king as a gutless failure while Egyptian warplanes cruise their skies.'

'This . . . this will be most difficult. . .'

'Then we have a deal, Minister?'

He hesitated once more – but there was no reason to do so. 'We have a deal, Madame,' he said. 'If His Highness agrees, our forces will pull back immediately.'

Juma Mahmud Hijazi walked into Zuwayy's office several minutes later, his face completely expressionless. 'Where the hell have you been, Juma?' Tahir Fazani asked irritably. It appeared as if Jadallah Zuwayy was even more morose and depressed than before.

Hijazi ignored Fazani. 'Listen, Jadallah, I think we have a solution to the problem,' he said. Fazani looked quizzically at his longtime friend and coconspirator, but wisely kept silent.

'What are you talking about, Juma?' Zuwayy asked.

'A . . . a back-channel contact I've been developing in the Egyptian government,' Hijazi replied carefully. 'I just got a call from them. They're willing to talk. The government wants to negotiate a ceasefire.'

'I will only accept a surrender,' Zuwayy said. 'The Egyptians surrender to me, and they allow us to occupy the Salimah oil fields as reparations for the death and destruction they've caused in Libya.' Both Hijazi and Fazani both rolled their eyes in exasperation – now, they realized, Zuwayy had gone completely over the edge. He wasn't thinking clearly at all anymore.

'Don't worry about anything, Jadallah,' Hijazi said. 'The Egyptians will agree to all our demands. They will cease attacking our bases, they will lay down their weapons, and they will withdraw from the frontier.'

'I want Salimah too. They will cede Salimah to me immediately.'

'Jadallah, they're not going to just cede Salimah to us or anyone – we have to pay to become part of this cartel.'

'*Pay?* I'm not going to pay them to belong to something that is already ours!'

'Jadallah, we will become equal partners with the consortium of Western oil companies that built the pipeline and are drilling the wells – and we don't have to lift one shovel or get our hands messy,' Hijazi said. 'Our investment could be returned to us a hundredfold *per year*. They will also allow Libyan workers in to work there.'

'What good is that?'

'We need to show that we won something from this battle,' Hijazi said. 'We can say we forced them to give us a stake in that oil project, but they can't say we forced them into giving it to us. We also take care of our workers by giving them access and jobs in the world's largest and richest oil project. They look weak because they handed over part of their project to us, and we look like a partner because we paid for our percentage.'

Zuwayy shook his head in confusion. 'I don't know what you're talking about, Juma,' he said. 'I want to just go in and take that oil field. Tahir says our troops are in place –'

'Then we risk getting bombed again by the Egyptians and whoever else they have working for them,' Hijazi said. 'We haven't been able to touch the forces that attacked Samāh or Jaghbub – we certainly won't be able to get them over Egypt.' He glared at Fazani, silently ordering him to start arguing on his side, or *else*.

'We need time and money to regroup, rearm, and reorganize our forces,' Fazani said tenuously. Hijazi nodded. 'This deal will give us the time and the money to do that.' Zuwayy looked at both his friends and advisers, and seemed to be relenting.

'And all we have to do is endorse Susan Bailey Salaam as president of Egypt,' Hijazi added quickly.

'*What?*' both Fazani and Zuwayy asked in unison.

'We need to do this, or this whole thing unravels,' Hijazi explained. 'Salaam is seen as the hero in all this, even though she did nothing but screw some American commander into bombing targets in Libya for her. She is inexperienced, naive, and idealistic. She will allow Muslim Brotherhood representatives into Egypt to argue before the People's Assembly for membership – that alone is worth the price. If Egypt becomes a full member of the Brotherhood, all African and Middle East nations will soon follow suit. But in order for this to happen, Salaam must become president of Egypt. If you endorse her, and get all the other Brotherhood leaders to do the same. . .'

'*What?* Have all of the other members *endorse an American to be president of Egypt?* Are you insane?'

'Jadallah, the Muslim Brotherhood can step out of the shadows and take its place in the center of the world stage if this happens,' Hijazi argued. 'Salaam is that powerful, that well known – and after this offensive against us, she looks more and more like a defender of Egypt. We need to tap into that power – and the best way for that is to embrace her as an equal, not as a victor. Only you can make this happen. She needs this from us as much as we need Salimah, Jadallah. Do it.'

Fazani was still looking quizzically at Hijazi, still trying to figure out what his game was, but he nodded as he turned to Zuwayy. 'Let's do this, Jadallah,' he said. 'Once we have our people in Egypt and get our cut of the oil revenues, then we can set about destroying Salaam and taking over. We'll put our spies in place all over Egypt, and we'll keep an eye on every move her military forces make. We'll play her game for a while, let her think she's won – and then, when she's gotten a little fatter off the oil money, we'll stomp her once and for all.'

Zuwayy still didn't look pleased. He looked warily at both Hijazi and Fazani. 'I will not wait long for all this to happen,' he said. 'A month or two, no more. We get our concessions from Egypt, and then we move in – and Salaam dies, this time for good.'

Alexandria, Egypt
the next night

At Amina Shafik's urging, Susan left the balcony of her Alexandria home late at night, got undressed, showered, then stood in the steamy bathroom for several minutes, staring at the hazy reflection in the mirror. She had plenty of questions for that person in the mirror, but no answers were forthcoming.

Her eyes roamed over her wet, naked body, pausing on the still-unhealed scars from the blast that took her husband's life. Her breasts were spared, but the blast had chewed and scorched large segments of her left shoulder, arm, and hand – a few more feet closer, the doctors said, and the blast would've taken her arm. Her left eye was still intact and would require several more surgeries to get any vision at all, but the doctors warned that if the vision in her right eye started to get worse, they would have to enucleate the left eye to keep it from sympathetically damaging the right.

She was lucky to be alive, she thought. Somebody up there still likes me. It also meant that if she was still alive, her mission here on Earth was still not yet finished. But what was her mission? Was it to avenge her husband – or was it something else? It was too late, and she was too tired, to think about it any more.

Susan shook her head at the sad, scarred reflection in the mirror, mercifully shut off the bathroom light, and stepped into
. . .

. . . a dark figure standing directly in front of her.

'Major! Ilha'uni!' she shouted. She swung with her right fist, but her blow was effortlessly turned away.

Behind the figure, the bedroom door burst open. Amina Shafik, crouching low behind the doorjamb with her side arm pointed inside, shouted, *'Wa'if! Yiden ala tul! Imshi!* Stop! Hands up! Move away!' But Susan felt a crackling of electricity, like stiff cellophane being crunched inside her skull, and Shafik collapsed to the floor.

'Amina!' Susan cried. She tried to rush to her bodyguard's side, thinking she was dead, but the dark figure roughly pushed her away onto the bed. *'Who are you?'* Susan shouted. She hoped one of the outside guards might hear her, but they were all probably dead too. 'What do you want?'

The figure reached out and flipped on the bedroom light. To Susan's immense surprise, it was one of the American commandos, dressed for full combat in the electronic battle armor and strength-enhancing microhydraulic exoskeleton. *'Patrick?* Is that you?'

321

Patrick McLanahan turned, lifted Shafik in his hydraulically augmented arms, carried her into her bedroom next to Susan's, and gently laid her on the bed. Susan felt the breeze blowing in off Abu Qir Bay through the bedroom patio doors and realized that Patrick had to have climbed up seventeen floors, or jumped at least a hundred feet from the nearest building, to get over to her bedroom balcony. He returned to the bedroom moments later and removed his helmet, rage blazing in his eyes.

'I thought you were dead,' Susan said, pulling on a thin, silky dressing gown.

'I thought we were going to go after the ones who killed your husband,' Patrick said. 'I thought you were going to help me find my wife and my men.'

'I am helping you.'

'By making a deal with Zuwayy to take the prisoners to Mersa Matrûh and lock us up in the bunker so he could wipe us – and your political rival Khan – out with a nuclear weapon?'

'You think *I* had something to do with that awful attack? I'm as horrified as you are,' Susan said. 'I've been under house arrest here in Alexandria. I never heard from Zuwayy or anyone from Libya. As for Khan – I'm glad he's dead, the murderous bastard, but I had nothing to do with it. He was double-crossed by his buddy Zuwayy – why, I don't know. It's all part of Zuwayy's twisted scheme for power.'

'And you didn't bother telling me about this? We thought you had turned us all in – we got out as soon as we could.'

'You didn't bother telling me you were going after Zuwayy.'

'I told you I was going to try to recover Wendy and my men, or go after Zuwayy to force him to give them up – that was the best way I thought of doing it,' Patrick said. 'I didn't tell you because I didn't know if I could trust you. Apparently I was right.'

'So what are you doing here now?' Susan asked. 'Why risk climbing a seventeen-story building and confronting a dozen armed guards? You won't find your wife here.'

Patrick clenched his fists in anger, the flexible electronic armor in his gauntlets and exoskeleton making little humming noises. 'I'm going to go home, Susan. I've already attacked Zillah and Al-Jawf. I'm tired, and my men are tired.'

Susan's mouth dropped open in surprise. 'How can you do

this? You and your men alone couldn't possibly have the power to do this.'

'It's done.' He paused, looking at her with a strange, faraway expression. 'What will you do?'

'I'm going to fight – what else do you think I'd do?' Susan replied hotly. 'I don't care if Zuwayy attacks my country and blows up my bases – I'm going to stay and fight! While my name and my dead husband's name still mean something in this country, I'm going to use them to bring peace and justice to Egypt.'

'So you can become president?'

'I want to see General Ahmad Baris made president of Egypt. He has the experience, and he is completely loyal to Egypt.' She saw Patrick imperceptibly nod his approval. She moved off the bed and stepped toward him. 'Patrick, I need your help.'

'What am I supposed to do?'

'Be my instrument of war,' Susan said. 'I can't trust anyone: not the military, not even my personal guards – Khan had them all on his payroll, and I think they're just looking for an opportunity to strike again without revealing their treason. The Muslim Brotherhood in Egypt will certainly move to assassinate me and make Egypt a theocracy. They mean to create a strong union between Egypt, Libya, and the other Muslim Brotherhood states – with Zuwayy pulling the strings. If I can uncover the plot or conspiracy to undermine the law in Egypt in favor of Libya, I can pave the way to elevate General Baris to the presidency.'

'What kind of conspiracy?'

'The conspiracy to kill my husband, for starters,' Susan said bitterly. 'I know Khan and Zuwayy were both involved. I also suspect there was some kind of conspiracy to force withdrawal of foreign oil companies from Egypt.' Susan stepped closer to him and placed her hands on his chest, looking deeply into his eyes. 'Will you help me? As the wife of a martyred president, I can offer much assistance to you.' He hesitated, his eyes staring at a spot beyond her shoulders. 'Is your mission complete? The reason you came here, the reason you attacked Libya – is it over?'

For a moment, it looked as if Patrick might crumble. His shoulders slumped, his eyes drooped, and his Adam's apple bobbed. 'Yes,' he finally responded woodenly.

'Then take on a different mission – help me uncover and remove the traitors from Egypt,' Susan said. 'Egypt is in danger of becoming another theocratic dictatorship – or, worse, a stooge of Jadallah Zuwayy. Help me stop this. Use your power for real justice, not just for a few dollars.'

He looked down at her, and she could see his eyes roam from her eyes to the wounds on her shoulder and arm, the anger in his eyes turning to empathy. She turned her eyes away from his and backed away from him. 'What's the matter?' Patrick asked.

'Don't look at my wounds, dammit,' she said. 'Don't take pity on me.' She pulled her gown down off her shoulders – purposely a bit farther down her chest than necessary to show the majority of her wounds. 'You want to take a look? Take a good look.' He did – including the parts of her naked body that were not damaged, she noticed. Maybe this guy didn't have quite the stone heart she once thought. Now was the time to drive the message home. . .

'Don't you dare pity me, McLanahan,' Susan went on. 'I don't wear a suit of armor like you – I'm fighting this battle with all the weapons I have, which is just about what you see here. I don't need your pity.' She took his armored hands into hers, squeezed them, then placed her right hand on his chest. 'I need these fighting hands, Patrick, and I need this heart. Be my champion, Patrick. Help me. If you've had enough of fighting for money, then try fighting for justice. Fight for me instead.'

He didn't say anything – but his eyes replied for him. The pity had turned to something else – not quite trust, not quite friendship. But he would be back.

'You're going to leave me, aren't you?' she asked sullenly.

'I have to.'

'To bury your brother. I know.' She lowered her eyes. 'And to mourn your wife. I know all about mourning – I've done a lot of that lately.' She pulled up her robe over her shoulders, but did it in such a way that covering up was even more seductive than exposing herself. Patrick picked up his helmet, fastened it in place, and then stepped to the bedroom patio. 'Patrick.' He turned, the helmet's bug-eyes looking sinister and comical at the same time. 'You will always have an ally here in Egypt. I will always be here for you.'

He nodded, once, slowly, and then turned. In a blink of an eye and a loud hiss of compressed air, he was gone. Susan thought she heard a clunk of boots on the rooftop across the street, but she couldn't see anything.

McLanahan was an emotional wreck right now – his brother dead, his wife blown to atoms, his men decimated, his mission failed and shattered. Did she actually expect him to be able to fight?

The quicker he was out of the country, she decided, the better.

Chapter Eight

Coronado, California
days later

The answering machine picked up for the sixth or seventh time that evening; again, Patrick ignored it.

It was an exceptionally warm evening, so Patrick was out on the big bayview balcony, sipping a Grand Marnier and watching the activity in San Diego Bay. He could see all the way from the Thirty-second Street Naval Base to the south to North Island Naval Air Station and Point Loma Naval Base to the north. North Island, the home of the Navy's Anti-Submarine Warfare Center, was a buzz of activity – it usually was, with aircraft of all sizes buzzing down the Pacific beaches of Coronado, right behind the Del Coronado Hotel, coming in for a landing. To the south on Coronado was the Navy Basic Underwater Demolition Service Training Center, the home of the Navy SEALs; one could usually see inflatable boats going up and down the coast all year long, day and night.

It was hard to tell from the level of activity in the harbor what was happening in the world. North Island had two carriers in port right now – that was unusual. Thirty-second Street Naval Base was busier than Patrick had ever seen it before – every pier looked occupied. Would it be busier if war was imminent as ships prepared for deployment, or would it be quieter because all available warships were heading into battle? Patrick didn't know. A trained spy might be able to deduce the answer to that, but Patrick wasn't a spy.

He wasn't anything right now – not a military man, not a Night Stalker. Just a man with a young son, a missing wife, a dead brother, and not much else – not even a future.

After the last strikes against Libya by the Night Stalkers and the Sky Masters Inc's EB-52 Megafortress, Patrick finally got his men out of Egypt. They first flew by CV-22 Pave Hammer tilt-rotor aircraft to an isolated base in southern Israel, where they sanitized their gear and received civilian travel documents. They drove to Tel Aviv, flew via commercial airlines to London, then to Los Angeles, and finally to San Diego.

Coming home was without question the happiest – and the saddest – day in Patrick's life. Little Bradley was brought to San Diego-Lindbergh International Airport by Patrick's mother and sisters; they hugged Patrick warmly, but they wore stony, stern expressions on their faces – they were silently accusing him of killing both Paul and Wendy and nearly orphaning his son. Patrick ignored their anger. He hugged his son long and hard right at the Jetway door, ignoring the aggravated comments of the others who had to maneuver around them. One look at Hal Briggs, Chris Wohl, and David Luger, however, and the complainers fell silent and went about their business.

But no sooner did they turn away from the Jetway than five-year-old Bradley asked, 'Dad, where's Mom?'

Patrick was dreading this moment. He took his son aside to an isolated set of seats near a big picture window, motioned the others to go on ahead, and sat his son beside him. Despite his request, his mother and sisters stayed, respectfully apart from them but close enough to watch and listen.

'Brad,' Patrick said, 'Mommy's not coming home with us.'

Bradley's blue eyes instantly filled with tears. 'Why?'

'Mommy was hurt,' Patrick replied. 'She was helping me, and Uncle Paul, and Uncle Hal, and Uncle Dave, and Uncle Chris, and a bunch of our other friends, and she got hurt real bad.'

'Is she dead?'

Patrick took immense comfort and drew a lot of strength from little Bradley's maturity. He wasn't sure if Bradley completely understood what death was, but the very fact that he asked if she was dead made Patrick think that he understood a little of what death meant. Bradley watched a lot of movies that should probably not be watched by young children, and then he liked to act out the fight scenes with his father and baby-sitters. But in the movies, the dead guys all came back to life when he replayed the movie; in their playacting, Daddy always got up moments after Bradley delivered the coup de grâce with his plastic laser-sword. Was that his only concept of death?

330

'She's missing,' Patrick told him. When Bradley furrowed his eyebrows, Patrick went on, 'The bad guys got her, and they took her to a place where a lot of people were killed. We haven't found her yet.'

'Mommy was killed?'

'I don't know, buddy . . .'

'Mommy's *dead?*' Bradley asked, louder this time. Patrick's mother rushed over and grabbed Bradley in her arms. The suddenness of her movements startled him, and he started to cry. Patrick's sisters looked at their brother with a strange, painful mixture of pity and contempt as they followed their mother out to the parking garage.

That was a few days ago. They had gone back up to Sacramento for Paul McLanahan's memorial service and interment beside their father in City Cemetery in downtown Sacramento. His sisters offered to take Bradley, but Patrick insisted on bringing his son home with him to their high-rise condominium on Coronado Island. That did not please them at all.

Patrick also did not offer any explanations to his family on what happened to Paul or to Wendy. That made them even angrier. His mother and sisters hugged Bradley tightly as they got on the plane to San Diego, but Patrick could have hugged pieces of plywood that had more warmth or tenderness than he felt from them.

He had an entire day by himself with Bradley. They made their usual stops: out to North Island Naval Air Station to watch the Navy planes come and go and to see if they could spot any submarines over at Point Loma; a visit to the Star of India, the old sailing barque on the San Diego waterfront, standing on deck pretending to be pirates; out to the Windsock Grill at San Diego-Lindbergh Airport to have lunch and watch the airliners as they seemingly threaded between the high-rises of the downtown district and skimmed the top of the parking garage on their way to the runway; then out to the lawns on Shelter Island where they tossed a Frisbee around and watched the Navy warships, yachts, and tour boats head out to sea. By then Bradley was ready for a nap; Patrick carried him to his room, as he usually had to do after all-day outings like this.

331

While Bradley napped, Patrick checked his e-mail – no messages. That meant they had been dumped or erased by Sky Masters Inc, or intercepted by the Feds. He checked his cell phone – no service, which meant either that service had been cut off or the secure system was detecting eavesdropping and deactivated itself. He tossed the phone onto his desk – frankly, he was glad to be rid of it.

The phone calls started shortly thereafter. The first one, which Patrick let the answering machine pick up, was from former President of the United States Kevin Martindale. 'I heard you were back in town, Patrick. Call me right away.' The second call was also from Martindale just ten minutes later; Patrick again did not answer. By the third call, Patrick had shut off the ringer.

After a one-hour nap, Bradley came into the living room, biting his red blanket. He had given up his blankets almost a year earlier, calling them silly and childish. Patrick had cut up all but one of them, making little kid handkerchiefs out of them, but Wendy had insisted on keeping one intact, the red one, his favorite. Patrick hadn't seen it in many months; he didn't know how Bradley found it, but he did, and he held it tightly against his face and chest as he walked into the room. 'Hi, big guy,' Patrick greeted his son.

'Where's Mommy?' he asked, his voice muffled by the blanket.

'Mommy's not here, Bradley,' Patrick said, choking down yet another lump in his throat. He wondered where his glass of Grand Marnier was right now. 'We're going to look for her soon, remember?'

'I want my mommy,' Bradley said tearfully.

'I know, big guy. Don't worry. Everything will be okay.' Patrick rose to go hug his son, but Bradley ran back to his room and closed the door. When Patrick went inside, he found him curled up in the middle of the floor. Oh, shit . . .

He picked him up and held him tightly. Bradley wasn't crying; he bit his blanket and stared straight ahead, hardly blinking. Scared, Patrick went back to the living room and held him until, thankfully, he fell asleep again, and then carried him into his bedroom and put him under the covers, on Wendy's side of the bed.

Patrick stayed with him and waited to see if Bradley would

wake up soon for dinner, but his heavy breathing told him he was down for the night, so Patrick took his shoes and clothes off and tucked him under the covers once again. Patrick usually did not allow Bradley to sleep in his bed – 'big boys sleep in their own beds,' he would often admonish his son – but tonight, having him sleep anywhere else was completely out of the question.

He didn't usually drink when caring for Bradley, but this time he poured himself a stiff shot of the orange liqueur and went out to the patio. These past few days were simply hell, he thought. If Bradley started going to pieces, he would too – it was as simple as that.

'Muck, we're on our way up,' he heard Hal Briggs call on the subcutaneous microtransceiver. 'Feel like some company?'

'Sure.' A few minutes later, Hal Briggs, along with Chris Wohl and David Luger, let themselves into Patrick's condo. They found seats in the living room; Patrick knew they wanted to talk business, which was why he did not go outside again.

'You drinking that sissy stuff again, Muck?' Hal asked. Patrick did not reply. Hal found something he liked in the liquor cabinet; David and Chris did not drink. 'How are you doin', man?' Still no answer.

A few quiet minutes later, they heard crying from the bedroom. Patrick shot to his feet to go check on Bradley, but Chris Wohl silently waved him back to his seat, and he went inside to check on him. He saw Wohl carry Bradley to the kitchen, give him a glass of milk, and start fixing him a fried bologna and cheese sandwich on toast, Wohl's favorite meal. Briggs and Luger stayed behind with Patrick on the patio.

'Big bad-ass Marine is really a sucker when it comes to kids,' Briggs observed.

'President Martindale's been calling,' Dave Luger said to Patrick.

'I know.'

'He's worried about you.'

'Like hell he is. He just wants to know when we're ready to go back out there.'

Luger couldn't argue with that observation. 'Fair enough – but *I'm* worried about you,' Luger said, 'and I want to know when we're going back out there to look for Wendy.'

'As soon as my son stops crying himself to sleep,' Patrick replied bitterly. Again, Luger had no reply for that.

'Been watching the news?'

'No.'

'Susan Bailey Salaam was elected president of Egypt,' Hal Briggs said. 'She's got the Libyans, Sudanese, Syrians, Lebanese, Iranians, Iraqis, Jordanis, and Saudis cheering for her like she's some kind of rock star.'

'Good for her.'

'There's talk of another United Arab Republic,' Luger added. 'Egypt and Syria merged for a few years back in the late fifties and early sixties under Nasser – they're saying that Susan Salaam might be able to unify the entire Arab world.'

Now Patrick's interest was piqued a bit. 'Interesting. So I'll bet Martindale is calling because the Central African Petroleum Partnership called. . .'

'Exactly – wanting to know if we're going to stay on the case,' Briggs said.

'What's going on out there?'

'Salaam has brought Libya in as a partner in the cartel, for starters,' Luger said.

'Libya? Partnered up with Egypt?'

'Hey, they're all huggy and kissy lately,' Briggs said. 'Egypt is giving out work visas to Libyans and Sudanese to work in Salimah like crazy – almost ten thousand persons have migrated to Salimah in just the past few days. There's already talk of Sudan, Syria, and Jordan joining the oil partnership.'

'Sounds like Egypt decided to trade jobs for peace,' Patrick observed. 'Good move.'

'And so far it's paying off big-time,' Luger said. 'Not only are they not fighting, but they're praising and cooperating with each other unlike anything anyone's ever seen.'

'So Egypt becomes the new center of the Arab world,' Patrick mused.

'Makes sense,' Luger said. 'Egypt is by far more powerful than any of the other countries, and they're more centrally located and strategically important, with the Suez Canal and the Salimah oil fields. They have strong ties to the Muslim world, the African world, Europe, and the West all at the same time.'

'And, last but not least, Egypt has Susan Bailey Salaam – they're calling her the reincarnation of Cleopatra,' Hal Briggs added. 'She was elected in a landslide and cheered in eight different African and Middle East capitals the night of her election. It's pretty amazing to watch. Less than a month ago she had almost gotten herself blown up and was on the run, being hunted down by assassins – now, she's not only president, but being considered the up-and-coming leader of the whole freakin' Arab world.'

'And naturally, the Central African Petroleum Partners are not happy with this arrangement – right?'

'You got it,' Luger said. 'Egypt is the majority partner, and Salaam has been allowing more Arab and African workers in to work at Salimah, displacing the Asians and Europeans.'

'And with the price of oil hitting new highs, all those folks are getting mighty rich,' Briggs added.

'Speaking of which.' David Luger held out three envelopes. 'Wire-transfer receipts: our payment from the Central African Petroleum Partners. Paul made you executor of his estate.'

Patrick looked at the receipts in the envelopes, closed his eyes, then dropped them on a table. 'It's a lot of money,' he said softly. 'But was it worth it, guys?' he asked.

'It's never worth it when you take losses, man,' Briggs said. 'But we all volunteered. We're all doin' what we want to be doin'.' He looked carefully at Patrick; then: 'Aren't we?'

Patrick did not – *could* not – answer.

Sky Masters Inc test facility, Tonopah Test Range, Nevada the next morning

Jon Masters found Kelsey Duffield asleep at a computer work-station in the research library, sound asleep, with a blanket thrown over her shoulders. Her mother Cheryl was asleep in a chair in a corner of the room, but awoke immediately when Jon entered – and she did not look happy.

'I've been looking for you guys. Your phones are off,' Jon whispered.

'Kelsey has been working all night – she refused to leave,'

Cheryl said. 'She's been on the phone to scientists and laboratories all over the world. I finally had to shut it off – we had no chance of getting any rest otherwise.' She awakened her daughter and told her to go to the bathroom. Kelsey walked out, rubbing her eyes and shuffling along like kids who just woke up do.

'Poor kid. She's a trouper, that's for sure.'

'"Trouper"? She's being overworked – and I'd say this verges on abuse,' Cheryl said angrily. 'Keeping her locked up in this place . . . spending days on end on that computer or in the lab. It's ridiculous. You can't expect her to keep on working like this.'

'Cheryl, I'm not expecting her to do any of this,' Jon said. 'Kelsey is the one who walked into the library and hasn't come out.'

'Come out? How can she? Security officers besiege us every time we turn around. It wastes almost half a day going in and out of security. Kelsey feels less intruded upon by just staying here.'

'Well, that's the conclusion most of us come to,' Jon admitted with a sheepish grin. 'It's almost as if the Air Force designs the security this way to make us work harder.'

'It's not funny, Dr Masters.'

'No one is forcing her to do this, Cheryl. She's doing it all on her own.' He looked at her carefully. 'You really are worried, aren't you?'

'Of course I am.'

'Are you telling me that Kelsey's never worked like this before? This is the first time she's been so . . .'

'Obsessed? Single-minded? Manic?' Cheryl exploded. 'That's what I'm saying, Dr Masters. Sure, she's worked hard before – she works hard on everything she's ever done. But never like this. I'm really worried about her.'

'I don't have kids, Cheryl, so I'm no expert,' Jon said, 'but if I didn't know better, I'd say Kelsey is . . .'

'What?'

'Having fun,' Jon said. When Cheryl rolled her eyes in disbelief, Jon went on, 'No, really. Putting together inertial confinement chambers and laser generators is like . . . like putting together a doll house or a Lego castle is to most kids.'

'Jon, you're wrong. Completely, absolutely wrong.' But even as she said the words, Jon could see that she really didn't believe

336

they were true. 'I wish this never happened. I wish Kelsey was just a normal, everyday kid.'

'Cheryl, she *is* just an everyday normal kid – but with an incredible gift,' Jon said. 'I think you see the security and the weapons and the horror and destruction all this could cause, and you wonder and worry about how this will affect your daughter.'

'Of course I'm worried!'

'But have you looked at your daughter lately . . . I mean, stepped back and *really* looked at her?' Jon asked. 'I mean, I've never had kids, but I'm a kid at heart. And I've seen supersmart kids before. Some of them are really full of themselves. They'll talk about the offers they get from universities and big companies and consultants to work for them; they'll talk about their stock portfolios and patents and the money they're making.'

He paused, staring out into space as if reliving some scene in his mind's eye. 'I know about those kids – because I was one. I am probably *still* one.' He chuckled. 'Man, I used to love stuffing one down some four-star general's shirt. He thought he knew everything – I couldn't wait to blow him away. Every tactic, every procedure, every concept he had, I had a response or an alternative that he never thought about. I used to cream the big corporate CEOs daily. They wouldn't give me the time of day – until I showed them a design for something they absolutely *had* to have. I was a third of their age and had bank accounts and portfolios bigger than theirs. I . . . was . . . the greatest.'

Jon looked at little Kelsey napping at the computer and smiled. 'Kelsey has done all that stuff too,' he said softly. 'She's built companies, lectured at Cornell, given presentations in front of the National Science Foundation and the Lawrence Livermore Laboratories. She has almost as many patents as I have and she's a fourth my age. But you know the difference between Kelsey and those other Generation-X nerds? The other bozos tell you all the stuff about themselves – myself included. I had to go out and *find* out all the stuff about Kelsey. She doesn't brag about all her accomplishments.' He looked at Cheryl and smiled. 'Maybe that has as much to do with you as it does with her?' For the first time in a very long time, Cheryl Duffield smiled.

Jon smiled back, then looked around. 'Where did she go?'

'Bathroom.'

'That was a few minutes ago,' Jon said. 'Uh-oh. If I know Kelsey, she's not going to come back here right away. I know where she is.' Jon was correct: He walked directly to the AL-52 laser lab and found Kelsey with her laser goggles on, punching instructions into a computer beside the large mounting racks where the components of the plasma laser were mounted. Kelsey wore only a pair of socks on her feet, and her Top Secret ID badge was pinned to the tops of her underwear peeking over the top of her pants.

Jon was simply and unabashedly dumbfounded whenever he walked into this lab. In an amazingly short period of time, he and Kelsey had managed to build a full-scale working model of a laser that had been virtually unheard of. The bench that the laser was mounted to was the same size as the interior of the B-52 aircraft; the laser waveguides were mounted in an adjacent room, and the power capacitors and other support equipment were mounted in other rooms as well, networked here for the tests.

The room was dominated by a large aluminum sphere seven feet in diameter, with a number of electrodes and cables running around the outside. This was the main component – the inertial confinement chamber. Set on the inside surface of the sphere were four hundred diode lasers, like powerful laser pointers, aimed into the center of the sphere. Inside the sphere, magnetrons – magnetic guns – were also set up, pointing into the center as well. A tube ran through the center, and there was an opening in the front end of the sphere that connected the confinement chamber to a large cylinder with thousands of rectangles etched into it – the laser generators – and from there to the Faraday oscillator that would collect the light energy from the generators and produce a laser beam.

The tube fed tiny pellets of deuterium and tritium into the sphere, and the laser beams bombarded the pellets. The deuterium and tritium elements in the gaseous cloud that formed in the center of the sphere released energy particles but were then trapped, focused, and squeezed by the laser beams until the heat built up to a point where the elements no longer repelled one another but were fused together. When they fused, they created a massive release of heat and energy. Further squeezed by the

338

magnetrons, the fused particles suddenly snapped apart, creating a cloud of free electrons and positively charged particles called ions – a plasma field. The magnetrons then focused the field and sent it to the laser generator, where the plasma energy stripped high-energy particles from neodymium, creating laser light.

Despite its size and complexity, it was a perfect example of simplicity and functionality. It weighed less than thirty thousand pounds, less than half the weight of the chemical laser it was replacing. The inertial confinement chamber was a simple re-engineering of the plasma-yield warhead Jon Masters had invented years earlier – instead of simply releasing the plasma energy created inside, the chamber was designed to channel it to the laser generator. It used virtually no power – just enough to light up the diode lasers inside the confinement chamber and to keep the magnetrons firing.

Unfortunately, that was the problem – and Kelsey's current headache. 'How's it looking, Kelsey?' Jon asked, ignoring Cheryl's concerned expression – better get a status update fast before Cheryl decided to escort her daughter out of here.

'Horrible,' Kelsey said. 'I still haven't been able to control the heat buildup and keep it away from the magnetrons.'

'That's a problem I never had to contend with,' Jon admitted. 'With the plasma-yield warhead, I *wanted* to let the heat build up – we got a bigger plasma field and we could do more damage. Here, we want to control it.'

It took an incredible amount of heat to create a plasma field – a hundred million degrees Fahrenheit, ten times hotter than the sun. The heat only lasted for a tiny fraction of a second, but it was still devastating to ordinary man-made materials. Further, cooling the sphere or magnetrons was not an option – the only way to do away with the heat was to build the heat up enough to create a plasma field, at which instant it would cool to safe limits and the plasma field would disappear. Even if the creation of the plasma fields was pulsed, excess heat eventually built up to the point where even the strongest materials would begin to corrode and weaken.

'What's the pulse interval looking like?'

'The optimum safe range is between ten and twenty-five milliseconds,' Kelsey replied, 'but I only get a yield of point four one megawatts – almost half the level of the chemical laser we're replacing. Not good.' Kelsey had been experimenting with trying to vary the spacing between plasma pulses. Spacing the pulses out farther resulted in manageable levels of heat but decreased the power available to the laser generators. 'If I can go to five to ten milliseconds I can get to one megawatt of power. I'm shooting for one millisecond – then I can beat TRW's chemical laser output by twenty-five percent. But at that power level, I can get maybe ten ten-second shots off before the magnetrons let go.'

'Letting go' was a nice way of saying 'exploding.' The magnetrons in the confinement chamber served two purposes: they squeezed the plasma energy down to a smaller size to increase the power of the plasma field, and it then channeled the plasma stream into the laser generator. The magnetrons signaled imminent failure by vibrating rapidly as the magnetic material began to disintegrate molecularly and the magnetic fields began alternately attracting, then repelling one another at incredible speed. If the magnetrons failed and the plasma reaction wasn't stopped in time, the plasma field would grow uncontrollably, unleashing one hundred million degrees of destruction on anything within one or two miles.

Building two smaller confinement chambers instead of one large one was an option, but there wasn't enough room for two of the right size in the B-52's fuselage; besides, Jon's and Kelsey's initial computations suggested that one large confinement chamber would do the trick, so they went for it, and now it would take weeks, maybe months, to redesign everything for two chambers.

'I don't think we have any choice – we drop back ten, punt, and go for two confinement chambers,' Jon said. 'We need to build a little more safety into the system too, or else we can't market to the Pentagon. We need to get more than thirty shots and we need at least one point five megawatts, preferably two megawatts.'

'I know I can do it,' Kelsey said. 'By varying the time between plasma pulses, making bigger magnetrons, increasing the power to the magnetrons, adding more laser generators, and perhaps redesigning the oscillator, I think we can get one point five megawatts out of this system with a good margin of safety. Those changes would be simpler than tearing everything apart and redoing it with two smaller confinement chambers.'

'Frankly, Kels, we make more of a splash with a two-megawatt system even if we only get ten to twelve safe shots out of it,' Jon said. 'It's not important now – tuning up an unworkable system is a mental exercise, not a business one. We'll redesign the system for two confinement chambers.' He squeezed her shoulders appreciatively. 'You've done an extraordinary job, young lady. You've designed and built a powerful, sophisticated laser pumping system that's never been tried before, and in record time. It's got some bugs, but we've actually fielded a working system. You should be proud of that. Let's let the concept engineers work on the new drawings and take a break from this one for now.'

'Okay, Jon,' Kelsey said.

Jon Masters nodded, winked at Cheryl, then headed for the door, fully expecting Kelsey to follow him, even holding his hand as she sometimes did. But Jon was out the door before he realized that Kelsey had not followed him – had, in fact, not even gotten up out of her chair.

He was about to go back inside and ask her – no, *order* her – to get up and go home. But then Cheryl reached over and, instead of taking her daughter out of there or trying to convince her that she needed her sleep, started to massage her daughter's little shoulders.

Who was abusing whom here? Jon asked himself. Did Cheryl want the best for her daughter, or was she mostly interested in making sure she was happy – and what in heck was the difference? Jon wasn't a parent – he could never know the answer to that question. The closest he came to family had been Paul and Patrick McLanahan – one was dead, the other an emotional wreck.

Best to just get out of there and let them have their time together, Jon thought. Cheryl obviously treasured even these little moments, as long as they could be together – even if it was at the control terminal of a fifty-million-dollar laser.

President Anwar Sadat Unity Stadium, Cairo, Egypt
several days later

'My brothers and sisters, may God bless and protect you, and may He grant all of us everlasting peace and happiness,' Egyptian president Susan Bailey Salaam began. The military memorial service for the slain, injured, and missing of Mersa Matrûh had concluded, and then came the political rally and the speeches. Last to step up to the dais was the president herself, making her first political speech since taking office. The cheering was deafening: It rattled seats, made the flags high atop the rim of the stadium flutter, and even caused car alarms in the parking lot outside to go off.

'We are here to pray for the victims of the terrible tragedy that claimed so many lives,' Susan went on. 'I pledge to you, on the memory of my beloved husband, to work tirelessly to bring to justice those that perpetrated that horrible deed. They will be brought before the people of Egypt, and they will feel our wrath – this I guarantee you.

'But we are here not just for vengeance or retribution, but to profess our strength and unity in the eyes of God and to everyone in the world,' Salaam went on. 'None may challenge us. None may stay our hands or our voices, because God is on the side of the believers, and he will defend and protect those who stand for justice and peace.'

Seated beside her, General Ahmad Baris, Egypt's new foreign minister, looked on, applauding enthusiastically and rising from his seat each time she was given a standing ovation. Outwardly, he was proud and overwhelmed by the effusive show of support for his friend . . .

. . . but inwardly, he was confused and, yes, a little frightened.

'My friends, we are here in the presence of God for one reason: to show Him that the faith, the solidarity, and the unity of His people is stronger than ever. We have an opportunity to do exactly that.

'We have seen the birth of an exciting and promising new venture: the opening of the Salimah oil project to all Arab workers. My goal is simple but powerful: share the wealth of our land with all of our Arab brothers and sisters. We have opened our borders to friends. We pledge Egypt's protection and support to all who enter peacefully. Salimah promises full employment, wealth, and happiness to anyone who is willing to take a chance and brave the Sahara. Egypt recognizes the bravery and sacrifice of everyone who ventures to Salimah, and we will defend and protect you in your travels and your labors – this I promise.'

After waiting nearly a full minute for the applause to die down, Susan continued: 'My friends, the spirit and promise of Salimah shows us one important ideal: that if we work together, we truly can be happy, wealthy, and fulfilled children of God. That important ideal is unity. We must become as one. Salimah is only the beginning. You can look out across that wasteland and see nothing but sand and rock, but I see much more: I see one people, one message, one common goal: peace, prosperity, and happiness. I see the future, secure and full of hope and promise for our children. I see all Arabs and all Africans working together to secure our borders, sharing in the wealth of our land and our seas, and contributing to a brave new society where we show the world what it's like to be free. I see our future, my brothers and sisters: I see the new United Arab Republic. God wills it, my brothers and sisters, and so let it be done.'

The cheers and joyful screaming reached an almost feverish pitch. This is what the crowd had been waiting for, and now they had heard it from the 'queen's' own lips: She was calling for the formation of the United Arab Republic.

It was not a new idea. In 1958, Egypt formed a United Arab Republic, mostly to fight against lingering European domination in Middle East affairs. With Egyptian president Gamal Abdel Nasser as its leader, the United Arab Republic flourished for three years and grew strong; the Republic was largely responsible for reuniting the Arab world following its defeat in the first Arab-Israeli War, and for strengthening the individual power of its member nations by removing foreign domination of Arab interests and instituting self-rule and determination.

The United Arab Republic foundered for a variety of reasons: The nations involved were too diverse, too wrapped up in their own domestic difficulties, and too dependent on non-Arab nations, mostly the Soviet Union, for their military strength. But assembling a new United Arab Republic was a dream of almost every Arab leader since the fall of the first – if Europe could establish a European Union, as different as they all were in language, geography, wealth, and history, why couldn't the Arab world do so as well?

Susan Bailey Salaam's speech did not last longer than a few minutes – but the crowd cheered and applauded her for almost

343

fifteen. It was truly an awe-inspiring demonstration of trust, loyalty, love, and respect for the American-born non-Muslim wife of a slain politician . . .

. . . for everyone except Jadallah Zuwayy. 'There she goes again – calling for a United Arab Republic!' he shouted at the television set in his office at the Royal Palace in Tripoli, United Kingdom of Libya. 'How dare she? Who does she think she is – Nasser? Kennedy? Cleopatra?' Zuwayy got up out of his seat and started stalking the room. 'I thought we had a deal to get a piece of Salimah, Juma,' he said to his Minister of Arab Unity, Juma Mahmud Hijazi. 'What happened?'

'The deal was that we got twenty percent from Salaam once we paid for ten percent to the cartel,' Hijazi replied. 'About nine hundred million American dollars.'

'*Nine hundred million dollars?* That's insane! I'm not going to pay any bunch of European bastards or anyone else almost a billion dollars!'

'They insisted on their money up front – we couldn't get them to agree to take the fee out of our royalties,' Hijazi went on.

'Jadallah, let's just pitch in and buy the damned shares so Salaam will release her shares and we can start taking in some cash,' Tahir Fazani, the Minister of Defense, said. 'In exchange for this investment to the cartel, we'll be receiving one point eight billion dollars US worth of value in the organization.'

'What good is that to me?' Zuwayy thundered. 'I don't have a billion dollars to spend!'

'We'll earn that investment back in less than three years if the cartel increases production as planned,' Fazani added. 'With an additional investment, we can enlarge the size of the new pipeline and –'

'Now you want me to pay *more?*' Zuwayy thundered. 'Did you hear what I said? I don't have a billion dollars to invest now – how do you expect me to invest more? And just breaking even in three years doesn't exactly appeal to me either – while I'm waiting for my money, Salaam and the fat cats in Europe and America are raking in money hand over fist. It's not right, and I won't stand for it!'

'Jadallah, if the project is expanded, we can all stand to make an enormous profit in coming years,' Hijazi said. 'And in the meantime, the cartel is providing employment for thousands of Libyans.'

'That's another question we're going to tackle – taxing Libyans working in Egypt!' Zuwayy said. 'Why should our people pay Egyptian taxes?' He slapped his desktop. 'I want Salimah destroyed, Fazani. I want it nuked, then I want to send in a ground force and take the entire complex. We've got the troops in place, lined up in Libya and Sudan – let's do it.'

'Don't be crazy, Jadallah. We'll think of something else.'

'I want all Libyan workers to return to this country or they'll be considered traitors and enemies of the state,' Zuwayy said hotly.

'We've got over twenty thousand workers in Egypt right now,' Hijazi said. 'It'll take weeks to get them back.'

'And I want Salimah shut down,' Zuwayy went on. 'Use those neutron weapons again – that'll work. We kill all the foreigners and Egyptians, and then we can just march right in and take over.'

'But what if Salaam calls up those American bombers again?' Fazani asked. 'We'll get clobbered. We haven't found a way to stop them – we don't even know where they came from or what they are!'

Zuwayy turned angrily on Tahir Fazani. 'You will do as I tell you, Fazani, or you can turn in your uniform and get out.'

'Don't be an idiot, Jadallah – we're all working together on this, remember?' Fazani said. The two men stared at each other for several long moments – Zuwayy looked almost psychotic, Fazani's expression turning from angry to scared and back to angry again.

'Do it, Fazani,' Zuwayy told him. 'I want the bombers airborne or the missiles on their way by tomorrow night. I'll give Salaam one more chance to conclude our deal – and if she doesn't agree, I'll turn her precious oil fields into a *graveyard*.'

The White House Oval Office
days later

'President Salaam, this is Thomas Thorn. It is a pleasure to speak with you,' President Thomas Thorn said. He was on a secure

345

videophone link from his study next to the Oval Office. 'I'm here in my study with Secretary of State Kercheval and Secretary of Defense Goff.'

'It's a pleasure to speak with you, Mr President,' Susan Bailey Salaam replied. 'With me is my senior adviser and defense minister, General Ahmad Baris. Thank you for speaking with me.'

'First, Madame Salaam, I'd like to extend my sympathy and condolences for the terrible tragedy that has occurred in Egypt,' Thorn went on. 'All of the relief, rescue and recovery, and scientific resources of the United States are yours for the asking.'

'Thank you, Mr President. The United States has long been a strong ally of Egypt, and I hope this will continue.'

'You're welcome, Madame President. Let's get down to business, shall we? Secretary Kercheval?'

'Thank you, Mr President. Madame President, I understand you have received a message direct from the king of Libya,' Secretary Kercheval said without further preamble, 'stating that a situation has developed involving the safety of Libyan workers in Egypt, and that the Libyan government sees this as a direct threat to its national security and peace in Africa. King Idris has said that it is unsafe for Libyan workers in Salimah and he has ordered all Libyan workers to leave Egypt immediately. He also warns Egypt to use every resource to protect Libyan lives.'

'You are very well informed, Mr Kercheval,' Susan said.

'Our intelligence agencies have examined the situation, and we've analyzed all of the press reports coming in from Egypt from news agencies all over the world covering the explosive growth of the Salimah complex, and we don't see any evidence of mistreatment,' Kercheval went on. 'If anything, we see a very high incidence of anti-Egyptian government sentiment rising in the settlements and housing areas, but mostly from non-Arab countries that resent the sudden and very large influx of Arab workers. That represents a slight danger for Arabs, but not targeted specifically against Libyans, in our view.'

'That's correct, Mr Kercheval.'

'But despite this, you believe this threat to be credible? You actually believe that Idris will attack Salimah, even if there are Libyans still working there?'

'I do, sir.'

'Are you considering military action of your own?' Secretary Goff asked. 'Some kind of preemptive strike?'

'Fully one-fifth of our military forces were decimated at Mersa Matrûh, including almost a third of our naval forces,' Salaam said. 'We redeployed troops to protect the capital; we have only a token ground force in Salimah. General Baris informs me that it would take several weeks at a minimum to recall the reserves and generate enough forces to stage an effective attack. Besides, we don't want to make war on Libya.'

'So why don't you tell us what the real problem is, Madame President?' President Thorn asked. 'Why is the president of Libya, this King Idris, threatening you?'

'The real issue is, Mr President, that Zuwayy of Libya wants Salimah – and he's willing to kill everyone there with more neutron weapons if he doesn't get what he wants.'

'What makes Zuwayy think he can have Salimah?' Robert Goff asked.

'You would have to ask Zuwayy that, Mr Secretary.'

'We're asking you, Mrs Salaam.'

'I'm sure I don't know, sir, except for the obvious reasons – money, power, influence.'

'Is it possible that perhaps Zuwayy was promised a piece of Salimah?' the President asked.

'Salimah belongs to Egypt, Mr President,' Susan responded.

Thomas Thorn lowered his head briefly and tightened his interlaced fingers together. 'Mrs Salaam, I feel as if we're dancing around the issue here,' he said with more than a hint of exasperation in his voice. 'You requested this videoconference with us, Madame – why don't you just tell us what's happening here?'

'Sir?'

'What the President is saying, Mrs Salaam,' Kercheval interjected angrily, 'is we think you promised Zuwayy something, and for some reason you can't or won't fulfill that promise, so he's threatening to attack Salimah. Why don't you just fill in the blanks for us, ma'am?'

Susan Bailey Salaam hesitated, lowered her head, then nodded. 'You're right, Mr Kercheval. I promised Zuwayy that I would grant him twenty percent of the ownership of the partnership that's developing Salimah.'

347

'Very generous of you,' Thorn said.

'However, Zuwayy was supposed to purchase ten percent of the outstanding shares from the Central African Petroleum Partners for nine hundred million dollars. Naturally, he reneged,' Salaam went on. 'He wanted the payments taken out of his royalties. I refused, and he got angry.'

'Will you agree to do so now?'

'I don't know. It depends on what you say, Mr President.'

'Why should it matter what I say?' Thorn asked. 'The United States is not part of this.'

'Because Egypt is powerless to stop Zuwayy,' Salaam said. 'I believe he will use neutron weapons against Egypt, certainly against Salimah and most likely against a major Egyptian city or another military base, as he did against Mersa Matrûh.'

'Do you have evidence that Libya was behind that attack, and that he used neutron weapons?' Goff asked. 'I know he's the main suspect, and he would have the most to gain by slaughtering all those people at Mersa Matrûh, but as far as I know, there's no direct evidence that Libya did it.'

'I know he did it. He's crazy.'

'Certifiable, I'd say,' Goff said. 'But that still doesn't mean he did it.'

'If I got you your evidence, Mr Secretary, then would you help me?' Salaam asked. 'Would you send your stealth bombers and armored commandos in against him and shatter his military, destroy his weapons of mass destruction, and kill Zuwayy if possible so he won't threaten to do this again? What's your price to assure peace in Africa? Whatever it is, I'll pay it.'

'President Salaam, first of all: If you were briefed anything about this administration by General Baris or your intelligence staff, you'd know that the President will not order US forces to get involved in squabbles between sovereign nations,' Edward Kercheval said. 'The United States's position has been that we will not interfere militarily with such matters unless it directly threatens the national security or vital national interests of the United States. That has been our policy since the beginning of this administration, and it has not changed. We will be happy to act as a disinterested third party in negotiations, but we will not commit American troops to help.'

'Second, we have no idea what bombers or armored commandos you're talking about,' Robert Goff added. 'The United States has bombers, of course, but they have not been deployed or sent on any missions anywhere. And we have no armored commandos. None.'

'What about Patrick McLanahan?'

There was a slight uncomfortable rustle of hands and shoulders; but, as if he were reading the words from a cue card, Robert Goff responded, 'We have heard of Mr McLanahan, and we know he has been linked with various organizations, none of which have any connection whatsoever with the US government. Mr McLanahan is under indictment in the United States for a variety of charges, the specifications of which are sealed by the Justice and Defense Departments. He is currently free on bond and awaiting a court hearing.'

'You're lying,' Susan said. 'He helped me. He has saved Egypt from Zuwayy's attacks.'

'If that's what he told you, I wouldn't believe it,' Goff said.

'You're all lying,' Susan repeated. 'He's a hero. He's been here. He saved Egypt from a terrible assault from Libyan military forces.'

'We may ask you to testify to that, Mrs President,' Kercheval said, 'at McLanahan's trial.'

'This is some kind of trick,' Salaam said, the anguish apparent in her voice. 'He saved us. He has powers . . . weapons . . .'

'Any of which are either fabrications or stolen, ma'am,' Goff said. 'I'm sorry if he's bamboozled you. You may of course file charges against him in federal court, and the US Attorney General will see to the matter personally. But I wouldn't place my trust, or the safety of my nation, in his hands.'

'Why are you doing this to him?' Susan asked, almost pleading. 'He's a wonderful man. He cares about his wife and his men. He loves the United States and he fights for justice. Why won't you support him?'

'We neither support nor try to hinder him, Mrs Salaam,' Kercheval said. 'He hasn't violated any laws in the United States that we know of. He is under investigation, but I can't discuss that. He's a private citizen. If we have any knowledge or evidence of wrongdoing, we'll prosecute him to the fullest extent of the law. Otherwise, he's free to do whatever he wishes as a free man.

But he is not part of the US government, and his actions are not under the direction of or sanctioned by the United States government in any way.'

'Mr President, gentlemen, I'm asking for your help in defending Egypt against probable attack from Libya,' Susan said. 'I know you have two aircraft carrier battle groups sailing in the Mediterranean Sea right now; I would like to offer you unlimited use of Egyptian ports and air bases for your crews.'

'Frankly, Madame President, after the warning you just gave us, I don't think it would be prudent to send any of our warships near an Egyptian port right now,' Robert Goff said.

'My warning is real enough so you won't send your ships anywhere near Egypt, but not real enough to assist us?'

'Mrs Salaam, I will discuss your situation with my advisers,' President Thorn said. 'But at this point, I don't think we'll be in a position to help. If the Libyan president's threat is that great, perhaps you might be better served by letting him have what he wants.'

'You're suggesting I *give in* to him?'

'I don't see that you have much choice, Madame President,' Thorn said earnestly. 'If the attack is as credible as you say, and if Idris is as unstable as Secretary Goff seems to think he is, then the presence of American warships in Egypt won't deter him – in fact, it might attract a heavier attack with an even larger loss of life. You can appeal to the United Nations or go in front of the world press, perhaps initiate an investigation on where Idris got those weapons and hope that exposing him and publicizing his threat will keep him from attacking – if you predict he'll use neutrons weapons on Egypt, he might be less likely to do so.'

'Perhaps an appeal before the Muslim Brotherhood might be the strongest deterrent,' Kercheval suggested. 'You seem to have been very successful in bringing the diverse factions of the Muslim Brotherhood together in Tripoli – they were even looking to you for leadership in a United Arab Republic. You may be able to head him off.'

'But I cannot count on help from the United States?'

'Not military help, Mrs Salaam.'

'No matter how many Americans are killed if Zuwayy attacks?'

'We're concerned about any loss of life, American or not,' Thorn said. 'We have condemned any use of nuclear weapons anywhere in the world, and if there was a threat against the United States, we would take swift and deadly action.'

'Pretty brave words, Mr President – how about putting them into action?'

Thorn paused, letting the caustic remark wash over and past him; then: 'But . . . the United States will not interfere militarily in the affairs of sovereign nations, Mrs Salaam. We are not a police force – you can't dial 911 and get an American aircraft carrier battle group to protect you because a deal you made goes south.

'We will discuss and analyze the situation there, Mrs Salaam, and we'll decide on a course of action,' Thorn said. 'But I suggest you give the man what he wants until you have the backing of your fellow Arab nations and can rally enough support to counter-act his threats.'

'I don't believe you would actually turn your back on Egypt, Mr President,' Susan said. 'You would actually stand back and watch as Libya destroys Africa's largest oil field and kills tens of thousands of innocent workers, when all it would take is to sail a few ships through the Gulf of Sidra and show him that you disapprove of his threat? What kind of superpower leader are you?'

'A superpower that shouldn't need to throw its military weight around to promote peace, Madame Salaam,' Thorn said. 'Peace comes in many different packages and for many different prices, Madame. You appear to be too proud to give in to Idris's threats, but not proud enough to ask the United States to invade Libya and kill its leader. This is a situation I'd rather not have the United States involved in. Once we learn more about the situation and have had time to confer, we'll contact you if we feel we can be of help.

'But again, I suggest you think about saving lives and give Idris or Zuwayy or whatever his real name is whatever he wants. From what you said, he's still willing to pay for the shares of the part-nership – you just need to take the money out of his earnings over a period of time. Why not agree to that for now? You all continue to pump oil and make money: Most importantly, everyone lives.'

351

'Thank you for your suggestion, Mr President,' Salaam said sarcastically. 'It must be a great comfort to you, giving sage advice from six thousand miles away, from the safety of your continent and your bombers and missile shield.'

'I wish you luck, Madame President,' Thorn said. But the call had already been terminated by then.

Kercheval shook his head. 'Ouch,' he said. 'That had to hurt.' But Thomas Thorn looked fairly unperturbed – he went back to his computer and started to make notes about the conversation. 'You're *really* not going to do anything, Mr President?' he asked incredulously. 'You're not going to reposition the fleet?'

'I'm going to do what I said I'd do, Edward – I'm going to ask for an independent assessment of the situation, get some satellites repositioned over there to keep an eye on things, and when we have our own take on what's really going on, I'll make a decision,' Thorn said as he typed. 'But no, I'm not going to send any ships anywhere near there. Robert's right – it's too dangerous. They're likely to be caught in the crossfire.'

'That "crossfire" could be a *nuclear war,*' Kercheval said. 'If Salaam is correct, tens of thousands of lives could be lost.'

'I'm aware of that, Edward,' Thorn said. 'But my problem is not to go rushing in and risk American lives in a fight we didn't start and one in which we don't know what's going on. I'll direct CIA to brief me on the current political situation in Egypt and Libya; I'll get Justice to brief me on the situation with that oil partnership; and I'll get Robert to brief me on the military situation and the threat to our forces in the Med. Until then, I'll direct all US forces to stay away from the area, and I'm directing you to issue a warning to all American citizens not to travel to Egypt – in case there are any Americans still in Egypt, after what happened in Mersa Matrûh.'

Edward Kercheval shook his head in undisguised disbelief. 'I'll get right on it, Mr President,' he said, and he departed. There was no secret of their almost continual policy disagreements – their debates, sometimes emerging as outright contradictions, were legendary. But their disagreements served two purposes: One, it proved that Thomas Thorn didn't hire yes-men to serve him in his Cabinet; and second, it showed that Thorn was firmly in charge. Edward Kercheval was considered one of the world's most respected political and foreign affairs experts – and for him to continue to serve under Thomas Thorn, a relative foreign affairs rookie, was a sideways tribute to both Kercheval's and the President's personal integrity. No one understood how it worked, but it did.

After he departed, Goff looked at his longtime friend and waited for him to say something; when he didn't, and the aggravation factor built up to the point he couldn't contain it any longer, he asked, 'So, what are you really going to do, Thomas?'

'I already said what I want done.'

'You're *really* going to do nothing? What if Libya really does attack Egypt? Could we stand the political heat and world condemnation if we received a credible warning directly from the Egyptian president but did nothing?'

'I'm not doing "nothing." I'm going to independently assess the situation . . .'

'I heard what you said. But you're not going to call Zuwayy? You don't want to position a few more bombers over in the region, say, in England or Diego Garcia?'

'No.'

Goff nodded knowingly and smiled. 'I get it. You want me to find out where McLanahan and his forces are – maybe give them a heads-up?'

'I *especially* don't want you to do that,' Thorn said firmly. 'In fact, I'm going to direct the Justice Department to shut Sky Masters down. I want all their planes grounded. And if McLanahan and the Night Stalkers are in the country, which I believe they are right now, I want them detained.'

'You're serious?' Goff asked incredulously. 'You really don't want to get involved in this thing at all, no matter how covertly we try or no matter how much it might cost you politically?'

'That's right,' Thorn said. 'You know, Bob, I'm really impressed with McLanahan and his bunch. They got their teeth knocked in pretty good from what we can tell, and they still fought like badgers. Their aircraft acquitted themselves pretty well, if all the reports about attacked Libyan bases and destroyed airfields are all attributed to them.

'But that's precisely the reason we need to put a muzzle on them: They're *too* good. They did so well that Zuwayy of Libya

353

might attack Egypt with nuclear weapons. That's why we need to shut him down. Unless I can somehow bring him and his people under control again, he's got to be shut down.'

'That's easy,' Goff said with a wry smile. 'Ask him to join your Cabinet. Make him your national security adviser. Make him defect from Martindale's team and join yours.'

'*You're* my national security adviser, Robert – I don't need another one.'

'I'm not your national security adviser, Thomas – I'm your national security *nudjen,*' Goff said. 'I haven't told you a thing in twenty years. You need a guy like McLanahan to tell you when you're wrong.'

'I want McLanahan in jail, Robert, not in the White House,' Thomas Thorn said stonily. 'He's a loose cannon. I want him shut down and shut off.'

'O-kay,' Goff said. 'So . . . that means you're not going to ring him up on your little subcutaneous walkie-talkie, then?' Thorn scowled at him, then turned back to his computer. Goff smiled and got up to leave.

'I'll be very interested,' the President said as Goff was leaving, 'to find out whom Susan Salaam calls next.'

Goff paused, then nodded. 'Yeah . . . me too,' he said. 'Me too.'

Akranes, Iceland
a few hours later

'Well, well,' Pavel Kazakov said. His initial anger at being awakened in the middle of the night vanished in an instant. 'Madame Susan Bailey Salaam, the esteemed president of Egypt, calling me personally? I'm flattered.'

'Let's cut to the chase, Kazakov,' Susan said angrily. 'We all know you are the puppet master behind Jadallah Zuwayy. He got the neutron weapons from you; you've been arming him with hundreds of millions of dollars' worth of weapons over the past several months; you talked him into blowing up Mersa Matrûh. . .'

'I don't know what you're talking about, Madame,' Kazakov said. 'I'm a prisoner, a witness for the United Nations, not an arms dealer.'

354

'I said, let's cut to the chase,' Susan said. 'Zuwayy wants his filthy claws in Salimah – but so do you. You want back into the world oil game, and Salimah is your latest target. Fine. Help me stop Zuwayy, and you can have Salimah.'

Pavel Kazakov was fully awake now. He buzzed for Ivana Vasilyeva, his aide. 'I'm listening, Mrs Salaam.'

'Shut down Zuwayy – I don't care how,' Susan said. 'Order him, bribe him, kill him – it doesn't matter to me, just stop him from blowing up my oil fields and killing the workers. You take Zuwayy's shares.'

'What will that give me? Thirty percent of a graveyard in the Sahara?'

'Not thirty – *sixty* percent of Salimah,' Susan said. 'Because if you do this, I'll buy out the Central African Petroleum Partners cartel and turn over their share of the partnership to you. I remind you, Mr Kazakov, that Salimah represents the largest known oil reserves in all of Africa. Zuwayy only wants to rape it or destroy it, not develop it. You're smarter than he is. Shut him down, and you can have a majority stake in the biggest known oil reserves in the world west of the Caspian.'

Pavel Kazakov was virtually shaking with anticipation. This was exactly what he was hoping for when he first struck this deal with Jadallah Zuwayy: a way to take control of Salimah without *appearing* to take control of anything. John D. Rockefeller once said that the key to wealth was 'own nothing, control everything' – that's exactly what Kazakov wanted.

'I'll try to stop Zuwayy, my dear Susan Bailey Salaam,' Kazakov said. 'But even if that ridiculous pig gets off a few shots, you will agree to this deal with me. You will ensure that a majority of shares in the partnership is transferred to me, and I'll see to it that Zuwayy moves to that ranch in Vietnam he's always wanted.'

'You keep Zuwayy from attacking Salimah, or the deal's off.'

'Madame, I'm not in Libya – I'm not Zuwayy's wet nurse,' Kazakov said. 'You're the one with the American white knights coming to your rescue – why not call on them to save you again?'

'If bombs fall on Salimah, Kazakov, the deal's off.'

'If you try to cancel this deal, Salaam, I'll send a transcript of this conversation to every media outlet in the world – see how long your popularity in the Arab world lasts then,' Kazakov said.

'On the other hand, you give me what I want, and I'll make Zuwayy and his goons heel. Count on it.'

There was silence on the line for several long moments; then: 'I guess I have no choice. But I want Zuwayy out of the picture. No more threats from him.'

'I'll make you a side deal, Mrs Salaam – you give me the white knights, and I'll serve you up Jadallah Zuwayy.'

'What?'

'You give me the Americans, the ones in the electronic battle armor, the ones with the fancy electromagnetic guns and the jump boots, and you can take control of the entire Muslim Brotherhood. Zuwayy will be a traitor to all loyal Arabs, and you slide right in as the leader of the Muslim world.'

'I can't do that if Salimah gets wiped out.'

'I can't help that,' Kazakov said. 'But if he does attack Salimah, he'll be slamming the lid shut on his own coffin. You, on the other hand, will have every bit of the power you want. You just have to give me the Tin Man.'

'How am I supposed to do that?'

'You're a very beautiful, beguiling woman – you figure it out,' Kazakov said. 'I wouldn't be surprised if they're on their way to save you right this minute. If they come back to rescue you, all you have to do is tell me.'

There was more silence on the phone – but it was shorter this time: 'All right,' Susan said. 'Do everything you can to stop Zuwayy, and I'll do everything I can to bring you McLanahan.'

'*McLanahan*, you say?' Kazakov asked incredulously. 'That's his name? McLanahan?'

'General Patrick McLanahan.'

Kazakov searched his memory. He had heard of that name before . . . where was it?

My God . . . he remembered where he had heard that name. The prisoners . . . the prisoners that he had ordered Zuwayy to segregate from the others before they were taken to their deaths in Mersa Matrûh. *One of the American prisoners still being held by Jadallah Zuwayy in Libya was a woman by the name of McLanahan.* That was too much of a coincidence. It had to be the same . . . a relative? Certainly not a sister or wife? This seemed too good to be true!

'Why is that name important to you, Kazakov?' Susan asked. 'Why do you sound so . . . ?' And then she stopped – she knew exactly why. 'You have her,' Salaam said breathlessly. 'No, not you . . . Zuwayy. Zuwayy has the woman named McLanahan.'

'Who is she?'

'She is your death sentence if Patrick McLanahan finds out she's alive,' Salaam said. 'She's the reason he's fighting this battle – just to get her back. You're a captive in a fancy Icelandic jail – you're easy to get to. I guarantee, Patrick will move heaven and earth to get to her – and he'll destroy an entire nation if she's harmed.'

'Call this General McLanahan off,' Kazakov said, his voice fairly shaking with anger. 'I don't care how you do it, but call him off. Threaten him, entice him, screw him – I don't care.'

'So he's worth something to you, then?'

'Don't try to dicker with me, woman. I can get McLanahan on my own time.'

'You don't sound so sure to me – if you could get him, I think you would have done it by now,' Susan said. 'Perhaps I should tell him that you ordered her execution, and you'll find yourself ripped into pieces by him. I assume you've seen his powered exoskeleton and electronic shock weapons in action? Don't think your lawyers will stop him.'

The 'powered exoskeleton' was a new one for Pavel Kazakov – it made his already fearsome battle armor sound even more fearsome. 'All right, all *right*,' Kazakov shouted. He thought quickly. There was an opportunity here – but Salaam had to play along. What did she want? What was *her* overriding desire? Certainly not this general . . . 'Here's the deal, Madame,' Kazakov said. 'You convince McLanahan not to attack us anymore. You keep the sixty percent majority ownership of Salimah, the Central African Petroleum Partners keep their thirty percent, and I'll take the remaining ten percent for myself.'

'You cannot give me something that I already own, Kazakov,' Salaam said. 'Zuwayy extorted Egypt for twenty percent of Salimah, yet he has done nothing but threaten his neighbors and waste your money – and now he's put your very life in danger. He is a psychopathic killer with delusions of grandeur. He thinks he's a Libyan king, yet his henchmen are stealing money from their treasury as if it's free for the taking. Why do you support him?'

'Because he controls an organization that potentially controls forty-five percent of the world's oil reserves,' Kazakov replied. 'What is it you control? What do you –?'

And then he stopped. He remembered the recent items in the news, the rallies, the editorials on this beautiful, opportunistic, charismatic woman – they were calling her the 'next Cleopatra.' Could this work . . . ?

'Are you still there, Kazakov? We'd better come to an agreement soon.'

'Of course,' Kazakov went on. 'I know just what might change your mind.'

'Oh, really? It had better be good – for your sake.'

'Everyone calls you the reincarnation of Cleopatra, an empress of the new United Arab Republic . . .' He paused, and he noticed that she did not rebuff him – interesting reaction! 'Why don't we make you . . . an emperor?'

'What are you blathering about, Kazakov?'

'The next Muslim Brotherhood Unity Congress, to be held in Tripoli,' Kazakov said. 'You will attend – and you will be elected president of the Muslim Brotherhood.'

Again, Kazakov noticed, no rebuke, no derision – she was not only listening, but considering the thought as well! Finally – much too late – she asked, 'What are you talking about, Kazakov? How can you do this?'

'Madame, do you really think the Muslim Brotherhood would even exist without my support?' Kazakov asked. 'Zuwayy is president of the Brotherhood because I give him the money to bribe the other members into voting for him. With him, it is a meaningless title – he doesn't care at all about Muslims or brotherhood, only money. But you . . .'

'I am not Muslim, Kazakov.'

'But you were on the verge of becoming Muslim, Madame – the world knows this,' Kazakov said. 'I know you have worshiped with your husband; I know you have taken the baths, read and studied the Koran, fasted during Ramadan, and given the *zakah*, the poor-due – I believe you even registered yourself as a Muslim so you could accompany your husband on the *Hadj*, the pilgrimage to Mecca and Medina. All you need to do, from what I know about converting to Islam, is publicly give the *Shahada*, the testament of faith. Besides, this whole Muslim Brotherhood thing is one of Zuwayy's concoctions to make himself look good and increase his perceived power. You have a thousand times more charm, charisma, and leadership qualities than he does. You would captivate the world, Susan.'

'This . . . this would never work, Kazakov. You know nothing about it.'

'I know I can turn the Muslim Brotherhood away from Zuwayy – I can expose him as an impostor, a pretender,' Kazakov said. 'With a little cash and the right information dropped here and there, I can destroy him without hardly lifting a finger. This paves the way for you to take over the Muslim Brotherhood. But with you controlling Salimah, you would be more than just a figurehead – you would be a true leader, a true savior. An empress.'

Another long pause – she was actually considering it. Man, Kazakov thought, the one thing more powerful than money just *had* to be vanity.

'And all I have to do . . . ?'

'Tell McLanahan to stay out of Africa,' Kazakov said. 'Tell your boyfriend and his bombers not to interfere with our operations again. You give me a taste of Salimah – just ten percent. Then you and I will talk about your future . . . as the leader of the United Arab Republic.'

There was another pause, but much shorter this time. 'Not one bomb falls on Egypt, Kazakov,' Susan Bailey Salaam said, 'or the deal's off. Destroy Zuwayy. Destroy him.'

'Yes . . . Empress,' Kazakov said. He hung up, stood up, and had to bite a knuckle to keep his excitement in check. Ivana Vasilyeva looked at him strangely as she entered the room. 'For a moment there, Madame Salaam,' he said half aloud, 'I thought you cared for this McLanahan. I guess everything – and everyone – has a price and a value.'

'What is it, Comrade?' Vasilyeva asked.

'You've got your orders now – you're going to Libya,' he told her. 'Get close to Zuwayy, report on his every move, find out where he's keeping any American prisoners, and get ready to kill that pig.'

'Yes, sir,' Vasilyeva said. 'He won't be difficult to manipulate.'

'I have no doubt. Take control of the situation in that palace. But most importantly: Save those prisoners. I believe they're in Tripoli – they may even be right in the palace.'

'I'll find them, Comrade.'

'And if you find a woman named McLanahan being kept prisoner by Zuwayy, capture her and get her out of there. She could be the key to getting our hands on the bastards that put me in this dreary place. If you find her, I want her taken alive and brought back to me.'

'What is she to you, sir?'

'If I can use those captives to lure the Tin Man into a trap, then Salaam can go to hell,' Kazakov said acidly. 'I'll get around to eventually burying that little bitch too.' He looked at Vasilyeva. 'But my real target is the husband, General Patrick McLanahan. If you encounter him, you are to kill him without fail. Do you hear me? *Without fail.*'

'Why don't I just kill them all, Comrade?' Vasilyeva asked with an evil smile, 'and we will let God sort them out?'

King Jadallah as-Sanusi Stadium,
Tripoli, United Kingdom of Libya
several days later

No one in the entire Arab world had seen anything like it in more than forty years – and, some surmised, nothing like this had been seen in northern Africa in more than *two thousand* years.

King Jadallah as-Sanusi Stadium was packed: more than two thousand spectators in the stands, another fifty thousand on the field, plus another five thousand dignitaries from all over the world in a specially set-up seating section, celebrating the opening of the First Muslim Brotherhood World Unity Conference. News agencies from around the world were carrying the celebrations and speeches live. It had the atmosphere of the opening day of the Olympics. Security was tight, almost oppressively so, but it did not deter from the festival atmosphere of this unprecedented gathering.

One by one, the presidents or representatives of the member

360

nations of the Muslim Brotherhood – Sudan, Palestine, Algeria, Syria, Jordan, Yemen, Somalia, Albania, Iraq, and Afghanistan – filed into the top VIP section of the stadium, to the delighted cheers of the crowd. Once these ministers were welcomed and seated, the provisional member nations of the Muslim Brotherhood, representing most of the rest of the Muslim world, entered. It was an incredible sight to see longtime enemies and adversaries greeting and embracing each other, and each time it happened it delighted the crowd even more.

The last representatives to enter were the most important: the host nation and the leader of the Muslim Brotherhood, King Jadallah as-Sanusi of the United Kingdom of Libya; and two of its most important provisional members – Crown Prince Abdallah bin Abd al-Aziz al-Sa'ad, the deputy foreign minister, commander of the Saudi National Guard, and heir to the throne of Saudi Arabia; and President Susan Bailey Salaam, the newly elected president of Egypt. The presence of the Crown Prince was significant in two ways: It signaled a more favorable change in attitude of the Saudi royal family toward the Muslim Brotherhood and, secondarily, to Jadallah Zuwayy; yet, because King Fa'ad himself did not attend, it was apparent that the Saudi royal family wasn't ready to commit to joining the Brotherhood quite yet.

The stir caused by the appearance of the Saudi Crown Prince was muted in comparison to the appearance of the president – some said the 'queen' – of Egypt. Susan Bailey Salaam was greeted with thunderous applause, singing, cheering, and chanting – and when she lifted her arms, palms upward, to acknowledge the crowd, their roaring redoubled. The eventual appearance of the host and leader of the Muslim Brotherhood, Jadallah Zuwayy, was hardly noticed – Zuwayy tried to delay his appearance on the dais for as long as he could to allow time for the cheering for Bailey to subside, but he finally had to step up anyway because it was obvious he would be waiting an awful long time.

There was a brief prayer service, followed by performances by dancers and singers from each of the member nations, and then each representative was allowed to give some brief remarks. Some of the representatives were better speakers than others; some others ran longer than their allotted five minutes. The crowd became restless. Everyone knew why: They were waiting for *her* to speak. Jadallah Zuwayy had no choice but to speak last: As the host, he was obligated to let all of his guests precede him. There was nothing he could do.

Zuwayy knew it was going to be a long and wasted day the moment Salaam stepped up to the microphone and the crowd saw it was her – they cheered for five minutes straight even before she uttered a single word.

The erstwhile king of Libya waited patiently for the cheering for Salaam to die down; when it was obvious it was not going to do so right away, Zuwayy signaled his Director of Arab Unity, Juma Mahmud Hijazi, to call for order – and it made it doubly embarrassing for Zuwayy when the crowd virtually ignored Hijazi's request. A sound technician finally had to inject some feedback into the sound system, and the loud squeal reverberating through the stadium finally helped to silence the crowd. Zuwayy read his welcoming remarks quickly, without any passion, and got off the dais as quickly as he could.

The members of the audience and those watching around the world who expected Susan Bailey Salaam to give one of her impassioned, fervent speeches on peace, freedom, prosperity, and unity among the Muslim nations might have been disappointed. Susan's speech lasted only a few short seconds – but she could not have uttered any more important or rousing words than the ones she chose that afternoon.

Susan stepped up to the microphone, waited a few moments for the cheers and shouting to subside, then touched her forehead with the fingertips of both hands, took a deep breath, and sang, '*Ash-Hadu anla elaha illa-allah wa ash-hadu anna Muhammadan rasul-Allah!* I bear witness that there is none truly to be worshiped but Allah, and I bear witness that Muhammad is the messenger of Allah.'

The crowd burst into insane cheering and applause. Susan raised her hands and repeated the words of the *Shahada*, the testimony of faith, but her words, even amplified, were easily drowned out by the cheering crowd.

Zuwayy was thunderstruck. She had done it: She had stolen this conference, this demonstration of his power, cleanly away from him. He might as well have closed the ceremonies and given her the mantle of presidency.

It was not until after the closing ceremonies that Zuwayy could finally see her alone in his palace office. He meant to have her wait for him in his office to at least try to reassert some control in their discussions, but since the media had followed Salaam to this meeting, Zuwayy had to make a show of welcoming her to his palace and showing her some of its antiques, treasures, and artifacts of Libyan history.

He quickly dropped all pretext of friendship with her once they were alone in his office. 'So, Mrs Salaam, you've had quite a week here. You have the entire world eating out of your hand.' Minister of Arab Unity Hijazi and Chief of the General Staff Tahir Fazani were also on hand with Zuwayy; General Ahmad Baris, Salaam's defense minister, and Captain Amina Shafik, Susan's new chief of staff, accompanied her.

'I think it was a most successful conference, Your Highness,' Salaam said, 'thanks to you and your staff.'

'No, no, no – I think the credit all goes to you, Madame President,' Zuwayy retorted irritably. 'Everywhere I went I heard cries of "Republic! Republic!" and "Queen Susan!" You must be very pleased with your newfound popularity, Madame.'

'I am proud and happy that our people are starting to think and speak as one, Your Highness,' Salaam said, wearing her most diplomatic smile and tone of voice.

'I'm happy that you're happy, "Queen" Salaam,' Zuwayy said.

Susan's smile never dimmed – but Ahmad Baris's eyes narrowed in concern. 'Have we done something to offend you, Highness?' he asked.

'Of course not,' Zuwayy replied curtly. He looked as if he was going to sit at his desk, but swung the chair out of his way and continued to pace around his desk. 'But it seems I'm being forced to remind a lot of folks here this week that the Muslim Brotherhood doesn't seek a republic. Our purpose is not to form one nation or even a federation of nations. Our purpose, Madame, is to assist Arab governments in forming and maintaining a *Shura*, a government based on Islamic law. We don't want to go through the trouble of erasing centuries of history for our member nations – we only want to encourage and assist governments in embracing Muslim holy law in its activities. Do you under*stand*, Madame?'

'Yes, Highness,' Susan replied. 'I understand perfectly.' She did not take her eyes off him, and the smile remained as well, which only served to make Zuwayy angrier. 'Is there something specific you wished of me, Highness?'

'Wish? What do I *wish?* I'll tell you what I wish, Queen Salaam!'

'What His Highness is trying to say, Madame President,' Juma Hijazi interjected, glancing at Zuwayy, hoping that he could keep his anger in check for just a few more minutes, 'is that His Highness is still waiting for a conclusion to the contract between yourself and the Central African Petroleum Partners for the kingdom's share of the partnership. As you remember, Madame, you said that in exchange for His Highness's support during your elections, the kingdom would receive a one-third share of the partnership –'

'It wasn't one-third, Minister, it was thirty percent,' General Baris interjected.

'One-third, thirty percent – it's all the same damn thing,' Zuwayy retorted.

'You're right, General – it was thirty percent,' Hijazi said. 'But the fact is, the agreement has not been concluded. Egypt has graciously and effectively opened its borders to many Arab nations and instituted the work visa program in record time, which has helped tens of thousands of workers from all over the Arab world. It is a shining example of the spirit of cooperation that we hope to continue.'

'Thank you, Minister.'

'But what about the rest of it?' Zuwayy interjected hotly. 'Part of the deal was a third of the partnership, a third of the revenues. We haven't seen a dinar yet. If you try to back out of the deal now, Salaam, you'll find yourself at the bottom –'

'Do you have some explanation for the delay, Madame Salaam?' General Fazani interjected before Zuwayy could threaten Salaam's life right in front of witnesses.

'I'm sure there's a reasonable explanation, Majesty,' Baris offered.

'Yeah? What is it, Baris?'

'Perhaps it is that you haven't paid for it yet, Majesty,' Susan said. Her smile never wavered, but her eyes suddenly lit up in slow-burning anger.

'*Paid* for it?'

'Majesty, the CAPP cartel invested a total of three point six billion US dollars towards the project,' Baris said. 'Egypt has promised in writing to grant the kingdom of Libya one-third of its shares in the partnership, but only if Libya agreed to purchase one-fourth of the shares owned by the cartel. That requires an investment by the kingdom of Libya of nine hundred million US dollars.'

'*What?* You expect me to pay a bunch of fat-cat Western oil companies almost *a billion dollars* for oil that belongs to *me?*'

Hijazi couldn't stop Zuwayy from stating his claim to the Salimah oil fields, but both Salaam and Baris pretended not to notice what he said. 'I think what His Highness is saying, Madame,' Hijazi interjected, 'is that perhaps we can come to some sort of accommodation.'

'What's that?'

'Allow us to pay our fee to the cartel out of our share of the oil revenues,' Hijazi said. 'It can be paid over, say, five years – they can take it right off the top of our share. We will even agree to pay a reasonable interest rate – it can be a loan of sorts, secured with the oil revenues from Salimah.'

Susan paused for a moment, then nodded. 'I don't think the Central African Petroleum Partners cartel would object, Minister,' Susan said.

Hijazi and Fazani breathed long sighs of relief, smiled, and nodded at each other. 'That's good news, Madame President. I think that we –'

'But *I* object,' Susan added.

The Libyan ministers' mouths dropped open. Zuwayy was stunned – he couldn't believe what he had just heard. To the Libyan ministers' surprise, they noticed that even Ahmad Baris had a shocked look on his face. 'Madame President, you . . . you are saying you will not accept a payment option based on our revenues? I don't understand.'

'It is quite obvious, Minister,' Susan said, looking directly at Zuwayy, her smile gone. 'Libya made this deal by threatening Egypt with war if we did not agree to your demands. You have no right to any part of the Salimah project – it is not your land, nor did you invest in any part of the production infrastructure. Yet I accepted your demand, even though I felt my country was under duress, because I wanted peace and prosperity for all of Egypt's neighbors. I made only one request – that you reimburse the European cartel for their shares in payment for their substantial investment in the project. That was more than fair – it was the right thing to do.

'Now, as Libya has done before, you are reneging on your promise. Not only do you demand the shares that Egypt was going to give you for free, but you then demand that you take the next six years to reimburse the European cartel for their shares. This tells me one thing: that Libya cannot be trusted, that Libya – no, that *you three* – want nothing more than to rape and steal from your own country.'

'*What did you say?*' Zuwayy thundered, his eyes bulging in sheer fury. 'How dare you? How *dare* you accuse me of such a thing? I will have you executed!' Zuwayy lunged for his desk drawer. Fazani, knowing exactly what he was reaching for, used his body to keep the drawer closed. 'Get out of the way, Fazani! I'm going to kill this Anglo bitch for what she's just said!'

'No, Jadallah!'

'I said, get out of the way –'

'Madame Salaam,' Hijazi said quickly, 'I strongly urge you to immediately and sincerely retract that statement and beg His Majesty's forgiveness.'

'I will not,' Salaam said, rising to her feet. She kept her hooked-crook cane in her hands, as if keeping it at the ready – Hijazi knew what she could do with that cane – but stood calmly right in front of Zuwayy's desk while he still grappled with Fazani.

'You're *dead!*' Zuwayy shouted. 'You are *dead!* Yours will be the shortest presidency in Egyptian history. Your husband will look like Adonis compared to what your body will look like after I get done with it!'

'Good day, "King,"' Susan said, making an exaggerated bow. 'Don't worry about your people – they will be perfectly happy in Egypt. Where do you think you'll be headed next? I think Brazil is nice this time of year.'

'Get out!' Zuwayy cried out. 'And I'd make sure you know

where your bomb shelters are in Cairo – you'll need them!' Salaam and Baris departed, with Shafik backing toward the door right behind them, her right hand invisible under her jacket. 'I want her dead, Fazani!' Zuwayy shouted after they departed.

'You can't kill Salaam now, Jadallah – she's more popular than God right now,' Fazani said. 'If anyone finds out you put out a contract on her, we won't even be able to hide in Brazil. We'll have to live in Antarctica.'

'I don't want a piece of Salimah anymore – I want the whole damned thing destroyed!' Zuwayy shouted. 'That American bitch has insulted me for the last time!' His eyes spun wildly as he thought. 'Launch the attack immediately.'

'Jadallah, only a few hundred of the twenty thousand-plus Libyans working there now have returned,' Hijazi said. 'You can't attack now! We'd be slaughtering our own people!'

'No! Launch the attack immediately!' he shouted. 'Do it. Let Queen Salaam be the ruler of the largest graveyard in Africa.'

Jadallah Zuwayy stomped off to his private residence, kicking furniture and individuals out of his way with equal fury. 'How *dare* she?' he shouted as he slammed the door to his apartment closed. 'How dare that bitch spit in my face like that? Who does she think she is?'

'Who, my lord?' a woman's thickly accented voice asked behind him.

'An Egyptian whore that has the unmitigated *balls* to tell me what to do!'

The woman approached him, naked, holding a crystal glass of thick, potent *arkasus*, or licorice brandy, in one hand, and a silver tray with a linen napkin covering it. He tossed down the brandy in one gulp. She set the tray down on a nightstand beside a lounge sofa, then kissed the back of his neck and started to massage his shoulders. 'Why don't you just eliminate this Egyptian whore, my lord?' the woman asked.

'Because she was just elected president of the Muslim Brotherhood, and she is a guest in my country,' Zuwayy said. 'Do you know nothing of Arab culture, Russian?'

Ivana Vasilyeva felt for the knot of bone at the base of Zuwayy's long, scrawny neck, then counted the right number of vertebrae up – right *there*. Snap that bone and Zuwayy would become a helpless lump of flesh on the floor, unable to do anything – except feel pain. But she simply continued her massage. 'Forgive me, my lord,' Vasilyeva said. 'You must instruct me about your country and all its customs.'

Zuwayy turned, ran a hand roughly over a nipple, then pinched it, hard. Vasilyeva opened her mouth in a half-yelp of pain and half-moan of pleasure. 'The first lesson is: Women must learn to be subservient,' Zuwayy said. 'You are nothing but bleeding, whining creatures who respond better to the lash than to reason or reality. The quicker you understand this, the happier your life will be.'

'Yes, master,' Vasilyeva said.

Zuwayy kissed her lips roughly, released her nipple, then lay down on the lounger. He rolled up the sleeve of his right arm. 'You were recommended to me because you had a unique talent. Show me. And if you disappoint me, you shall pay dearly for it.'

'I understand, master.' Vasilyeva removed the linen napkin from the tray, revealing a hypodermic syringe and a rubber hose. She wrapped the hose around Zuwayy's biceps, kissed his right hand, then curled his fingers for him, silently telling him to make a fist. Zuwayy never felt the needle slip into his vein; never felt a thing as Vasilyeva injected the drug.

What an idiot, Vasilyeva thought. She had bribed a Tripoli drug pusher to spread her name around as a trained nurse and anesthesiologist; she had been admitted to the residence almost immediately. Zuwayy liked whores and he liked heroin – he was a slave to both. But apparently he disliked having his nurses and his whores around for too long, so he usually had them killed after about a week in the residence.

That was not going to happen to Vasilyeva.

The drug she had administered was not heroin but thiopental sodium, an ultra-fast-acting, short-duration sedative. Zuwayy was not unconscious, just very relaxed. Vasilyeva removed the rubber tube from his arm and swabbed the injection site. 'Do you feel all right, Highness?'

'You can leave me now.'

'Not quite yet, Highness. Where is the female American prisoner, the one called McLanahan, and the other American prisoners?'

'The American spies? In my interrogation facility.'

'Which ones? Where?'

'Who are you, woman? Why do you care about the Americans?'

'I'm here to take care of your problem with the Americans, if you just tell me where they are.'

'I don't care to tell you.'

Vasilyeva had to remember to be patient. Thiopental sodium, also known by its brand name Sodium Pentothal, was just a mild sedative, not the much-vaunted 'truth serum' fiction writers made it out to be..If the subject didn't want to talk, thiopental sodium couldn't make them do it. Eventually, however, she could get the information from him. She needed to learn a little more about his peccadilloes, fantasies, fears, and weaknesses. One or two more days and she would have him eating out of her hand.

She prepared a small dose of heroin and, as expertly as the first time, injected it into a vein, 'jacking it off' by drawing blood into the syringe in and out several times before injecting it all into his arm.

He looked at Vasilyeva with half-closed, dreamy eyes. 'Are you going to kill me now?' he asked.

'I have no such orders, unless you resisted,' she said.

'Good. I was hoping to get rid of those damned Americans anyway – I should've shipped them off to Mersa Matrûh and had them zapped with the neutron bombs along with the others.'

'How very interesting. So you deliberately killed those prisoners at Mersa Matrûh with a neutron weapon? It wasn't an Egyptian insurgency group or Hamas or Hizb'allah or any of the other right-wing Islamic terrorist groups? It was you?'

'Sure. I wasn't going to let the Egyptians get the glory for saving them. I wish I did the Americans too.'

'Of course. So, is it true that you are not really a Libyan king, but just an ordinary army soldier who is pretending to be a king?'

'Pretty good scam, wasn't it? I've got half the world believing I'm a fucking god. It's priceless. Some fools will believe anything you tell them as long as they think they'll get something good out of it.'

'How clever of you. What will you do now, Highness?'

'Attack Egypt, again,' Zuwayy said. 'That bitch Salaam won't back me with the oil cartel, so I'm going to have to destroy

369

Salimah. Actually, not destroy it – just the workers. I'll keep the oil fields for myself. I've got enough troops to take the whole southern part of Egypt.'

'Did you already give the order to attack?'

'Yes. And that cowardly bastard Fazani better follow my orders too.'

She picked up the phone beside the lounger. 'Call off the attack, Zuwayy. Killing all those workers won't get you any closer to the oil.' But he had already drifted off into his drug-induced world, oblivious to the real one.

Surt Air Base, northern Libya
the next evening

As soon as the three fighters lit their afterburners, the copilot started counting: *'Talaeta, itnen, waehid . . . daeyikh!'* The pilot released brakes and slowly moved the throttles up to full military power, let them stabilize a few seconds, then pushed the throttles into afterburner zone. He waited for the inevitable *kohha* – the 'cough' – as the old fuel valves struggled to keep raw fuel flowing into the afterburner cans. Half the time, especially if the pilot advanced the throttles too fast, a valve stuck or failed and the afterburner would blow out completely. But it didn't happen this time – the nozzles opened, the fuel-flow needles jumped, and the Libyan Tupolev-22 bomber leapt down the runway. Six seconds behind him, the second Tu-22 bomber began its takeoff roll.

A third bomber wasn't so lucky – both of its Dobrynin RD-7M-2 turbojet engines' afterburners blew out seconds after engagement. The pilot quickly yanked the throttles back to military power and tried once more to light the afterburners, inching the throttles up over the detent in slow, careful increments. But it was no use, and the third Tu-22 bomber aborted the takeoff, its screeching, smoking brakes barely managing to stop the two-hundred-thousand-pound bomber before it rolled off the end of the runway.

Libyan air force major Jama Talhi, the pilot and flight leader, said a silent prayer as he retracted the landing gear and flaps, watching the hydraulic needles jumping wildly in their cases. Hydraulic fluid was even more expensive than fuel or weapons, and because it was not changed as often as it should be, contamination was a problem. Amazingly, everything was working. Talhi, a ten-year veteran of the Al Quwwat al Jawwiya al Jamahiriyah al Arabiya al Libya, was the Libyan air force's most experienced Tu-22 bomber pilot, with a grand total of just over three hundred hours in this ex-Soviet medium supersonic bomber. In any other air force, three hundred hours would mean you were hardly out of flight school – in Libya, surviving that many hours usually meant a promotion. Tupolev-22 bombers were notorious maintenance hogs – they routinely cannibalized as many as ten planes to keep three in the air. This time, even that ratio wasn't enough. Talhi had experienced every possible malfunction and inflight emergency in a Tu-22, but had never crashed one. That made him top dog in the Libyan air force.

'*Sahra* flight, check.'

'Two,' his wingman replied. The third plane had already reported aborting its takeoff, and the timing on this mission was so critical that they could not wait for him. They would have to do the mission with one-third less firepower.

'Dufda flight, Sahra flight checking in.'

'Sahra flight, acknowledged,' the leader of the flight of three Libyan Mikoyan-23 fighters replied. They had launched from Surt Air Base in northern Libya just ahead of the bombers and were already at patrol altitude at twenty thousand feet. It took just a few minutes for the two formations to join up, and they proceeded east, flying in loose formation as the crews completed checklists and got ready for the attack. 'No contact yet, but we expect company any minute.'

Just ten minutes later, Major Talhi began a slow descent, keeping cruise power in all the way down until his airspeed approached six hundred knots. They received a few bleeps of their Sirena radar-warning receiver from the Egyptian air defense base at Siwah, but they were below radar coverage in moments, cruising at nearly the speed of sound across the northern Libyan Desert.

But they were not low enough for Egypt's main air defense system – a former American Navy E-2C Hawkeye radar plane,

371

orbiting over the desert just north of Al-Jilf Air Base in south-west Egypt. The powerful AN/APS-145 radar of the E-2 Hawkeye spotted the Libyan planes two hundred miles away, and the radar controllers immediately vectored in Egyptian alert fighters – a mixture of former Chinese, French, and even Russian jets from three different bases in central and southern Egypt.

'Sahra, Sahra, be advised, Egyptian fighters inbound, range fifty miles and closing,' the lead pilot of the MiG-23 fighter escorts reported.

'Sahra flight copies,' Talhi responded. 'Sahra flight, go to point nine.' The pilot pushed his throttles until the airspeed indicator hit six hundred and sixty knots – eleven miles a minute, or nine-tenths the speed of sound.

Talhi's copilot, Captain Muftah Birish, sat in the rear upper cockpit compartment of the Tupolev-22 bomber. The copilot's seat swiveled around the rear compartment so that he could fly the plane (not very well, but better than nothing) by facing forward, or operate the electronic warfare equipment and the remote-controlled 23-millimeter tail gun by sitting facing backward. Right now he was studying the SRO-2 threat warning display with alarm. 'At least two fighters, maybe more, closing in from the northeast,' Birish reported. Thankfully Talhi had his unit's most experienced copilot with him, although that wasn't saying much – systems officers, even copilots, got even less flying time in the bombers themselves than pilots. 'India-band search radar – Mirage 2000s.'

'Don't tell me – tell our fighters!' Talhi shouted. Birish got on the command radio and frantically passed along the information. He pushed the bomber's nose down even farther. The terrain was flat and rolling, so terrain wasn't a problem – but the waves and waves of heat swirling up from the desert floor created turbulence so bad that it felt as if they were riding a dune buggy across a mountain of rocks. The twenty-year-old ex-Soviet bomber's aged fuselage shrieked in protest with every bump.

'They're closing in fast,' Birish shouted. 'They're right on us – the E-2 Hawkeye radar plane must be vectoring them in.'

'Five minutes thirty seconds to go,' Talhi's bombardier, Captain Masad Montessi, shouted on intercom. 'Hold steady for fifteen seconds.'

'Fifteen seconds? Better make it quicker than that, navigator!'

'I said fifteen seconds, or at this speed we'll be lost and flying over downtown Cairo before we know it!' Montessi shouted back. He was in a tiny compartment of the Tupolev-22 bomber below the pilot, with only a ten-inch RBP-4 Rubin navigation radar, an optical bomb sight between his legs, some mechanical flight computers, a compass, a Doppler radar system, and two small windows. He had just finished laying his crosshairs on a small mountain peak ten miles ahead, then changed to the second aimpoint – another peak on the other side of courseline.

The crosshairs were off just a small amount. He double-checked his aiming on the first aimpoint, switched back to the second, verified the aimpoint, then moved the crosshairs on the second peak using a large tracking handle he called the 'goat turd.' As soon as he moved the crosshairs, he could hear the *clack-clack-clacking* of the mechanical navigation computer as it updated itself. He switched back to the first aimpoint, and the crosshairs rested right on it – all of the heading and velocity errors in the system had been corrected. 'You're clear to maneuver! Go! Go!'

'Sahra flight! Take tactical spacing! Lead is maneuvering south!' Talhi executed a quick turn to the south, rolled out momentarily, then executed a tighter turn around a very short valley. He wasn't going any lower, so left and right maneuvering was all he had to escape the Egyptian pursuers.

No use. 'Mirages still on us, estimate twenty miles – coming within lethal range,' Birish shouted. 'I've got fighters going after our wingman.'

'Sahra flight, you've got company, coming in fast!' Talhi reported on the command frequency. 'Do you have him?'

'Negative! Negative! Our threat receiver is down!' the pilot aboard the second Tu-22 responded. 'Our navigation radar is down too!'

'Then get the hell out of here,' Talhi said. 'If you're blind and deaf, you're no use to us out here! Return to base!'

'Negative, lead,' the other pilot reported. 'I've got dead reckoning and I think I can find enough landmarks to proceed. I'm inbound to the target.'

Talhi didn't blame him too much at all – he wouldn't want to face the wrath of President Zuwayy and his henchmen either if he returned to base without completing his mission. 'I under-stand, Sahra. Do you have a good DME on us?' Each of the Tu-22 bombers was equipped with radio direction finders that gave range and bearing to the other.

'Affirmative.'

'Then keep us in front of you – we're inbound to the target too,' Talhi said. He banked southeast and lined up on the navigation steering bug, then pushed the throttles all the way to full military power. 'We're target direct now, crew. Our wingman has got no other way to find the target, so he's going to follow us in to the target.'

'Mirage moving in to lethal range,' Birish said on intercom. 'All jammers active, countermeasures ready.' On the command frequency, he said, 'Sahra flight, we've got Mirages moving in to radar missile range. Use side-to-side jinks and make sure your jammers are active.'

'We're jinking, lead, we're jinking,' the second bomber pilot acknowledged. 'Just find the damned target. We'll be right behind you.'

But they were losing this race. The Egyptian fighters were moving in faster – they must be 'headed down the ramp,' zooming in from high altitude to use the extra speed to rapidly close in for the kill. 'Rapid PRF – fighter locked on!' Birish shouted. 'Vertical jinks! Find any terrain you can! Let's lose this guy!' The Egyptian fighter's radar changed from rapid-pulse-rate frequency to a constant tone. 'Uplink active! Missile launch! *Break left!*'

But just as Talhi began to yank the control wheel to the left, Birish reported, 'Uplink down! Radar down! The fighter disap-peared!'

'Did he shut down his radar?'

'Could be, but he wouldn't do that right after firing a missile.'

They heard the reason a few moments later: 'Sahra flight, Dufda flight, this is Fadda flight of six. Your tail is clear. Now shove a few down their throats!'

Talhi whooped for joy. Fadda flight was a flight of six MiG-25s, some of the fastest fighter planes in the world. Originally designed to chase down and destroy high-flying supersonic American bombers over the Soviet Union, the titanium-armored MiG-25 could attack targets at over three times the speed of sound. Based in Tobruk, the Libyan fighters covered a lot of ground very quickly and caught the Egyptian pilots from behind.

Talhi climbed his Tu-22 back up to fifteen thousand feet above ground level, and his bombardier programmed his weapons for their attack. Talhi's bomber was in what was called the 'overload' condition – it carried three Kh-22 air-to-surface missiles, called 'Burya' in Russia, one under the fuselage and one under each wing. The Kh-22, powered by its own liquid-fueled rocket engine, was the size of a small fighter jet and could fly at over six hundred miles per hour. It carried an inertial navigation system, a thousand pounds of fuel – and a three-thousand-pound high-explosive warhead.

One by one, Montessi dumped navigation and heading information into the Buryas' computers, aligned their inertial navigation gyros, and let them fly. Although he had done many simulated Kh-22 attacks, Talhi had never actually seen one of those behemoths fly before. The rocket engine firing up sounded like an explosion right under their belly, and when it blasted free, it seemed as if a fiery spear from Allah himself had just missed them.

The missiles started a rapid climb on tongues of fire and headed for their targets – Egypt's network of early-warning surveillance radars along its western frontier. The Burya missiles used passive radar homing devices to zero in on the early-warning radars, and once they had computed the radar's exact position, they could not miss. With devastating accuracy, the huge Kh-22 missiles struck their targets, obliterating the radar installations and flattening any aboveground buildings or objects for over a mile around the impact point.

Meanwhile, the Libyan MiG-23 and MiG-25 fighters went to work themselves – on the Egyptian E-2C Hawkeye radar aircraft. The Hawkeye was over one hundred miles away and had its own flight of Mirage fighter escorts, and when the radar plane detected the Libyan MiGs heading eastbound, it shut down its radar, headed northeast toward safety, and sent its fighter escorts after the intruders. But the Libyan attackers hopelessly outnumbered them. The MiG-25 fighters merely blew past the Mirages with their superior speed, and the MiG-23s pounced when the Egyptian defenders turned to pursue. The MiG-25s took care of the Hawkeye radar plane after losing only one fighter to enemy missiles.

With both the airborne and ground radar sites destroyed, the way was clear for the second Tupolev-22 bomber to climb to a safer altitude and pick its navigation waypoints with care. With Talhi's Tu-22 leading the way, the bombardier aboard the second Tu-22 lined up precisely on his preplanned bomb run course. The courseline had to be perfect: Although the weapons did not need to be directly on target to be effective, they would get maximum effect by being no more than one or two degrees off the desired course. One by one, he seeded the area with small two-hundred-and-fifty-pound bombs fitted with radar fuzes.

Far below was the massive Salimah oil complex, Egypt's newest oil project. Comprising over thirty thousand square miles of southern Egypt, it was the largest known oil and natural gas reserves in northern Africa. Seven wells had been drilled every day for the past two years, and none of them showed any signs of lessening their output. Five thousand workers, mostly Arabs and Africans from Sudan, Chad, Kenya and Ethiopia, worked around the clock in Salimah, housed in rows and rows of trailers and huge tent cities stretching as far as anyone could see.

One of Egypt's two field armies, known as the King Menes Army, was in charge of the defense of Salimah. Although it was seriously under its full strength, the King Menes Army comprised well over a third of all of Egypt's fighting forces, including two full armored divisions, three mechanized infantry divisions, one infantry division, five artillery battalions, two fighter-interceptor squadrons, two fighter-attack squadrons, and one helicopter squadron. The eighty thousand troops were distributed with the bulk of the forces, mostly heavy armor, arrayed along the borders of Libya and Chad, with the other lighter, more rapid-response forces deployed mostly north of the oil fields as a reserve. The two westernmost military Areas of Responsibility were Al-Jilf and Al-Kabir, and these were the two areas targeted by the weapons dropped by the Tu-22 bombers.

One might believe the bombardier missed his target, because the gravity weapons detonated a thousand feet in the air, producing nothing more than a loud *BANG!* and a puff of sand below. The explosion was repeated sixty-three times in the space of six minutes, ten weapons per minute, as the Libyan bomber sowed its deadly seeds. Curious soldiers below looked up when they heard the explosions, and they jumped and felt the sudden gush of air and a little bit of pressure in their ears – nothing more severe than a slammed door or a slug of mud popping out of a new well. But there was very little heat unless the explosion was directly overhead, no trace of vapor or liquid, and no shrapnel or caltrops. Before most folks realized it, the noisemakers were gone. They could have been fireworks, except these fireworks were in the morning, which didn't make sense at all.

It still didn't make sense later that day – even when the soldiers started dying in massive, horrendous numbers.

The ones directly under the airbursts were first, complaining of headaches that increased in intensity quickly, eventually causing loss of eyesight and loss of equilibrium. Hours later, they were coughing up blood. By the time they were able to get off work later that day, they were usually unable to take themselves to the infirmary. Many of them died in their beds or in their living rooms, surrounded by their puzzled comrades and worried corpsmen. The ones that were as far as one mile away from the bursts didn't start having symptoms until the next day, but their fate was the same – crushing headaches leading to blindness, loss of balance eventually leading to incapacitation, and sudden loss of blood leading to hemorrhage and death within eight hours.

The soldiers in bunkers and even chemical weapon-resistant shelters were not spared – even those in underground storage areas and shielded command centers could not escape. Eventually the deadly neutron and gamma radiation from the sixty-four neutron bombs detonated over Salimah, unrestricted by the uranium outer shell as in regular fission weapons, claimed over twelve thousand lives . . .

. . . without harming one piece of oil-drilling equipment, spilling one drop of crude oil, or ruining one piece of precious military hardware.

Chapter Nine

Naval Amphibious Base Coronado,
Coronado, California
days later

Patrick detested running, but it was the only aerobic exercise he cared for, and he knew he'd probably blow up like a 'bunker-buster' bomb if he didn't do it. When he was in town he usually jogged the short distance from his condo on Coronado Island, across the bay from San Diego, to the base gym at the Naval Amphibious Base Coronado. This time, however, he had Bradley with him, so he drove. It took longer to go down to the garage, strap Bradley in, and pull out onto busy Silver Strand Highway than it did to get to the base.

Going to the gym was one of the few things he liked to do alone, just for himself – but not anymore. It was another of the little changes he had to make in his life, with Wendy gone.

Security was tight on base – even the sticker on his windshield with the white star on blue background of a brigadier general didn't help speed things up. Along with an ID check, Patrick's car was checked underneath with a mirror, and the inside of the car from bumper to bumper was checked visually and also with a military working dog. Bradley liked the dog, and he enjoyed having his car seat sniffed by the dog after Patrick had to lift him up and out of his seat. After clearing security, he headed off to the gym. He checked Bradley into the base gym's day-care center – one of Bradley's favorite places to go, even for an hour or two – and changed into workout clothes in the locker room. Five minutes on the elliptical trainer, then five minutes on the stretching chair to warm up, and he was ready to go.

The news on the televisions surrounding the workout room was full of information on the Libyan attack on the Egyptian military forces defending Salimah. The death toll in just one day was simply staggering. Patrick had a tough time conceiving of the five thousand killed at Mersa Matrûh, and now the deaths at Al-Jilf and Al-Kabir were probably going to triple that toll.

The toll that most likely included Wendy. Oh, God . . . That thought made him tear into his workout with a vengeance.

The tail end of the news reports focused on the American response to the attacks on Egypt – or, more accurately, the *lack* of response. There were two aircraft carriers with almost a hundred combat aircraft plus ten thousand US Marines within helicopter distance of Egypt, yet the United States made no move to help. There were stern warnings to Libya not to use any more neutron weapons, that using them increased the danger of the conflict spreading and growing to a full-scale nuclear war in a short time – but the response was far short of what most folks expected of the President.

Well, Patrick thought, that was typical of this President – speak softly, but carry a big twig.

Soon, Patrick found he had disregarded his workout log completely and finally ended up just picking a weight from the racks, in some cases fifty percent more than he was able to throw around before, doing repetitions until he lost count, then continuing doing more reps until his muscles gave out completely. After twenty minutes of an absolutely blistering workout, finally something gave way in his left shoulder during an incline bench press, and he was forced to toss a seventy-pound dumbbell aside in pain.

'Are you all right, General McLanahan?' he heard behind him. He turned and saw Captain Fred Jackson, the commanding officer of Naval Amphibious Base Coronado, standing behind him, a look of serious concern on his face. Jackson was a tall, powerful-looking ex-SEAL who still looked as if he could command a team on a mission – he sometimes worked out with Patrick in the gym or at the SEAL Training Facility across the street, and even though Patrick had been working out for many years and Jackson was at least five years older, Patrick found it impossible to keep up with him.

Patrick nodded. 'I'm okay, Fred,' he said ruefully.

'My guys told me you were on the base, so I thought I'd stop by and say hello,' Jackson said. 'I'll get a corpsman to look at that shoulder for you.'

382

'Not necessary. I'll just get some ice on it.' But Jackson was not accustomed to anyone saying 'no' to him – he already had someone on the way. A few minutes later they were sitting down together, Patrick with a bag of ice on his shoulder.

'You upset about something, sir?' Jackson asked. 'You looked like you were about ready to toss those dumbbells through the mirrors.'

'No – just cranky because I'm getting more and more of these little pains,' Patrick said.

'The price of getting old . . . I mean old-*er*,' Jackson said.

Patrick nodded at the TV as well. 'I don't understand why we're not doing more over in Egypt, and that's upsetting me as much as my shoulder.'

'I expected you to be in Washington advising the President on what to do,' Jackson said.

'Why do you say that?'

'According to what I've been reading, you're still the number-one candidate for national security adviser,' the Navy SEAL said. 'I thought you'd be out there in the thick of things, writing your policy papers, getting your classified briefings, and getting ready to testify in front of the Senate Armed Services Committee after your nomination.'

'So that's why you're over here looking me up, eh, Fred?' Patrick asked with a smile. 'Thought you'd get a little face time with the rumored number-one guy?'

'Now, would I do that, sir?' he asked with a toothy grin. 'Oh, by the way, I'm letting your son play in my office. I got him his own SEAL to watch him, and I brought in a gourmet chef from the Del to fix him lunch. Is that okay?'

'Sorry to disappoint you, Fred, but I haven't been anywhere near Washington or the White House in many moons, and I'm not likely to be,' Patrick said. 'We don't see eye to eye on much of anything.'

'Which is why all the pundits are saying you're "it" – Thorn likes surrounding himself with ideological opposites,' Jackson said. 'You just remember your buddies who give you their tee times and let you fly your plane from their airstrips, the next time you talk to the President about the next chief of naval operations, okay?'

'Don't hold your breath, Captain,' Patrick said with a laugh – his first laugh in many, many days.

'How's the missus?' Jackson asked.

Patrick tried not to let his smile completely wash away. 'Still away. She should be back in town next weekend.'

'Good. Can't wait to see her again. You still owe my wife and me a rematch of our last golf match.'

'You're on, Fred.'

Jackson could tell something was wrong, but he decided not to pursue it further. He nodded toward the televisions. 'So what do you think we'll do over in Egypt? Anything?'

Patrick shrugged as he readjusted the ice pack on his shoulder. 'Move up the *Kennedy* battle group to the Red Sea to defend the Suez Canal, keep the two carrier groups on station in the Med, and try to keep the conflict from spreading to the Persian Gulf or Israel,' Patrick said. 'Purely defensive moves – I don't think the President wants to send in any military forces. If Libya stays on the move, destroys Salimah, takes the Suez Canal, and crosses over the Red Sea into Israel, then I think the President might make a move. But I think he's really hoping Susan Salaam will pull the Arab countries together to fight off Libya.' He looked at Jackson. 'So what do you think we'll do?'

'What I think we'll *do*? Same as you – *nada*,' Jackson replied. 'What I think we *should* do? We should go pay President Zuwayy of Libya a little visit, blow up a few of his palaces just to get his attention, and then deprive him of his bombers, fighters, airstrips, and rockets – and that's all for starters. My guys can do all that in one night. Two at the most.' Jackson was definitely not above a little hubris when it came to sending Navy SEALs into action. He looked carefully at Patrick. 'Of course, scuttlebutt says someone or some group of someones might have been already mixing it up with the king. Wouldn't know anything about that, would you, sir?'

'Not a thing. But if they did, they should have their heads examined.'

'Maybe they can show our commander-in-chief how it's done,' Jackson said.

'President Salaam needs to fight for her country too. She's got a military – she needs to use it to defend her people.'

'If anyone can do it, she can. Not bad for an Air Force puke, I guess.'

'No Air Force cracks – unless you want to lose those four stars I had planned for you.'

'Oops – sorry, sorry, sir, sorry,' Jackson said with a smile – he was one of the few Navy SEALs Patrick had ever met that actually seemed to like to smile. He shook Patrick's hand warmly. 'If there's anything you need, sir, please don't hesitate to ask. And I hope you don't mind I have my spies out keeping an eye on you. You're the biggest celebrity we've had hanging around the area since Dennis Conner. We'll be sorry to see you and Wendy head back to Washington.' Before Patrick could protest again, Jackson added, 'I know, I know, you're not in the running. I'll remember you said that when I see you at your confirmation party in Washington. You sure you don't need a doctor to look at your shoulder?'

'I'm fine, Captain. And you can let your spies go home too.'

'Yes, sir. Take care of that shoulder – I want to beat you fair and square on the golf course.' Patrick noticed Jackson motion to a young sailor who had been standing near the entrance to the workout room with a cell phone, who departed with Jackson. The base commander was a good guy, Patrick decided, but there was no doubt that he played the political battles as well as he undoubtedly played the real-world military battles – and making friends with potentially influential persons was one way to get ahead in the Navy.

Too bad he was sucking up to the wrong guy.

Patrick toweled off, tossed the bag of ice, then experimentally flexed his left shoulder. It felt pretty good, so he decided to forgo the steam room and instead take his son Bradley to the pool. He checked Bradley out of the day-care center and took him back to the locker room.

He didn't notice a janitor set a bucket of smelly water and a mop in front of the door to the locker room after Patrick entered, put up a sign that said, 'DO NOT ENTER' on the door, and then lock the door after he entered.

Patrick put Bradley in a pair of swim trunks he kept in his gym bag for just this purpose, changed himself, and led his son to the pool. He found the door to the pool locked. He turned to ask someone why the door was locked when he noticed that the locker room was very quiet – unusually quiet. No one else was in there. The place usually had at least a dozen men in there all hours of the day, but it was empty now . . .

. . . except for an Arab-looking man who stepped out from behind a row of lockers – carrying an automatic pistol in one hand.

Patrick immediately grabbed Bradley and dodged behind a row of lockers. The man didn't follow – that meant there were others in the room, waiting for him.

'Dad? Aren't we going swimming?' Bradley asked. He was obviously more concerned about not going to the pool than he was about being carried protectively by his father like a slippery football through onrushing linebackers.

'Shh,' Patrick whispered. He crouched as low as he could, almost duckwalking through the locker room.

He saw the second guy's knees before he saw the rest of him, and he prayed it wasn't an innocent sailor – because Patrick lashed out with his right foot, snapping out in a driving thrust against the stranger's left knee. The knee buckled outward at an unnatural angle.

'Dad? Why did you kick that guy?' Bradley asked amid the stranger's animal-like howling. 'Is he a bad guy?'

Patrick wasn't sure how to answer – until another automatic pistol clattered to the tiled floor. 'Yes, he's a bad guy,' Patrick replied as he picked up the gun. 'We're getting out of here.'

'Good job,' Bradley said.

Patrick decided not to go to the front door but try for the equipment manager's office, which had an exit into the gymnasium. He heard footsteps sliding around the tile floor behind him. He kicked a chair over toward the front door to try to make it sound as if he was headed in that direction, then ran as hard as he could to the equipment manager's office. Good – no one around. He tried the door – even better, it was unlocked. Patrick dashed in . . .

. . . and immediately a fist rapped him on the side of his head. He went sprawling. Bradley screamed. Patrick raised the gun, but he couldn't make his eyes focus, and he didn't dare try to aim at any shape he saw in front of him, fearful it would be his son. 'Get the hell away from me!' he shouted over Bradley's screaming.

'Get away or I'll shoot!' But at that instant a large blur raced across his eyes, and the gun was knocked from his hand. 'Bradley!' he shouted. He curled himself over his son, pressing him into a corner up against a file cabinet, shielding him as best he could. 'Stay down!'

'It's all right, General, it's all right,' he heard a familiar voice say. 'Tell your son to calm down. You are in no danger.'

'Who . . . who is it?'

'Just relax, my friend. Relax.' His vision did clear a few moments later . . .

. . . and when it did, he saw the smiling, boyish face of King Idris the Second of Libya, Muhammad as-Sanusi, hovering over him. 'You . . . Your Majesty, what in hell are you doing here?' Patrick said. He got Bradley up and calmed him down.

'Whatever I'm doing, I don't think I'm doing it very gracefully,' Sanusi said. He gave commands in Arabic, and his two men disappeared. 'I need to speak with you immediately, General McLanahan. It is most urgent. Where can we meet?'

'For Pete's sake, Your Majesty, a phone call would've been better,' Patrick said. He couldn't help but smile at Sanusi's wry grin.

'I apologize, my friend,' Sanusi said, 'but my men went about their task too enthusiastically, and you reacted most unexpectedly. But I need to speak with you. It is very important.'

'How did you get on base?' Patrick asked. 'The security on this base has never been tighter. How . . . ?'

'It is about your wife, Wendy McLanahan,' Sanusi said.

Patrick's mouth dropped open in surprise. Bradley stopped whimpering and broke out in a wide, teary-eyed smile. 'Mommy . . . ?'

'Fifteen minutes. Silver Strand State Park, east side, near the boat rental shop.'

'I know where it is.'

'Then be there in ten minutes,' Patrick said. Sanusi disappeared – Patrick had no idea how he expected to get out of the gym after the commotion they started, but somehow he knew he would. 'Let's go, Bradley.'

'Are we going to see Mommy?' he asked excitedly. Patrick did not – *could* not – answer.

*   *   *

It took longer than ten minutes for Patrick to explain to Fred Jackson and his security police units what all the yelling and screaming was about. But Patrick explained everything to Jackson, including where and when he was going to meet with Sanusi. Jackson offered to have a few of his men tag along, but Patrick declined.

He already had someone on the way prepared to do that.

It was thirty minutes later when Patrick arrived at the rendezvous point, a small glass-and-concrete white building between the base and the Loews Coronado Resort where folks could rent sailboats during the summer. Sanusi and his men didn't arrive for another twenty minutes. Patrick was somewhat dismayed to see them – he had thought security at the naval base was tighter than that.

Patrick's concern was assuaged after he met up with Sanusi and greeted him. 'I am sorry to be late, my friend – the naval security forces detained us momentarily,' the king said. 'I am grateful you explained who we were. They agreed to release us under your supervision – after they took away our ID cards.'

'You had false ID cards?'

'Real ID cards with false photos on them,' Sanusi said. 'It is laughably easy to take IDs from lockers in your recreation facilities. We had no trouble crossing the Mexican border with false Israeli passports, and getting on base was simplicity itself – does no one patrol the shores at your seaside bases?'

'What about my wife, Your Highness?' Patrick asked.

'Ah yes – enough of the security lecture,' Sanusi said. 'I believe your wife is alive, my friend. She and several Americans are still held by the pretender Zuwayy in Tripoli, in one of his underground bunkers south of the city.'

Patrick knelt down and put an arm around his son, hugging him with joy. Bradley was more interested in Sanusi's men, one of whom now had a splint around his left knee. 'Have your men seen her? Are you certain?'

'We have not seen her,' Sanusi replied. 'But the guards have reported to my men that the woman spoke her name, and that name was McLanahan. When this was told to me, I ordered my agents inside Tripoli to try to stay in contact with her, and I made arrangements to travel here to tell you myself. Because of you, my men and I are still patrolling the desert, probing for weaknesses in the Libyan army. We will help you all we can.'

'I'm grateful, Your Highness,' Patrick said. 'I just hope we can reach her in time.' He turned away and spoke: 'Patrick to Luger, Briggs, and Wohl.'

'Luger's up.'

'Wohl's up, in sight, your four o'clock.' Patrick turned, and Sanusi looked in the same direction – just as Chris Wohl peeked his head above the low concrete rim of an adjacent rest room building about a hundred yards away. Patrick had called and asked that he cover him and Bradley during this meeting – just in case.

'Very wise precaution, General McLanahan,' Muhammad as-Sanusi commented, his smile beaming. He waved at Wohl; his wave was not returned. None of them could see what weapon Wohl was carrying, but there were no doubts in anyone's mind that he was more than proficient with it at this close range.

'Just a heads-up, Muck – Naval Intelligence has just initiated a foreign-contact log on you,' David Luger reported. 'They'll start setting up surveillance on you, probably tap your phones, all that stuff. The contact log said that Muhammad as-Sanusi made contact with you right there in Coronado?'

'He and his men are with me right now,' Patrick said. 'So I should assume we're under surveillance right now, correct?'

'I think that would be a safe assumption. What's happening?'

'The king says Wendy and the Americans are alive.'

'Holy shit! That's great! Can we confirm it? Do we have a location?'

'No, and no,' Patrick said. 'But I want to get the force loaded up and headed back to Jaghbub right away.'

'You got it, Muck,' Luger said. 'But just to let you know, the feds have really cracked down on Sky Masters. They've got us in virtual lockdown as we speak, and Jon has received notice of an FBI security inspection team that wants unlimited access to inspect the base tomorrow morning. My guess is that they're not there to do a security audit – they'll shut down the facility. I'm sure we've got Defense Intelligence Agency guys on our butts, and now we'll have to contend with Naval Intelligence.'

'Which means we start immediately,' Patrick said. 'I'll go with the king and Dave to Libya and get the base set up; you and Chris will split up and help Jon get our planes airborne with as many weapons and as much fuel as we can carry.'

Tonopah Test Range, Nevada
a short time later

The Suburban screeched to a halt in front of the security gate, and six men in plain dark business suits hopped out and assembled at the electric gate. The man from the front passenger seat picked up the phone mounted on the fence beside the gate. 'Special Agent Willison, FBI, Los Angeles. My office called this morning.' The gate was buzzed open by the guards inside, and the agents rushed in.

They were met inside the guardhouse by a young man who extended his hand to welcome them but was greeted instead by upraised ID cards and stern, intimidating expressions. 'I'm Special Agent Larry Willison, FBI,' the lead agent said. 'And you are?'

'John Landow, assistant security director of Sky Masters Inc, the prime contractor in this facility.'

'I asked to meet directly with Dr Masters or General McLanahan. Where are they?'

'They're both in the lab right now,' Landow said, 'but they can meet you as soon as you clear security.'

'I happen to know that General McLanahan is in San Diego,' Willison said angrily, 'and Dr Masters was told to meet us here. Now I want you to call him and have him meet us right outside. I've been ordered to consider any more delays as obstructing a federal investigation, and I am authorized to take him, and anyone else who doesn't cooperate fully, into custody.'

'Agent Willison, I assure you, no one is trying to hamper any investigation,' Landow said. Landow was tall, in his early sixties, with bright blue eyes and a ready smile – but when the smile vanished, he looked very mean and serious. 'I was informed the general was here – if I'm mistaken, then I apologize. And I promise you, Dr Masters will be right outside by the time you clear security.'

'What do you mean, "clear security"?' one of the other agents asked. 'We submitted all of our credentials yesterday. We're demanding immediate access. That means *right now*.'

'Agent, if you knew anything at all about this facility, you know that *no one* gets immediate access,' Landow said. 'The security requirements in this facility are established by folks very much higher than our pay grades or even our boss's pay grade, and I'm not allowed to violate them. I faxed your office a copy of the entry procedures – I trust you received them?' The FBI agents nodded. 'That is exactly what we'll do. My time estimate is accurate – no more than fifteen minutes to clear security. Shall we get started?'

Willison and the others had no choice but to agree. 'But I want no one else to enter or leave this facility,' he said. 'That outer gate remains locked. All aircraft movement will cease immediately, all aircraft engines will be shut down, and all external power carts will be detached from all aircraft. If we see one aircraft with even so much as a courtesy light on, we'll arrest each and every individual in this facility.'

'Your cease-and-desist order and the search warrant spelled out everything, Special Agent,' Landow said, 'and our attorneys have told us it's in our best interest to cooperate. I've advised all the labs to comply one hundred percent. Your IDs and firearms go in the turntable there.'

Landow had moved a weapon-clearing barrel into the guardhouse, and the agents went about unloading and clearing their weapons by pointing them at the sand inside the barrel, then placing them on a turntable surrounded with bulletproof glass. The guard inside the secure room collected the weapons and placed them in lockers, then turned the locker keys back over to the agents. Meanwhile, another guard began checking IDs and taking digital photos.

As they were waiting for their IDs to be checked and their clearances issued, they were surprised to see a young girl step into the guardhouse, escorted by a security officer. The girl was wearing what looked like the proper identification badges – but it certainly looked strange to see a youngster inside one of the most secure compounds in the United States of America. It was even more surprising when the officer dropped the girl off in the guardhouse without anyone else appearing to be supervising her.

The biggest, leanest, most menacing Doberman Pinscher that any of them had ever seen accompanied the girl.

The girl walked over to Willison; the Doberman sat right beside her and stared at the FBI agent. 'Hi. I'm Kelsey.' She motioned to the dog. 'This is my friend Sasha. Who are you?'

'My name is Mr Willison.'

'Pleased to meet you,' she said politely. Willison turned when the officer checking their IDs offered them back. 'Oooo,' the girl said when she noticed the badge holders. 'Are you a police officer?'

'Yes, we are.'

'How exciting,' she said. She reached for his ID as he was putting it back in his jacket. 'Can I see?'

'Not now,' Willison said curtly. The girl looked perturbed. Willison went over to the guard window. 'Hey, what's the story with the kid?'

'That's Kelsey.'

'So I heard. What's she doing here?'

'Her mom is one of the owners. She comes here every now and then. The dog is her bodyguard.'

'A bodyguard? Inside the compound?'

'Everywhere she goes, I guess. She has class-C access.'

'How in hell did a little kid –?'

'Hey, mister?' the girl asked. She was back again, a look of determination in her eyes. 'Can I please see your badge?'

'No, you cannot,' Willison replied.

'But I said "please." My mommy said I have to be more polite, and when I'm more polite, I get more things.'

'She's right, but you still can't see my badge,' Willison said sternly.

'But I said "please."'

'I said no.'

'Pul-leese?' She stopped asking and was whining now.

'No!' Willison barked. His kids were grown, but when they were even younger than this girl, they learned respect. 'Now go sit down over there.'

'You can't make me. You can't tell me what to do. You're not the boss of me!'

Willison turned again to the guard. 'Where's her mother?'

'Somewhere in the facility. She goes with her kid when they're getting ready to leave, but then she usually gets waylaid and sends the kid on ahead. We usually end up picking her up in the break room and escorting her here.'

'My mom won't like you telling me what to do,' the girl said.

'I don't care. Now go sit down.'

'Just let me please see your badge? I promise I won't hurt it or get it dirty.'

'For the fourth time, I said no.'

Suddenly the girl reached over and actually tried to pull the badge case from his inside jacket pocket. Willison practically leapt backward in surprise. The other agents were suppressing amused snickers at the girl's persistence and Willison's mounting aggravation. The girl actually managed to get two little fingers on the badge holder and was pulling it out of his breast pocket. Willison heard a faint ripping and realized she was taking most of his breast pocket with her. 'Hey! Watch it!' he shouted, louder than he intended.

He may have pushed her a *tiny* bit, just because he was surprised at her quick move and to keep his pocket from ripping right off. If he did, he didn't put any force behind it. But whatever he did, suddenly the little girl yelped in pain and flew backward as if she had been body-slammed by a WWF wrestler. She hit the linoleum floor hard. She lay on the floor, staring straight up; at first, Willison thought – no, *prayed* – that she wasn't hurt. But he knew kids better than that. Seconds later, the little girl let out an earsplitting scream so loud that he thought for sure she had cracked open her skull or fallen on an ax or something.

The only reason they stopped being concerned for the child's welfare was that they were more concerned about their own – because now Sasha the Doberman was all teeth, hair, and eyeballs. None of them had ever seen a more vicious-looking animal in their lives. They instinctively backed away and reached for side arms before realizing they no longer carried them.

'Get that animal away from us!' Willison shouted. The girl screamed even louder. Finally one of the guards behind the counter, a younger one with kids, was able to pick her up, and he carried her to a chair and let her cry on his shoulder for a while until the security guard waved the FBI agents through. The dog watched them, snarling, facing them the entire time. By then, the girl was over her crying, and she watched silently, tearlessly, as the FBI agents departed. With one word from the little girl, the Doberman stopped snarling and sat down, impassively watching the door close behind them.

'For Christ sake, Larry,' one of the other agents admonished him, going over to the little girl. 'What'd you do?'

'I didn't do anything!' Willison protested. 'She came at me, and I –'

'She "came at you"? Who'd you think she was – Freddie Krueger? Hannibal Lecter?'

'Her mom probably makes more dough than all of us combined,' another agent said over the now ear-piercing screams.

'I hear the new office in Greenland needs a janitor,' another joked.

'Har har.' Willison looked mad enough to chew the chain-link fence as he walked through an X-ray machine, then submitted to a pat-down search. 'What in hell is a little kid like that hanging around this facility, anyway?' he grumbled. 'I'm going to look into that next. This place is not a day-care center. And what the hell is it with that dog? I thought we were goners!'

'Let it go, Larry,' one of the other agents said as they emerged through yet another chain-link entrapment area into the street behind the hangar complexes. They saw the assistant security director, Landow, just emerging from a hangar, coming to meet them. 'You just forgot how to handle little kids, that's all.'

'Hey, we're here on business, not to entertain some rich bitch's kid.' He looked around. 'Masters is still nowhere to be found. I want some butts here today, gentlemen. Nothing goes by us. I don't put up with this shit from anyone, especially not from some snot-nosed egghead. I want –' Just then, he heard a high-pitched whine – the unmistakable sound of heavy jet engines spooling up. 'What the hell?' He shouted at Landow, pointing in the direction of the noise. *'I thought I ordered no engine starts! What in hell is that?'*

At that moment, over the growing roar of jet engines not far away, they heard, *'Freeze! Hands in the air! No one move!'* In the blink of an eye, heavily armed security officers with M-16 rifles leveled at them surrounded the FBI agents.

Willison casually reached for his ID inside his jacket. 'Put your guns down, boys. We're FB—'

'*I said hands in the fucking air!*' Before they knew it, the officers pounced, using their rifles as pugil sticks to knock the agents to the asphalt. They spread-eagled the stunned FBI agents and began patting them down. To their immense shock, Sasha the Doberman was back, her jaws just inches away, snarling and growling louder and meaner than ever.

'What in hell are you doing?' Willison shouted. 'We're FBI, dammit! We just got clearance inside!' The dog snapped its jaws, and Willison felt the gush of its breath on the back of his hand – he thought his bladder was going to let go.

'Don't move!' The guards secured their hands with nylon handcuffs, then continued pat-searching them.

John Landow strolled over to them a few moments later. 'Landow! You tell them who we are, *right now!*' Willison shouted.

'I suggest you stay quiet and cooperate, whoever you are,' Landow said. 'You're in serious trouble.'

'What are you talking about?'

'Got one,' one of the guards said.

'I got one too,' another said, who had been searching the younger agent who had picked Kelsey off the floor.

Both guards brought small devices, resembling small ballpoint pens with wires attached to them, over to Landow. Landow examined them, then stooped down beside Willison so he could see what he had in his hands. 'Where did you get these, Special Agent?' he asked.

'Get what?' He looked at the objects Landow had in his hand. 'I never saw those things before in my life.'

'We'd better read you your rights,' Landow said. 'I advise you right now not to say another word.'

'What are you talking about? What are they?'

'Then you agree to waive your right to remain silent?'

'Don't fuck with me, Landow! I'll close down this facility so fast it'll make your head spin! Now, cut these cuffs off and tell those pilots to shut down those engines, and that's an order!'

'I don't think you're in a position to be issuing orders right now, guys,' Landow said. 'You've just entered a secure government research facility operating under Threatcon Delta with

Kryton nuclear trigger devices in your possession.'

'What?'

'Our electronics sensors detected them in your clothing. You're under arrest for attempting to bring a weapon-of-mass-destruction component inside a secure government facility.'

'That's bullshit!' Willison stared bug-eyed at the objects. 'I've never seen those things before! I have no idea what they are! This is a frame-up! You planted those things on us . . . no, that girl! That girl planted them on us!' He continued his loud protests as the security officers were hauling him and his men away at gunpoint.

Landow met up with Jon Masters a few minutes later. 'Good job, John,' he said. 'Those old triggers from the museum sure did come in handy.'

'It's a ridiculous stunt that won't hold up for a moment,' Landow said.

'But it sets off the security procedures, and once they go into action, it'll take someone in Washington to stop it,' Masters said happily. 'This is the first time I'm actually *thankful* we have such tight security. How long are they going to be out of the picture?'

'We can hold them incommunicado for about six hours,' Landow replied, 'unless you intend on just locking them away somewhere.'

'The thought had crossed my mind.'

'Even a terrorist with a gun would get a phone call,' Landow pointed out. 'I think you should count on locking them away until just after five P.M., so they'll have to contact a duty officer instead of their own office for help – that'll slow things down a little more. But once the call goes in, your time runs out fast. The FBI will probably fly a supervisor or a US attorney out from LA shortly after they hear about this, but they won't have clearance to enter, so that'll delay things another few hours. But they might fly a Hostage Rescue Team out here to guard the place until the men can be released – that'll take them no more than one or two hours. After that, the game will be up. I'm sure they'll shut this place down tight and have all of us in federal prison in a heartbeat.'

'Plenty of time,' Jon said. 'We'll all be long gone by then. We'll have to hope that Patrick's benefactor can keep the heat off us so there's a company to come back to after this is all over.' He held out his arms when Kelsey Duffield approached, then picked her up and gave her a kiss on her cheek. Sasha sat down beside Jon, proudly puffing out her chest. 'Good job, Kelsey,' he said. 'You too, Sasha. Kelsey, I didn't know you were a pickpocket too.'

'Thanks, Jon. My dad always told me everyone likes a good pickpocket – but just as a joke. It's easy. I never picked a pocket to put anything *in* before, though.'

'The support aircraft will be ready to launch in about four hours, fully loaded with every weapon we can carry,' Jon said. 'The bombers should be airborne a few hours after that. They'll be loaded to the gills too with external weapons, so they won't be stealthy, but we'll have to risk it. I hope Patrick and Megafortress Two will be up there clearing a path for us.'

'Is this going to work, Doc?' Landow asked. 'We've broken just about every federal law in the books already – we're going to make it a million times worse by flying those planes to Libya. Libya is a prohibited country – technology export and import sanctions, terrorist support sanctions, money sanctions, travel and immigration restrictions, the works. If we don't get our asses shot down by the Libyans, we could all be in prison for the rest of our lives.'

'Nah. Everything'll be okay,' Jon Masters said confidently, giving Kelsey a reassuring hug. 'You haven't been with the company too long, John. We do this sort of thing all the time.'

'And you've never been caught?'

Jon shrugged, then gave Landow a sheepish grin. 'Well . . . we've always gotten away with it before,' Jon admitted. 'That's just as good.' He turned to Kelsey. 'Unfortunately, the only plane we won't have with us is the second Dragon airborne laser aircraft. We can't fly it in its current state unless we remove all the plasma-pumping equipment you've put on it and reassemble the diode pumping system on the laser. You gave it a good try, Kels.'

'Jon, I promise, it will work,' Kelsey said. 'Don't keep on thinking in two-dimensional ways. The plasma generator doesn't need to be a multimegawatt monster – all we need is a large pulse for a hundredth of a second to excite the neodymium lasing amplifier chips. Let's reassemble the plasma generators we have, install them, and try it.'

'We're going to lose our lab in less than eight hours, Kels –'

'Then we better hurry, shouldn't we?' Kelsey asked. 'We have a plasma generator we know will work on Dragon Two right now. Let's load it up, put the screws back in, and leave before that angry Mr Willison comes back.' She smiled and touched Jon's hand. 'Jon, we'll have time to write up the documentation and the engineering later – right now, we have to get Dragon flying, before they come and take her away. You're worried that you won't know how it works if it does, and so you won't be able to start preparing marketing plans and prospectuses for the project. Don't worry about all that stuff, Jon – let's see if it flies first, then worry about selling it later.'

Jon Masters looked at Kelsey with a grin. Her enthusiasm was indeed infectious. 'Kelsey, you know there's no way this should work,' Jon said. 'It's too dangerous. We still haven't gotten the right yield out of the single-generator system to be an effective weapon with the proper safety tolerances. We won't know if it's ready to let go until just before it blows up. And all these unknowns will be going on with two human beings riding on top of it.'

Kelsey took Jon's face in her hands, pulled his head down, and kissed his forehead. 'You're silly, you know that?' she said. 'I know we don't know all these things, Jon – doesn't that want to make you go and try it out?' When he hesitated in replying, Kelsey added, 'Jon, wasn't there once a time when you would have given anything – even your own life – for one chance to try?'

In fact, there was such a time: Jon Masters put himself in the fuselage of an airliner loaded with several hundred pounds of TNT to prove his electronic armor called BERP, or Ballistic Electro-Reactive Process, would protect the aircraft in case of a terrorist bomb going off in the cargo hold. The demonstration had horrified the airline and government representatives to the point that they refused to fund the program, but that didn't matter – it worked, and Jon risked his own life to prove it. That BERP material eventually became the Tin Man battle armor system, which would one day revolutionize American infantry fighting.

Kelsey paused, still holding Jon's hand, like a brother and sister taking a stroll. They found themselves standing in front of Dragon One's open hangar door. There was a flurry of action around it, with dozens of technicians and crew members rushing to get it ready to fly. Right next door was Dragon Two – virtually ignored except for the four security guards stationed around it.

'Doesn't it look lonely?' Kelsey asked her new big brother. 'It needs some love and attention. We can do it, Jon. We put Dragon's new plasma generators in, give it some gas, and take it on a trip to help the general find his wife.' She saw Jon's smile vanish and his shoulders slump. 'I know Wendy is still okay, Jon. I know she is. But we need to help Patrick so he can go back and find her.'

Jon smiled at his little partner, then nodded. When he looked at Dragon Two, he had to agree – it was a good-looking bird, and right now it did look pretty lonely.

He pulled out his secure cell phone: 'Doug? How's it going . . . ? Excellent. Listen, pull Ken and Duncan's crews off Dragon One and have them start installing the plasma generators on Dragon Two . . . yep, right now. As soon as Joel's crew signs off their preflight on One, have them jump over to help, and get the rest of the crews on Two as soon as One launches. We're going to bring Dragon Two with us . . . yes, and I want it operational . . . yes, *operational*, not just flyable. . . We've done all the lab testing we're going to do. Dr Duffield and I are standing out front right now to help. We have about six hours to do it . . . yes, I said *six*, and I'll be surprised if we don't get a visit from the Feds before then. Let's hustle!'

Sky Masters Inc World Headquarters, Arkansas International Jetport, Blytheville, Arkansas later that evening

The twin-engine Aerostar aircraft taxied quickly off the two-mile-long runway right up to the doors of Sky Masters Inc's main hangar. The pilot wheeled the light twin around so it was pointing back down the taxiway toward the runway, then shut down engines.

In less than two minutes, two dark sedans pulled over to the plane, blocking it fore and aft. By the time the pilot opened the split clamshell doors and stepped out, the plane was surrounded by agents in black fatigues emblazoned with 'FBI' and 'FEDERAL AGENT' front and back, all carrying M-16 assault rifles at the ready.

'General McLanahan?' one of the agents in a simple dark suit and tie announced.

'That's me,' Patrick replied.

'Special Agent Norwalk, FBI, Memphis office. I'd like you to come with me. Anyone in the plane with you?' Instead of waiting for a response, another agent pushed past Patrick and shined a flashlight inside, then shook his head, indicating it was empty. Another agent checked the baggage compartment in the back – it, too, was empty. He even checked the wheel wells, but they were too small to hide anything bigger than a small dog.

'Something wrong?' Patrick asked.

'We'll explain everything inside,' the FBI agent replied. 'Your plane will be secured inside the hangar.'

'You guys ever move a plane like this before? The nose gear is sensitive.'

'We'll be careful,' Norwalk responded, definitely sounding like he wasn't planning on being careful at all. He spoke into a radio, and before long one of Sky Masters Inc's technicians came out riding an aircraft tug, accompanied by another agent. The tech scooped up the Aerostar's nose wheel with the lifter. Meanwhile, the main hangar door opened. The plane was pushed back into the hangar beside one of the company's DC-10 mission support/launch/tanker aircraft.

Patrick was taken to his office in the headquarters facility. Special Agent Norwalk and another officer stayed inside with him. 'Now, mind telling me what's going on?' Patrick asked once they were seated inside.

'First, General, I advise you that you are hereby under arrest,' Norwalk began. 'You have the right to remain silent; should you choose to give up the right to remain silent, anything you say can and will be used against you in a court of law. You have the right to an attorney and to have the attorney present during questioning. If you cannot afford an attorney, one will be provided for you at no charge. Do you understand these rights as I've explained them?'

'What am I being arrested for?'

'General, do you understand your Constitutional rights as I've explained them to you?'

'Yes. Now can you tell me –?'

'Do you waive your right to remain silent?'

'I've done nothing wrong.'

'Are you willing to answer questions for me?'

'Yes. Now tell me what's going on here.'

'Do you know where Dr Jon Masters, Dr Kelsey Duffield, and the Sky Masters Inc crew members that were stationed at the Tonopah Test Range are right now, General?'

'I thought they were at Tonopah. Are they missing?'

'You're telling me you have no idea where they are?'

'What's going on, Norwalk? Has something happened? And why am I under arrest? Do you think I had something to do with it?'

'Did you have anything to do with Dr Masters and Dr Kelsey recently, say, in the past two days? Have you been in contact with them?'

'Hold it, hold it,' Patrick said, raising his hands and shaking his head in confusion. 'You're not answering any of my questions, and I'm getting confused. I feel like I'm being tricked into admitting something, and I think I should stop this questioning until I get my lawyer.'

The last thing Norwalk wanted was for McLanahan to 'lawyer up' now, so he nodded and put on a faint smile. As long as McLanahan only said 'I *think* I should stop' and not 'I want a lawyer' or 'I *want* to stop,' he could still question the suspect, even if the suspect believed his responses wouldn't incriminate himself. 'I'm sorry, sir. We just got here, and it's been a long day. Let's all relax and just talk.' He looked around the office. 'You got any coffee around here? It's been a *really* long day.'

'Sure,' Patrick said cheerfully. 'It's been a busy day for me too. Call in the rest of your guys – there's plenty for everyone.'

'Nice plane you got out there,' Norwalk said as Patrick went out to the outer office to start the coffeemaker. 'What is it?'

'An Aerostar – the fastest piston-powered twin you can buy,' Patrick said proudly. 'It's got six seats in it, but it's really only

401

good for two persons with full fuel and luggage.'

'You fly out from San Diego?'

'I keep the plane out at North Island Naval Air Station – the base commander is a friend of mine. It's about a seven-hour flight, plus a couple potty breaks – eleven hours total, including the time zone changes.'

'It sounds pretty fast.'

'It's a rocket ship,' Patrick said. 'I just wish it could hold more people and baggage. Me, the wife, and my son pretty much max it out.'

The armrest of the rear bench seat inside the Aerostar flopped down, and one eye peeked out from behind the seat. Seeing it was all clear, both seat backs in the split bench seat flopped down, and Chris Wohl and Hal Briggs unfolded themselves from the small baggage space behind the seat. 'Oh, God,' Briggs said, groaning as he stretched and flexed his sore legs and back. 'My leg cramps have cramps.' As he usually did, Chris Wohl ignored his friend and former commanding officer, but it was obvious he was experiencing much of the same difficulty unfolding his legs.

After he got feeling and circulation going in his limbs, Briggs crawled over the bench seats, staying low, then peeked out the smoked side windows into the hangar. No guards visible on the hangar door side; none visible out the forward windscreen. He looked out the right windows and saw one armed guard seated up on the concrete stairway landing leading into the flight department offices. Briggs made hand signals to Wohl where the guard was, then made his way to the forward entry hatch.

Meanwhile, Wohl knocked twice on the rear bulkhead. Behind the pressurized cabin was the unpressurized baggage compartment, which in Patrick's plane was normally mostly filled with an auxiliary fuel tank. But gloved fingers popped the false steel cover off, and two Night Stalkers emerged from the space normally occupied by the fuel tank. They were clothed in heavy winter-weight flight suits, jackets, boots, hats, and gloves, and each had a green oxygen bottle and mask. They, too, took a few moments to stretch and get their limbs going again, then donned

FM commlinks and readied automatic pistols. 'Cargo One is up,' one of them reported.

'Stand by,' Wohl said. 'One guard in sight. Pop your hatch and get ready.' The Night Stalkers unlatched the baggage compartment door as quietly as they could but did not open it.

Meanwhile, Briggs made his way to the split clamshell entry hatch, unlatched it with a twist of its handle, opened the top half just an inch or two, then unlatched and lowered the lower half. He hoped the guard couldn't see the open lower half from where he was sitting. Briggs stepped out and then lowered the upper half of the door all the way. 'Let's go, Sarge –'

'*Freeze!*' he heard. '*Hands where I can see them! Now!*' The lone guard had seen the hatch open and had quickly sneaked around the Aerostar, his rifle lowered.

Briggs shot his hands up in the air. The guard braced his rifle against his right hip, then pulled his walkie-talkie from his web belt and keyed the mike button: 'Unit Three to Control . . .'

'Cargo! Out now! Hard!' Wohl whispered into his commlink.

The lead Night Stalker in the baggage compartment threw himself out the baggage compartment, landing about five feet in front of the startled FBI agent. The agent pulled the trigger on his rifle. The single round missed the Night Stalker by a few inches, then ricocheted off the side of the Aerostar, missing Briggs's head by scant inches as well.

The second Night Stalker inside the baggage compartment aimed and fired his weapon. Tiny crystalline darts about the size of a short golfer's pencil hit the FBI agent. The darts instantly exploded into a fine dust that penetrated the agent's black fatigues. The agent had just enough time to realize that he was hit before the nerve agent in the dust completely immobilized his entire voluntary nervous system and he collapsed to the concrete hangar floor.

Briggs, Wohl, and the two Night Stalkers quickly split up, taking separate exits into the building. They were gone before any other FBI agents had responded.

Special Agent Norwalk was in the middle of a sip of coffee when he heard the shot, and he nearly dumped the coffee on himself. '*What the hell . . . ?*'

'Don't worry – that's just the cavalry showing up,' Patrick said matter-of-factly. Norwalk was reaching for his service pistol when Patrick touched a hidden switch on his desk, then covered his eyes with his arm and tightly closed his eyes just as the room lights went out and an immense flash of light completely blinded the two FBI agents. The room lights then came back to normal. Patrick was able to simply walk over and disarm both men by plucking their weapons from their hands – the sudden flash of light disoriented them so badly that they could hardly tell up from down. Norwalk was shouting for help as he bumped and caromed off the furniture; the other agent couldn't stay on his feet any longer and finally slumped to the floor.

Briggs and Wohl rushed into the office moments later. Briggs looked at the two writhing on the floor. 'There's the last two. All present or accounted for,' he said, then shot both with the crystal nerve darts. 'I think the guy out in the hangar shot your plane.'

'Bastard. He'll pay for that,' Patrick deadpanned. 'Let's go.'

Within minutes, Patrick started up the DC-10's auxiliary power unit and powered it up while one of the Night Stalkers drove one of the company jet fuel trucks over to the DC-10. After Patrick directed him on how to use the DC-10's single-point refueling system, he went up to the cockpit and started getting ready for their flight out of the country. Meanwhile, Briggs and Wohl loaded up as many sets of the Tin Man battle armor, the powered exoskeletons, the electromagnetic rail guns, and as much ammunition, spare battery packs, tools, and as many other devices as they could carry in the DC-10. In less than twenty minutes, they had completely refueled the DC-10, loaded it up, and were all on board.

'All that cargo space, and no weapons aboard,' Briggs said as he looked down the cavernous cargo area. They had enough cargo space and payload to carry two Megafortresses' worth of air-launched weapons – but they had no time to get any out from the storage bunkers. 'Too bad.'

'We got the fuel, the battle armor, and the rail guns – that'll do for now,' Patrick said. 'The nerve agent will wear off in another thirty minutes – we need to be long gone before they wake up.'

Jaghbub, United Kingdom of Libya
the next morning

'Unfortunately, we weren't able to bring many weapons with us,' Patrick said to Sayyid Muhammad ibn al-Hasan as-Sanusi. They were back in the big aircraft hangars at Jaghbub's military airfield, supervising the refueling of all the planes. One of the Megafortresses had to abort while over the Atlantic; in addition, all of the EB-1C Megafortress Two aircraft had been returned to their Air National Guard unit. Their remaining force: two EB-52 Megafortress flying battleships and two AL-52 Dragon airborne laser aircraft, Dragon One and Two, with Dragon Two carrying its untested plasma laser on board. 'But I would sure like to take another look at your weapon storage areas, Your Highness.'

'I think we may be able to help you there,' Sanusi said. Patrick hadn't had time to explore it yet, but the underground warehouses here supposedly held a lot of the latest military hardware. Some of it could be adapted for the Megafortress – if they had time to load it, mate it, program the weapons for release by the computers, and perhaps test them.

Patrick was amazed at the assortment of weapons they found in the weapon-storage bunkers a few minutes later. Zuwayy had collected a large and very impressive arsenal of Russian air-launched weapons: the BetAB series of antirunway penetration bombs, the largest of which could create a three-foot-deep crater the size of a football field in twenty inches of concrete; a large variety of KAB series laser-guided bombs, resembling copies of the American Paveway series, ranging from five-hundred- to well over three-thousand-pounders; almost the entire range of air-to-air missiles, from the tiny R-60 heat-seeker to the massive R-33 long-range radar-guided missile with nearly a hundred-mile range; and a good selection of air-to-surface missiles, including the Kh-27 antiradar missile, the Kh-29 laser-guided missile, and the Kh-15 long-range attack missile, a copy of the AGM-69A short-range attack missile, except these had only three-hundred-pound high-explosive warheads, not nuclear ones.

'Can you use any of them, my friend?' Sanusi asked.

405

'I think so,' Patrick replied with a grin. 'All of the weapons have the Russian-standard two-hundred-and-fifty-millimeter suspension lug spacing, so we need to get busy resetting all of the squibs on the bomb racks to accommodate them. Fortunately, our engineers in Nevada had thought of the real possibility of using pirated Russian-bloc weapons in the field, so it should be easy to do the conversion in the field. And most of the weapons are in surprisingly good shape – others look brand new, as if they just came right "out of the box."'

The Libyan weapons were hauled out of storage bunkers near the air base with block and tackle, makeshift trailers – most of the vehicles on the base had been destroyed by the fuel-air weapon attacks by the Megafortress days earlier – and pure old-fashioned muscle work. The weapons were dragged, pulled, or manhandled across the runway and to the largest and most undamaged hangar on the field, on which a large canvas tent had to be erected to hide the Megafortresses' protruding tails, which had to remain outside the hangar. Muhammad as-Sanusi's men had devised a bomb-loading 'jammer' out of an engine jack for the larger weapons; the smaller weapons were simply carried into position by however many men it took to do the job. Once they were loaded, it was simple to get them ready for release – the Megafortresses' attack computers already had ballistics information for every possible air-launched weapon in existence, even Russian ones, so it was just a matter of telling the computers which weapon was on which station.

The first EB-52 Megafortress battleship that would lead the attack carried longer-range standoff weapons, including four Russian Kh-27 antiradar missiles in the forward bomb bay, eight Kh-15 long-range inertially guided missiles on the rotary launcher in the aft bomb bay, four R-60 heat-seeking air-to-air missiles on each external pylon, and two FlightHawk unmanned combat aircraft on wing pylons – unfortunately, the FlightHawks did not carry any weapons of their own. The second EB-52 Megafortress battleship carried a rotary launcher in the rear of the bomb bay that held sixteen one-thousand-pound unguided bombs in eight two-round clips, with inflatable parachutes attached to each one to allow them to be released from low altitude if necessary. The slant racks in the forward bomb bay held thirty-six five-hundred-pound unguided cluster munitions in six rounds of six bombs; and the external weapon pylons held two Kh-27 antiradar missiles plus four R-60 heat-seeking missiles on each pylon.

Even though the Russian guided weapons were state-of-the-art, they couldn't interface well with the Megafortress. The anti-radar missiles were programmed on the ground to detect and attack any height-finder radar, an integral part of a surface-to-air missile or fighter ground-controlled intercept radar; the air-to-air missiles' seeker was caged straight ahead and would only report if a bright enough heat source crossed its path – they would never know if it locked on or hit its target. The inertially guided missiles had to be programmed with a target on the ground before takeoff, and then their guidance systems had to be aligned on the ground before takeoff – and their accuracy couldn't be updated while in flight.

Patrick took the king on a quick tour of the AL-52 Dragon. Workers from Sky Masters Inc, including Jon Masters himself, were still poring over it, adjusting components and voltages while a laptop computer measured magnetic fields and predicted power yields and safety margins. 'A truly impressive weapon, Dr Masters,' Sanusi said after he had been introduced.

'I wish I could take all the credit for it,' Jon said. He motioned inside the belly of the AL-52 just as a little girl emerged, covered in grease and dirt but wearing a big smile. 'Your Majesty, may I present Dr Kelsey Duffield of Nevada, my partner and chief engineer of this particular weapon system. Dr Duffield, may I present the king of the United Kingdom of Libya, His Majesty, Muhammad as-Sanusi.'

'Jon, for Christ's sake!' Patrick gasped. 'Pardon me, Your Highness, but . . . Jeez, Jon, you *brought* Kelsey Duffield . . . to *Libya*?'

'I couldn't keep her away, Patrick,' Jon said. 'If you're going to yell at me, stand in line – Kelsey's mom isn't done chewing on me yet. Patrick, this is Dr Kelsey Duffield, our new partner; Kelsey, Brigadier-General Patrick McLanahan, retired, our VP in charge of operations.'

'Pleased to meet you, General,' Kelsey said, giving Patrick a big hug and a kiss. 'Don't worry about Dr Wendy, sir – we'll get her back for you and Bradley.' She gave Sanusi a little-girl curtsy, then went back inside the Dragon's fuselage and back to work.

'Not exactly what you expected, huh?' Jon asked.

'I expected anything but a nine-year-old in a war zone, Jon,' Patrick said. 'We will get her out as soon as we can.'

'She's advancing the state of the art in high-power lasers by five years every hour she works on the Dragon,' Jon said. But when Patrick glared at him, he held up his hands. 'Okay, okay, as soon as we launch, Kelsey goes home.'

While Sanusi's men and the Sky Masters tech crews loaded up the planes, Patrick and Sanusi met up with Dave Luger, Hal Briggs, and Chris Wohl in a meeting room, where charts and diagrams had been spread out on a table. 'I have never before seen the defenses in Tripoli so strong and tight,' the king said. He took out a notepad from his tunic, then started drawing circles and crosses on the charts. 'Zuwayy has definitely pulled in and reinforced his forces around Tripoli to prepare for air attacks. These are new mobile antiaircraft missile and gun emplacements – at least ten new units brought in within the past several days. We haven't been able to actually count the number of fighters stationed at Al-Khums and Miznah, but we believe all of their alert aircraft shelters are occupied – that's twelve fighter-interceptors on alert twenty-four-seven at each base.' He looked seriously at Patrick. 'With all due respect to your men and machines, my friend, it would be suicide to attack Tripoli now.'

'We don't have any choice, Your Highness,' Patrick said.

'Perhaps,' Sanusi said. 'But even if you do penetrate those air defenses, there is no way you can locate your wife and your men in the Garden labyrinth. We've narrowed the area down to the southeast complex, which is the presidential palace area, but that only narrows it down to two or three dozen rooms, defended by perhaps five hundred troops.'

'I know a way to find her quickly,' Patrick said.

Sanusi looked into Patrick's eyes, and his round eyes grew sad and his lips pulled taut. 'I think I know how you intend to do this,' Sanusi said. 'It's madness. Your son will lose both his parents.'

'It's the only chance we'll ever get, Your Highness,' Patrick said.

He looked down, tracing his finger over the air defense circles surrounding their objective. 'I don't think I can go back without her again, Muhammad. The pain on my son's face was almost too much to bear.'

Chapter Ten

Presidential Palace, Tripoli, United Kingdom of Libya
that night

'He is with that new whore every hour of every day now,' General Tahir Fazani, the Libyan military chief of staff, commented disgustedly in a low voice. He and the Minister of Arab Unity, Juma Mahmud Hijazi, were in Fazani's office in the Libyan Presidential Palace, where a military briefing had just wrapped up – minus the king, Jadallah Zuwayy, again. They had dismissed the rest of the military advisers and were preparing to brief the king on the military-readiness reports. 'We're getting ready to go to war with Egypt, and he's over there getting laid.'

'Or worse,' Hijazi mused. 'Do you think he's on the drugs again?'

'God, I hope not,' Fazani said. 'We're screwed if he is.'

'Tahir, why the hell don't we just blow town?' Hijazi asked.

'You know why, Juma – if we don't control the money or don't bump off Jadallah, we come away with nothing – and worse, he'll be coming after us for the rest of his life. We need to get those bank account numbers and passwords first.'

'Maybe if he was back on horse, we could get them easier,' Hijazi surmised. He nodded to the reports. 'How are we looking?'

'It couldn't be better,' Fazani said. 'Exactly as the planning staff predicted, the intelligence staff tells us Egypt pulled so many forces back toward Cairo that they're unable to set up any kind of meaningful defense, let alone mount an offensive. We don't have enough troops to take Salimah yet, in my opinion, but if Jadallah wanted to mount an offensive, now would be the time to do it. We set up a forward base inside Egypt, move a large number of troops and aircraft there, and we can hold off the Egyptian army forever.'

'And if the Americans intervene?'

'They won't – President Thorn is a spineless weakling,' Fazani said. 'But if he does, we withdraw – but not before destroying Salimah. We blow all the oil wells, just like Saddam Hussein did as his forces left Kuwait.' Just then, the outer door opened, and Fazani's aide stepped quickly in. 'What is it, Captain?'

'Sir, an American has been arrested by the security forces outside the gate of the Presidential Palace. He was demanding to see the king.'

'Why are you bothering me with this drivel, Captain? Have him arrested and taken to the interrogation center.'

'He also demands to see the prisoners.'

'What prisoners?'

'He says, the American prisoners,' the aide said. 'The ones captured after the attacks in the Mediterranean Sea – including the woman, Wendy McLanahan.'

Fazani and Hijazi looked at each other in complete surprise. No one, they wordlessly reminded each other, knew about the prisoners – and they sure as hell didn't know any of the prisoners' names! 'Does this man have a name?'

'Yes, sir – he called himself McLanahan too. Brigadier General Patrick McLanahan.'

Both Libyan ministers jumped to their feet in surprise. 'McLanahan? He's *here*?' Fazani shouted. 'Is he armed?'

'Just a small pistol, sir.'

Thank God he didn't visit them as he visited Zuwayy in Jaghbub – with his bombers buzzing overhead destroying the place and wearing his medieval armor with the built-in bug zapper, Fazani thought. 'Bring him up here, right now!'

'I'll tell Jadallah –' Hijazi said.

'Not quite yet,' Fazani said. 'Maybe this McLanahan has information that is valuable to us. We'll tell Jadallah . . . in good time.'

A few minutes later, Patrick was standing before both Hijazi and Fazani, his hands shackled in front of him with handcuffs and a chain around his waist. He was wearing plain civilian clothes, similar to urban Arabs. One of the guards set a bag on the desk. 'He was found with this, sir,' the guard said. Fazani examined the bag: It contained a fake beard, Libyan citizen documents, Libyan money, a small digital camera, a palm-sized radio, a Russian Tokarev pistol – common in both Libya and Egypt – and a fake Egyptian passport. The guard held out another smaller

414

bag – this one held colored contact lenses. 'He was wearing these as well. His hair is dyed black, too.' Fazani felt his hair – quick, cheap hair dye. 'No other weapons.'

'Very clever, General,' Fazani said in halting but good English. 'Fake documents, fake hair, even fake eye color. What do you hope to accomplish here, General?'

'I'm looking for my wife and my men,' Patrick said. 'I know you're holding them.'

'Oh, I am sure you will be joining them soon enough,' Fazani said. 'But we have questions first.'

'I'm not answering any questions. I want the Americans. If I don't come out with them, I'll destroy this palace.'

'You will? With what? This pistol?'

'You know how,' Patrick said ominously. 'The same way I destroyed Samāh, Jaghbub, Al-Jawf, and Zillah.'

Both Fazani and Hijazi looked decidedly uncomfortable at that point. Fazani paced around Patrick, thinking hard; then: 'Then I have a better idea, General: You will recall your bombers immediately, or I will execute your wife and all your men right before your eyes.'

'If I don't report in to my unit by the bottom of the hour, Minister, this palace will be destroyed.' Hijazi looked at his watch: ten minutes to go. 'There is no abort code, Minister – either I report I'm still inbound, or I report I'm coming out with the prisoners, or this place gets leveled. I'm not afraid to die.'

'Then it was a suicide mission,' Fazani said. 'Because I assure you, we will be safe from any of your weapons – unless you intend on dropping a nuclear bomb on us. After the attack, we will all appear on the world news together and tell the world all about your doomed rescue mission and your homicidal bombing raids on Libya.'

'Then you'll be doing that report from the rubble of your government buildings and palaces,' Patrick said, 'because I guarantee you, you won't be able to stop my bombers from attacking this city.'

'Then right after your appearance on CNN, General McLanahan, perhaps you, your wife, and your spies will be dragged out of that rubble yourselves,' Fazani said. 'Either way, we will be safe, and alive, and you'll be dead and disgraced.'

'I have a better idea, Tahir – let us tell Jadallah's financier whom we have now,' Hijazi suggested. Fazani's eyes brightened at that idea. 'I think he will pay handsomely for this man delivered alive to him.'

'Don't count on it,' Patrick said. 'I don't work for any government, but I command a lot of firepower – whoever you bring me to will suffer the same fate as you will.'

'I doubt that very much,' Hijazi said. 'Pavel Kazakov commands many forces as well, and I'm sure he's far wealthier than you are.'

'*Kazakov?*' Patrick exclaimed. 'Zuwayy is working with Pavel Kazakov? I should have known.'

'I see you've heard of him? Good. He will pay a very generous bonus to the ones who bring you to him – alive if possible, but dead if necessary. Perhaps we can negotiate a package deal for all of you Americans together – I think Kazakov would love to use you all as an example to others of what happens when you cross him. But first we need to know all about your bombers and other infantry forces you have in Libya. The king has described some very amazing forces – perhaps you can tell us all about them.'

'Go to hell,' Patrick said.

'Well, that is a little more defiant than the things your wife has been saying while in captivity, General,' Fazani said with a smile. Patrick angrily tested his shackles yet another time – they were securely locked. '*Imshi. Enta tiqdar ta'mel ahsan min kida.* Get him out of here, now.'

After the guards had taken McLanahan out, Hijazi said, 'I'll get Kazakov on the phone right away. I think he's been looking for this guy – I'll bet he'll pay a lot for him.'

'You handle Kazakov – I'll notify Jadallah,' Fazani said. 'This way we cover our asses in case Kazakov blabs that we told him and not our boss.'

'Good idea.'

'We've also got to get all those captives out of here as soon as possible,' Fazani added. 'It can't be a coincidence that McLanahan just waltzes in here – the exact spot where we happen to be keeping his wife and his fighters. He's doing a probe. The faster we get him out of here, the better.'

416

Fazani walked over to Zuwayy's residence and notified the Republican Guards that he wished to speak with the king. Ten frustrating, aggravating minutes later, Fazani was told the king was unavailable. Not daring to push aside one of Zuwayy's Republican Guards – they were absolute fanatics about security; their lives depended on it – Fazani asked again, and after another ten-minute wait, he was admitted into the king's private residence.

He could see it immediately. Tahir Fazani had known Jadallah Zuwayy for more than fifteen years, including two years in Sudan where Zuwayy got hooked on heroin. He and Hijazi had nursed him, covered for him, threatened him, and cajoled him into giving up the stuff. They *thought* they had been successful. 'Damn you, Jadallah,' he muttered. 'What the hell is wrong with you? We're going to war with Egypt any day now, and you're up here getting high.'

'What the hell do you want, Tahir?' Zuwayy asked. He was slumped in a chair, drinking something; his head lolled around every now and then as if he were on some sort of sailboat race on the Gulf of Sidra.

'We had a little visit by someone tonight – one Brigadier General Patrick McLanahan.'

'An Anglo? So what? Is he an arms dealer? A mercenary? If not, kick him out of the country and . . .' Zuwayy stopped and looked at Fazani through bloodshot, bleary eyes and blown pupils. 'Did you say . . . McLanahan?'

'The woman we have in your interrogation center is his *wife*,' Fazani said. 'He came here to demand we return her and his men to him.'

'And you have him? He actually tried to walk in here and demanded we release the prisoners? Was he deranged?'

'I think it's some kind of setup,' Fazani said seriously. 'I had him taken to the detention center, but I think he should be moved as soon as possible.'

'Moved? Yes, he should be moved – straight to Kazakov,' Zuwayy said. 'This might be our chance to get back in his good graces. Where is he now?'

'The interrogation center,' Fazani said. 'It should be useful for us to interrogate him as much as possible before we turn him over.

He might be able to give us a lot of information on Egyptian defenses as well as exactly what he used to attack all our bases. And if we can find out who he works for, maybe they'll pay even more to get him back than Kazakov will.' Zuwayy got unsteadily to his feet; Fazani practically had to catch him to keep him from falling over. 'Why don't you let me handle McLanahan, Jadallah? Give me some time to see what he'll do. If he's as tough as his men we captured, it might be easier just to hand him over to Kazakov; but if we can break him quickly, maybe we can explore alternate opportunities.'

'*Ma'lesh, ma'lesh,*' Zuwayy said. He returned to his chair and collapsed into it. 'You and Juma take care of it. I'll be okay in a few hours.' Fazani was thankful Zuwayy didn't put up a fight about that, and he headed for the door. But just before he left, Zuwayy shouted behind him, 'Wait, Tahir! Did you say you were going to take him to the interrogation center?'

'*Na'am.*'

'Did you search him first?'

'Of course. We found disguises, fake travel documents, a gun . . .'

'What about a radio?'

'We found a radio too.'

'A small one? A very small one?'

Now Fazani was getting anxious. He turned back toward Zuwayy. 'Well . . . yes, it was small,' he asked. 'Palm-sized, smaller than anything I've ever –'

'No, you idiot, I mean *small*, like a tack or bead!'

'What are you talking about, Jadallah?'

'The woman, the other McLanahan – she had some kind of transceiver implanted in her arm!' Zuwayy shouted. 'If this one has one too . . .'

'Then they know exactly where he is,' Fazani muttered. 'God . . . he *was* doing a probe, and he's led his forces right to us!'

'Get that transceiver off of him – I don't care if you have to cut all his limbs off!' Zuwayy shouted. 'And then evacuate this entire facility *right* –!'

And at that moment, the first explosion shook the Presidential Palace like an earthquake.

Sirens and alarms sounded everywhere. Zuwayy was immediately escorted – dragged might be more accurate – through one

418

of the myriad of escape tunnels that led from the Presidential Palace to the Ginayna, the maze of rooms, prisons, and military barracks under the city of Tripoli. He ran virtually headlong into Tahir Fazani and Juma Mahmud Hijazi, also running for their lives.

'Unidentified aircraft detected all around the city,' Fazani said to Zuwayy. 'It looks like a massive attack – perhaps the entire Egyptian air force!'

'Get to a phone and commence the rocket attack on Salimah,' Zuwayy shouted. 'I want Salimah destroyed! *Now!*'

'Forget about Salimah,' Hijazi said. 'Let's just get out of here and regroup at one of the alternate command centers.'

'I will tell the world that the Americans are conducting a preemptive, unprovoked attack on the kingdom,' Zuwayy shouted. 'I must make a television broadcast to the entire nation immediately! And I want the attack on Salimah started right *now*. I'm going to evacuate and flee the country before everything is destroyed!'

Hijazi looked at Fazani – and they made a silent agreement. 'Good idea, Jadallah,' Hijazi said carefully. 'Tahir will call in the rocket attack. But . . . before the Americans freeze all our assets and destroy our communications, I should transfer cash from the treasury to our personal accounts. I can do that from the command center. I just need your account numbers and passwords.'

'I can do that myself after I get out –'

'There's no time, Jadallah! You can't use a cell phone to call the banks, and if the Americans take down all the communications facilities, we'll be stuck. If I get your account numbers and pass codes, I can transfer funds right now.' Zuwayy hesitated. Another explosion shook the walls and sent dust sprinkling down on their heads. 'For God's sake, Jadallah, we're running out of time! Their next action will be to cut off all communications!' Hijazi handed him a pen and a pad of paper. 'Hurry, Jadallah! It could be our only chance.'

To the two henchmen's immense relief, Zuwayy scribbled something down on the pad, then handed it back to Hijazi. Hijazi tried to read his writing – it was all numbers. 'What is this, Jadallah?' he asked.

'The combination to my safe upstairs in my bedroom,' Zuwayy

replied. 'Do you think I've memorized all those bank account numbers and passwords? The numbers are locked in the safe.'

'And you didn't think of taking it with you before you ran off, Jadallah?' Hijazi asked incredulously.

'Go get it,' Fazani told him. 'I'll call in the rocket attack. Jadallah, get going – we'll be right behind you.' Zuwayy needed no more prompting to get out. Hijazi gulped fearfully but returned the way they had come.

There were only two words that could describe the performance of the Russian missiles that were loaded onto the lead EB-52 Megafortress – and those words were 'dead weight.'

'Another alignment failure message, dammit!' Kenneth 'KK' Kowalski, the mission commander aboard the lead EB-52 Megafortress, cursed. 'That's the fifth failure!' He was trying to fire one of the Kh-15 inertially guided missiles from the aft bomb bay; but like one of the Kh-27 antiradar missiles and three of the other Kh-15 missiles he tried to launch, this latest one failed as well. 'I'll power it down and bring it back up and see if it'll realign.'

'Good thing the Libyans can't seem to shoot straight,' the aircraft commander, Randall 'Fangs' Harper, commented. 'Otherwise we'd be Swiss cheese by now.' They had successfully fired two Kh-27 missiles at Libyan surface-to-air missile sites; one site was apparently destroyed, and the other shut down before the missile hit and never came back on the air again. Out of six attempts to launch Kh-15 attack missiles from the aft bomb bay, only two were successful, and of the four unsuccessful launches, they had to emergency-jettison two of them because their internal chemical batteries had overheated and threatened to blow the missiles – and the Megafortress – up with them. They had to stay at high altitude, above thirty thousand feet, to stay out of range of anti-aircraft artillery and short-range antiaircraft missiles – the Libyans even still used searchlights to try and find the bombers.

Their mission was pretty much a bust, thanks to the unreliable Russian standoff weapons – except for the FlightHawk unmanned combat aircraft. Although they were not armed, they still had enough gadgetry and magic in them to affect the outcome of this mission.

'Coming up on the release point, sixty seconds . . . now,' Kowalski announced. 'Both birds are in the green and ready.'

'It's about time something we're carrying works,' Harper mused.

At the planned launch point, Kowalski launched both FlightHawks within two minutes of each other. Their thirty-minute flights would take them on a zigzag track within ten miles either side of an ingress corridor they had planned for the second EB-52 Megafortress. The cruise missiles descended to fifteen thousand feet aboveground, powering up their turbofan engines and unfolding their wings as they fell from altitude.

The FlightHawks were small and stealthy enough that they were almost invisible to Libyan search radars. At irregular intervals along their flight, however, they would suddenly begin sending out bursts of radar and radio energy and deploying small radar reflectors that would instantly make them appear on radar as if they were the size of Boeing 747s. When the Libyan air defense radars popped on, the FlightHawks would instantly plot their position and type of system, transmit the enemy threat locations to the Megafortresses, then deactivate the reflectors and emissions to virtually disappear from radar. In just a few minutes, the FlightHawks had flushed out almost a dozen new antiaircraft threats. The tactic worked great . . .

. . . until both FlightHawks were shot down within seconds of each other, one by random, sweeping bursts of antiaircraft artillery fire, the other by a MiG-23 fighter with a radar-guided missile that had just showed up over the capital on air defense patrol.

'Zero, this is Fangs,' Harper radioed. 'Be advised, we've got bandits in the area.' He stole a glance at Kowalski's supercockpit display, which showed the entire battlefield area, along with their wingman and the inbound infantrymen, in a 'God's-eye' view. 'Closest one is at your twelve o'clock, twenty miles, high. He got one of our 'Hawks.'

'Copy, Fangs,' George 'Zero' Tanaka, the aircraft commander of the second Megafortress battleship, replied. 'We've got him. What's your status?'

'We've got a bellyful of duds now,' Kowalski replied. 'I'm going to try inflight-aligning them to see if we can't lob a few more in, but I have a feeling we're done for the day. We'll stand by at waypoint Lima in case you need any assistance.'

421

'Roger,' Tanaka said. To his mission commander, Greg 'Gonzo' Wickland, he said, 'Better check those Russian antiradar missiles – they're likely to dud on us too.'

'They're looking pretty good right now,' Wickland responded. He had reluctantly agreed to go with Tanaka on this mission – the possibility that his friend and mentor, Wendy Tork McLanahan, might still be alive down there in the heart of Libya changed his mind about being afraid of dying during a secret mission in the EB-52. 'Our first launch point is a pop-up target at two o'clock, twenty-eight miles, an SA-10 SAM site. I'll start the –'

But as Wickland watched the supercockpit display, he saw the icon representing the Libyan MiG-23 fighter turn toward them, and the green cone that represented his radar beam sweep in their direction. 'Shit, that MiG is heading our way,' Wickland interrupted himself. 'Step it down to five hundred feet and accelerate.'

'Set clearance plane five hundred, hard ride, and set four-eight-zero knots true,' Tanaka ordered the flight control computer. He carefully monitored the aircraft as the throttles advanced themselves and the terrain-following computer reset the height above ground the autopilot would continue to fly the bomber.

'He's still coming around,' Wickland said. The radar cone had changed from green to yellow – now the fighter had an azimuth-only lock-on. 'He's got us. Deploy towed array.' Behind them, one of the tiny towed array antennas unreeled itself in the bomber's slipstream. 'He's still up pretty high. Give me thirty left – let's see if he follows us.' Sure enough, the fighter turned left with the Megafortress, but his range did not increase. Every now and then the radar cone depiction on the supercockpit display flashed red – that meant the fighter's radar switched into range mode, the last measurement needed before missile launch – but it never stayed on very long. 'He's hanging out there at eleven miles, matching our airspeed, and just hitting us with his ranging radar long enough to keep up,' Wickland said. 'He's not letting our trackbreakers get a chance to wipe out his picture.'

'Waiting for instructions?' Tanaka asked.

'Give me forty right, nice shallow bank,' Wickland said. 'Let's see how aggressive he is.'

*   *   *

422

'But I have a target! I have another unknown aircraft at my twelve o'clock, seventeen kilometers, very low!' the pilot of the Libyan MiG-23 shouted.

'*Hibr* flight, you are ordered to return to patrol altitude and proceed north to intercept inbound aircraft!' the ground radar controller shouted again. 'And you do not have permission to open fire!'

The Libyan pilot whipped off his oxygen mask in frustration. 'I tell you, Control, there are numerous enemy aircraft out here!' he shouted again. 'I am tracking one now, and there were one, maybe two others up here as well. I think Tripoli is under attack from the south!'

'You are ordered to proceed immediately to point *Amm* and intercept and identify unknown aircraft inbound toward the capital!' the ground controller said. 'Backup aircraft are being prepared now. Proceed immediately!'

The MiG-23 pilot had no choice. No ground radars had picked up these low-flying bandits. Aircraft north of the city could mean anything – inbound passenger airliners, cargo planes, anything but an attacker. Low-flying unidentified aircraft weaving and jinking around south of the city could mean only one thing: enemy aircraft. But the controller was telling him to chase the target he could see. He was an idiot – but he had complete authority, too.

He angrily jammed his throttles forward and yanked the stick hard right, zooming northward. He didn't even think of his wingman, trailing to his right and slightly higher – he hoped he was paying attention and didn't get fried as his leader cut right in front of him.

It took only four minutes for the pair of MiG-23s to reach the intercept anchor point. '*Hibr* flight, proceed on heading three-zero-zero. Your bogey will be at your twelve o'clock, range fifty K, descending through four thousand meters.'

'Acknowledged, Control,' the pilot said. 'How about sending some fighters up to track down the bogeys I found near Kadra?' No response from the controller – he couldn't see any targets down south of the city, so he wasn't going to send any planes there.

'*Hibr* flight, bogey at your twelve o'clock, forty-five K, still descending, now through three point five K meters. Report when tied on.'

The MiG-23 flight leader activated his intercept radar and found the aircraft almost instantly – it was a solid radar lock-on, not weak and intermittent like the other one. '*Hibr* flight has a bogey at my twelve o'clock, forty-two K meters range, three point zero K meters altitude.' He keyed two switches on the instrument panel near the throttle that sent out coded interrogation signals. 'Negative mode two, mode C, and mode four IFF.'

'That's your bandit, *Hibr* flight.'

The target was in a shallow descent, heading right for Tripoli at close to six hundred kilometers per hour. Every now and then it would make a sudden move – a sharper descent, a fast turn one direction or the other, and at one time it even appeared to be doing a one-eighty. Large bombers needed to transfer alignment maneuvers for inertially guided air-launched weapons – maybe that's what this aircraft was doing. But one thing was for sure: It was definitely heading for Tripoli, and it was unidentified.

The rules said shoot it down.

'*Hibr* two, take tactical spacing,' the leader called to his wingman.

'Acknowledged.'

The lead MiG-23 pilot flew above and past the target, then started a rapid left descending turn that quickly brought him right on the bandit's right rear quarter. The aircraft had no exterior lights whatsoever, and no lights were visible on the side of the fuselage either – definitely not an airliner. He moved in close enough so he could clearly see the outline of the plane against the growing brightness of the horizon as Tripoli came closer and closer; then he turned on his identification spotlight.

'Control, *Hibr* flight has visual identification,' the leader radioed. 'Bandit is a DC-10 aircraft. It has a US registration number, N-three-oh-three Sierra Mike. I see no weapons or any unusual protrusions or devices. The aircraft is completely dark, and . . . Stand by, Control.' The pilot slid forward, letting the searchlight shine in the copilot's side of the cockpit. 'Control, it appears the bandit's right cockpit sliding window is open, and there appears to be smoke trailing out from the window, repeat, the bandit seems to be venting smoke from his cockpit. Smoke is also trailing from what appears to be an open cockpit escape hatch. There are only flashlight beams in the cockpit – no lights whatsoever. This aircraft may be having an inflight emergency. If he has shut off all aircraft power, that could be the reason why he has not responded to us and why he has no lights on.'

'*Hibr* flight, be advised, *Suf* flight of four and *Kheyma* flight of two are joining on you, ETE three minutes.'

'Control, I don't need any more fighters up here,' the leader said perturbedly. 'This is a commercial aircraft with what appears to be an inflight emergency. He's not a combat aircraft. I think I can get him turned away from the coast myself – I don't need six more fighters in the area. Have those extra planes go look for the bogeys I found south of Tripoli.' But his suggestion went unheeded.

Within minutes there were three different kinds of jets buzzing around the stricken American-registered cargo plane: *Hibr* flight of two MiG-23s, *Suf* flight of four MiG-29s, and *Kheyma* flight of two MiG-25s. The problem was, no one could decide exactly what to do about this intruder. He was obviously a noncombatant, and he was obviously in trouble. They tried light signals, but it wasn't clear if their searchlights were penetrating the smoke in the cockpit. They couldn't see inside, and it was obvious no one in the cockpit could see out.

Finally the MiG-23 flight leader switched his number two radio to the international UHF emergency frequency: 'Unidentified American cargo plane, this is *Hibr* flight of two of the United Kingdom of Libya Royal Air Force. You are in restricted airspace and in violation of Libyan law. You are ordered to reverse course immediately. I say again, reverse course immediately or you will be attacked.'

There was no answer. The flight leader repeated the message on the VHF GUARD emergency frequency; still no response. He was about to switch back to his controller's frequency to request permission to open fire when he heard a scratchy, frightened voice say, 'I hear you, Libyan fighters! I hear you! This is November three-oh-three Sierra Mike on VHF GUARD channel. I am on a handheld emergency radio. Mayday, mayday, mayday, can you hear me, Libyan air force?'

'I can hear you, Three Sierra Mike,' the flight leader replied. 'You must reverse course immediately! In ten kilometers you will enter restricted Libyan airspace, and we will attack. Reverse course immediately! Acknowledge!'

'This is Three Sierra Mike, we have a catastrophic fire in the cockpit and we were forced to evacuate the cockpit. The aircraft is on autopilot, and we are trying to put the fire out. As soon as we put the fire out we can retake control of the plane. Don't shoot! We are a cargo plane. We're carrying relief supplies bound for Khartoum, Sudan, on an international flight plan. We have twenty-two relief workers on board plus a crew of five. Give us time to get the fire out. Over.'

'Three Sierra Mike, you are flying into restricted Libyan airspace during a time of severe emergency flight restrictions,' the flight leader said. 'This is a wartime situation. If you do not reverse course in two minutes, I will have no choice but to open fire. You must do everything you can to reverse course or at least stay out over the Gulf of Sidra. I will be forced to open fire if you do not comply.'

'Please, for God's sake, don't shoot!' the pilot cried. 'We'll have control of our plane in less than two minutes! Please, stand by!'

'Think he's for real, lead?' the wingman radioed.

'I know I'd have a tough time if my cockpit was filled with smoke like that,' the flight leader said. 'We'll wait until he crosses the twenty-kilometer mark, then open fire if he doesn't turn away.'

It seemed to take forever – the big American plane was definitely slowing down. The other Libyan fighters circled, jockeyed around, and generally tried their best to fly night-staggered formation with the crippled American plane. No one departed – all the pilots wanted to watch when *Hibr* lead fired his missile and brought the big plane down.

Tripoli Air Defense Control confirmed the orders moments later: shoot to kill if the plane crosses the twenty-kilometer ring.

'Three Sierra Mike, this is *Hibr* flight, you are ordered to turn away now,' the flight leader radioed. 'I am ordered to shoot you down if you do not comply. This is your last warning.' He then angled upward, clearing the DC-10's powerful wake, and started to maneuver behind the big plane. The lights of Tripoli were brilliant, filling the horizon below – he was afraid that maybe he was too late, that twenty kilometers was still too close. Even if the plane was hit, could it still glide on fire and hit the city?

At that moment, the smoke stopped streaming out of the DC-10's cockpit, and the big plane started a slow ten-degree bank turn to the left. It took almost ninety seconds, but finally the big plane was heading away from Tripoli. It was just thirty seconds – about three kilometers – away from the flight leader pressing the button on his control stick that would send the DC-10 crashing to earth.

'Too bad, *Hibr* flight,' one of the other pilots radioed. 'We thought you'd finally get a chance to hit something this time.'

It wasn't funny, the lead pilot thought – he was *sure* that this was nothing but a feint for an attack from the south. This plane had managed to draw off nearly all of Libya's alert fighter patrols away from the capital. *Something* was not right here. . .

'*Suf* and *Kheyma* flights, this is *Hibr* lead. I'm getting close to bingo fuel,' the flight leader radioed. '*Hibr* flight is going to depart the formation and head to base. Escort this bastard out of our airspace.'

'You got it,' one of the other pilots said. '*Suf* flight has the lead. We'll stay in formation with the American until he's well away.' The leader of the flight of two MiG-23s descended to five hundred meters below the American cargo plane, then turned south; a few moments later, his wingman was in loose fingertip formation.

'*Hibr* flight, this is Control. Understand you are declaring bingo fuel at this time.'

'Negative, Control,' the flight leader said. 'We're twenty minutes from bingo. I want vectors to the last position of those unidentified radar contacts south of Tripoli.'

'Cut it kind of close, didn't you?' the DC-10's flight engineer asked as he removed his emergency firefighting mask. He collected the empty casings of the smoke signal flares he had been shooting out the window and put them in an empty canvas survival bag. 'That fighter departed to get behind us to shoot our asses down, didn't he?'

The pilot of the DC-10 rechecked that the pressurization system was indeed pumping the cabin back up and that his side storm window was securely closed. 'It wasn't enough time,' he said. 'Our guys needed another five minutes.'

'Maybe we can turn back in – keep the fighters around for a little while longer?'

'I think we used up all our lucky charms on that last stunt,' the pilot said. 'Those Libyan bastards could've pulled the trigger just to see what color the fire would've been as we plummeted to earth – we're not going to risk twisting the tiger's tail again. It's the bomber's turn now – we did our job.' He switched to the command channel and spoke: 'Headbangers, this is Three Sierra Mike, we've made our turn northbound. We kept eight bandits with us as long as we could. Good luck.'

'We copy, Sierra Mike,' George 'Zero' Tanaka responded. 'Thanks for the assist.'

The second EB-52 Megafortress, with Tanaka and Wickland back at the controls, swept in at low altitude over the rolling sand- and rock-covered hills of southern Tripoli inbound toward the Presidential Palace. Wickland's supercockpit display was a nightmarish presentation of destruction: Every Libyan air defense site discovered by the FlightHawks was highlighted, and the route of flight adjusted accordingly. Because they had no standoff weapons – both of their Kh-27 antiradar missiles worked, but they had to expend both of them early on the inbound run because so few sites had been taken down by the first Megafortress – they were forced to zigzag in between the threat computer's guesstimate of each site's lethal radius.

'Coming up on a right turn, thirty degrees of bank, ready, ready . . . now,' Wickland said, and the modified B-52 Stratofortress bomber banked hard in response. 'We've got a ZSU-57-2 site at our nine o'clock, seven miles.' Wickland glanced out the cockpit just as the radar-guided twin-barreled fifty-seven-millimeter anti-aircraft artillery guns opened fire – their jammers and track-breakers did not even need to jam the Libyan radar because they were well out of range. Tracers fluttered through the air in eerie snakelike patterns across the sky – a few rounds twisted in their direction, but most of the rounds were behind them as the site's radar locked onto the countermeasures array towed behind the

Megafortress. 'Coming up on a hard left turn, forty degrees of bank . . . now.' It was like being on an indoor roller coaster.

Wickland activated the laser radar arrays for two seconds to take a snapshot of the sky and earth surrounding them. 'Those fighters are headed this way,' he said. 'First flight of MiGs is north of us at forty-three miles, coming in hard. The other two flights of MiGs are still heading north with the DC-10 . . . and now we got another flight of three MiGs lifting off from Mitiga Airfield, one o'clock, eighteen miles. They'll be on top of us in no time.'

'How are we doing on the bomb run?' Tanaka asked.

'Thirty seconds to the first target,' Wickland responded. 'This will be a pull-up push-over release on an SA-3 site. I need full military power for this release.'

'You already got it.'

'All trackbreakers and jammers active. Acquisition radar at eleven o'clock, eight miles.' Wickland magnified the last LADAR image of the target area. This SA-3 site consisted of four quadruple-missile fixed launchers with a trailer-mounted long-range radar and another trailer-mounted fire-control radar, all in a five-acre hand-shaped site. The Megafortress's attack computers programmed the coordinates of the center of the "hand" and the "thumb," where the radars and control systems were located. At the exact point as directed by the attack computer, the rear bomb doors opened and retracted inward, and the Megafortress began a steep climb.

'Warning, SA-3 target tracking mode,' the threat warning computer blared.

'Trackbreakers active . . .'

'Warning, missile launch, SA-3 uplink!' The threat computers automatically ejected decoy chaff and flares, and the jamming signals coming from the towed array came on continuously.

'C'mon, baby, toss those suckers!'

The Megafortress nosed over, then began a hard left bank. At the very apex of the roller-coaster-like arc, the attack computer released two one-thousand-pound high-explosive bombs from the rotary launcher. Like the last kid in a 'crack-the-whip' line, the bombs sailed out of the bomb bay with such force that they flew nearly three miles through the air. Just as two SA-3 missiles streaked from their launcher, the bombs hit, destroying the fire-control radar with an almost direct hit.

The first missile self-destructed seconds after launch when it lost its uplink signal; the second missile was able to switch to command line-of-sight guidance signals from the SA-3 long-range radar. Fortunately, the long-range radar was locked onto the towed countermeasures array, not the Megafortress itself, and the blast from the second missile's one-hundred-and-thirty-pound warhead destroyed the towed array – well over two hundred feet behind the bomber. The Megafortress's jammers completely shut down the long-range search radars and defeated a second two-round missile volley launched moments later.

The Megafortress made another hard left turn, correcting on course, dropping six air-retarded cluster bomb canisters on a power substation at the periphery of the palace grounds before making a hard right turn back toward the Presidential Palace. Wickland ordered a climb to one thousand feet, then sixty seconds later released another stick of six cluster bomb dispensers on the security guard barracks and headquarters outside the palace gates. The last releases were virtually simultaneous: two gravity bombs on the front gates themselves, the last stick of cluster bombs on the entryway to the palace, and two more gravity bombs on the palace itself.

The Megafortress then continued eastbound, passing right over Matiga Airfield, the old American Wheelus Air Force Base on the eastern side of the city. Antiaircraft artillery units fired into the sky all around them, but the Megafortress's jammers and track-breakers kept any of the radar-guided heavier-caliber units from locking in on them. The final bomb run was right across the center of the airfield, dropping the remaining gravity bombs on the runway, radar facility, and control tower, then seeding cluster bombs throughout the aircraft parking areas. Almost a dozen air-craft of all kinds, from fighters to cargo planes to helicopters, were destroyed.

'Set clearance plane COLA,' Tanaka ordered. The Megafortress turned sharply northward away from the coast, but Tanaka had to override the autopilot because it appeared they turned right toward a large Libyan warship in the Gulf of Sidra.

'We've got company,' Wickland said. 'MiG-23s, coming in fast, seven o'clock, eleven miles.' At that same instant, they received another warning: 'Missile launch, SA-N-8 from that Libyan warship!' The threat defense computers ejected chaff and flares, and the Megafortress did a hard right break back toward the coast near Ed Dachla. The naval surface-to-air missile exploded less than a hundred feet off their left side, violently shaking the big bomber.

'I think we got some fuel leaks from the left wing, and we're losing pressurization,' Tanaka reported. 'I've also got a fault on the left ruddervator trim system.'

'We got a "MISSILE HOT" light on the left weapon pylon,' Wickland said. He acknowledged the fault, but by then the weapons computer had ejected first the left pylon and its remaining air-to-air missiles, and then the right pylon to balance out the aircraft. 'There goes the last of our heaters.' He checked the supercockpit display. 'I think we're clear of that ship, but the fighters are coming in hot,' he said. 'Let's continue southeast. We'll try to make it to the Cussabat Mountains – the MiGs may not be able to find us there.'

But they were too late. The first MiG-23 moved in almost at the speed of sound and fired a heat-seeking missile from point-blank range. The Megafortress detected the missile launch and immediately initiated a right break, ejecting chaff and flares from the left ejectors. The combination of the decoys and the active laser countermeasures system steered the missile away from a direct hit, but the Russian-made R-60 missile exploded just ahead of the left wingtip.

'Shit, we lost the entire left wingtip!' Tanaka shouted. The vibration coming from the left wing was tremendous – it felt as if the entire wing was going to snap right off. 'I've got to slow down or we'll lose the whole wing!'

'The second MiG coming in fast!'

'Stinger airmines!' Tanaka shouted. 'Blast that sucker!'

But the second MiG-23 was already firing its twenty-three-millimeter cannon as the airmines were launched, and the bullets hit first: Warning messages flashed on all of the multi-function displays in the Megafortress's cockpit. Wickland looked out his window and saw the number-four engine throwing off tongues of flames and flashes of fire. 'Oh, Jesus!' he shouted. 'We're hit!'

'Just make sure you smoke that MiG!' Tanaka shouted. He kept his eyes flying over the system readouts, hands on the controls and throttles and his feet on the rudder pedals, ready in an instant to take over if the Megafortress's flight computer didn't immediately respond. But the computer was in charge for now: By the time the warning messages had flashed on the screens, the computers had already shut down the number-four engine, discharged the fire extinguishers, isolated the hydraulic, pneumatic, electrical, and fuel systems to that engine, and had reconfigured all of the aircraft systems to take up the load from the destroyed engine.

'The second MiG is breaking away,' Wickland said, checking the supercockpit display. 'I think we got –' He stopped when the computer issued a fresh warning: 'The first MiG is heading for us again. Nine o'clock, eight miles and closing fast.' A moment later: 'Another MiG inbound, six o'clock, twenty-five miles. Both are locked on.' With a shut-down and shattered number-four engine, the radar cross-section of the normally very stealthy Megafortress was multiplied a hundred times, making it an easy target.

Tanaka started a hard right turn. 'We're going to have to take them over the desert,' he said. 'No other way to do it.' He looked over at his partner. 'Make sure your straps are tight, Gonzo. Put your clear visor down and zip your jacket all the way up.' Wickland looked as if he was going to shrivel up and die as he hurriedly pulled his shoulder and lap belts as tight as he could stand, his hands shaking uncontrollably.

They had not quite finished their turn when the computer reported, *'Warning, radar lock MiG-23, two o'clock, fifteen miles . . . warning, missile launch, MiG-23 R-24 . . . missile launch, MiG-23, R-24.'*

'Jammers and countermeasures active,' Wickland said tonelessly. 'Active laser countermeasures firing . . . decoys out . . .' Everything had to work perfectly now – they were well outside their absconded Libyan air-to-air missile's range. Tanaka started up and down jinks, trying to get the radar-guided missiles to overcorrect and overshoot their target. For a moment Wickland thought he could see the missiles heading toward him, but he knew that was impossible – traveling at night over three times the speed of sound, the naked eye could never see them. His hands closed over the handles of his ejection seat.

'Don't wait for my order,' he heard Tanaka say. 'If the missiles hit, just go. Don't wait for me. Don't wait . . .' And just then, Wickland saw a tremendous burst of light and a huge fireball blossom directly in front of him. His fingers tightened on the lever and he began to rotate them upward, exposing the ejection initiation trigger. . .

Central Libya
a short time later

Within a few minutes after receiving the call from Tripoli, the crews aboard two dozen mobile SS-12 missiles, armed with a variety of warheads – ranging from one-thousand-pound high-explosive to chemical to subatomic neutron – prepared their missiles for launch. Within five minutes of receiving the final launch order, one by one, the rockets lifted off into the dawn sky on columns of fire.

'*Giant zero! Giant zero!* Rockets detected!' the mission commander aboard the second AL-52 Dragon reported. After refueling, the Dragon had gone on patrol over west-central Egypt, covering both the Salimah oil fields and Cairo from any rockets launched from Libya.

Long before the mission commander even keyed the microphone, the most sophisticated computer system ever placed aboard any aircraft was already prosecuting the attack. The mission commander merely watched in fascination as the chemicals they carried in the tail section of the plane mixed and created their magic, and the Dragon came to life once again. The crew watched through the telescopic optics as the SS-12 rocket was blown apart by the COIL laser.

'Yeah, baby, *yeah*!' the mission commander crowed. 'We got it!' The LADAR warning system bleeped again as more SS-12 rockets were detected. But one by one, the AL-52 Dragon aircraft detected and attacked every SS-12 that rose out of the desert.

As it attacked each one, coordinates of the launch points were transmitted to US Air Force B-2 Spirit stealth bombers orbiting over southern Libya and northern Chad. The coordinates of the launchers were instantly programmed into satellite-guided AGM-158A standoff missiles, which were launched from well over one hundred miles away within moments after the rockets were

433

launched. The missiles, called the Joint Air-to-Surface Standoff Missile, carried a one-thousand-pound high-explosive warhead and an infrared terminal seeker. The missile flew toward the rocket's launch point, detected the red-hot launcher and support trucks with its heat-seeking terminal sensor, and destroyed them with pinpoint accuracy.

Over southern Tripoli, Libya
that same time

'Wait!' Tanaka shouted, pulling Wickland's hand carefully away from the ejection handle. 'That wasn't the missile!' The fireball became a fat comet, arcing across the night sky. Seconds later, a second fireball appeared, this one spinning crazily across the horizon like a burning tumbleweed blown across a prairie. 'What the hell . . . ?'

'Yo, Zero,' a voice came over the long-forgotten command radio channel. 'Is that you out there?'

'Bud? Is that you?'

'Roger that,' John 'Bud' Franken, at the command of the second, improved AL-52 Dragon aircraft, replied. 'Looks like we got here right on time. What's your status?'

'We're short one engine and we have a few more holes now than we did at takeoff,' Tanaka said, 'but we're still flying. Can you clear our six for us so we can get the hell out of here?'

'Roger that,' Bud Franken replied. He turned to Lindsey Reeves in the mission commander's seat. 'You got them, Linds?'

Lindsey Reeves, Franken's mission commander, checked her supercockpit display. The LADAR attack computer already highlighted the fighters for her – both of them were converging on the crippled Megafortress bomber. 'Got 'em!' she crowed. 'Nine o'clock, sixty miles, heading northeast at six hundred knots, one thousand feet AGL.'

'Let's see what this baby can do,' Franken said. 'Light 'em up, Linds.'

Reeves touched the MiGs' icon on her display, then said, 'Attack Dragon' into the voice-command computer.

434

'*Attack commit Dragon, stop attack,*' the attack computer responded. A few moments later, capacitors in the rear fuselage started receiving and storing power from the aircraft's generators. At the same time, the deformable mirror turret in the nose unstowed and pointed itself at the Libyan fighters. When all of the capacitors reported full, the attack computer reported, '*Laser ready.*'

'Laser commit,' Lindsey said.

Franken flipped his consent switch. 'Go get 'em, kiddo.' Lindsey did the same on her side.

'*Laser commit, stop attack,*' the computer reported.

The laser radar system tracked and measured the target, then also sampled the atmosphere at the target and sent corrective and focusing instructions to the deformable mirror. At the same instant, the capacitors in the rear of the aircraft started pumping massive waves of energy into the plasma generators. Four hundred diode lasers focused laser light onto the center of a small aluminum chamber, burning a pellet of deuterium-tritium fuel the size of a grain of sand, creating a ball of deuterium-tritium-enhanced gas. Confined and heated by the lasers and now weighing thousands of pounds, the superheated ball of gas quickly reached a temperature of one hundred million degrees Celsius – ten times hotter than the surface of the sun. At that temperature, the atoms of deuterium and tritium were blasted apart, creating a mixture of free electrons and ions – also known as plasma. The plasma field lasted for only a millionth of a second; three other plasma generators acted in series to generate an almost continuous wave of plasma energy.

Corralled and steered by a magnetic waveguide chamber, the plasma field, more powerful than all the nuclear explosions ever created but existing for only a few trillionths of a second, pounded into the laser generator chamber, where the massive pulse of energy excited thousands of glass disks containing neodymium, a rare earth element. The plasma energy stripped the neodymium atoms off the glass, creating an immensely powerful pulse of light. The light was reflected into the Faraday oscillator, which bounced the light back and forth between cooled mirrors until the light was in perfect synchronization, then fired it out into the laser waveguide. An amplifier intensified the beam even more, and spatial filters focused the beam down to a tiny spot, then expanded the beam to three feet in diameter, where it was projected onto the deformable mirror, then reflected into space.

In the cockpit, it was anticlimactic – there was no loud hum, no recoil, and no sound at all except for the faint vibration of the turret moving as it tracked the target. Lindsey did receive some warning indications dealing with the plasma generators. The plasma generators were in effect plasma-yield weapon warheads, capable of destroying all matter around them for hundreds of feet in all directions – the explosion was simply controlled and shortened into pulses contained by magnetic fields. They were setting off thousands of plasma-yield explosions every second in the back of the AL-52 aircraft – not exactly a safe or secure situation. The technology was very new, virtually untested, and in rough design stage only – they had few safety devices installed simply because they did not have enough information on what the really dangerous subsystems were. The whole system was a hazard.

But despite the warning messages, Lindsey let the laser sequence go – and in the next few seconds, history was made.

The laser beam that hit the first Libyan MiG-23 fighter was akin to a blowtorch against a stick of butter – the fighter's fuselage was not merely melted, but vaporized at the same instant. The beam focused on the fattest section of the aircraft – the fuselage between the wings, containing the midbody fuel tank, the fighter's largest fuel tank. The superheated metal ignited the three thousand gallons of vaporized jet fuel in the blink of an eye, creating a fireball over a mile in diameter that swallowed the fighter and sent burning clouds of fire spreading across the night sky like a man-made aurora borealis. The explosion was plainly visible from over one hundred and fifty miles away.

'Lost contact,' Lindsey said matter-of-factly, still monitoring the laser engagement on her supercockpit display.

'My God,' Bud Franken gasped, dropping his mask in surprise. 'We did it. We nailed it.' He had to pull himself back into the present – he was astonished, thinking of the power of this incredible weapon. They were over sixty miles away from the target. In one instant, the image of the MiG-23 fighter, magnified by the laser's telescope and deformable mirror, was sharp and clear – the next instant it was gone, lost in a ball of superheated gas. There was almost no debris – nothing except a wave of fire quickly dissipating in the sky. 'Let's tag that last fighter.'

'Attack target Dragon,' Lindsey repeated, touching the screen again. Seconds later the second MiG disappeared from their screens as well.

'Zero, this is Bud, splash two fighters,' Franken said. 'Your tail is clear. Clear to head to the rendezvous point. We can cover you almost until you reach Israeli airspace.'

As they watched the EB-52 retreat to the northeast, to rendezvous with the DC-10 tanker for its refueling anchor, Reeves also monitored another aircraft – this one a small, slow one, flying at barely treetop level, across the sands toward southeast Tripoli. This aircraft was datalinking its threat receiver information to the AL-52 Dragon, and now a pop-up threat displayed itself on Lindsey's supercockpit display. 'The MV-22 has got an SA-10 at his twelve o'clock, thirty miles,' Wickland said. 'His signal is pretty strong – he'll get within detection threshold in less than five miles.' On the command channel, he radioed, 'Motorboat, this is Dragon, you've got a threat ahead that's locking on you. Reverse course.'

'Can you tag him, Dragon?' the pilot of the MV-22 Pave Hammer tilt-rotor aircraft asked.

'Stand by,' Franken replied. He turned to his young mission commander. 'Can you get him, Linds?'

'I'm slaving on him now,' Reeves said. She slaved the laser's telescope to the threat location datalinked from the MV-22. 'I got the command vehicle,' she said happily. She moved the target cursor from the radar dish itself to the command cab, located on the back of the same vehicle. 'Let's see what happens –'

But before she could commit, their threat receiver changed from a 'SEARCH' warning to a 'LOCK' warning and instantly to a 'MISSILE LAUNCH' warning. 'SA-10 in the air!' Wickland shouted.

'Reverse course, Motorboat,' Franken said. 'Full countermeasures.' To Reeves he said, 'Nab that sucker, Linds!'

Lindsey Reeves had already switched from slaving mode to the laser radar, and the system instantly picked up the two incoming SA-10 missiles. 'Got the SAMs,' she said. 'Attack SA-10 missiles Dragon.'

'*Warning, plasma generator number three not ready,*' the computer spoke.

'What does that mean, "not ready"?' Franken asked.

'We've gotten several warning messages from about a dozen different components of the laser,' Reeves said, 'but I've bypassed them all. I think the plasma generator vessels are becoming too hot, both from the heat of the fusion reaction and the stray radiation leakage impregnating the aluminum. The magnetic fields can't contain all the particles, and it weakens the reactor vessel.'

Franken checked the supercockpit display. 'We've got no choice now, Linds,' he said. 'If a reactor fails, we jettison it and we're done for the day.'

'I agree,' Reeves said. To the computer she said, 'Deactivate generator number three, reset warning, and attack Dragon.'

'*Laser commit, stop attack,*' the computer replied. '*Caution, plasma generator number one overtemp, stop attack.*' Computer cautions did not require an override: Lindsey simply remained silent, and the computer processed the attack. Seconds later both SA-10 missiles were destroyed, and Reeves turned her attention back to the saved set of coordinates for the SA-10 command vehicle. 'C'mon, baby,' she said. 'Show me what you got.'

The laser radar system couldn't fully compensate for the massive atmospheric distortion caused by shooting down through the atmosphere – but this time, it didn't need to. The plasma laser beam could only focus down to two feet in diameter – but with over two megawatts' worth of power, it was enough. The laser instantly burned through the dielectric fiberglass panel covering the face of the phased array radar, melted several hundred emitter arrays underneath, then burned clear through the thin metal radar structure. The beam stayed on target long enough to weaken the steel supporting the radar, and the radar collapsed backward against the command cab, knocking the entire unit out of commission.

'Oh, man,' Lindsey gasped. 'The radar's down . . . I mean, it's *down*, on top of the command cab. We just destroyed a ground vehicle with a laser fired from an airplane.'

As the MV-22 continued toward its objective – the presidential palace in Tripoli – the AL-52 Dragon moved farther west until it was in a patrol orbit north of Tripoli. There were fighters everywhere, but Lindsey dared not use the laser to shoot at any of them – she had no idea what it would do. She could do nothing but stay in orbit, watch the last aircraft in their attack formation make its way in to the target, and wait.

But minutes later, just as the MV-22 had lined up for its final few miles to its objective, Lindsey expanded her supercockpit display and took another laser radar snapshot. 'I've got a formation of two enemy aircraft, MiG-25s, twelve o'clock, thirty miles from Motorboat and closing, descending, speed eight hundred forty knots,' Lindsey reported. 'I've got a *second* formation of aircraft right behind them – my God, they're MiG-29s, four MiG-29s. I'm not sure if the laser will get them all.'

'Bud, can you keep these guys off us until we make it to the infil point?'

'I'd bug out if I were you,' Franken responded. 'We're getting continuous faults on the laser, and we've already lost one generator.'

'Give us thirty seconds and we'll be outta here,' the pilot of the MV-22 aircraft said. 'Keep 'em off us for as long as you can.'

'No promises, boys,' Franken said. To Lindsey Reeves: 'What's it look like, Linds?'

'Pretty bad – we should be bugging out of here ourselves,' Reeves replied. 'I'm getting overtemp warnings on the plasma generators even though the system isn't powered on, and I think the heat is affecting the magnetron that channels the plasma field into the laser generators. If the magnetic field's not strong enough, and the plasma field touches the inertial confinement chamber before the reaction stops – we'll be turned into stardust in a millisecond.'

'Roger that,' Franken replied. On the command channel: 'Sorry, boys, but I suggest you bug out now – we'll use the last bit of juice we have left in the laser to cover your retreat.'

'Twenty seconds, Dragon. Fifteen.'

'Lindsey . . .'

'We're pushing it, Bud – but okay.' She touched the icons for the MiG-25 fighters, then spoke: 'Attack commit Dragon.'

'Warning, overtemp on plasma generator number one . . . caution, magnetron voltage approaching tolerance limit . . . caution, overtemp on plasma generator number two.'

'Override overtemp warning and attack.'

'Warning, magnetron voltage at tolerance . . .'

Franken looked over at his young mission commander. No sign of airsickness this time – she was all business, steady and focused. 'Override all magnetron warnings and attack,' Lindsey said.

'Warning, plasma containment –'

'Override *all* warnings and attack!' Lindsey shouted.

'Attack commit Dragon, MiG-25, stop attack.'

Suddenly there was a deep, high-pitched vibration coming from the back of the AL-52 Dragon, so great that Franken had to take a firmer grip on the control stick. He was about to order her to stop the laser from firing, but at that moment she announced, 'MiG one destroyed.' But the vibration didn't stop – in fact, it was getting worse.

'Lindsey –'

'Attack commit Dragon,' she announced.

'Warning –'

'Override all warnings and attack,' she ordered.

'Lindsey –'

'Attack commit Dragon, stop attack,' the computer warned.

The vibration was getting worse – finally, Lindsey was starting to notice it. 'What is that?' she asked.

'Eject,' Franken said flatly.

'What?'

'I said eject!' Franken shouted.

'I'm getting this second MiG,' Lindsey said.

'No!' Franken shouted. But at that moment the laser fired, and the second MiG-25 bearing down on the MV-22 disappeared in a cloud of fire.

The vibration was louder and harder now, so hard that Franken had trouble taking a normal breath. He had to force the air out of his lungs to scream, *'Eject! Eject! Eject!'*

All aircrew personnel at Sky Masters Inc had extensive training in aircrew survival, including twice-a-year ejection seat qualification. Lindsey Reeves was not prior military, like John Franken, but she had been so thoroughly indoctrinated by Patrick McLanahan and his staff that every flying scientist was as thoroughly familiar with aircrew survival procedures as their military counterparts.

She did hesitate when he said it once – every crew member has a moment of disbelief when they hear that word. But the real command to eject was the word 'Eject' three times. So when Franken gave the proper command to eject, Lindsey Reeves didn't hesitate again. She sat back in her seat, pressed her head, back and butt as deeply into the seat as she could, jammed her heels back, kept her elbows in tight, tucked her chin down, rotated the ejection handles upward, and squeezed the exposed triggers. Her overhead hatch ripped away, and the seat disappeared in a cloud of gray-blue smoke that disappeared in the sudden vacuum as quickly as it appeared, replaced by a cold fog and an impossibly loud roar of wind.

'Hope you make it okay, kiddo,' Franken said into his oxygen mask. He entered some commands into the attack computer – a complete system data dump, sending the entire mission's worth of stored system information to a satellite, where the engineers at Sky Masters Inc could retrieve and analyze it. That was something Lindsey would do, if he had given her a chance to do it. She turned out to be a pretty good crewdog, Franken decided – she overcame her fear and nearly debilitating airsickness enough to take an untested warplane into combat halfway around the world. Amazing. The least he could do for her was to make sure that everything she worked and sacrificed so long and hard to build survived.

There were dozens of warning and caution indications on the instrument panel, but Franken no longer cared. He turned the AL-52 Megafortress north, toward the oncoming MiG-29 fighters. At this closure rate – the MiGs were flying at almost twice the speed of sound to catch the MV-22 – he would catch them in no time.

Sure enough, Franken could actually see two bright flashes of light, then two more, as the lead MiGs fired air-to-air missiles. He saw the four streaks of fire arc across the sky – but suddenly the sky seemed to brighten, as if dawn was approaching, but at ten times the normal speed. The dawn then seemed to turn silvery and warm.

The Dragon, the four missiles, and then all four MiG-29 interceptors disappeared in an uncontrolled plasma field that had formed, expanded to nearly ten miles in diameter, engulfed its prey in a cloud of free electrons and ions, and then disappeared without a trace – all in the space of a few millionths of a second.

'Bud, this is Zero. Is our tail clear? We're losing our electronic countermeasures system. What's your status?' No reply. 'Where are they, Gonzo?'

'No sign of 'em,' Wickland replied.

'What?' Tanaka switched one of his multifunction displays to the LADAR tactical view. There were no aircraft at all within fifty miles. 'Oh shit, they're gone. All of them – the fighters and the Dragon. They must've taken each other out.'

'They're *dead*?' Both men fell silent. Then Wickland checked his display again. 'Holy shit – a target in the air, but almost hovering. I'm getting another LADAR shot.' Wickland activated the laser radar again, then magnified the new target. Neither of them could believe their eyes – it was the first time they had ever seen something like this on a laser radar display. 'My God, it's a parachute! Someone in a parachute! I can't believe it! What do we do? What *can* we do?'

'We turn around and follow it down, then hope there are some friendlies we can send into the area in case it's one of ours,' Tanaka said. 'I have a feeling it's one of our guys – judging by how slow it's going down, I'll bet it's Lindsey Reeves. At this rate, she'll be falling all night. My God, I wonder what went wrong . . .'

Over the Presidential Palace, Tripoli, United Kingdom of Libya that same time

'Twenty right,' Hal Briggs said. The pilot of the MV-22 Pave Hammer tilt-rotor assault aircraft banked in response. Briggs was studying the data display on the electronic visor of his Tin Man battle armor's helmet, watching the range and bearing of his objective countdown as they flew closer. They had followed the clear path of destruction created by the second Megafortress and had zoomed in at treetop level right to the Presidential Palace, virtually unmolested. 'Five more right . . . hold it. Range point four hundred meters . . . three hundred . . . steady at three hundred . . . steady at three hundred.'

'Matches range to the rooftop,' the copilot reported, checking the range straight ahead displayed on his targeting visor. After checking the range, he switched his targeting visor to slave the chin turret and infrared sensor and used the twenty-millimeter Gatling gun in the turret to force down any small-arms fire from security units on the roof he could see.

'Make a couple holes,' Briggs said. 'Night Stalkers, stand by.'

The pilot activated his weapons panel and selected 'HELLFIRE.' Two weapons pods unstowed themselves from the left and right landing gear sponsons. He activated the missiles and squeezed a trigger. One Hellfire laser-guided missile from each weapon pod shot out from its canister, and together the missiles and their twenty-pound penetrating warheads blew a large hole in the roof of the Presidential Palace. The pilot swung the MV-22's nose to the right, and he made a second hole about fifty feet from the first with two more missiles.

The MV-22 came in fast, then swung quickly to a low hover over the first smoking hole they had just created. Door gunners suppressed machine-gun fire from more rooftop security guards while the rear cargo ramp of the tilt-rotor motored down, and eight men in dark gray electronic battle armor, composite micro-hydraulic exoskeletons, and electromagnetic rail guns marched from the belly of the tilt-rotor aircraft.

One of the commandos felt bullets ricochet off his armor and instinctively dropped down and tried to take cover. 'Don't try to cover from small-arms fire unless your power drops below twenty percent,' Hal Briggs radioed over their secure commlink. 'And don't waste projectiles on infantry, or doors and walls your sensors can see through. We do different tactics here, gents: You work alone, you work quickly, and you let the armor defend you and feed you information. Follow the position signals, check every room. Let's move out.'

'I'm getting a power-level warning,' one of the commandos said. 'It's reading twenty percent already.'

'You have a bad power pack,' Briggs said. 'Withdraw, change packs, follow us down once it checks out. Move out.' The one commando went back inside the MV-22, where technicians in protective armor quickly helped the commando out of his exoskeleton. Meanwhile, the other Tin Man commandos split up into two groups and dropped through the holes in the roof to the floors below.

Hal Briggs led the first group of four. Holding his rail gun on his left hip, anchored to his exoskeleton, he walked quickly without running through the corridors of the Libyan Presidential Palace; the others split up, taking different corridors. Terrified workers and other persons, presumably relatives or other staffers, ran past him, some running headlong into him. He ignored everyone he didn't recognize. Hal used his ultrawide bandwidth sensor to peer through walls and doors, and anytime he saw someone inside, he kicked the door open to see who it was. But he kept on moving, sometimes simply walking right through a wall or door to get inside an adjacent room.

'It's hard to take stairs with this exoskeleton,' one of the commandos radioed.

'Don't bother with stairs,' Hal responded. When he reached the end of the hallway, he simply turned, tossed an explosive charge onto the floor, blew a hole in the floor, and jumped through.

Once they finished the top floor, the other floors went more quickly. On the ground floor, Hal had to contend with massed Republican Guard soldiers, now with heavier machine guns and grenade launchers. The battle armor's electric shock system took care of any close-in security he encountered; he had to fire one hypersonic projectile at the security booth just inside the front palace entry, where Republican Guards had set up a twenty-millimeter Gatling gun. One Tin Man had to jet-jump outside and retreat back to the roof after taking nearly two thousand rounds from the cannon before Briggs put it out of commission. Briggs left one Tin Man on the ground floor to watch for any heavy security responses, while the rest started down to the subfloors.

The entire search of the above-ground floors took them less than two minutes.

Now that the assault was on, they moved faster through the subfloors, following the location signal. They came across interrogation rooms, zapped anyone inside carrying weapons, and released all others. Chris Wohl found an infirmary, and next door was a makeshift autopsy room and morgue. 'I found two of our

444

guys in the morgue,' Chris radioed. 'Looks like both of them have been tortured to death.' His voice started to tremble with rage. 'I'm going to kill someone for this.' He zipped both corpses into their black body bags and carried them to the roof.

'I found survivors,' another of the commandos reported. 'I'm bringing them out.' Within minutes, eleven more Night Stalkers were on board the Pave Hammer tilt-rotor, all of them injured from torture and near-starvation but all still alive.

Briggs and two other commandos had just moved to the bottom subfloor when Briggs heard one of the lookouts say, 'We've got trouble, One. Heavy armor on the way in. We're engaging, but we're running out of time.'

'We'll be finished searching the building in three minutes,' Briggs responded.

'No good, sir,' Chris Wohl interjected. 'We're going to be surrounded in one minute. The Pave Hammer is too vulnerable. Make your way upstairs.'

'We can't leave without Patrick and Wendy.'

'Sir, we'll be walking out of Libya if we're not airborne in sixty seconds.'

'Then get airborne.'

'Negative, sir. Everyone gets on board. I've stopped picking up life signs from the general.'

'That's an order, Master Sergeant.' Briggs sent the last two commandos upstairs to get on the MV-22. 'Two more on the way. I'm staying until I find the McLanahans.'

Briggs hurried toward the source of the location signal – and he was horrified at what he found. There, a desktop was covered with blood – and moments later he found Patrick's microtransceiver, tossed into a corner.

'I found the transceiver – minus the general,' Briggs reported solemnly. He did another sweep of the area – no sign of him. 'I'm coming up.'

Ivana Vasilyeva waited until the loud, rhythmic beat of the heavy rotors far above her subsided, then crawled out of her hiding place in the steel-lined weapons locker in an isolated corner of the room. She checked that her submachine gun was cocked and ready, then carefully searched the hallway outside the small armory. All clear. She then returned to the locker and grabbed a woman by the back of her neck, pinning her left arm behind her to steer her out of the room.

'Well, that wasn't much of an assault,' Vasilyeva said to the woman in English. 'It appears your friends have left already, before their work was done.'

'They'll be back,' Wendy McLanahan said. 'Count on it.'

'But we will be long gone by then, Dr McLanahan,' Vasilyeva said. 'I am sorry we did not meet up with your husband. But I do not think he would like how you have been keeping yourself.' Wendy's face was badly beaten; one eye was swollen shut and bleeding; her nose was broken in several places – and she had trouble breathing because of cracked ribs, a partially deflated lung, and a torn abdominal diaphragm. Blood had been oozing out of several orifices and wounds for many days, making her look pale and ethereal.

'I think he'll understand. Besides, I'll get better – you and your friends will just get dead.'

'You'll be alive long enough for us to lure your husband to us, and then you'll both be dead, at Comrade Kazakov's hands.'

'Pavel Kazakov.' Wendy chuckled. 'The only thing worse than being his whore or his drug pusher is his assassin.'

Vasilyeva twisted Wendy's arm higher up her back, causing her to cry out in pain. 'Pain must be something you enjoy, Dr McLanahan.'

'Am I turning you on, bitch?'

'Shut up and move,' Vasilyeva said. 'We have a boat waiting for us in the harbor. A short ride to Zuwarah, a plane ride across the Sahara to Algeria, and then another private jet to meet Comrade Kazakov. Then we set a trap for your –'

They heard a loud scream behind them. Vasilyeva turned just as a body came flying at her, pinning himself against her submachine gun and pulling it out of her hands. The gun went spinning across the hallway. Wendy twisted away. Vasilyeva struggled to her feet, madly searching for her weapon – and then saw him. 'There . . . you . . . are, General McLanahan,' she cooed softly.

Patrick stood between her and the weapon. He still wore the handcuffs, waist chain, and manacles; his left shoulder was an

446

ugly mass of blood from where Zuwayy's men had roughly cut the microtransceiver out of his body. He backed up, looking for the weapon with his feet in the semidarkness of the hallway.

'Wendy?'

'Patrick!' she cried.

'Get out of here,' he said. 'Go back. Get away from here.'

Vasilyeva reached back, grabbed Wendy by the hair, and pulled her up to her feet. 'Is this who you came for, General? I would not have wasted my time.' Patrick quickly searched for the gun around his feet. Vasilyeva pulled Wendy to her, wrapped her left arm around Wendy's neck, and applied pressure with her right hand. 'Do not move, or I will snap her neck,' Vasilyeva warned.

'Let her go.'

'Kharasho,' Vasilyeva said. 'It is you I want anyway.' And in the blink of an eye, the former Russian officer withdrew a knife from her belt and drew it quickly across Wendy's throat. Wendy's eyes rolled up inside her head, and Vasilyeva let her drop to the floor.

'No!' Patrick shouted. 'You bitch! You murderer!'

'It was you Comrade Kazakov wanted all the time,' Vasilyeva said, advancing on Patrick with the bloodied knife at the ready. 'But where is this Tin Man armor he spoke of? No matter. Comrade Kazakov only desires you dead. I think I shall bring him a finger – that should be proof enough.'

Patrick's bulging eyes shifted rapidly from his wife's inert form to his attacker. He backed away a few steps – that only made the Russian smile. Patrick raised his hands. 'Cut these handcuffs off and let's make it a fair fight.'

'I do not wish a fair fight,' Vasilyeva said. 'Comrade Kazakov only wanted you dead, not for me to give you a fair fight.' In the blink of an eye she was on him, and before he knew it her blade had sliced once across his right arm and once across his chest. She smiled evilly. 'But he did not say it could not be slow and agonizing for you.' Patrick tried to back away, but he tripped and fell straight back. He tried to get back on his feet, but with his hands cuffed in front of him and his feet manacled, he was helpless. 'I think,' Vasilyeva said, her teeth shining as she smiled at him, 'that you should have matching cuts across your throats. Do you not think it would be fitting, General?'

A shot rang out and a bullet ricocheted off the wall. Vasilyeva turned and saw Wendy McLanahan, her torso a hideous blouse of dark red, not fifteen feet from her, leveling the submachine gun at her. 'Very impressive, Comrade Doctor – to the very last,' Vasilyeva said. She spun the knife around until she was holding the blade, then threw it. The blade sunk into Wendy's chest, and she toppled over backward. 'How very touching. You must be proud, Gen—'

She never got to finish her sentence. Patrick had gotten to his feet, kicked the back of her knees to send her down, then jumped up, wrapped the chain connecting his ankle manacles around Vasilyeva's neck, and rolled around to twist it tight. He rolled several more times until the chain was tight, then locked his feet together.

Vasilyeva was a fierce, powerful woman. She was able to struggle to her feet, actually pulling Patrick's body up as she fought to free herself. The Russian clubbed his legs, swung at his groin, and snarled like a wild animal. She started to swing his body around, jumping up and down wildly in an effort to loosen his legs. He hit the walls several times and saw stars. With Patrick stunned, this time she was able to pin his legs back and land on top of him, the chain still wrapped around her neck, her face a contorted mask of pain and rage, with blood vessels breaking all over her face, making it appear as if she were wearing some sort of primitive war mask. She punched his groin, his legs, his chest, and his face, trying desperately to get him to release his grip.

Patrick was bent over in two so far by her weight that he found he was able to grab her head with his hands, tangling his fingers in her hair to help his grip. Using all his strength, he pushed with his legs. Now both of their faces were hideous contortions of pain. They both screamed in unison, loud, furious screams – until suddenly there was a loud *snap!* Ivana Vasilyeva's eyes rolled sideways, her bloated dark red tongue unreeled itself from her mouth, and her body went totally limp.

Patrick lay on the floor for what seemed like a long time before untangling himself from the dead Russian, then crawled over to his wife. He carefully removed the knife from her chest, then held her lifeless body and wept.

He didn't even notice when strong armored mechanical arms

448

lifted him and Wendy up, carried them carefully outside, and placed them in a waiting tilt-rotor aircraft to evacuate them out of Tripoli.

Alternate National Military Command and Communications Center, Sidi Salih, Libya
a short time later

'My brothers and sisters, my fellow Libyans, we have been shame-lessly and cowardly attacked by the great Satan, the United States of America,' Jadallah Zuwayy intoned. He was sitting in a small, cramped communications center in an underground alternate command post thirty miles south of Tripoli. 'Tonight, while you slept peacefully in your beds, the forces of the United States, with help from their stooges the Zionists, launched a brazen sneak attack against the capital of the Kingdom of Libya, attacking the royal palace itself and killing many scores of innocent men, women, and children.'

Zuwayy raised his hands as if praying, then slowly curled them into fists. 'As Allah, may His name be praised, is my witness, today the people of the Islamic world declare war upon the infi-dels, the destroyers, the crusaders from across the oceans who attacked our capital,' he went on. 'May He deliver upon the faithful the strength to crush the enemies of Islam.

'Thanks to the brave efforts of the Republican Guards and the soldiers of the kingdom, I am safe. I will return to the capital and immediately plan the destruction of our enemies. Death to all who oppose us. Death to –'

There was the sound of shattering glass, then the *BANG!* of a door thrown open. Zuwayy half rose to his feet, looking scared and confused. Men in military dress forced him to his seat again, and two unidentified soldiers stood behind him. Gunshots were heard off-camera – Zuwayy jumped and closed his eyes at each report, expecting it to hit him next. The television viewers then saw Zuwayy's eyes widen in astonishment as a chair was slid beside Zuwayy's and a young man sat down beside the king. He took off his red-lensed goggles, unwrapped his scarf, and took off his helmet . . .

449

. . . and Sayyid Muhammad ibn al-Hasan as-Sanusi, the true king of Libya, smiled at the camera.

'*Es salaam alekum*, Captain Zuwayy,' Sanusi said. He clasped Zuwayy on the shoulder. 'Don't you think you should consult the *real* king of Libya before declaring war?'

'Muhammad? Prince . . . I mean . . . King Muhammad . . . You . . . you are *alive*?' He forced himself to smile, then reached out to Sanusi to embrace him. 'My brother . . . you are *alive*!' He hugged Sanusi, then said to him under his breath, 'Play along with me, Sanusi, or we're both dead. I'll see to it that the Republican Guards spare your life.'

Sanusi pushed him away. 'I am not a ghost, despite all your attempts to turn me into one,' Sanusi said. 'And you are not my brother. There is a nice prison cell awaiting you, Jadallah. You shall stand trial for the murder of my family, the desecration of my family tombs, for stealing millions from the treasury, and for perpetuating a fraud upon the people of Libya.' He motioned toward the door, and Zuwayy was dragged out of sight.

Sanusi turned to the camera and folded his hands before him. 'My brothers and sisters, I am sorry for the pain and lies Jadallah Zuwayy has burdened you with for all these years. But even more, I am sorry for the pain and isolation the world has burdened you with since the revolution. Libya has endured much – not only because of the actions of its leaders, but because of the people's search for the truth: the truth of our past, and of our future.

'I am not here to steal your future, like Colonel Qadhafi and Captain Zuwayy have done,' Sanusi went on. 'I am here because I wanted to expose the fraud, present my evidence of Zuwayy's embezzlement, try to stop the fighting, and so I could return home once more.

'But I only return as a fellow Libyan, not as your monarch, unless that is what you wish,' Sanusi said. 'I have only a handful of fighters and not much money. Zuwayy commands the Republican Guard, and their loyalty lies with him. I may not live long after I sign off with you tonight. But before I leave, I want to give you some promises. Under the eyes of God and guided by the spirits of my beloved family, I tell you this is the truth:

'The Americans did attack Tripoli tonight, but to liberate it, not

450

to destroy it. Jadallah Zuwayy had planned to destroy the Salimah oil fields, where many thousands of Libyans and fellow Arabs live and work – this after he attacked and killed many thousands of Egyptians with neutron weapons sold to him by Russian black-market arms dealers. Jadallah Zuwayy conspired with Ulama Khalid al-Khan of Egypt to assassinate Kamal Ismail Salaam so that the Muslim Brotherhood could set up a theocracy in Egypt; but then Zuwayy killed Khan and many other innocent Egyptians at Mersa Matrûh so that he could disrupt the Egyptian government enough to take control of Salimah. I swear by the blood of my father and the memory of my mother that this is true.

'I will never again raise a hand against a fellow Libyan,' Sanusi went on. 'My men and I have attacked and harassed Zuwayy's troops in the desert long enough. I only want peace. I shall head toward the Great Mosque in Tripoli and pray at the former final resting place of my mother, before Qadhafi removed her body from there and discarded it in the desert. I will order my men not to fight. If you want me to return to Tripoli, if you want me to live, you must take back the streets of the capital from the Republican Guard. Help me to return to our capital, and I promise you, I will help restore our country to its former greatness. If you wish me to do so, I will help bring peace to Libya. Otherwise, I wish to live in Libya as a teacher and engineer and help Libya rebuild. The choice, and the decision, is up to you, my brothers and sisters. *Misae el kher. Ma'as salaama.*'

When Sanusi rose from his seat, every man and woman in the room bowed – not only his men, but the Republican Guards captured there as well. He exited the communications facility and stepped outside into the growing dawn.

Sidi Salih, on the foothills of the Tarhûna Mountains of northwest Libya, was on a slight rise, so Muhammad as-Sanusi could see north past the wide expanse of desert all the way into Tripoli. The Tripoli International Airport, closed during the conflict, was slightly to the west; but the city itself, and even the Mediterranean Sea, could clearly be seen. It was a beautiful, awe-inspiring sight. He was about to put on his helmet, but he changed his mind, unwrapped the turban from the helmet, then wrapped it around his head. He had had enough of fighting.

But there was a sight even more beautiful than the sunrise

over Al-Khums to the east or the view of the ancient city of Tripoli on the Mediterranean – the sight of thousands of cars, trucks, bicycles, and buses roaring south down the highway toward Sidi Salih. At first he thought it might be the Republican Guards; but before long he noticed that none of the flags he saw were the Socialist Arab Republic flags or Zuwayy's bastardized imperial flag, but the old imperial flags with his family crest on them. Those flags had been outlawed since the revolution.

Muhammad Sanusi climbed into his desert vehicle and took his place in the gunner's seat in the back – but then he unbolted the big twenty-three-millimeter machine gun from its pedestal and threw it to the ground. His driver then took him to meet his people so they could welcome him back to his capital, his country – and his true home.

Epilogue

Off the coast near San Diego, California
several days later

Even young Bradley realized right away that it wasn't just another boat ride with his 'uncles' Hal, Chris, and Dave. They had no fishing poles, no scuba gear – just the strange aluminum urn.

'Mommy is really dead, Daddy?' Bradley asked.

'Yes, son,' Patrick replied.

He touched the urn. 'Is she in there?' A lump formed in Patrick's throat – he couldn't answer. 'Those are Mommy's ashes, aren't they?' Patrick looked at the deck of the boat – how in hell do you answer something like that? 'I remember in *Star Wars*, when Qui-Gon Jinn was killed by Darth Maul, they put him in a fire and prayed for him. Is that what we did with Mommy?'

The tears burst forth, despite every effort Patrick made to be strong. Through tear-streaked eyes, he looked at his son. 'Is . . . is that okay, son?'

'I . . . guess so.' He started to cry, and it tore into Patrick's heart like a sword.

'Mommy . . . Mommy was just like Qui-Gon Jinn,' Patrick said. 'She was a warrior. She was gentle and she loved us very much, and she was so smart and built wonderful things, but when the bad guys attacked, she fought like a Jedi Knight.'

'She sure did,' Chris Wohl said. 'She was as brave as a Jedi Knight. Even as brave as a US Marine.'

Bradley smiled, then looked at the urn. 'So we can keep this?'

Patrick tapped Bradley's chest, then his head. 'Mommy's here, in your heart; and she's here, in your memory. And she'll always be there. Forever. She's not in there.'

'Then why do we have Mommy's ashes in there?'

Patrick had thought about this moment since he left Libya: how to explain death to his young son. The only thing he could

455

decide is to try to not explain too much at once. He was young; he would eventually understand.

'Brad, I told you about the soul, remember?'

'Yes,' Bradley said proudly. 'The soul is the tiny bit of magic that makes a person.'

'Right. And what did I tell you about the soul?' Bradley looked a little confused. 'Can the soul ever die?'

'You said "no."'

'Right. The soul can never die. Everything that we loved about Mommy was in her soul, and that can never die. Right?' The little boy nodded. 'But our bodies can die. They wear out, get old, and get hurt. Doctors can fix our bodies, but our bodies will eventually die anyway. Like trees and flowers and all living things, they die.'

'Like Mufasa in *The Lion King*?' Patrick smiled and nodded – thank God for kids' movies. 'Are you going to die too, Dad?'

Patrick hugged his son, then looked him straight in the eyes. 'Someday I will, son – but right now, I'm here with you, and so are Uncle David and Uncle Hal and Uncle Chris. We'll always be here for you.

'But do you know what happens when you die, Bradley? Your soul is ready for a journey. Mommy's soul gets to go into another body. We don't know who, or where, or when, but it does.'

'Cool,' Bradley said. 'She's dead, but she's not *really* dead.' He looked up into the blue-gray sky and squinted, searching until his eyes hurt. 'Is that what heaven is?'

'A soul can go to heaven too. There are lots of worlds and things to see and do for the soul. But you know what we have to do before the soul can go on its journey?'

'What?'

'We have to tell Mommy's soul that it's okay for her to go,' Patrick said. 'You see, Mommy doesn't want to leave you and me. She'd rather stay here. She knows how sad you are, and that makes her feel bad.'

'Then she can stay here with me?'

'If you really want her to, yes, she can,' Patrick said carefully. 'But remember: Mommy's soul can also go into another body. Once it's inside someone else, the things that made us love Mommy, the magic that was inside her soul, will be alive again.'

456

'So . . . so someone else is waiting to love Mommy?'

'Exactly, son.' Damn, Patrick thought, thank God his son was smart and open-minded enough to think on his own – he was making this whole ordeal much easier.

'But I still don't want Mommy to go.'

'You know that Mommy will never be far away from us – we just have to think about her, and her soul will return,' Patrick said. 'Sometimes when you're sleeping, Mommy will visit you in your dreams – other times, you'll be doing something else, or maybe be having a problem, and then poof! All of a sudden, Mommy will be there. But we can share the magic in Mommy's soul with the rest of the world. That way, maybe other little boys and girls can enjoy some of Mommy's soul too and love her just like we do.'

'But how do we do that, if she's . . . dead?'

'We have to tell her that it's okay to go on her journey to find those other people that need her,' Patrick said. 'Remember, her soul will never die – but we have to say good-bye. So what do you say? Is it okay?'

'I . . . I guess so.' He looked fearfully at the urn. 'What do we do?'

Patrick nodded to David Luger, and he cut the engine. Patrick led his son back to the built-in swim platform on the stern, and they knelt at the very edge. He unscrewed the cap on the urn. Bradley at first couldn't look, but eventually his curiosity took over. He peered into the urn, and his eyes grew wide with fear. The tears started to flow again, and his lower lip quivered.

'Bradley, listen to me,' Patrick said, holding his son tightly. 'This is a pretty grown-up thing we have to do. Most little boys can't do it. I'm a grown man, and it's hard for me to do.' Bradley looked at his father, now curious to see what his father looked like when he was afraid – and he was comforted to see that he looked pretty much the same, just very sad. 'You have to help me do this, son. I can't do it by myself. You have to say it's okay first, and you have to help me. Please.'

To Patrick's amazement, Bradley took the urn in his hands. He looked as if he was going to simply pour the contents into the water – but instead, he stopped, then turned toward David Luger. 'Uncle David?'

'Yeah, Brad?'

'Go fast,' he said. 'Go real fast.' He turned to his father. 'Mommy liked going fast, didn't she? She liked flying.'

'She sure did, big guy,' Patrick said with a tearful smile. How in hell did I get so lucky to have a son like this? he thought. 'She sure did.' He reached out, kissed the urn, and said, 'Good-bye, sweetheart. I love you. Have a nice journey.' He then stepped back into the cockpit and held tightly on to Bradley's life jacket as Luger gradually eased in the throttle. The big MerCruiser stern drive leapt to life. The speedometer topped sixty miles an hour, close to sixty-five – the Cobalt was fast, but it had never gone this fast ever before. Suddenly the ocean was as smooth as glass – there wasn't a ripple as far as they could see, when moments before there was a light chop.

Bradley held the urn tightly, tears flowing down his cheeks. He kissed the urn, whispered, 'Good-bye, Mommy. I love you. Come see me anytime,' over the loud hum of the engine, then held the urn up over his head and tipped it slightly. In the blink of an eye, the urn was empty, and he let it fly out of his hands.

The silvery ash never seemed to fall to the surface of the ocean, but gently floated upward into the sky until, several long moments later, it disappeared inside a sunbeam that had appeared through the clouds.

It seemed as if Patrick never let his son leave his arms for the next eighteen hours as they traveled from San Diego to Washington, DC. They arrived and checked into the Hay-Adams Hotel, across the street from the White House, in a suite of rooms reserved for them by former president Kevin Martindale.

Patrick's sisters Nancy and Margaret came in a short time later; they were going to be Bradley's baby-sitters during the Night Stalkers' post-action debriefing on the Libyan conflict and their role in it. The first of several meetings was scheduled for eight A.M. the next morning in the Old Executive Office Building with the senior White House staff, followed by more briefings at the Pentagon and the State Department – and then the congressional committees and subcommittees were going to hold hearings, both classified and unclassified. There was no telling how long the

458

debriefings were going to last – and there was no indication yet on what the final outcome might be. They were all betting on confinement – Patrick had already had custody documents drawn up so his sisters could legally take Bradley with them, just in case.

Bradley was still on West Coast time and so wasn't tired, so he, his father, and Hal Briggs walked around the White House and the Capitol Mall until after ten P.M. On their return, it was Hal who noticed the first one: a plainclothed agent standing inside the lobby across from the hotel entrance. Several members of the hotel staff looked apprehensively at them as they went past, then smiled and nodded nervously. As Patrick walked by, the first agent spoke into his sleeve. Another agent was at the top of the stairs; another was standing at the door to Patrick's suite of rooms. The Secret Service agent nodded to Patrick and opened the door for him; he stopped Hal long enough to take his .45-caliber automatic from him before he stepped into the room.

'I should have known you weren't going to be tired,' President Thomas Thorn said, rising from the chair as Patrick entered. 'How are you, General McLanahan?'

'Fine, sir,' Patrick replied stonily. He looked at his son. 'Bradley, this is the President of the United States, Thomas Thorn. Mr President, my son, Bradley James.'

'How do you do, Bradley?' Thorn asked. He extended his hand, and Bradley shook it, then stepped back to be beside his father.

'Who are those guys?' Bradley asked, pointing to the Secret Service agents inside the room.

'Those are Secret Service agents,' Thorn replied. 'They're called the Presidential Protection Detail. They watch out for me.'

Bradley pointed to Hal Briggs, David Luger, and Chris Wohl. 'Those are my uncles,' he said, 'and they watch out over my dad.'

'I know they do – and they do a very good job,' Thorn agreed. Patrick's sisters came and took Bradley into their room, closing the door behind them.

'I'm sorry about Wendy,' Thorn said. 'I wish I had gotten to know her like President Martindale did. She sounded like an extraordinary woman.'

'She was,' Patrick said woodenly.

'I'm off to Israel tomorrow, then Egypt, and probably to Libya,' Thorn said. 'Muhammad Sanusi is going to be proclaimed the

459

monarch of Libya, the true Idris the Second – that's something that hasn't happened in over fifty years, so I'd like to be there, if we can set up security in time. His first official act is going to be a call for national elections – and he says his name won't be on the ballot. He says he's happy just being a Libyan again. Libya will be a constitutional monarchy.'

'So I heard.'

'President Salaam asked to speak with me,' Thorn went on. 'She wants to normalize relations with the United States, both for herself and the Muslim Brotherhood. She hinted that she's going to step down as leader of the Muslim Brotherhood – she's nominated King Idris the Second to be its leader. She also said she's going to step down as president of Egypt.' Patrick looked at Thorn in surprise. 'She's going to name General Ahmad Baris as acting president until new elections are held; I think he'll be elected. What do you think?' Patrick made no response. 'I wonder what Susan Bailey Salaam is going to do?' Still, Patrick said nothing.

'I think most of official Washington wants to interview you,' Thorn went on. 'I think you're going to get grilled for a few days. At least you picked a nice hotel for Bradley to hang out in . . . until you're done.' He studied his hands for a moment. 'But from where I sit, there's only one thing I have to know.'

'I'm not going to join your administration,' Patrick said. 'I can't be your national security adviser.'

'Why do you say that?'

'Because we both feel strongly that we're right.'

Thorn nodded. 'I agree.' He paused for a moment, then said, 'Thomas Jefferson once said that a Council of War is at the same time the most valuable thing and the worst thing for a democracy. But he did have one – and the office was right next to his, not because he consulted them frequently, but so he could keep an eye on them. I think that's what I need to do with you, General McLanahan – put you somewhere so I can keep an eye on you.'

'I can't support you as part of your administration,' Patrick repeated. 'I'd be a serious liability.'

'But you would be in a suit and tie, not in a flight suit – or in Tin Man battle armor,' Thorn said. 'You'd be in Washington, where the bureaucrats can stifle a thought or an action more swiftly and more surely than an entire Marine division. More importantly, I

460

can keep an eye on you. With all due respect, General, I like that idea.'

Patrick looked warily at the President. He was being trapped – he knew it. It was going to be a choice between prison or some office position, locked away amid classified briefings, mountains of paperwork, and nameless, faceless bureaucrats looking for a strong back on which to step on their way up the ladder of power.

Thorn stepped over to Patrick. 'Yes, sir. Keep you in line, keep you in check, pick your brain when I need to but otherwise keep a tight hold on your leash. Hell, any man who names his son after the White House's perennial mad-dog warmonger has *got* to be looking for trouble. Besides, I figure the one thing that will punish you better than hard labor in prison is a *desk job*. Yes, I like that idea a lot . . . but I'm not going to do it.'

He reached into a pocket . . . and pulled out silver major general's stars.

'Take them, General,' Thorn ordered. 'There's a new base in northern Nevada called Battle Mountain Air Force Base that's almost ready to be activated. You're going to command it.

'I'm going to fill that base with all of the aircraft and weapons you've been taking from Sky Masters Inc for the past several years – every model of the Megafortress you've designed, built, and flown over the past fifteen years, and every new air weapon you've developed at Dreamland, including the new airborne laser,' Thorn went on. He turned to the others in the room. '*General* Luger will be your deputy commander. *Colonel* Briggs and *Sergeant Major* Wohl will command a special-ops unit based at Battle Mountain – equipped with the Tin Man battle armor technology and trained to be the ground force that mops up after the Megafortresses attack.

'The Air Battle Force at Battle Mountain will be the tip of the spear. Every conflict around the world, every emergency, every potential war zone will have one of your Megafortresses deployed there first. I think it's about time you stop freelancing and start fighting for your country again, don't you – Major General McLanahan?'

Patrick looked into Thorn's face – then reached up and took the stars from his hand. Thorn smiled and nodded. 'Very good. Nice to have you back on *America's* team – where you belong.' He and Patrick shook hands to seal the deal.

461

'Next problem,' President Thorn said. 'Where is Sergeant Major Wohl?'

Pavel Kazakov's terms of his protective custody agreement allowed him two hours a week supervised release outside of his apartment, and he usually spent those hours playing golf. Akranes, in west Iceland, had two excellent courses, Thorisstadir and Leynir, and in two hours he was usually able to get in nine or more holes and lunch before being returned to his apartment.

His guards/caddies today were two hulking blond Icelanders assigned to him from the World Court. Golf carts were usually not allowed in Iceland, but a cart driver kept one nearby while the three men walked the course – the cart had the heavy firepower in it, enough weapons to hold off a helicopter assault, while the guards themselves wore bulletproof vests and carried submachine guns. Two platoons of commandos were stationed around the course, also heavily armed.

Kazakov played quickly, getting in as many holes as he could before his release was up. He already had the next three shots lined up before he approached the ball; he never spent any time enjoying the spectacular rugged scenery of the small fishing village. He strode quickly to the ball every time – he already had the club selected – and he addressed the ball and swung. He never had to worry about other players on the course – the guards cleared the course twenty minutes before and after he played anyway. Kazakov stopped only long enough to take a sip of tea from a Thermos bottle to ward off the cold.

The rest room and snack bar at the turn was a simple but sturdy log cabin building, set in what looked at first to be an empty frozen tundra. There was always a roaring fire in the stone fireplace, hot tea and coffee, and a section of cakes, confections, and even smoked fish on hand. The guards checked the building out first – the staff at the snack bar had been escorted off the course, along with all the other players – and then Kazakov was allowed inside.

Kazakov sampled some of the smoked fish as he stood by the fire to warm up. 'Other than playing golf itself,' he told his Icelandic guard in Russian, 'this little cabin is perhaps the best part of playing golf in this country.' The guard said nothing –

462

Kazakov didn't know, or care, if the guards spoke Russian – but kept on checking doorways and windows. 'Why, you ask?' Kazakov went on. 'Because, my Norse friend, Iceland has to be the shittiest nation on Earth. Yes, your women are very beautiful. But if this isn't the end of the Earth, one could certainly see it from Iceland. Everything about this place is stark, bland, rugged, and cold. You people all look alike – you have bred every bit of color and interesting features out of your race. You live in one of the harshest climates on Earth and you smile all the time – I don't mean you, but you Icelanders in general. You must be crazy from the cold and isolation.'

The guard nodded, smiled slightly as if Kazakov had just given him a compliment, and continued to scan for intruders. Kazakov snorted his contempt and went to use the lavatory. Big dumb Norseman, he thought. Why did Iceland even bother to have a military? Who would ever attack *Iceland*? And why would they not assign him a guard that spoke Russian, if for no other reason than to collect any possible intelligence? The guard checked the men's room first, then allowed Kazakov to enter.

Kazakov had just turned on the tap to wash his hands when the guard came back in to check on him. 'I will be out in a moment, you big dumb Viking,' he said in Russian. 'Can't I even –?'

A hand grabbed his throat and spun him around. Kazakov was suddenly face-to-face with the biggest, meanest, most chiseled man he had ever seen. His nose looked as if it had been smashed several times, and he looked much older, but his steel-blue eyes burning with pure hatred could have belonged to a youngster. Kazakov tried to pry the man's hand off his throat, but he couldn't budge the fingers one millimeter.

'Good morning, Comrade Kazakov,' the man said in English. 'Having a nice game?' The fingers around his neck squeezed, not allowing any sound to escape. 'My name is Master Sergeant Christopher Wohl, United States Marine Corps, Retired. I have a message for you from General Patrick McLanahan.' Kazakov's eyes bugged when he heard that name . . .

. . . but they bulged even more when the commando held up a four-inch-long double serrated-edge T-bar push knife.

The knife easily pierced Kazakov's jacket, then his flesh, and then his diaphragm, twice, with two fast, powerful thrusts, filling the Russian drug dealer's lungs with blood. 'Those are for my two men your friend Jadallah Zuwayy tortured to death.' He raised the blood-soaked knife, showing the glistening wet blade to Kazakov. 'And this is for Dr Wendy McLanahan.' And he plunged the knife into Kazakov's neck and slashed sideways, nearly slicing the neck in two.

The Icelandic guard stepped into the men's room just as Wohl let the blood-covered body drop to the floor. Wohl calmly took off his bloody jacket and dropped it too.

The two commandos looked at each other for a long moment; then Wohl said in Russian, '*Ya abasralsa na vannaya. Prasteetye.* I really fucked up your bathroom. Sorry.'

'*Suhadrochka. Nye za shta. Fseevo samava loochsheva,*' the Icelandic commando replied in perfect, fluent Russian. He handed Wohl his own clean overcoat – it fit him very well. 'No problem. Don't mention it. Have a nice day.'